FROM THE FANTASTIC LUXURY
OF A MILLIONAIRE'S GUARDED VILLA

TO THE UNSPEAKABLE SORDIDNESS
OF A PRIVATE CLUB
WHERE EVERY VICE WAS POSSIBLE
AND NOTHING WAS FORBIDDEN,

From these two places, a network of secret power extended
its control over human beings in the highest circles of power
and in the lowest depths of depravity.

Statesmen and strippers . . . policemen and perverts . . .
respectable businessmen and greedy pimps . . . they were
all trapped, all part of the plan. All were tangled in a net
of diabolical cunning and total ruthlessness, moving in-
exorably toward hell. And in hell, everyone is destroyed
but the devil . . .

THE AFFAIR OF NINA B.

Don't even try to guess the ending!

Also by Johannes Mario Simmel and
available from Popular Library:

THE BERLIN CONNECTION
THE MONTE CRISTO COVER-UP
THE CAIN CONSPIRACY
THE CAESAR CODE
DOUBLE AGENT, TRIPLE CROSS
I CONFESS

THE AFFAIR OF NINA B.

SIMMEL

Translated from the German by Catherine Hutter

POPULAR LIBRARY • NEW YORK

Published by Popular Library, a unit of CBS Publications,
the Consumer Publishing Division of CBS Inc.,
by arrangement with Paul Zsolnay Verlag, Gmbh.

January, 1978

ISBN: 0-445-04160-9

In memoriam:
"Mila Blehova"

Original German title: *Affäre Nina B.*

Prologue

He had many enemies. I was his greatest enemy. Many people hated him. No one hated him as much as I did. Many people wished he were dead. I was determined to bring it about, the death of the man I hated so implacably.

And the day had come. I had waited a long time. Now that waiting was at an end. I had hesitated for a long time. That period was over too. Now it was a question of my life—and of his.

It was already very warm in Baden-Baden. The gently wooded valley in which the town had been built was bathed in the strong spring sunlight; the dark, fruitful earth received it, clung to it. So many flowers were in bloom—yellow, blue, white. I saw primula, cowslips, crocus, violets on the banks of the sleepily murmuring Oos River as I drove the heavy car through the Lichtentaler Allee. It was his car, one of the three he owned, and it suited him: a huge, showy, red and black Cadillac with whitewall tires.

Everybody on the street looked friendly. The women were smiling, there was a slight air of mystery about them. They were wearing light, bright dresses. Quite a few wore dashing hats. I saw a lot of dashing hats that morning as I drove to the police station. This was going to be a hat spring, I decided.

The men were wearing grey, light brown, light and dark blue suits; most of them had left their coats at home. The men looked at the women, and took their time about it. They weren't in a hurry. Nobody was in a hurry on this spring day in Baden-Baden, except myself. I was driven by my hatred. I was driven by an invisible, inaudible clockwork which I had set in motion. There was no escaping its zero hour, not for him, not for me.

Children were playing under the dusty old poplars that grew alongside the *allee*. They were rolling colored hoops and riding in circles on tricycles. Balls flew in the air. The children sounded jubilant. There were a few French children. I heard them cry, *"Armand! Armand! Rends moi la bicyclette!" "Mais non, Loulou! Laisse-la moi encore un peu."*

On a curve I saw my face in the rear-view mirror. It was white. I looked ill. There were black circles under my eyes. My lips were bloodless, and beads of sweat glistened on my forehead. I took off my visor cap and wiped them away. My cap was grey; it matched my double-breasted gabardine suit. My shirt was grey. Poplin. My tie was a dull shade of blue, my shoes were black. I was his chauffeur and that was how I was dressed: like the chauffeur of the man who went by the name of Julius Brummer.

Julius Maria Brummer. That was his full name. Very few people knew his middle name. He told me about it one night, on some autobahn or other. "I was a great disappointment to my mother. She had longed for a daughter, whose name was to be Maria. Mother was terribly unhappy after my birth. The least she could do was saddle me with the name . . ."

I had arrived at the Atlantic Hotel. A few guests were breakfasting on the terrace. They sat in the shade of tall red-and-white-striped umbrellas. The hotel had been freshly painted sandstone color, "Kaiser yellow." The hedges below the terrace shone wet and dark green. Opposite the hotel, the windows of the casino glittered blindingly in the sun. The pink shell of the spa orchestra stage showed rosily through the blossoming trees. So much color. Even the air seemed to glitter. The day was going to be hot. I stepped on the gas. I was driven by time. I had something to report, and I was in a hurry to do so.

The policeman at the entrance of the police station in the Sophienstrasse lifted his hand to his cap in a vague salute as I entered. He was smiling. Then he looked at the two letters on the left lapel of my jacket. Most people

6

looked at them when they saw me. The letters J and B in gold were attached to my left lapel with a gold pin. They were his initials. Julius Brummer seemed to like his name. Anyway, he liked his initials. He put them on everything—on his properties, on his apartment houses, on his villas, on his three cars, his yacht, and on the uniforms of his employees. His wife had a lot of jewelry. She could wear the most costly pieces and take them off again; but there was one piece she couldn't remove since a goldsmith had locked it around her ankle years ago: a thin band of gold with two initials engraved on it . . .

"What do you want?" asked the officer.

"I have something to report."

"Have you lost anything?"

"No. Why?"

"I thought you were going to report something lost," he said. He was still looking at the letters J and B.

"I want to report a crime."

"On the left. Second floor. Room 31."

"Thank you."

The station had been built in the middle of the nineteenth century, the stairwell was plastered white, the whole place radiated Prussian sobriety. On the second floor I stopped in front of the door to Room 31 and thought of Julius Brummer's wife, Nina, and that I loved her, and why I loved her. Then I thought of Julius Brummer and how much I hated him and why.

I didn't think too long about Nina, but I did give a lot of thought to her husband. And I decided that I hated him more than I loved Nina, a lot more. I couldn't possibly have loved anyone as much as I hated Julius Brummer. Transformed into a different type energy, the intensity of my feelings for Julius Brummer would have sufficed to build a cathedral, to construct a dam, to light a whole city. Standing there in the empty passageway in front of Room 31, I fingered the two gold letters on my lapel. They felt smooth and cool. Feeling them gave me the strength to knock on the door to Room 31. Hatred was a fine thing.

"Come in." The voice of a man.

Room 31 was large and pleasantly furnished, not at all like the usual drab municipal office. Apparently the spa Baden-Baden liked to cater to their visitors' feeling for beauty, even at police headquarters. Pictures on the wall depicted hunting scenes in the style of well-known English originals. Gentlemen in red jackets and black trousers, silver buckles on their boots, lace jabots over silk shirts, were riding fast horses across autumnal fields, with the hunted animal falling victim to a wild pack of hounds.

The furniture in Room 31 was modern and utilitarian. There were comfortable upholstered chairs in green and brown, light wood file cabinets, a wide desk. Larchwood. The desk stood in front of an open window and the sunlight streamed through it into the room and across the broad shoulders of a man, seated in front of a desk. As I entered he was writing with two fingers on a small typewriter. Now he let his hands fall into his lap and looked up.

"What can I do for you?"

I removed my cap and bowed. "They told me to come here. I have something to report."

The sympathetic man behind the desk, who appeared to be about thirty, gestured amiably in the direction of a nearby chair. I sat down and crossed my legs. I let one hand rest on the desk. I was anxious to appear casual. The police officer had thick, black hair, cut short. It stood away from his head like a brush. His eyes were light blue, his mouth was large and sensual with astonishingly red lips. He was wearing grey flannel trousers and a beige sport jacket. His green tie didn't match the pattern of his jacket, but his shirt did. So did his brown loafers.

As usual, his eyes wandered from my face to the eighteen-karat gold letters J and B. He was looking at them as he said, "I am Kriminal Kommissar Kehlmann."

"My name," I said coolly, "is Holden. Robert Holden."

"You reside in Baden-Baden, Herr Holden?"

"No. In Düsseldorf. I am a visitor in Baden-Baden. I am a chauffeur. I drove my employer here in his car. My employer is Julius Brummer."

"Oh," said Kehlmann, softly. Judging by his controlled reaction, the Chief Investigator was evidently an extraordinarily diplomatic man. Of course he knew Julius Brummer. Everybody in Germany knew Julius Brummer. In the last six months he had frequently provided the German press with headlines. He was as famous as a film star. Over and over again his flat, pasty face with the watery button eyes and the pale moustache had been pictured in newspapers, illustrated magazines, newsreels, and on television. He had been written about and photographed when his arrest in Düsseldorf had shaken society, and when his equally sensational release had led to an inquiry by the Social-Democrat faction in parliament. Yes, Julius Brummer was a famous man.

I told Herr Kommissar Kehlmann, "In case you are surprised that my employer is in Baden-Baden—the investigation was broken off months ago."

"Oh," the chief said again. Then he asked drily, "Do you want to file a complaint against Herr Brummer?"

Evidently it seemed the obvious thing to him. Complaints were constantly being filed against Julius Brummer. Kehlmann looked as if he would be quite pleased to receive such a complaint.

"No," I said. "I do not want to file a complaint against Herr Brummer."

"Against whom then, Herr Holden?"

I had given great consideration to my reply to this question. I had learned it by heart for so long and so precisely that the words I now spoke seemed quite strange and senseless, without meaning or content. I said, looking Kehlmann straight in his blue eyes, "I want to report a theft, criminal slander, breach of peace, and embezzlement." Whereupon Kehlmann asked quietly, "Is your report directed against anyone specific?"

"Yes," I said, just as quietly. "Against one man."

"Not bad—for one man," he said.

"That isn't all," I went on. "In a short time this man will also commit a murder."

Now he looked at me for a long time without saying a word. I had known all along that at this point he would take just such a hard, long look at me, he or whoever would be listening to me. I let him stare at me, my own face expressionless, and began to count. One, two, . . . I got as far as seven. I had expected to get to ten.

"Are you filing this report against an unknown person?"

"No."

"You know the man?"

"Yes."

"You know his name?"

"Yes."

"And what is his name, Herr Holden?"

I thought of how I hated Julius Brummer more than I could possibly ever love anyone. I thought of my determination to bring about his death. I said, "The man's name is Robert Holden."

The Chief looked at the initals on my lapel. I didn't hurry him, I gave him time. I had known that at this point he would need time. I began to count again. This time I got as far as four when he said, "Your name is Robert Holden and you want to bring charges against Robert Holden?"

"Yes, Herr Kommissar."

A heavy truck drove by on the street below. I could hear the gears grinding as the driver put them in reverse. "Is there a second Robert Holden?" asked Kehlmann.

I had also given the answer to this question a lot of thought. "No, there is no second Robert Holden."

"In other words, you want to bring charges against yourself."

"Yes, Herr Kommissar," I said politely. "That's what I want to do."

BOOK ONE

1

What I told Chief Investigator Kehlmann took over three hours. He listened attentively, then told me to drive back to my hotel and wait. I was forbidden to leave Baden-Baden without first notifying him. They would proceed with an investigation, he said; I would be notified.

Actually it would have been his duty to hold me, but the story I had told him wasn't all that simple. It was an extraordinarily complicated story and will fill the following pages of my report. He didn't *dare* to arrest me then and there; he simply didn't dare. He sent me home.

So here I am in my hotel room, shaking with fear. My hands are ice-cold, my head is bursting, and I keep thinking, thinking . . . always the same thing. Did Chief Kehlmann believe my story? Was I convincing? If he didn't believe it, I was lost. Then it had all been for nothing—the caution, the smart thinking, the careful preparation.

But would he have accepted my story and let me go if he hadn't believed me?

No. Not likely.

So he believed me.

But perhaps he let me go just because he didn't believe me. To make me feel secure; in order to be able to watch me for days, weeks, perhaps months. My nerves are shot. I've been through too much. I can't, I daren't go through much more. I must calm down. No rashness, not at this point. I must think in an orderly fashion. Writing it all down is going to help me to collect myself and think clearly. Only in that way can I hope to cope with the last difficult steps I have to take.

There is a certain amount of irony in the fact that today, of all days, on the afternoon of April 7, 1957, I will begin a diary for the first time in my life. I was born forty-one years ago today. But in no way is calm reflectiveness at the beginning of the fifth decade of my existence the impetus that drives me to set down on paper certain secret and dangerous events of my life; actually my decision is the result of having just returned to my cool, shady room in the hotel after a long interview at the police station.

There can be no doubt about it, look at it as you will, but on this seventh day of April, 1957, the most decisive period of my life has begun. For lack of a better or more original explanation, I'll use the old cliché—with my statement to Chief Investigator Kehlmann I have started a snowball rolling and even I can't foresee the dimensions of the resulting avalanche.

Five hundred sheets of paper lie on the table in front of me. I bought them after leaving the police station, after I had come to the decision to keep a diary from now on. In the last few hours I have written about a dozen pages. I have mentioned the fact that I hate Julius Brummer. I have not mentioned why. I have described my visit to the police station and the first part of my report to Chief Investigator Kehlmann. I have told how I brought charges against myself. But now I am stuck.

Because what I went on to tell Chief Kehlmann was as fantastic as practically everything that has happened to me in the last six months. What I told him was objectively true but subjectively untrue. But if this diary I am starting today is to have any sort of meaning, then its content must be true objectively *and* subjectively. And to do that makes it impossible to go on with the story I told Chief Kehlmann. To tell the objective and subjective truth I have to go back farther; I have to start at the beginning and tell how the gruesome pattern of obvious madness developed, by which I find myself living today. I must go back to that rainy evening in August of last year on which I met Julius Brummer for the first time. Beginning with this meeting, I shall report chronologically what has taken

14

place up to the present day. So, until I have caught up with the present, I am really not writing a diary, but a memoir. I think therefore that I'd better place the dozen pages I have written at the beginning of my book. As a prologue.

The more I get used to the idea of this unusual thing I am about to do, the easier I feel. Writing it all down will distract me. It will help me to see things more clearly and to act more coolly during these last weeks before the end of the bastard.

When I was still in school there was a time when my teachers were very pleased with my compositions because they were so "discriminating." My parents had hopes that I might be a writer. They were poor, and they had read in an illustrated paper something about the yearly income of the writer, Ludwig Ganghofer.

I was a disappointment to my parents, not only in respect to the literary career they had hoped for me, and I have to smile when I think that even this late literary activity, on which I am embarking on my forty-first birthday, is not likely to be a financial success either.

There are two possibilities for the future of these pages. On the one hand, what I have embarked on could succeed. In that case the world will be minus a villain and I shall breathe freely again and be safe. In that case I'll keep what I've written to myself and read it from time to time in order to realize again that in a world of dispirited judges and bribed witnesses there still exists a kind of incorruptible justice that chose me as its tool.

On the other hand, what I have embarked on could fail. In that case Chief Investigator Kehlmann may consider this manuscript my confession.

2

I met Julius Maria Brummer for the first time on the evening of August 21, 1956. It was raining in Düsseldorf. The old bus on which I was proceeding from the center of town to Cecilienallee was crowded. Laborers and minor civil servants were going home. There was a smell of wet clothing, cheap shoe polish, rancid fat, and the sad, stuffy miasma that seems to surround the poor. The overhead light fell dismally on exhausted faces. A few men were reading. One of them was pockmarked, the black dead stump of a cigar was stuck in the corner of his mouth. The women stared into space with lacklustre eyes. The young girl sitting next to me tried to make up her lips. The bus lurched, the rouge slipped over the edges of her lips. Patiently she wiped it off. Her second try succeeded. She opened her powder case and tried various ways of smiling into the small mirror.

The conductor shoved his way through the passengers who were standing. He was in a foul mood. Raindrops ran down the panes and the street lights glistened. More and more people got out. I watched them fight the east wind with their open umbrellas until they were swallowed up by the darkness. The girl with the made-up lips left us at the Malkasten stop, in front of the large movie house. I saw her hurry happily toward a young man, but he was looking up at an illuminated clock and his handsome face was angry. She was late. Sadly she lowered her head. As the bus drove on I saw the two of them, bathed in neon light, standing under the gigantic picture of a bosomy American beauty, and witnessed the end of an affair. He was too handsome, she was too humble. She laid one hand on the sleeve of his wet coat. He shook it off, threw away his cigarette, and left her standing there. She ran after him,

16

stumbling on her high heels, bumping into people; she ran her fingers helplessly through her wet hair, then stood still in the rain, discouraged and small . . .

"Hofgarten!" yelled the disgruntled conductor.

We had reached the river and the long rows of elegant villas along its banks. I got out. The cold rain struck my face. Many cars were parked in front of the Rhine Terrace. I saw lighted windows. An orchestra was playing in the bar. Four couples were dancing. I couldn't hear the music. They were moving silently across the floor.

I turned up the collar of my raincoat and walked down Cecilienallee. Then I stopped under a tree and rolled up the cuffs of my trousers. I didn't want them to get dirty. The blue suit I was wearing was the only one I had. I also owned two old pairs of flannel pants, one grey, one brown, a leather jacket, and a sport jacket. The grey flannel pants were thin in spots and the lining of my jacket was torn, but my double-breasted blue suit still looked quite decent in artificial light. In daylight the elbows and knees were shiny. It was shiny over my rear end too, but you couldn't see that. My jacket covered it.

I also still owned two pairs of shoes, brown and black. The sole of the left black shoe was thin, in spite of which I had chosen to wear them today. Brown shoes didn't look right with a blue suit. And I was determined to make a good impression this evening. I still had one mark and thirty-one pfennigs. I owed a month's rent; my landlady and I weren't on speaking terms.

The east wind was whistling in the trees; a foghorn was blaring across the water. Here the road curved. Suddenly I saw a lot of people. They were standing in front of a gate that was lit up brightly by the headlights of several cars. As I drew closer I could see three cars in the park, beyond the gate. The police were everywhere.

Cecilienallee 486 was inscribed on a small enamel sign on the fence. I pushed my way through the crowd, at least thirty men and women. Some had their umbrellas up, others were letting the rain trickle down their faces. They were watching the police hurrying across the wet grass in the park, to their cars, to the majestic villa visible behind the old trees. The heavy rain slanted in silvery streaks

17

across the bright beams of the headlights. The whole thing looked like a film set, unreal, staged for the moment.

Two old women were standing beside the gate. "With gas," said one.

"Nonsense," said the other. "With muriatic acid and lysol."

"With gas," the first insisted. "I heard what the fellow from the ambulance said. She's dead."

"If she's dead, why did they take her away so fast? With the sirens and all."

"You should have that much money," said the first one.

"It *was* muriatic acid," said the second one, and coughed.

"What's going on here?" I asked.

The old women stared at me. The light from the cars lit up their mean faces.

"In God's hand," said the second one and sneezed noisily. "We are all in God's hand."

I walked through the open gate. A police car blocked the wide gravel driveway that led to the villa. It was idling unevenly. I walked past a young policeman who was talking into a microphone. "Hello . . . central . . . this is Düssel three . . ."

A crackling sound, then a voice on the loudspeaker, "Come in Düssel three . . ."

"The ambulance is on its way to Marien Hospital," said the young policeman. The rain was running down his neck into his collar. "Düssel four is getting hold of her husband at his office . . ."

I walked on. Nobody paid any attention to me. A bed of tiger lilies. A bed of roses. A bowlegged, misshapen dog walked out of a rhododendron bush. He wobbled when he walked. His yellow coat was wet, but he was wagging his stubby tail.

The sad old boxer bumped into a tree, after that he ran between my legs. When his heavy head knocked against my knee, he began to whimper. I leaned down and patted him. His floppy ears hadn't been clipped. Now I saw why he had bumped into me. His bloodshot, milky eyes looked up at me. He was blind. Suddenly he fell down, got to his feet again and shuffled off, back into the bushes.

A man came tearing up to me, out of breath. "Are you the photographer from the *Telegraph?*"

"No."

"For Christ's sake, where is the guy?" and he dashed off into the darkness.

Finally I reached the villa. Every room was lit up, the front door was open. There were terraces and balconies. Shadows moved across some of the lighted windows. Over the entrance I saw two letters in gold, large as platters: J and B.

I walked up three steps and into the hall. There were many doors, a fireplace, and a wide dark wood staircase. It led to the second floor. Dark pictures hung on the white walls. Old pewter was arranged on the mantle. The blind dog came waddling into the hall, up to the fireplace. A big fire was burning in it. He lay down in front of it as if he wanted to die.

There were a lot of people in the hall: a doctor in white, three policemen in leather jackets, four men in plain clothes. The latter wore hats. They were standing in a corner, taking notes. All the doors leading to the rooms were open and all the men were smoking.

A fifth civilian was sitting in front of the fire. He was holding a telephone on his knees and talking rapidly. "Whaddayamean—no more room on the front page? Scrap the two columns on Algiers. What I've got here is a damn sight more important. The whole house reeks of gas . . ."

He was right. Since entering the hall I had grown aware of a sickly sweet smell. I noticed that all the windows were wide open. The rain was spraying onto the heavy carpeting.

"Coffee?" A voice behind me.

I turned around. A little woman with white hair, carrying a tray with steaming cups of coffee. Over her black dress she wore an apron. Her eyes were red. "Would you like a cup of coffee, sir?" She spoke with a strong Czech accent.

"No, thank you."

She walked to the policemen and reporters. "Coffee?" she said. "Would any of the gentlemen like a cup of coffee?" She seemed lost in her grief.

19

A hand on my shoulder. I turned around. A policeman was eyeing me suspiciously. "Who are you?"

"My name is Holden," I said politely. I didn't want any trouble, especially not with the police.

"Are you here officially?" He was tired, his left eyelid was twitching, his leather jacket was wet.

"No."

"Then how did you get in?"

"Through the door."

"Don't get fresh with me."

"That was not my intention," I said meekly. Anything but trouble with the police. "I really did come in through the door. I've come to be interviewed for a position."

"What sort of position?"

"As chauffeur." I tried to smile. It didn't come off. I'm unlucky, was what I was thinking. When Julius Brummer's secretary had written, telling me to come for an interview, I had seen it as life giving me another chance. Five minutes ago, walking through the rain, I had felt good. I'd still been full of hope. Now I could feel the old fear crawling over me, slimy and cold, the fear that had followed me all my life.

"Do you have any identification?" asked the policeman. He was looking at the rolled-up cuffs of my trousers. He saw my old socks, my old shoes with the rainwater still dripping from them.

I gave him my passport.

"German citizen?"

"I wouldn't have a German passport if I wasn't."

"Keep a civil tongue in your head, Herr Holden, if you know what's good for you."

"I haven't done anything. Why are you treating me like a criminal?"

"You live in Düsseldorf?" he asked, instead of answering my question.

"Grupellosstrasse 180."

"Here it says you live in Munich."

"I used to live in Munich."

"When?"

My hands began to tremble. I couldn't take it much longer. "A year ago. Then I moved . . ." My voice. Surely he'd notice . . .

20

"Married?" He didn't notice.

"No."

"Do you know Herr Brummer?"

"No."

"Frau Brummer?"

"No. What's going on here anyway?"

"Frau Brummer," he said, and pointed thumb-down with his left hand.

"Dead?"

"Not yet."

"Suicide?"

"Smells like it, doesn't it?" He returned my passport with a tired smile. "Over there. Second door. Have the cook give you a cup of coffee. It'll be a while before Herr Brummer gets home."

3

Her name was Mila Blehova and she came from Prague. She had a broad nose like a duck's, magnificent false teeth, and the kindest face I had ever seen in my life. When you looked at her, you knew—this woman has never told a lie, this woman is incapable of doing anything mean. Tiny, bent, her white hair combed straight back, she stood beside the open window of the big kitchen and worked while she spoke. She was preparing a meal—stuffed rolled beef. Four flat pieces of meat lay in front of her, dark red and juicy. She salted and peppered them.

"Such a tragedy, sir. Such a terrible tragedy." A few tears rolled down her wrinkled cheeks. She wiped them away with her right elbow and went on. "You must excuse me for breaking down like this, but she's like my child, my very own child, Nina is . . ."

I sat opposite her and drank my coffee and smoked, and, although the windows were wide open, the kitchen still smelled of gas. In the dark garden behind the house, I could hear the rain.

"You've known Frau Brummer for a long time?"

"More than thirty years, sir." Now she was smearing mustard on the meat. Her work-worn, cleanly scrubbed hands were deft. Above her apron, on her left shoulder, two initials were pinned to her dress: J and B. "I was her nursemaid. Nina's nursemaid. I taught her how to walk, how to eat with a knife and fork and comb her hair and say the Lord's Prayer. I was never away from her, not for a single day. Her parents liked to take me along on trips. I was always with my little Nina. Oh dear God, when she had the measles, and whooping cough . . . And then, when her parents died, so quickly one after the other . . . we went through it all together, my poor little Nina and I . . ."

She was cutting thin slices off a large slab of bacon and laying them neatly side by side on the mustard and meat, and from somewhere in the house you could still hear the voices of the reporters and police.

Mila Blehova said, "She is so beautiful, sir. Like a living angel. And so good. If she dies, I don't want to live any more either." She began to cut up onions in thin, small rings. "She's a part of me, after all we've gone through together. The misery in Vienna, the war, the bombs, and then—such good fortune."

"What good fortune?"

"Well . . . when Herr Brummer fell in love with my little Nina. The wedding. Such a lot of money. A mink coat, diamonds, this beautiful house . . ." The tears were rolling down Mila Blehova's cheeks and she made a noise as if she had drunk soda water too fast. "You see, I'm belching again," she said in a resigned tone. Suddenly, by the expression on her face, I could see she was in pain. "Always, when I get excited. It's my thyroid. Overactive."

There was a thin, tortured howl. It was the boxer. The dog was curled up beside the stove and was looking at us with its bloodshot, half-blind eyes.

"Yes, my Mitzi, my poor Mitzili, it's terrible. I know . . . I know . . ." She nodded sadly, and the dog whimpered and came to her and rubbed its head against her leg.

Mila Blehova began to roll up the first piece of meat.

"Oh dear, oh dear . . . our Mitzi, our good little Mitzi . . . if it hadn't been for her, my Nina wouldn't be alive . . ."

"How's that?"

"Well, today is Wednesday, and on Wednesday all of us have the afternoon off, and my Nina said to me, 'Why don't you go to the movies?' But I said no, I'd rather go for a nice walk with Mitzi." Again the helpless old dog whimpered. "We walked down to the Yacht Club, and all of a sudden, Mitzi started to howl and pull on her leash, back to the house. She must have felt what was going on, the poor animal." The first roll was finished, and the little old woman pierced it with an aluminum pin. "So I began to get nervous too, and went back home with the dog, and when I got to the kitchen, there she was, lying in front of the stove with all the taps on, and she was as good as gone." She belched again.

"How long were you away?"

"About three hours."

"And in three hours . . ."

"She took Veronal too. Twelve."

"How old is Frau Brummer?"

"Thirty-four." She rolled up the second piece and threw the dog some bacon. The animal tried to catch it, but failed.

"Why did she do it?" I asked.

"I don't know. Nobody knows."

"Was she happily married?"

"Happiest marriage in the world. A bed of roses, that's what he gave her. All the money she could possibly want, nothing to worry about. I don't understand it, I just don't understand it."

The door opened and the policeman who had looked at my passport came in. "Got any coffee left, *Mütterchen?*"

"As much as you like. Here's the pot. Help yourself to sugar. And milk."

"We just phoned the hospital," he said amiably as he poured his coffee. "Herr Brummer is on his way here."

"And Frau Brummer?" Her slack old mouth was trembling. "How is the *gnädige Frau?*"

"They've got her in an oxygen tent and they're trying Cardiazol. For the heart."

23

"Oh dear Jesus, is she going to live?"

"If she gets through the night," said the policeman, and went back into the hall.

As if she had understood every word, the old dog began to whimper again. In spite of her stiff legs, Mila Blehova knelt down beside the animal and stroked her swollen belly. In her harsh tongue, so unintelligible with its many consonants, she tried to comfort the dog, but the animal went on whimpering, and in the kitchen there was still a smell of gas.

4

The telephone rang. It was small and white and was attached to the tiled wall next to the door. The old woman hurried over to it, picked up the receiver. During the last half hour she had prepared a meal. The red cabbage and potatoes were done. "Yes, please," said Mila Blehova.

She listened, belching nervously, one hand on her stomach, which was obviously hurting. "Yes, very good, *gnä' Herr*. I'll dish up right away."

I would have liked nothing better than to leave; in fact I had been wanting to leave for some time, but where was I to go? Not back to my furnished room with only one mark and thirty-one pfennigs in my pocket. My interview with Julius Brummer was the only hope I had left in the world and I clung to it.

Mila Blehova had grasped all this some time ago. Now she nodded in my direction and said into the receiver, "The chauffeur is here. He was told to come here, *gnä' Herr*. He's been waiting a long time."

Again she listened. "Good. I'll tell him," she said, and hung up. As she hurried to the counter, where she began to set up a tray with plates and silver, she said, "You can come right along with me."

24

"But I don't want to disturb Herr Brummer at his supper."

"That's all right. Especially on Wednesday. Then the butler isn't here and I serve. I mustn't forget the beer." She took two bottles out of the refrigerator and set them on the tray. Then she placed the serving dishes on another tray and carried both to the dumbwaiter. She pressed a button. The dumbwaiter made a humming noise as it disappeared upward. Mila Blehova took off her apron and we left the kitchen. The sad old dog stumbled after us.

The hall was empty. The windows had been closed, and so had the front door. Police and reporters were gone. Stains on the carpet, ash trays full to overflowing, and empty cups bore witness to their recent presence. It was cold in the hall. The damp of a rainy night had penetrated.

We went up the stairs to the second floor. The wooden risers creaked under our feet and I looked at the dark pictures on the wall. I knew a little about paintings, years ago I'd had something to do with them. A peasant Breughel, probably an original. Trees by Fragonard, the real thing too. A copy of Tintoretto's *Suzanna and the Elders*. Lasciviously the bearded elders were watching the young girl with the voluptuous thighs and full breasts as she looked, abashed, into a pool.

The half-blind dog wobbled ahead of us along the corridor, past two doors; Mila Blehova opened the third. The dining room was huge. An antique table stood in the center, twelve antique chairs around it. Heavy dark red drapes covered the windows. Unlike the hall, the room was very warm. The silk wall covering had a design of leaves and vines in a silvery grey and light green. The sideboards were elaborately carved. I watched Mila Blehova set the head of the table for one person. She placed a silver candelabrum on the damask tablecloth and lit the seven candles. Then she turned off the ceiling light and the room was plunged into soft semidarkness. The old cook opened a wall panel and revealed the dumbwaiter. As she carried the dishes to the table, she said, "The dining room used to be downstairs, but now we have a conference room there. The dumbwaiter's new too. Everything's cold by the time it gets to the table."

25

The old boxer barked hoarsely and limped to a second door, which opened immediately. A man came in. The flames of the seven candles flickered and I saw a double-breasted black suit, a white shirt, a silver tie. The man was completely bald, very tall, and very fat. In spite of his weight, he moved gracefully on small, dainty feet in small, dainty shoes. He came floating into the room like a gigantic blimp.

His head was round, his forehead low. His face was a healthy, rosy color, his tiny watery eyes were embedded in cushions of fat. A pale blond moustache grew over his little womanish mouth.

The half-blind dog howled miserably. The fat man stroked her. "Yes, Mitzi, yes, yes . . ." Then he straightened up. "Herr Holden? Good evening. My name is Brummer." His hand was small and soft. "Excuse me for having kept you waiting so long. I'm sure you know what happened."

He spoke fast and to the point, and he made a powerful, self-controlled impression. I imagined him to be about forty-five.

"Herr Brummer," I said, "allow me to . . . to express my sympathy. I'm afraid this is a bad moment for me to introduce myself. Wouldn't it be better if I came back tomorrow?"

Julius Brummer shook his head and skipped five sentences of dialogue. "Are you hungry, Herr Holden?" Now I noticed that his jaw was moving. He was chewing gum. "Are you hungry?" he asked again.

I nodded. I was feeling sick with hunger.

"Set another place, Mila."

"Yes, *gnä' Herr!*"

"What's the matter, Herr Holden? It isn't going to make my wife feel any better if *we* don't eat. Nobody is more upset than I am. I love my wife. We were happy, weren't we, Mila?"

"Oh yes, *gnä' Herr*." The old cook belched painfully, as she set the second place. He went up to her and embraced her. Her white hair barely reached the gold watch chain on his vest. "Why did she do it, *gnä' Herr?* Why?"

"Nobody knows, Mila." His voice was warm and

resonant. "They wouldn't let me see her yet, but I'll find out what happened. You can depend on it."

"But if she dies, *gnä' Herr*. If our Nina dies . . ."

He shook his head vehemently in a way that said quite clearly, "She is *not* going to die." Infinite power lay in the way Julius Brummer shook his head. Mila Blehova looked at him, obviously deeply moved. For her he was a tower of assurance and strength. She spoke with difficulty. "It's rolled beef, *gnä' Herr*. With red cabbage."

"And bacon?"

"You said with bacon."

He lifted the lid of the serving dish. "*Four?*"

"I made two for the *gnädige Frau* . . . by mistake."

"Well, now we have Herr Holden."

"I'm a stupid old woman, *gnä' Herr*."

"It's all right, Mila. You're the cream of the crop," said Julius Brummer.

5

"Best beer in the world. As far as I'm concerned, there's nothing like Pilsner beer." He wiped the foam from his mouth with the rosy back of his hand. We were alone. "Draft beer. I order it by the case. See the sickle-and-hammer trade mark? Straight from Prague. The commies make good beer too."

He took one of the beef rolls, tore it in two and threw half down to the old boxer, who was standing beside him. The meat fell on the carpet. The dog began to eat, her jaws drooling.

"Can't see a thing any more, poor old Mitzi." Brummer licked his greasy fingers. "After her second litter she lost her hair too. But we don't care. We love you, don't we, Mitzili?"

27

"How old is she?"

"Eleven or twelve. I can't remember exactly. Nineteen forty-five, in that cold winter, I found her in a ruin, half dead." He threw another piece of meat on the carpet. "Mila's going to be mad at us, Mitzi, because we're messing things up." He loved the dog, no doubt about that. "I don't want you to get a wrong impression, Holden."

"About what?"

"Because I don't talk about my wife. I can't. When I think of my wife, I lose my head. And right now I need my head. All sorts of things are going on—against me."

I looked down at my plate. It was also initialed in gold J.B. The silver was engraved with the same letters.

"You're not curious?"

"Not very."

"Good. Help yourself to potatoes. And cabbage. First-rate cabbage, isn't it?"

"Yes."

"You know what, Herr Holden? I killed a man. Driving."

I helped myself to some more cabbage.

"That was a year ago."

I helped myself to potatoes.

"Terrible thing. He was deaf. Ran straight into my car. It wasn't my fault, it really wasn't. But I was on the way home from a party. Three, four martinis. Maybe five. But I was sober, cold sober, naturally."

I ate the cabbage, the potatoes, some of the meat.

"What a mess! Troopers. Blood test. Blood alcohol positive. Driver's license revoked. If they catch me behind a steering wheel again there'll be trouble. Big trouble. Bad luck, no?"

"Bad luck."

"Ever since then I've been dependent on chauffeurs. The last one I had got fresh. A pretty fellow. A fag. His boys were blackmailing him, so he tried to blackmail me. I threw him out. You can't blackmail me, Holden."

"I'm not a fag."

"I can see that. So what's wrong with you?"

"Nothing's wrong with me, Herr Brummer."

"Shit!"

28

I put my knife and fork down on my plate.

"So . . . say something."

I said nothing.

"I got seventeen answers to my ad." He was poking in his teeth with his fingers. The results seemed to disappoint him, and he went on eating. He spoke at the same time. "Your letter attracted my attention. Would you like to know why?"

"Why, Herr Brummer?"

"It was so humble. So fawning. So resigned. Why are you so resigned, Holden?"

I said nothing.

"Storm trooper?"

"No."

"Party member?"

"No."

"I see you don't want to talk."

He was picking his teeth again. The candles flickered. The dog was whimpering softly. I told myself I didn't have a chance with Julius Brummer. Now his little eyes were slits.

"I have a lot of enemies in Düsseldorf, Holden. But I also have a lot of friends. At police headquarters too. What did you say?"

"I didn't say anything, Herr Brummer."

"For instance in the detective bureau. The chief's name is Rohm. Good fellow. Will do anything for me. Gives me all the information I need. Good to know, wouldn't you say?"

"Must be, Herr Brummer."

"I think I'll give him a call. What's your first name, Holden?"

"Robert."

He walked over to the telephone that was standing on one of the sideboards. "Robert Holden. Very good. Date of birth?"

"April 7, 1916."

"Where?"

I said nothing.

He began to dial. "Do you have a passport?"

"Yes."

"Let me have it."

I didn't move. Every street I took was a dead end, every direction the wrong one. There was no way out for me.

"Come on, Holden, your passport."

I could hear them ringing the number. I said, "Hang up, Herr Brummer. I've been in jail."

"Well, there you are. For how long?"

I lied. My past was dead, I had atoned for my sins. I had left Munich in order to live free again, so that the past would be dead. Munich was far away. I lied.

"Two years."

"When did you get out?" He put the receiver down.

"Four months ago."

"And why were you doing time?"

I lied and could see he didn't believe me. "Bankruptcy fraud. I had a textile business."

"Really?"

"Yes, really."

Yes, I lied to Julius Brummer. I was in prison not two but nine years, and not for bankruptcy fraud, but for manslaughter. I killed my wife, my wife Margit, whom I loved more than anything else in the world. I never owned a textile business in Munich. I was an antique dealer and appraiser. I had an elegant shop in the Theatinerstrasse. When the war started I was happily married. Poland, France, Africa, Russia—all the time I dreamed of my wife, only of her. She was the only thing that kept me alive, because I hated the war, the uniform, the killing.

Then I came home. End of 1946. It had been a long war, and I lost more than anybody else.

She was lying in bed with him when I came, in bed and naked. That's when I did it.

I struck her, again and again, and the blood was flowing over my eyes from the wound on my forehead that the fellow had dealt me before he ran off, so I saw everything through a thick, sticky red curtain. I beat her and I heard her screaming until the neighbors tore me away and began beating me. She died the same night, Margit, my wife, my love.

They took the extenuating circumstances into consideration and gave me twelve years. After nine years I was pardoned.

I left Munich. I came here to forget Margit, to forget

my past. I had lost everything—my shop, my home. I wanted to begin life all over again. That was why I lied to Julius Maria Brummer.

He looked at me silently. I rose, because I had the feeling he was about to dismiss me. Who was going to hire an ex-con? I was unlucky. I should have realized right along that I was unlucky, and that I'd never be lucky again. Not with what lay behind me.

"Why are you standing, Holden?"

"Because I'm leaving, Herr Brummer."

"Sit down. Four hundred marks, with room and board. Okay?"

I shook my head.

He interpreted my helplessness incorrectly. "Too little?"

I nodded. Everything was going in circles around me.

"All right, then—five hundred. But you might as well know it—you're going to have to work hard. I'm on the go all the time—Hamburg, Munich, Berlin, Paris, Rome—I won't fly. Hate it."

"You're hiring me in spite of the fact that I've done time?"

"I'm hiring you because of it. People like you are loyal. Any more questions?"

"Yes. Could I have a month's salary in advance? I have debts."

He took a roll of bills out of his trouser pocket, licked his thumb and counted out ten fifty-mark bills on the table in front of me. My neck felt hot, my lips were dry. The violet banknotes lay spread out in a semicircle. They looked to me like a rainbow at the end of bad weather. I could feel Brummer watching me curiously. I looked up.

"Do you drink, Holden?"

"No."

"That's the main thing. Women?"

"In moderation."

"Can you start right away?"

"Yes."

The telephone on the sideboard rang. He left me, moved liltingly across the room and lifted the receiver. "Yes?"

Then he was silent, listening to a voice I could hear but couldn't understand. I gathered up the bills. The old dog crawled on her belly to her master. The rain was beating on the windows.

"I'll be there right away," said Julius Brummer. He put the receiver back on the hook and passed a hand across his forehead. The dog howled.

"You'll have to drive me to the hospital," he said. "My wife is dying."

6

"Faster!"

He was looking out at the rain, his jaws chomping nervously. There was a smell of peppermint. I stepped on the gas. The speedometer needle moved up to a hundred. We were tearing south on the Rhine highway, to the center of town.

I had noted three cars in the garage—a Mercedes, a BMW, and a black and red Cadillac. We took the Cadillac. The dog lay between us, whining. Her saliva dripped, thin and sticky, onto the leather seat.

"Faster, dammit, faster!" said Julius Brummer.

A hundred and ten. A hundred and twenty. A hundred and twenty-five. The wipers were flailing like mad. The car began to dance on the wet pavement.

"Keep your pants on, Holden. A car like this has got what it takes. Cost me a fortune."

I reached the Marien Hospital in seven minutes. The car hadn't come to a dead stop in front of the lighted entrance before Brummer jumped out of it, the dog after him, yapping. The revolving door glittered for a moment as it turned, then both of them were gone.

I drove the Cadillac slowly back down to the street and parked a few yards away, under an old chestnut tree. Here it was dark. The rain drummed on the car top. I turned on the radio.

32

". . . At the signal it will be ten o'clock. Here is the news from Station North-West, Germany. London: The United Nations disarmament committee met today. Toward a mutual security system against surprise attack through worldwide cooperation of air and ground control, the ambassador from the United States, Harold Stassen, proposed to the Soviet Union on behalf of Great Britain, France, and Canada, and with the consent of the governments of Norway and Denmark, the following plan: The territory north of the Arctic Circle in the Soviet Union, Canada, Alaska, Greenland, and Norway, as well as the territory of Canada and the United States and the Soviet Union, one hundred and forty degrees longitude west . . ."

The street was empty. The rain was beating down on the pavement. My left hand was in the pocket of my jacket. In the pocket of my jacket were ten fifty-mark bills.

". . . one hundred sixty degrees longitude east and fifty degrees latitude north, also the remaining portion of Alaska and the peninsula of Kamchatka, as well as the Aleutian and Kurile Islands, to be part of the surveillance . . ."

Five hundred marks. The rent paid. Working for a man who asked no questions. In a city where nobody knew me.

". . . as well as a European surveillance zone between ten degrees longitude west and sixty degrees longitude east, also forty degrees latitude south, which would thus run from England, through the Mediterranan and the Urals . . ."

But why had Nina Brummer tried to take her life? Why did a rich, spoiled woman try to commit suicide?

". . . the West European nations would include West Germany, almost all of Italy, France, England, Ireland, Portugal, a major portion of Greece . . ."

Nobody knew why. Not even Mila Blehova. What did she look like, this woman, Nina Brummer?

". . . and a portion of Turkey, all in all an expanse of three point five million square kilometers in the surveillance zone. In exchange the Soviet Union . . ."

A rich man. Probably a profiteer.

". . . would open its satellite area and all territories to the Urals . . ."

Should I have taken the money?

". . . all in all circa seven million square kilometers . . ."

Why did Nina Brummer want to die?

". . . to the surveillance . . ."

I wondered: Is she dead? Then I fell asleep.

7

The car door slammed. I woke with a start. The radio was still on, a saxophone was wailing, the clock on the dashboard pointed to eight minutes before midnight.

"I'm sorry, Herr Brummer."

But the man sitting beside me was not Julius Brummer. He was wearing a black slicker, gleaming wet from the rain. Drops of rain ran from his blond hair down his ascetic face. Metal-rimmed glasses hid his eyes.

"Where is Herr Brummer?" He spoke with a Saxon accent, his voice sounded teary. "For God's sake, talk! It's important. I've been looking for him all evening. I called the house. The cook said he was at the hospital."

"So why ask me?"

"I have to speak to Herr Brummer—I have something to tell him."

"So go and tell him."

He made a face like an unhappy child. "I can't do that. I don't have permission. My train leaves in half an hour. I must leave Düsseldorf . . ."

"Who are you?" I asked.

The man looked starved and ill. A few of his teeth were missing. When he talked, saliva sprayed through the holes.

"Herr Brummer knows me. My name is Dietrich."

"Dietrich?"

"Yes. He was waiting for my call. What's happened?"

"His wife. Suicide."

"Oh God," he said, "because of that?"

"Because of what?"

"You don't know why?"

"I don't know a thing."

He looked at me helplessly. "What am I going to do?"

I shrugged.

"People like me always come to a shitty end," he said bitterly. "Assignments, orders, instructions, guide lines . . . That she'd commit suicide is something nobody thought of. So now we're in one helluva mess." He blinked, looked at me trustingly, "Would you give Herr Brummer a message, comrade?"

"Sure."

"Tell him his friend is here. His friend from Leipzig. He'll bring the material. Tomorrow afternoon, five o'clock."

"Where to?"

"Hermsdorfer Kreuz. Autobahn exit Dresden."

"In the Zone?"

"Well, of course." He sneezed loudly. "I've got to get out of here before they catch me. I don't know whether I can trust you but at this point I don't give a damn. For once I'm going to think of myself. What a shitty profession. Nothing functions any more. The whole organization—nobody knows their ass from a hole in the ground."

The saxophone wailed.

"Hermsdorfer Kreuz. Dresden exit. At five," I said.

"He'd better be on time."

"Okay."

"His friend will be carrying a black attaché case, and he'll have on a black raincoat, like me. Got it?"

"Got it."

"Not that I give a damn. I've had it, comrade."

"*Gesundheit,*" I said.

"A shitty life," he said sadly. "You can end under the ground. Ahead of time. Got a cigarette?"

I handed him my pack.

"May I take two?"

"Take the pack."

35

"I didn't mean to impose. I just don't happen to have any."

"Forget it."

"Swell car," he said, obviously in an effort to exit on a sociable note. He passed his fingers across the gold letters J and B on the car door. "Sure, sure . . . guys like us never make it. Farewell, comrade."

"Good night."

He walked off fast, down the street, thin, sick, in his crumpled pants and worn shoes. The saxophone finished a slow fox-trot. "And now, ladies and gentlemen, Ray Torro and his new hit song, 'Two Hearts Full of Glory on the Lago Maggiore' . . ."

I got out of the car and walked through the rain to the entrance of the hospital. I had decided to look for Julius Brummer. His wife was evidently taking her time about dying.

8

It was a Catholic hospital. The nuns wore wide white robes and wide white caps. I was astonished to see so many of them at this late hour. They were hurrying up the stairs and along the corridors, and some of them were pushing little carts with medicine. They were very nice nuns and they seemed to have a lot to do. There was also a nun sitting in the booth at the entrance. She was fat and wore glasses. I asked for Herr Brummer.

"He is with his wife," she said, putting down the newspaper she had been reading. The old dog lay curled up beside her chair and blinked at me sadly. She was shivering but her stumpy tail was wagging. "Dog's aren't allowed in the hospital," the fat nun explained.

"How is Frau Brummer?"

"Not good, I'm afraid. We must pray to God to forgive her for her mortal sin."

I didn't understand at first, but then I remembered that in her eyes suicide was a mortal sin, perhaps not only in her eyes, but altogether, and that I hadn't prayed for a long time. The last time I could recall praying was in a cellar, when the house was hit by a bomb. But perhaps you couldn't count that as a prayer.

"I must speak to Herr Brummer," I said. "I'm his chauffeur."

"Go up to the second floor and turn left to the private room. Report at the nurses' station."

All the way up the stairs there were niches, and in each niche stood the painted statue of a saint, about the size of a child. They were painted blue and red and yellow. Their halos were gilded, and gleamed. There were a few male saints, but for the most part they were female, and in front of each one stood a vase with flowers. My steps echoed in the corridor. A bell nearby tinkled softly.

I found the floor nurse for the private rooms at the station. She was young and pretty, but very serious. "Herr Brummer is with his wife." She was standing in front of a medicine cabinet and seemed to be looking for something among several packages of syringes. The blue light of the ceiling lamp fell on her.

"Will she pull through?"

"Only God knows that." She had apparently found what she had been looking for, a package of syringes marked: *Veritol.* Now she walked off, down the bluely lit corridor. I followed her. To create a more friendly mood between us I said, "That was a terrible thing she did."

"A mortal sin. May God forgive her."

"Amen," I said.

"The oxygen tent didn't help. And she hasn't reacted to the vascular treatment. We keep losing her pulse. Dr. Schuster is going to try a dialysis."

"What's that?"

"We tap two thirds of the blood and replace it with plasma. At the same time Dr. Schuster is going to inject Veritol directly into the heart."

"So she does have a chance?"

"A small chance, yes."

37

She opened a white door, the top part of which had a window. The door fell shut behind her.

I walked up to the window. There was a curtain on the other side, but it wasn't drawn. I saw the young nurse, an elderly doctor, and Julius Brummer. And I experienced a shock, the like of which I had never experienced before. What I saw wasn't what was dreadful, but that I was the one who had to see it, I, of all people . . .

The three were standing at the bedside of a young woman. She was lying on her back, obviously unconscious. Her blond hair covered the pillow, her face was blue, her lips were bloodless. Blue lids, the mouth open . . . Nina Brummer might be beautiful in life, I thought, but at this moment she was not. She looked as if she had been dead for hours.

The doctor and the nurse were preparing a transfusion. They moved the metal stand with the plasma suspended from it close to the bed; they fastened a rubber tube and a small phial to Nina Brummer's arm. Her husband was watching. He had his back turned to me.

Now the doctor drew back the bedclothes. The unconscious woman lay naked to the hips on a white sheet. Her body was beautiful, her breasts were large and voluptuous. The doctor leaned over her and listened to her heart while the nurse snapped the top off a syringe. The Veritol, in a long glass tube now, was honey yellow. The doctor applied the needle to Nina Brummer's white skin and plunged it in.

I turned away. Suddenly I felt sick. I couldn't stand the sight of this woman any longer. I knew her. I knew this woman.

I walked down the hall to a small chapel. Here there was an altar with a prayer bench in front of it. A large, colorful Madonna with a Child on her arm stood on the altar. Two candles flickered restlessly. There were flowers here too. Three rows of chairs stood in front of the prayer bench. The chairs were hard. On the left, as you entered the chapel, there was a second, smaller altar in an alcove. Here there were two upholstered chairs. I reached one of them just in time. Everything was spinning around me. I took deep breaths to control my nausea. My heart was beating wildly. The Madonna with the Child on her arm looked down at me earnestly.

So short, I thought, is the life of a lie. I wanted to flee the past. Here, in this quiet hospital, it had already caught up with me. I looked up at the Madonna and thought bitterly: Why don't you leave me in peace? I have atoned. And I have suffered—yes, I have suffered.

The Madonna looked at me stonily.

Why, I thought—why?

Everything had been going so well until I had looked through the window of that door. And had seen her again, seen Margit, my wife, not yet quite risen from the dead.

It sounds fantastic when I write it down like this, but that's exactly how it happened. *Her* body was lying there, *her* face, *her* blond hair, Margit's eyebrows, Margit's little ears, Margit's long, delicate hands . . . Margit was lying there and wasn't Margit but a strange, wealthy woman called Nina Brummer.

And yet . . . and yet she looked exactly as Margit had looked after I had done it, before they dragged me away like a wild animal.

My teeth were chattering. Behind that door lay Margit who wasn't Margit, behind that door lay my past.

Why? Why?—I asked the Madonna bitterly.

But stone can't speak.

I had to get away, I told myself, panic-stricken. I couldn't stay with Brummer. Who, in God's name, could endure seeing the beloved wife one has killed, daily?

No one.

And if Nina Brummer died? Then I wouldn't have to see her. Then the past would be dead. Is this a test? I asked the stone. In vain.

I had to do something. Read. Look at something. If I went on thinking about it, I would go mad. I walked back to the door of the sickroom, but was overcome again by nausea and didn't dare look through the window. I went back to the chapel. In front of the second altar lay an open book, a pencil hanging from it. I picked it up. About half of its unlined pages were filled with prayers, pleas for help, outbursts of despair, and expressions of gratitude in a variety of handwritings. I began to leaf through it.

"Holy Mother of God, help me in my need. Don't let it

be a tumor. My family needs me. Johanna Allensweiler, Düsseldorf 15, Grothestrasse 45/III."

"Dear God in Heaven, I thank you with all my heart for my successful bladder operation that took place on 23.4.56. Your faithful Lebrecht Hermine, presently at Duisburg Ruhrort, Kiepenheuerweg 13."

"Oh dear Lord in Heaven, pity our poor mother. This is the third operation on her right eye. Don't let it be cataract. Adolf and Elisabeth Kramhals and children, Heinz-Dieter and Christa, Düsseldorf, Wallgraben 61."

Some of the handwriting was trembly, some was firm, some had written in big letters, others in small. At the end of every entry was the full address of the inscriber. On every fourth page I saw the round stamp of the hospital administration, and always the same, precise signature: Angelica Meuren, Supervisor.

"The pneumothorax was your will, oh Lord. Help me to work with it as I have worked before. I have six dependents. Civil Engineer Robert Anstand, Düsseldorf-Lohausen, Flughafenstrasse 44/III, left staircase."

"Dear God in Heaven, give me the strength to remain with Rosemarie. She has been a cripple for ten years. The doctors say her case is hopeless. Forgive my sinful thoughts and give me wisdom. Amen. Hans H., Düsseldorf, Farberweg 14."

On one page a child had painted a bouquet. "For the dear Lord because He fixed it so that Mammi doesn't have any more pains in her stomach. From his Liebknecht Rudi, Düsseldorf, Weymayrstrasse 1."

A sound behind me made me look up.

Julius Brummer had entered the chapel. He reeled up to the main altar. He didn't see me. I got the impression that he wasn't seeing anything. He was staggering as unsurely as his dog. The tears were streaming down his face. He fell on his knees on the prayer bench in front of the Madonna with a crash. It sounded as if the wood had splintered.

My first reaction—to make my presence known—gave way to overwhelming curiosity. Rooted to the spot, I watched this massive man who had broken down before me. The candlelight was mirrored on his bald head. He was groaning; he beat his head against the rail of the bench. His body swayed from side to side, then straightened up. He tore off his tie, opened the top button of his shirt, and stared at the Madonna and her Child.

Clumsily, like a little peasant boy, Julius Brummer folded his rosy hands. Awkwardly he began to pray aloud. "Please don't let Nina die. Help her. Let the blood transfusion work, and the Veritol . . ."

He was panting. Then he rose and staggered up to the altar, propped his hands on the brocade altar cloth. His little mouth was twitching.

"If you let her live . . . I'll atone . . . for everything. I'll go to jail . . . I'll accept my punishment . . . I won't fight the miserable bastards . . . I swear I won't. I swear by my life. *I won't go into the Zone again . . .*"

He grasped the Madonna with both hands. His body sagged forward, the Madonna was in danger of toppling.

"I'll stay here and wait until they arrest me," Julius Brummer gasped, "but don't let her die. Please don't let her die . . ."

With a soft cry he let the Madonna go, his hand on his heart. Then he swiveled around once and fell flat on his face. As he fell, the statue fell with him. It hit Brummer with a dull thud, bounced off, and broke in two.

I leaped forward and turned the motionless man on his back. His eyes were wide open, all I could see were the whites. He smelled of peppermint. I ran up the corridor, calling for the pretty night nurse. She came out of the station.

"Herr Brummer," I said. "In the chapel. Quick."

"What's the matter with him?"

"He's fainted. I don't want him to know I found him."

She gave me an odd look, then she picked up the receiver of the phone on her desk. "Dr. Schuster, please . . this is an emergency."

9

They put him in a private room and gave him Bellergal when he recovered consciousness. He asked for a cognac and the bill for the broken Madonna. "Buy a bigger and better one. I'll pay."

They didn't tell him who had found him. He wanted to know how his wife was, and was told she was still alive, whereupon he began to cry and they gave him some more Bellergal and turned out the light in the room and advised him to breathe evenly and lie on his back.

It was a long night. I helped the pretty nurse to clean up the mess in the chapel, then she made some strong coffee for the two of us. By now she was very friendly. She said that before she had taken her vows she had known a man who had looked rather like me. The antiaircraft fire over Warsaw had shot him down right at the beginning, in September 1939. I didn't listen very attentively while she talked about her life, and I paid even less attention to the old snapshots of the pilot. They were worn from handling. He really did look a little like me. But I kept having to think of Julius Brummer's strange prayer.

If you let her live, I'll atone . . . I'll go to jail . . . I'll accept punishment . . .

"I corresponded with his mother for a long time," the pretty nurse was saying. "She was very fond of me. We would have been married in October . . ."

I won't fight the miserable bastards. I swear I won't . . . I swear by my life . . .

"I had my wedding dress and my trousseau—everything. We were going to live in Hamburg. On the Innenalster. The apartment had a balcony . . ."

I swear I won't . . . I swear by her life . . . I won't go into the Zone again . . .

42

"Sometimes, when I close my eyes, I can still see his face." She turned her head away. "But not always. I used to see it all the time."

At 4:30 Julius Brummer felt better and asked for me. I went to see him. He was sitting on the edge of the bed, chewing gum as usual. "Sorry that your work with me had to start like this. Are you tired?"

I shook my head.

"What's the matter? I can see something's the matter." He looked at me sharply. "Have you heard something about me?"

"Heard something, Herr Brummer?"

"That I passed out in the chapel. Have the nuns been talking? Has there been any gossip?" He was defending his reputation, his dignity. I thought of his distorted face in front of the altar, his maudlin promises . . .

"Nobody has said anything. I was told you weren't feeling well. I . . . I have something to tell you."

"What?"

"While I was waiting in the car, a man came up to me."

"What sort of a man?"

I told him all about it.

He sat there, motionless. The curtain on the window behind him began to glow. The light of the rising sun was coloring it pink. Brummer licked his lips, then he went on chewing. When I was through he said, "That would be this afternoon, wouldn't it?"

"Yes. Five P.M. Exit Dresden. Hermsdorfer Kreuz."

"Do you know where that is, Holden?"

"Of course," I said, and added, on purpose, "In the Zone."

"In the Zone," he repeated.

I swear I won't . . . I swear it by her life . . . I won't go into the Zone again . . .

It had been a long time since I had witnessed a sunrise, and I was surprised by how quickly it happened. Now the curtain was blood red and so bright that Brummer was silhouetted black against it, a fat, stooped ape. Gold rays of light shot across the ceiling from between the cracks in the curtain.

"Have you told anyone else about this?"

"No, Herr Brummer."

There was a crucifix over the door. He looked at it. Then he walked over to the window and pushed back the curtains. The sunlight was blinding. He opened the window and looked out at the hospital garden, lying still and dewy in the dawn. I could smell the cool air, the damp grass. A bird began to sing. Slowly, stubbornly, Brummer shook his head.

The door opened. The pretty night nurse said in a serious voice, "God has forgiven her."

"Is she dead?" Brummer asked hoarsely.

"She is going to live," the nurse replied, and smiled. "The transfusion was successful. Her pulse is regular. All we're giving her now is Strophantin."

Three seconds, then Brummer said, "No!"

"It's true."

He was shaking, torn between fear and hope. "It's not true!"

"But it is. Dr. Schuster sent me to tell you. He wouldn't have sent me if he hadn't been quite sure. Your wife is going to live, Herr Brummer. God is merciful."

Three seconds more, then Julius Brummer began to laugh. He laughed uproariously. Like a prehistoric creature, like a Titan—that's what he looked like to me. As he laughed he beat his chest with both fists.

"She's alive!" He spat out his gum. "She's alive! My darling is alive!" He slapped me on the shoulder, then he embraced the young nun. And all the time he was laughing.

The nun looked disconcerted. "Dr. Schuster wants to see you," she said.

Brummer walked to the door. As he passed me, he grinned. "Lie down on the bed, man. Get some sleep. And just in case, have the oil changed."

"The oil changed?"

"It's quite a stretch through the Zone," said Julius Brummer as the door fell to behind him and the nun.

Now the sunlight filled the whole room. Birds were singing in the garden. I walked over to the window. A light east wind was blowing. The sky looked clean.

I took off my jacket, unbuttoned my shirt, and lay down on the hospital bed, my arms crossed behind my head. So she was going to live and I would have to go.

44

But why did I have to go?

Margit was dead. I didn't love her any more. She had been unfaithful. What difference did it make to me, to have to see a woman so exactly like her? No difference at all. It had just been a shock, that was all.

I'll stay, I told myself. Ridiculous not to feel equal to the sight of a strange woman. A few days, and I'll be perfectly used to her. On the contrary: I *must* stay, in order to get over it. Because it would be much worse to go and to know that, far away, there she was.

So that was what I was thinking, Herr Kriminal Kommissar Kehlmann, for whom I am filling these pages. That was what I was thinking that morning, as justification to stay. My thoughts were pretty transparent, weren't they? You're a man; you'll know what to conclude from them.

10

That day it was hot right after breakfast. I can remember it exactly because in the end, everything that happened was due to the infernal heat. The light flickered on the asphalt, the metal hood of the car shimmered in the heat as I drove into town to have the oil changed. The women were wearing white blouses, shorts, and colorful dresses. Their arms and legs were bare, and much of their breasts. Nearly all the men were in shirtsleeves. There were puddles from the last night's rain. The water was steaming.

While the mechanic in the Goethe Garage did a lube job and changed the oil, I walked over to Grupellosstrasse 180 and rang the bell. There was no man in my landlady's life; she was a bitter woman with stringy hair and hungry eyes.

"Now look here, Herr Holden, this won't do. I suppose the fact that you don't pay your rent isn't enough. I have to open the door for you because you're too elegant to open it yourself."

I said nothing, but walked into my ugly room, took my old suitcase out of the closet and began to pack the few things I owned.

"So what's going on?" She came shuffling into the room, her thin arms on her hips. "You don't think you can get away with this. I suppose I'll have to call the police."

"I'm giving you notice, Frau Meise. Write down what I owe you, to the first. Everything. Hurry up!"

"You don't have any money. You just want me to leave the room so you can scram—"

I took the fifty-mark notes out of my pocket and held them under her nose. She stared at them, then she rushed out of the room. I closed my suitcase. It felt damp. Everything in the room had always felt damp. It was a damp, dark room with the view of a brick wall. The bedding had always been damp, and my shirts in the bureau, and my papers. But it had been a cheap room, thirty-five marks, and all I had really done was sleep in it. I had always worn an old shirt in bed, and my socks, because I had no pajamas and the damp had bothered me.

My landlady came back with the bill and I paid. She took the money and left the room without saying a word. I put the house keys down on the table, picked up my suitcase, and left the room in which I had slept for four months of my life and had had many nightmares.

In the garage they were finished with the car. I had them fill it up and tossed my ugly suitcase into the back. On the red leather it looked even uglier.

"I'd like to make a call," I told the garage boy. He gestured with his chin in the direction of a glass phone booth beside the station. I called Julius Brummer in his office. He had given me the number. There was sweat on my forehead as I waited for the connection. It was as hot as a Turkish bath in the booth.

"Holden?"

"Yes, Herr Brummer. I'm ready."

"Good." He sounded matter-of-fact, as usual. "I need another two hours, then you can call for me. Go home. Tell my valet to pack a suitcase for me."

"Yes, sir."

"Do you know the Stadler flower shop on the Königsalle?"

"No. But I'll find it, Herr Brummer."

A few children were playing in the shade of the garage. They had on bathing suits. A little boy was spraying the others with a hose. They were laughing and screaming and hopping around, having a great time.

"Drive there and pick up the flowers I ordered. They're for my wife. Take them to the hospital."

"Yes, Herr Brummer."

Yes, Herr Brummer. No, Herr Brummer. Right away, Herr Brummer. How quickly one caught on, how quickly one got used to it again. Yes, *Herr Leutnant*. No, *Herr Leutnant*. Right away, *Herr Leutnant*. It had not bothered me at the time and it didn't bother me now. In Brummer's house there was a room for me and it wouldn't be damp. There was money in my pockets, I had work, I had a boss who asked no questions. No, Herr Brummer. Yes, Herr Brummer. Right away, Herr Brummer. So? In the war there had been shooting besides.

"What do I owe you?" I asked.

"Herr Brummer pays by the month."

"Okay," I said, and took my place behind the wheel. The air conditioning began to hum when I started the motor. Cool air flowed through the hot car. Smoothly it glided out into the street. When we got back from our trip into the Zone, Brummer had told me, I'd get a smart uniform, tailor-made.

A uniform was a uniform.

Yes, *Herr Leutnant*. Yes, Herr Brummer. I had work. I had peace of mind. No questions. No suspicious looks. That was a lot for a man fresh out of jail.

I stopped the car, got out, and put my old suitcase in the trunk. Such a beautiful car and such an ugly suitcase. Hirnschall, the warden, gave it to me when I was discharged . . .

11

Thirty-one dark red roses. They had been double-wrapped in cellophane. It was a huge bouquet, almost heavy to carry. "And please cut the stems before they're put in water."

"I'll see to it."

"Came from Holland. Nothing finer. Herr Brummer will be pleased."

"The bill . . .?"

"Herr Brummer has an account with us. Thank you. Good day."

Slowly I was beginning to learn how the rich lived. They had charge accounts. They paid monthly. Their credit was good because they could be counted on to pay their bills. That was the difference.

In celebration of the day, I was still wearing my blue suit, but in the sunlight the fabric over elbows and knees was shiny. I know the woman in the flower shop noticed it. She had looked away as if she had seen something disgusting, like an epileptic having a fit or a man vomiting. It was a very elegant flower shop and Düsseldorf was a very elegant city. Julius Brummer was one of its most affluent citizens, and what was more, I thought, as I walked back to "my" elegant Cadillac, I could have a new suit tailormade for me anytime I liked. And I was going to get a uniform . . .

In the Marien Hospital a different nun was sitting in the entrance booth, and there was a different nurse on duty in the private-room sector. The pretty nurse who had lost her fiancé in a bombing raid over Warsaw was gone. An older woman had taken her place in the hot little nurses' station. She looked at me sternly when she saw what was inside the cellophane wrapping.

"They're supposed to be cut before they're put in water."

She said coldly, "Must have cost a mark fifty apiece."

"I'd say so."

"Sinful. A lot of families have to live a week on that."

Of the five hundred marks Brummer had given me, a hundred and seventy-five had gone to the widow Meise. But even with only three hundred fifty marks in my pocket, I felt like a close relative of Julius Brummer, a participator in his business, a member of the establishment. I nodded and left the disgruntled nun.

As I walked down the stairs I was thinking that the first suit I'd have made for myself would be grey—not double breasted. I would wear a white shirt, a black tie, black shoes, black socks. One could really wear anything with grey . . .

"Wait a minute!"

I turned around. The elderly nun was hurrying after me. "Frau Brummer wants to speak to you."

"To me? Why?"

"I don't know. She hasn't really come to yet, but she wants to see you. Come along, please."

So I followed her back into the private room sector and she ushered me into Nina Brummer's room and said in a loud voice, "The *gnädige Frau* is still *very* weak. She shouldn't be seeing anyone." Then she disappeared.

It was hot in the room. Nina Brummer's head lay propped up on cushions. She had been washed, her hair was combed, but her face was still a bluish white. She looked bloodless and depleted, and again it was Margit's face. The similarity was incredible. But now the sun was shining, I had recovered from the initial shock, I could take it. The thirty-one roses lay on the bed cover. She passed a trembling hand across the blossoms. Her grey lips moved. She spoke, but so softly I couldn't understand. I stepped closer. She whispered agonizingly, "The . . . new . . . chauffeur?"

"Yes, *gnädige Frau*."

She took a deep, hoarse breath. She still seemed to find breathing difficult. I could see her breasts rise and fall under the covers. Her big blue eyes were milky and glazed, the pupils shifted from side to side. She was obviously not

49

fully recovered from unconsciousness. She was alive, but barely so. The poison was still in her system. No. This woman didn't know what she was doing, or what she was saying. This woman was moving her head jerkily like a mechanical doll, and she was mumbling the word "help."

I leaned over her.

When she opened her mouth, her breath smelled of gas. I felt hot, hot and sick.

". . . must . . . help . . . me . . ."

At that moment, the elderly nun came in. She came up to the bed, took the roses, and said, "I have found a vase." She walked back to the door where she said in a sharp voice, "The *Herr Doktor* gave strict orders that Frau Brummer was to receive *no* visitors, and she is *not* to speak. It would be very bad for her." Then the door fell shut behind her.

Nina Brummer spoke between twisted lips. Saliva was running out of the corners of her mouth. "Hate me . . . they . . . all . . ."

That I could believe. She was certainly not popular here—a rich, spoiled woman, an idler, a sinner who had tried to take her own life. No, nobody here liked Nina Brummer.

". . . can't . . . trust . . . anybody . . ." Her head sagged onto her shoulder, her breathing was raspy, as if she were fighting for her life.

Gas . . . gas . . . the smell of gas. I couldn't stand the sight of those sightless eyes any longer. I felt as if I were spying on her sleep, on the stammerings of a stranger under the influence of a narcotic. I looked at the bedside table. A white telephone was standing on it. Next to it lay jewelry: a ring, a wide gold armband, a wristwatch with glittering stones.

". . . nobody . . . nobody must know . . . not . . . not even Mila . . ."

Her right hand reached under the covers, appeared again, holding a letter. I didn't move.

"Take . . . take it . . ."

A ghastly look of surrender was in her beautiful, hazy eyes. "Please . . ."

The hand holding the letter was stretched out toward me.

This woman wasn't in her right mind, I told myself. There could be no question of that.

I took the letter. I read what was written on the envelope:

Herrn Toni Vorm
Düsseldorf
Stresemannstrasse 31A

The letters were big, they looked windswept, they trailed across the paper like a bizarre spider's web. The letters looked like madness, like nightmare and fever. I put the note down on the sheet where there was a little hollow between Nina Brummer's breasts, and shook my head.

"He . . . he must . . . get . . . the letter."

She tried to raise herself to a sitting position, but fell back. She didn't know what she was doing. She had surrendered herself to me. She was risking blackmail, her marriage, her future. She was risking everything—under the influence of Cardiazol, Veritol, weakness, loss of blood, gas poisoning. The woman was not in her right mind.

I couldn't stand the sound of her hoarse voice any longer. I didn't want to listen to it any more. I shook my head again, and pointed to the phone.

"He . . . he . . . doesn't have a . . . a . . . telephone."

I don't know when I began to love Nina Brummer. Certainly not that morning. One can't fall in love with a stranger, with a woman on the brink of death. It's impossible. But in a unique way Nina Brummer was no stranger to me. I had known her in a very special way for years, many years. I knew her face, her skin, her eyes, her hair. Because they were Margit's skin, hair and face; they were Margit's eyes. I am a realist. I despise every type of metaphysics, but apparently for those who love there is no such thing as death. My love for Margit had not come to an end when I had killed her, on the contrary—I had killed her because I loved her. That was why I hadn't been able to bear the fact that she had been unfaithful to me. And now I was standing in front of a woman who looked so much like her, in a completely incomprehensible fashion.

51

Margit had come to life again in her. My love for Margit could go on. That may be the explanation for what I did: *I took the letter.*

"All right," I said.

I could discern an expression of boundless relief in her glassy eyes.

"Wait . . . for . . . an answer . . ."

"Yes."

"Call me . . ."

The door flew open. The nun said, "If you don't leave at once, I shall have to call *Herr Doktor.*"

Nina Brummer's head fell sideways. She closed her eyes.

I said, "I'm just leaving."

12

Stresemannstrasse 31 was an old, two-story house. It stood behind two crippled trees, grey and forbidding. It must have been built at the turn of the century. Massive sandstone caryatids supported the balcony over the entrance. Beside the front door stood a pale young girl in a black dress. She was wearing a floppy black hat and thick glasses and she was holding a pamphlet in her raised hand.

"God lives!"

"He does?"

"His Kingdom has come. Jehovah's Witnesses are preaching everywhere!" She lifted the paper high and I could see the title: *The Watchtower.*

"How much?" I asked.

"You mustn't buy anything you don't want to buy," said the girl. Encouraged now, she was smiling. "The Judgment Day will come in our generation. The evildoers will perish in the Judgment, but Jehovah's Witnesses, who love justice as you do, will be saved in the flood, like Noah and his family. And the saved will take possession of this earth in God's new world. You can read it in Peter and Matthew."

I gave her a mark, and she gave me a copy and said, "It only costs fifty pfennigs."

"That's all right," I said, and walked into the cool, dimly lit entry. There was a metal plate on the wall with the names of the occupants and a bell beside each name. There were four—two on the ground floor, two on the second. I read: *Toni Vorm, Musician.*

He lived on the second floor. There was a peephole in the door, and after I had rung the bell, I could see an eye behind it, looking at me. The sight of the eye startled me because I hadn't heard a sound behind the door.

"What do you want?" asked the invisible mouth of the face to which the eye belonged.

"I have a letter. For Herr Vorm. Are you Herr Vorm?"

"Yes."

He didn't speak clearly. Either he had a cold or he was drunk.

"Then open up."

"Put the letter in the mailbox."

"I'm to wait for an answer."

"The mailbox. Put it in the mailbox."

I shook my head.

The eye looked angry, the voice said, "Then forget it."

"The letter is from Frau Brummer."

The door flew open. A man, twenty-five years old at the most, stood in the doorway. He had on a dark blue shiny robe with silver trim. He was an exceptionally handsome young man and he didn't have a cold, he was just terribly drunk. His big black eyes were glowering, his short, curly hair tumbled over his pale, perspiring forehead, his full sensuous mouth was slack and open. He had remarkably long, silky lashes and expressive, finely shaped hands. He was really a very handsome fellow, broad shoulders, narrow hips, and he was barefoot. That was why I hadn't heard him.

Now he leaned against the wall. "Are you from the police?"

"No."

I walked past him, into the apartment, and thought of

53

Nina with the blue eyes and the white, voluptuous body. Dark Toni with his silky lashes, blond Nina—a beautiful couple.

The shutters had been closed, the electric light was burning. There was a smell of cognac and cigarettes. Music was scattered over an open grand piano. There was a shelf with a lot of books and magazines lying on it in a disorderly fashion, a wide couch with a low, tiled table and three chairs in front of it. Crumpled bedclothing covered the couch, four morning papers lay on the tiled table, between them a half-empty bottle of Asbach-Uralt and a glass. Dirty ashtrays everywhere.

The light from a ceiling fixture fell harshly upon us and the bright sunlight lanced its way through the cracks in the shutters. I sat down on the disorderly couch and noticed a photograph of Nina Brummer on a wall shelf. A large picture. Nina Brummer on the beach, laughing and waving, in a tight-fitting black bathing suit. She looked very attractive, a good deal more attractive than she looked right now.

The young man came staggering up to me. I gave him the letter. With a groan he sat down on one of the chairs and tore open the envelope. His hands were trembling so much that the letter inside fell out. He picked it up and began to read. As he turned the page around he groaned again and ran a trembling hand through his short black hair. He drank. He must have been drinking for hours. I looked at the newspapers on the tiled table and counted the words in the headlines. Four times I read the word "Nina," four times the letter "B", three times the word "suicide," and three times the word "affair." Then I noticed that the pretty young man had finished reading the letter and was staring at me. Now he pointed a finger at me. "Who are you?"

"Herr Brummer's chauffeur."

Vorm fell back in his chair and repeated, "Herr Brummer's chauffeur." He closed his eyes. "She must have gone crazy. Where did she give you the letter?"

"In the hospital," I said. "I'm a friend. You can rely on me. Your affair is no concern of mine."

"What affair?" He sat up, with difficulty. "I don't know what you're talking about."

54

"Oh, come on . . ."

"Go away," he mumbled and tried to get up. But he fell back again in his chair. His robe fell open. Toni Vorm was really magnificently built.

I walked over to the door. Somewhere, someone was flushing a toilet; you could hear it in the wall.

"Hey! You!"

I turned around. I felt sorry for him. Such a handsome fellow. And I could understand Nina.

With great difficulty he rose to his feet, swaying as he walked toward me, and fell onto the swivel chair in front of the piano. Both his elbows hit the keys. He began to slide off sideways, and I just managed to catch him before he hit the floor. He said, "I can't do it. D'you hear me?"

"All right—then don't do it."

"What's going on in her mind?" He managed to get to his feet again. With his back to the piano he could stand fairly well. His breath stank of cognac. It was a morning of smells.

"It's in all the papers. The police are investigating. What happens if they find out? I have to have peace. To work. I have a good job. Do you know the Eden Bar?"

"No."

"A good job. Really. I'm just starting. I have to think of myself too. Look at this apartment . . . the furniture . . . the books. Bought all of it myself. With my money. I . . . I won a prize at the conservatory. Here!" He slapped his hand down feebly on a heap of loose pages of sheet music. "My rhapsody. Two-thirds finished. I was going to buy myself a Volkswagen next year. I told her I could never marry her. I never lied to her. Why did she do it? Why?"

I shrugged.

"Brummer will finish me if they find out. What does she mean—flee? Where to? I'm asking you—where are we supposed to go?"

"Don't ask me."

He slapped the flat of his hand on the letter. "Air France. Book tickets for Paris. Right away. What sort of an idiocy is this anyway? She's in the hospital. How does she think she can get out?"

"No idea."

"And what do we do in Paris? I don't speak French. I

55

have no money. She has no money." He grabbed me by the lapels. "Why did she try to take her life?"

"Don't," I said.

"Don't what?"

"Grab me like that. I don't like it."

He let me go. "What's so terrible that she can't stand it?"

"I don't know."

"But that's what she writes."

"It's her problem."

"So why is it mine? She's married, isn't she?"

Nina Brummer was smiling at us radiantly from her photo, blond, enticing and desirable—apparently not desirable and enticing enough.

"I can't help her." Toni Vorm reeled back to the table, filled his glass, spilling some of the cognac. "I don't want to have anything to do with it. I've always told her—my work comes first. I've never taken money from her," he cried proudly. "Not even gifts. I'm ten years younger than she is." His voice broke. "We had an absolutely clear agreement, right from the start. She came up to me—"

"She came up to you?"

"Yes, yes. In the Eden Bar." He passed a hand across his mouth. "She's so sweet. So beautiful. We . . . we had some good times together, we really did . . ." Again he slapped his hand down on the pile of sheet music. "But here . . . almost finished. I never concealed it from her . . ."

"I have to go, Herr Vorm."

"Tell her I can't. Tell her not to write to me again. If she'll just lay low . . . Then, perhaps, we could meet again. Later. Tell her I wish her all the best."

"But you're not going to book the flight to Paris."

"No. And I don't intend to write to her. Or call her."

"Okay," I said. "And now stop drinking and try to get some sleep."

"I can't sleep. I don't want you to get the wrong impression . . . I'm fond of her . . . very fond. I feel terrible about what she's done. But I can't help her. Tell her that! *I can't help her!*"

When I stepped out of the dark hallway into the heat outside, I heard a friendly voice. "Good day, sir."

"Good day."

"God lives," said the little Jehovah's Witness. She was still standing in the sun, fulfilled in her mission.

"Yes, yes," I said, walking over to the red and black Cadillac. "We've already talked about all that."

"Oh, I'm sorry," said the little girl, smiling. I was to remember that smile.

13

The office building was nine stories high, situated in the heart of Düsseldorf, glittering and transparent. A network of antennae rose into the sky from its roof. The glass entrance doors opened automatically when you approached them. An electric eye opened them. Above the portal, two gold letters, a meter high, had been inlaid in the facade.

The huge lobby was air-conditioned. A fountain was playing. Little fish were swimming in the pool around it. The water was illuminated by lights, red, green, and blue. Dull yellow and grey were the predominant colors in the lobby. Busy people were hurrying back and forth. I saw a lot of pretty girls.

There were three elevators. Men in blue uniforms stood in front of them, the gold initials on their lapels. On one of the wider walls there was a vast mosaic mural: peasants plowing the fields; miners working in a shaft; women picking grapes; masons building a stone wall; pilots in a cockpit; researchers bent over their instruments; sailors at the steering wheel of their ships, which were crossing a stylized ocean. MY FIELD IS THE WORLD was embossed in gold over this impressive mural. Below it, six employees sat behind a long mahogany desk, three men, three women. All of them wore the blue uniform and the gold initials. The one with the red hair smiled at me as I came toward them.

"I've come for Herr Brummer. I'm his chauffeur."

The redhead made the connection, then handed me the phone.

"Everything okay, Holden?"

"Yes, sir. Your valet has packed a suitcase—shirts, toilet articles, black suit."

"Good."

"The dog is in the car. The cook has sent along sandwiches."

"I'll be with you in five minutes."

"Very good, Herr Brummer."

I gave the phone back to the redhead. She was evidently in good spirits. All the people in the lobby were in good spirits, probably because it was so cool. I asked, "What sort of business is this, anyway?"

She stared at me.

"I'm new on the job. This is my first day," I explained and smiled.

"Export," said the redhead. And smiled.

"What do we export?"

"Oh, lots of things—lumber and steel. Machinery and synthetics."

"Where to?"

"Everywhere. All over the world."

"Hm."

"I beg your pardon?"

"I didn't say anything. I've got to make a call."

"The pay booths are over there."

I walked over to where six phone booths were lined up against the wall. Above them various clocks told the time, in Düsseldorf and all over the world. It was ten to eleven in Düsseldorf, ten minutes to five in New York, ten before seven in Rio de Janeiro . . . I walked into one of the booths and found the number I wanted. I dialed.

"Marien Hospital."

"Frau Brummer, please."

"Sorry. I can't put you through to Frau Brummer." That was what I had expected, also what came next. "Herr Doktor Schuster has forbidden all calls. The patient is still very weak. She is not supposed to speak."

I said, "This is Herr Brummer. Will you please put me

through to my wife immediately or I'm going to raise hell!"

"Oh, I'm terribly sorry, Herr Brummer. I was only obeying orders. I had no idea—"

"My wife," I said. "Please!"

And then, from far away, I heard Nina Brummer's voice. "Yes?"

"This is the chauffeur."

"Yes . . . and?"

And why didn't I tell her the truth? Why did I lie to her? Was it out of pity? Or was this already love?

Ridiculous. The whole thing was unthinkable. Things like this didn't happen. No, it had to be Margit, still Margit whom I loved. Nina Brummer had Margit to thank for my miserable lie.

"Herr Vorm is going to do what you suggest. Only he wants you to be patient."

"Patient?"

"The police were there."

Silence.

"He managed to placate the officer, but he can't undertake anything now without attracting attention."

"Yes . . . yes . . ." A choking cough.

"That's why he's not going to call you."

Silence.

Through the glass door of the booth I could see Julius Brummer emerging from one of the elevators. He walked over to reception and the redhead pointed to the booth I was in. I said, "I was to tell you that he loves you."

It was a merciful lie, nothing else. In two or three days this woman would be sufficiently recovered for me to tell her everything. I went on lying. "His thoughts are with you all the time."

Julius Brummer came over to the booth. I waved. He nodded. "You must be patient."

"Thank you," the voice moaned.

"Auf Wiedersehen."

I hung up and left the booth. Julius Brummer had on a beige summer suit, yellow sandals, and an open yellow sports shirt. "Had to say a quick farewell to your girl, eh?"

I nodded.

59

"A pretty brunette?"

"A pretty blonde."

He chuckled.

In Moscow it was four minutes past one. In Rio de Janeiro it was four minutes past seven. In Düsseldorf it was four minutes past eleven, and very warm.

14

It got hotter. We drove south on the autobahn, through Bonn and Koblenz to Limburg. Here I took State Highway 49 to Giessen and Lich, with which I cut off the curve around Frankfurt. Highway 49 was being repaired. We had three detours and two stops. Julius Brummer was watching me. "You're enjoying the car, aren't you?"

"Yes, sir."

"You drive well, considering you're not really a chauffeur."

I said nothing. I knew what he was leading up to. I discovered a new aspect of his personality—so *that* was something he enjoyed.

"Haven't driven for a long time, eh?"

"No, Herr Brummer."

"How long, Holden?"

I gave him the pleasure. "Since I went to jail, Herr Brummer."

He grunted. I stepped on the gas. He had told me he liked to drive fast.

In the forest it was cooler. We stopped once. The old dog, who had been lying between us, jumped out and ran into the grass.

I got the wicker basket with the sandwiches out of the trunk, and a big thermos bottle. In a container, in dry ice, lay four bottles of beer. The ice-cold green glass frosted up as soon as the air hit it, and the beer hurt your teeth, it was so cold.

We sat down beside a brook that flowed along the roadside. I could see the stones at the bottom, and a few small fish, and I thought of the fish in the illuminated pool in Düsseldorf. The fish in the brook looked happier.

It was very quiet. Somewhere in the woods, men were felling a tree. The sound of their axes was dry. There were three kinds of sausage in Mila Blehova's sandwiches, and cheese, radishes, peppers and tomatoes. Dragonflies were hovering over the brook. The old dog laid her head on Brummer's knee. "Now she's hungry again, our Mitzili." Brummer fed the dog a sandwich. Slobbering, she ate out of his hand. Because our wife is going to live." He looked at me. "I live with that animal as if she were human. Sleeps on my bed." (And where does Frau Brummer sleep, I wondered.) "Yes, my pet, you are the most beautiful of them all, even if they never did clip your ears." There was honest indignation in his voice. "Can you understand that, Herr Holden? There are people who clip their boxers' ears because it's chic. The bastards! If I had anything to say about it, they'd go to jail!" He began to roar laughing. "Ho-ho-ho! That's a word you don't like to hear, isn't it, Herr Holden?"

I thought this was the sort of thing I didn't have to put up with. I took a cheese sandwich and said, "Are you going to do anything about the *Tagesspiegel*, Herr Brummer?"

"The *Tagesspiegel*? What about the *Tagesspiegel*?"

"They write that you're having business difficulties, and that's why your wife committed suicide."

His face darkened. "Pigs!" He spoke with his mouth full. "There are difficulties, to be sure. And my wife was worried. Much too worried." His eyes closed to slits and he whispered, so low I could barely hear, "But I'll fight them. Just let me get back to Düsseldorf. They want to break me, the bastards. Just let me get back from the Zone, Holden. Then I'll finish them off, the whole shitty bunch." He threw the rest of his sandwich into the brook. "My poor wife. She takes it all too hard because she loves me. I have only three people in the world who love me." He hitched up his pants and walked back to the car. "My

61

wife, old Mila and my Mitzi. Get rid of the paper and bottles."

"Yes, Herr Brummer," I said, and thought of how Julius Brummer counted a dog among the three people who loved him, and thought of Herr Vorm with the silky lashes.

The dragonflies were still hovering over the water and the sun fell slanting through the trees. It had been pleasant, eating beside the little brook. The sandwiches had tasted so good and the beer so cool. Pilsner. Draft beer.

15

On the autobahn it was blazing hot. I drove a hundred and thirty kilometers an hour all the way to Alsfeld. The wind hummed around the car. The old dog lay between us and slept. Julius Brummer smoked a strong cigar.

We tore around the curves of the Knüll Mountains between Niederjossa and Kirchheim, up and down again into the valley of Bad Hersfeld. Little white clouds collected on the horizon in the east. There was good visibility in every direction. I could see for miles—green fields with yellow and brown acres in between; villages with white-walled houses and red-tiled roofs, and many churches.

After passing the exits of Bad Hersfeld and Fulda, the autobahn rose uphill again, and the forest moved closer to the highway. The trees were dark green; sometimes they looked black. The woods smelled good, and here it was cool.

We passed a long column of American army vehicles, two-and-a-half-ton trucks, black tanks, and jeeps and armored scout cars. Soldiers in camouflage uniforms with steel helmets sat in the trucks. Soldiers with leather helmets and earphones looked out of the turrets of the tanks. Officers sat in the jeeps. Most of the drivers were Negroes.

At every autobahn exit I saw colored flags and a soldier standing alone with a submachine gun. I counted up to seventy tanks and over a hundred trucks. I didn't count the jeeps; there were too many.

"Maneuvers," said Julius Brummer, and flicked the ash off his cigar. "The Amis seem to be on the move in a big way." He let down the window on his side and stuck out his rosy little hand and waved. Some of the soldiers on the trucks waved back. Some didn't.

"If I were a pretty young girl, they'd all wave," said Julius Brummer.

We passed the trucks, and after a while more tanks. They were painted green and brown. Everything was moving east.

"Were you a soldier, Holden?"

"Yes, sir."

"In what capacity?"

"Tank corps."

"What do you think of these? Impressive, no?"

"Impressive."

"Although it's really ridiculous when you think of the hydrogen bomb."

"Ridiculous, yes, sir."

"Would you like a cigar?"

"No thank you, Herr Brummer."

Signs began to appear on the right side of the road, in English and German. I read: *Achtung! Only 150 meters to the Zone border.*

The autobahn wove downhill again, into the valley. Far to the east there were villages with white houses and red rooftops, and many churches. The fields were green and golden yellow, and there were brown acres in between. I could see a large city with many smoking chimneys.

"Eisenach," said Brummer. "That's on the other side."

"Yes, sir."

But there was no difference in the landscape. Everything on the other side looked just the same. Now a few wooden towers and bunkers appeared on the edge of the autobahn. In the fields below us I could see men in green uniforms. They were armed. Some were pushing bicycles, others were leading dogs, a few were standing still, looking through binoculars at the smoking chimneys of the city called Eisenach that was on "the other side."

Suddenly the autobahn ended in front of a dynamited bridge. Here there were signs with instructions in three languages that said Zone Checkpoint Herleshausen-Wartha was twenty-five kilometers away on a side road. The Cadillac bounced over potholes into the valley below, where cows were grazing. During the last half-hour everything around us had grown increasingly silent. We met very few cars. Some had the white Zone license. The road was narrow and very dusty; we had to close the windows. The landscape grew poorer and poorer. The people in the fields looked somber. "The asshole of creation," said Brummer.

A forest with shattered trees. A filthy village. A gas station. A store. Children picking their noses. Sand and dust. Bare red brick houses.

"Nobody'll invest a cent here, not in this shitty area. Look at the streets. All ready for the next war."

"Yes, sir."

"Ha-ha! What luck! That one's not going to be *our* fault!"

"No, sir."

The roads were truly execrable, with dangerous curves, worn-out shoulders and potholes.

16

The villages grew smaller and smaller. In a place called Eschwege, Brummer told me to stop in front of a store. "Buy some candy." He gave me the money. "The cheapest you can get; the more the better. There are always children standing along the road in the Zone. It's no fault of theirs."

So I went into the little store and bought thirty marks worth of candy and chocolate. It amounted to an awful lot. The storekeeper put it in a cardboard box for me.

As we passed the church in Eschwege, the bells began to toll. It was three o'clock. A hearse stood on the square in front of the church, and I saw many peasants with their wives, all dressed in black. They were standing in the red sand, watching the volunteer firemen lifting the coffin from the hearse and carrying it into the church. The firemen were sweating. They had on black trousers and black boots, red jackets with gold trim, and silver helmets. Now the bells had stopped ringing. It was very still on the square, and as we drove past, we could hear the women praying.

"Funerals are lucky," said Julius Brummer, toying with a button on his jacket. The red dust began to settle in the car; I could feel it in my throat and between my fingers on the steering wheel. The old dog slept. She was breathing heavily in the heat, and the chocolate for the children in the Zone was melting.

The last place before the border was Herleshausen. Beyond the town a massive viaduct passed over the street. The autobahn ran across it. The road we were on ended, and a dirt road led to the West German checkpoint. A few trucks and passenger cars were parked near it. There was a small tavern, a gas station, painted red and yellow, and a lot of flies. We could hear music coming from the tavern. Frank Sinatra singing, "Hey, jealous lover . . ."

The border guards were friendly. They were wearing pea-green trousers and shirts to match, and they were sweating. We showed our passports. The officers saluted and wished us a pleasant trip. The toll bar under the black, red, and gold flag rose, and we drove from one Germany across a miserable road to another Germany.

In the other Germany, the guards were just as friendly, and here too a black, red, and gold flag hung over the toll gate. The People's Police, or Vopos, as they were called, wore brown uniforms and were younger than the border guards in the West. There were also girls in uniform. They had on blue pants and blouses, and were sweating just as much as the men in their brown uniforms and the older guards on the other side, in the West.

"What is your destination?" asked the young guard at the toll gate. By his accent I could tell he was a Saxon.

"Berlin West," said Brummer. (One wasn't allowed to drive simply to Hermsdorfer Kreuz and back again; one had to go to Berlin.)

"First barrack," said the Vopo.

To the right of the road there was a railway station with surprisingly many tracks. People were sitting in the shade of the station. They were waiting for a train. The name of the place was Wartha. Huge piles of coal lay beside the tracks, glittering in the sunshine. It was very quiet in Wartha too, that afternoon.

I put on my jacket and we walked into the passport control office, paid the toll for the autobahn to Berlin, and were given a receipt. They asked how much West German money I had on me and entered the amount—three hundred and twenty-five marks—in my passport. Then they asked Brummer, but he didn't know how much money he had on him.

"Well, why don't you take a look in your wallet, *Herr Direktor*," said the Vopo.

I looked at the pictures hanging on the barrack walls. Pieck and Grotewohl, Arndt and Lessing, Joliot-Curie, and men who were unfamiliar to me. Under the pictures there were poems and slogans. I read a few, then I went out again into the fresh air. There was music coming from P.A. speakers—a Leipzig orchestra was playing a potpourri of old Peter Kreuder melodies.

The trees behind the checkpoint stood out starkly against the light sky. Four Vopos were playing skat. A tenor's voice sang from the loudspeakers, "I don't need millions, I don't lack a penny's worth of luck . . ."

I walked over to the car. A young border guard was standing beside it. He was blond, very thin, and couldn't have been more than twenty years old. I showed him my pass and opened the door of the car. The old dog lifted her head. I took off my jacket again and was hanging it on the hook when *The Watchtower* fell out of my pocket, directly at the feet of the young policeman. I had forgotten all about it.

17

As I have already said—it was the heat. If it hadn't been so infernally hot, all of us would have reacted differently, the dog too.

"What's that?" the young blond officer asked. He leaned down and picked it up. "Jehovah's Witnesses. Are you a Witness?"

"No."

Without saying another word, he read aloud the title of one of the articles, and silently I read it with him: "Communism Cannot Silence the True Christian!"

Softly the blond Vopo asked, "What are you doing with this?" He looked as if he wished the brochure had never fallen out of my pocket; I probably looked the same way.

"Nothing," I said. "Throw it away."

"Where did you get it?"

"In Düsseldorf." I thought of the black dress, the pale face, the floppy hat, the thick glasses, the brave little voice—"Good day, sir. God lives!"

Julius Brummer came prancing up to us. He was smiling jovially. "Anything wrong?"

"Your chauffeur—" the blond Vopo began, but he didn't finish the sentence. Perhaps he made a sudden movement, perhaps his boots had a smell the dog didn't like, but I think it was simply the heat. Suddenly the old dog yelped, jumped out of the car, and bit the Vopo. Her yellow teeth dug into the man's corduroy pants.

"Mitzili!" Julius Brummer screamed, horrified. But the dog only growled angrily. The left leg of the Vopo's pants tore open with a ripping sound. You could see the man's skin, his shorts . . . no blood. He cursed furiously and kicked the dog in the side. The animal flew into the air, turned over and landed next to the barracks wall where she remained prone, groaning.

Two uniformed girls hurried over; the four Vopos who had been playing cards hurried over, other people came running up. All of them stood around us in the sunshine but nobody said a word. The thin blond Vopo looked at his torn pants. He was still holding *The Watchtower* in his hands.

Julius Brummer was breathing fast. He was frightened; I could sense it, and the others could sense it too. You could almost smell Brummer's fear. He stammered, "Excuse me . . ."

The blond Vopo looked at him, standing there—a big fat man with a red and black Cadillac with whitewall tires.

"Please excuse us. My dog is old. She doesn't see well any more. Sometimes things startle her. Anything . . ."

More and more people came. Nobody said a word. The tenor in the loudspeaker caroled, "All I need is music, music, music . . ."

"A very old dog," Julius Brummer pleaded. "Almost blind, really, almost totally blind."

They were looking at him like a creature from outer space. They were all very young, but their faces were old, and nobody was fat, like Julius Brummer.

"My pants are shot," said the blond Vopo.

"I'll replace them. I'll replace everything. Luckily you're not hurt. What did the pants cost?"

"I don't know."

"I'll leave money here; any amount you say. My insurance pays for any damage my dog does."

"Not here."

"What?"

"Your fucking dog would have had to tear my pants in the West."

He was right. Five hundred meters farther west, the torn pants would have been no problem. Brummer lost his head. "For God's sake, I'll *give* you the money! We have to get going. I've got to be on time for an important business appointment."

He made one mistake after the other. Now he took out his fat wallet and took some bills from it and held them out to the blond Vopo, who looked at them in silent rejection and made no move to take the money.

"Well . . . come on!"

But the blond Vopo shook his head and stood there in the sunshine, pale and thin, looking ridiculous in his torn pants, with his grey skin and white shorts showing, and the old dog came crawling up to Julius Brummer and licked his shoes.

The blond Vopo said to one of the other Vopos, "Get the officer in charge."

"What for?" Julius Brummer sounded desperate. "Take the money, for God's sake. I'm in a hurry."

"I have to file a report."

Now Julius Brummer yelled at me. "What are you standing there for like an idiot? Talk to the man! If you hadn't lost that fucking paper, none of this would have happened!"

"None of this would have happened either if we'd driven up in an old Volkswagen instead of a Cadillac," I said, to help Brummer out, and I grinned at the blond Vopo. "Am I right?"

"I'm sorry," he said, more friendly now, "but I have to report this."

"Oh come on, let the damn thing slide. The boss is really in a hurry."

"That breaks my heart."

"Listen—we're coming back this way. Take his money. As security."

"I have to file a report," he said.

The others stood around silently in the hot sun. Nobody spoke. Everybody looked at Julius Brummer dully, without sympathy, and he stood in their midst, his wallet in his hand, with all that German money in it which had lost its value half a kilometer ago.

The shift commander came, and we followed him to his little office in which the flies were buzzing. He sat down in front of an old typewriter and began to type a report, slowly, and slowly each one of us was interrogated—the blond Vopo, Julius Brummer, and me.

We sweated in that little office, Julius Brummer most of all. Now everybody was very polite again. There was a clock on the wall. I saw it read 4:00, 4:30, 4:45. At five I

69

looked at Julius Brummer. He shrugged. I thought of the pale little girl in Düsseldorf, dressed in black, and heard her soft, courageous voice telling of the end of the world and of Noah and his family. She had also mentioned those who loved justice, but I didn't recall that at the time.

18

At 5:15 we were finally allowed to proceed. In the end the incident cost Julius Brummer eighty westmark—a fine of twenty, and sixty for the pants. But he had two receipts for the amounts and everything could be considered in order. The *Watchtower* had been confiscated. Also in order.

"A hundred and sixty-three kilometers to Hermsdorfer Kreuz," I said, after we had passed the second toll gate and I'd read the sign. "If I step on it we can be there in seventy minutes."

"Don't go over eighty," said Brummer. "I don't want any more trouble." He was smoking a fat cigar again. "The fellow at the Kreuz will wait. After all, I'm paying him." It seemed to comfort him that there were still people who let him pay them.

The road back to the autobahn was just as bad as the side road in the West. The houses were just as ramshackle and the people working in the fields looked just as poor. At last we reached the autobahn. It ran across Eisenach, and every now and then we came to stretches that had been destroyed. Detour signs warned us again and again. The chimneys of Eisenach were smoking and many windows were aglow with the light of the sun, which now stood in the west. Beyond the city, white rocks rose above the black forest, and on some of them there were castles.

Half an hour later the autobahn was in good condition in both directions and led straight east across a wide plateau. Now we met long columns of Soviet military vehicles. Heavy tanks, open two-and-a-half-ton trucks, and jeeps. Russian soldiers in pea-green uniforms sat on the trucks. Officers wearing red caps sat in the jeeps, and soldiers with leather helmets and earphones were peering out of the turrets of the tanks. All the columns we met were proceeding west.

I began to count the tanks again, and Julius Brummer stuck his head out of the window and waved, and a few of the soldiers on the trucks waved back.

"Got to hold maneuvers here too, of course."

"Yes, Herr Brummer."

There were more and more tanks and trucks with soldiers and on the mountains I could see more castles. Some were black and gutted, others were brick-red and looked inhabited.

"An awful lot of tanks. I hope war doesn't break out before we get to Berlin. That would be something, wouldn't it, Holden. Ha-ha-ha!"

"Yes, Herr Brummer, that would be something."

Gotha. Erfurt. Weimar. Jena.

Five forty-five. Six P.M. Six-thirty.

Now the sunlight was red. The color of all things changed constantly. The old dog was lying in the back. She sensed that her master was angry with her. She had buried her face between her paws.

"If the fellow's smart, he'll go into the HO-store and have a beer," said Brummer. It was meant to sound casual, but it didn't. He turned on the radio, which was still tuned to a northwest German station. A voice said, ". . . Many a film star would consider himself lucky if he could lose nine pounds in such a short time. For Montgomery Clift, however, it has been a catastrophe. Exhausted by his various film commitments and thoroughly run down, the popular actor has consulted a specialist who has recommended a gourmet diet of lobster, caviar. . ."

Julius Brummer turned the radio off again. Now the fields were red-gold, the meadows were violet, and the sky in the east was losing more and more color.

We reached Hermsdorfer Kreuz at 6:45. Under the grey overpasses of the autobahn, which intersected here, we could see a crowd of people. Vopos were directing the traffic. An ambulance stood on the grass.

A Vopo stopped us. He said politely, "You'll have to make a detour past the HO-tavern, sir."

"Why?" asked Julius Brummer.

"There's been an accident," said the Vopo. "Two hours ago. A PKW ran over a man. Hit-and-run driver."

Julius Brummer's face turned grey.

The Vopo said. "He was dead immediately. Funny thing . . . something fishy about it, if you ask me."

"What makes you say that?" I asked.

"Well now . . . look here . . . The man's standing on the side of the road, in the bright sunshine. Gets run into and thrown two feet in the air. The bastard at the wheel doesn't even stop. How do you figure that out?"

"Does anyone know who the man is?"

"No identification on him. Elderly fellow. Was wearing a black raincoat. In this heat. Must have been crazy."

19

Other cars were stopping behind us, blowing their horns. The Vopo waved us on. As the car began to move, I noticed that Julius Brummer was sitting in a tense position—his legs stretched from him, his hands pressed down on the seat. His face was ashen, his lips were trembling. He was mumbling, "Go on . . ."

So I drove off the autobahn and stopped in the parking lot in front of the town hall, which dated back to the Third Reich and was built in that typical style, with endless rows of windows, huge square capitals, and columns. Julius Brummer didn't move. His face was blue, his mouth was open, his tongue hung out of one corner.

Now he tore open his shirt and I saw that he was wearing a thin gold chain with a gold disc the size of a five-mark piece hanging from it. Engraved on it were the words: *I am having a heart attack. Please look in the right-hand pocket of my jacket and put one of the capsules you will find there in my mouth. Thank you.*

Julius Brummer

In the right pocket of his jacket I found a small box. I took out a soft transparent capsule filled with a red liquid and put it in Brummer's mouth. Then I pressed his jaw closed. A small sound indicated that the capsule had burst open. I waited a few minutes. Brummer began to breathe again, his face lost its blue color, he opened his eyes.

"Is there anything I can do for you?"

"I'm all right. It happens sometimes." He buttoned his shirt modestly, almost as if ashamed. "Well, now you know. For the future. I have to rest for a little while. You go back to the scene of the accident. See if you can find out what happened to the attaché case that the dead man was carrying. It's important. I have to know what happened to the attaché case."

"Yes, sir."

I got out of the car and walked back to the autobahn. There were still quite a few curious people standing around. The dead man and the ambulance were gone, but the Vopos were photographing a pool of blood on the road, the green line, footprints.

I took up a stand beside two little boys and listened to what they were saying.

"No skid marks. Wild! He must have driven a hundred kilometers an hour straight into his ass."

"Political."

"What?"

"Must have been political. Probably an Ami."

"You're nuts!"

"Didn't you just say—no skid marks? And did he have any identification on him? Nothing."

"I don't have anything on me, either."

"You're just a kid. But when an adult doesn't have any identification on him, he's political."

"You're crazy!"

"Don't look at me right away," a whining voice behind me said. "Don't give any sign that you know me."

I lighted a cigarette, then I turned around slowly and handed the pack to the man behind me. It was Herr Dietrich, the melancholy agent with the faulty dentures whom I had met the night before, when he had been looking for Julius Brummer. In the light of day he looked even more pitiful. The sweat stood out on his pale forehead and his nose was red and swollen from his cold. His eyes were tearing. I could see them behind his shining glasses, dull and resigned. He had on baggy grey trousers, rundown shoes, and an old brown jacket. He was sitting on the ground. I sat down beside him. He smelled of liniment and camomile. The two boys ran after the Vopos, who were scattering magnesium powder on the highway for further clues.

Spraying saliva through the openings between his teeth, Dietrich said, "I was there. It happened at a quarter to five. I have the license number. I saw it all. They stopped, but slowly, so the Vopos wouldn't find any skid marks. One of them got out and ran back."

"Why?"

Dietrich cackled. "The briefcase. He went back for the briefcase. Where's the boss?"

"In the parking lot."

"Tell him I want to talk to him."

"Then come with me."

"Too many Vopos. I have to be careful. Tell him to wait another fifteen minutes. I'll start walking. On the right side of the highway. Toward Eisenberg. When you catch up with me, I'll get in. Tell him he's not to try anything. We're in the Zone."

20

The sun had set. Evening came, and it was cool. In the west the sky was red, in the east it was colorless. I drove through the woods, toward Eisenberg. "There he is," said Brummer. He had recovered.

In front of us, on the side of the road, Dietrich was walking slowly northward, like a tramp, his hands in the pockets of his baggy trousers. I stepped on the brakes. The dog growled when Brummer opened the door and Dietrich got in. "Be quiet, Mitzili."

Now we were sitting side by side, the three of us. The woods retreated from the side of the road, just before Zeitz, and a wide, flat stretch of land opened up. Dietrich spoke humbly, yet his tone was fresh and strangely contemptuous. "Sorry about what happened, Herr Brummer."

"How do you happen to be here, anyway?"

"I was tipped off. Last night. In Düsseldorf."

Brummer turned to me. "Stop at the next parking area. We two will get out and have a little talk."

"Yes, Herr Brummer."

"Out of the question," said Dietrich. Suddenly he grinned. "Any car that stops now is suspect, especially any car with a West license. You don't think I want to go to jail for this."

"Do you think I intend to talk to you in front of my chauffeur?"

"Then forget it." Pitiful little Dietrich was a changed man. "I'm not getting out. Either we talk in the car or not at all."

Silence. Brummer stroked the old dog and looked straight ahead at the white center stripe on the road as it flew toward us. He had lost the first round. Now he let it out on me. "Holden!"

"Herr Brummer?"

"You seem constantly to be a witness to my private affairs." His voice rose. "You're fresh out of jail, Holden. That doesn't bother me. I gave you employment. But if you talk, if you say one word about what you see and hear here, you're fired, and I'll see to it that, as far as the West is concerned, you're finished. I know how to have a man taken care of if I want to, don't I, Dietrich?"

Dietrich nodded.

"Tell him."

"Herr Brummer can get any man hit if he wants to, so keep your trap shut, comrade!"

"Is that clear, Holden?" Now he was a big shot again,

75

Brummer, the boss. Brummer who would brook no opposition. Brummer the Titan.

"Perfectly clear, Herr Brummer."

After this victory over me, his spirits rose. "And now to you, Dietrich. What about this tip?"

"That they're after our man. They want the papers."

"And where did this tip come from?"

"I'm a poor man, but I have friends. I got the tip from friends."

"Why didn't you let me know?"

"I couldn't reach you. I tried the hospital."

"You're lying."

"I'm a poor man."

"You're a bastard."

"A poor bastard, Herr Brummer. A poor bastard has to see where his bread is buttered. I've got sick lungs."

"Shit!" said Julius Brummer.

The road rose again. In the north the sky was violet and hazy. The light was failing.

"It's perfectly clear to me. You went to the Kreuz and waited. You didn't warn your comrade."

"He wasn't my comrade."

"You thought: Let's see who makes it. Brummer or the others. The others made it. So you waited for me. If I'd made it, you'd have sent the others after me."

"A poor man doesn't have much choice, Herr Brummer. When one's rich, like you, things look very different." Dietrich sneezed and the dog growled.

"Quiet, Mitzili. I could report you at the next checkpoint. You know that."

"Yes, Herr Brummer. Of course, Herr Brummer. They would interrogate me and I'd have to tell them everything I know. And there's plenty to tell, Herr Brummer. Oh God, oh God . . ."

"My chauffeur says you know the license number." That was a second defeat. Automatically he involved me in it.

"That's right."

"Who can guarantee that you're not lying?"

"Nobody, Herr Brummer. The car is still on the autobahn, but soon they'll get to the Berlin Ring. I have friends at the border. If we can get together on this, I'll get out in Schkenditz. There's an HO-store there. I'll phone my friends. They'll hold the car as soon as it comes in. Give it a thought. The papers are in the car. If we can't come to an agreement, the papers will be flown back to the West, early tomorrow morning."

"How do I know this isn't a trick? I've never seen the papers."

"But I have."

"You're a liar."

Dietrich said, with the pride of a proletarian, "I'm not going to take any abuse from you, Herr Brummer."

"Well now, look here—after all, this is blackmail."

"I've done dirty work for you for years. You didn't pay me well. Why? Because you've got something on me. Perhaps you've got something on a lot of people. But now *I've* got something on *you*."

"You don't know a thing."

"Just let those papers get into the West, Herr Brummer."

He took out a handkerchief, blew his nose, and looked full of self-pity at the results. "I've had enough of this life. I'm forty years old . . ."

He, too, I thought.

"At forty a man begins to think things over . . ."

Indeed, I thought.

"They say every man gets one chance in his life. Well, this is mine. I'm moving to Munich. I'm going to open an espresso there. I was a waiter once. I know a thing or two about it . . ."

We passed a sign: *HO-Gaststätte Schkenditz—17 km.*

"Look, Herr Brummer, even the little man has to think of his future. Security—it's a word for everybody."

"How much?"

"Twenty thousand."

"You're crazy!"

"I have expenses. I have to pay my friends in Berlin."

Twilight was falling. I turned on the parking lights.

"You know something, Dietrich? You can kiss my ass!"

"Twenty-five thousand, Herr Brummer. Five thousand for what you just said. I may be poor, but I'm a human being, just like you. I'm not going to take any insults from you."

"And I don't let myself be blackmailed, not by a filthy little bastard like you. Holden!"

"Herr Brummer?"

"Stop. Throw the man out."

I drew up at the side of the road. The air had grown damp and I slipped on the wet grass as I walked around the car and opened the door on Dietrich's side.

"Don't trouble yourself, comrade," he said, and got out. "Once those papers get to Düsseldorf, you can look for a new job too." He stuck his hands in his pockets and walked away.

Four steps, six steps, seven . . .

"Five thousand," said Brummer.

Dietrich lumbered on along the side of the road, into the twilight.

"Ten thousand!"

No answer.

"Fifteen! And that's my last word on it."

Dietrich walked on. A car with a West license plate passed us. The driver blew his horn.

"Herr Brummer, we can't stand here."

"Dietrich!" he yelled. It was the way one yelled at a dog.

Dietrich didn't react. By now he was fairly far away, a grey figure almost swallowed up by the night. The fog was creeping out of the woods, milky and thin.

Another car passed us. Again the driver blew his horn, long and furiously.

"We can't stay—"

"Drive after the bastard. Hurry up!"

So I got behind the wheel again and turned on the headlights. Their beams cut through the fog and lit up the old pants, the dirty jacket, the dull blond hair. I caught up with Dietrich. He jumped into the grass and began to run in the direction of the nearby woods. He had just witnessed what could happen when a car hunted a man down. I stopped.

Brummer threw open the door and yelled, "Come here!"

Dietrich stumbled on, in the direction of the trees.

"You can have your money."

Dietrich stopped, stood in the knee-high grass. "Twenty-five thousand?"

78

"Yes. Twenty-five thousand."

"How do I get the money?"

"A check," groaned Brummer. I thought he was going to have another attack. "On a bank in the West. A check you can't cash for three days. If it turns out you lied . . ."

"Write the check," said the ugly little man with a cold, standing in the midst of sage, cornflowers and thistles. Julius Brummer took out his checkbook. He wrote the check on his knees.

"Here, Dietrich."

The agent came back, through knee-high grass, thistles, cornflowers and sage. Brummer held out the check to him through the window.

"If I'm arrested when I cash it, I'll tell everything," said Dietrich. Then he became very businesslike and gave the license number of the car that had run down and killed the man at Hermsdorfer Kreuz, the color of the car, and the names of his friends at the checkpoint before West Berlin.

Julius Brummer wrote it all down. He had put on horn-rimmed glasses to write the check and now, in the precise handwriting of an A student, wrote in a notebook the information Dietrich was giving him. Then he looked at me across his glasses like a fat owl. "Get going to Schkenditz as fast as you can. The man's got to phone."

"Yes, Herr Brummer."

The fog that had crept in on us from the woods grew thicker. It swept across the autobahn, but the headlights were still above it. I drove fast, disregarding the speed limit. The sky turned black. Lights swam in the fog ahead of us. "That's Schkenditz," said the agent.

"Stop at the tavern," said Brummer.

"No, a little before that, please."

"All right."

As the lights came clearer through the fog, Dietrich said to Brummer, "Checkpoint Dreilinden. West Zone. Beside the barracks. A man will come up to you and address you by name. By your full name."

I stopped. Dietrich got out. "I'm going to get a new set of dentures, too," he said, nodded to both of us, and walked quickly into the fog.

"Fucking fog," said Julius Brummer. "Let's hope it

79

doesn't get worse." I thought of how our safety depended sometimes on papers, sometimes on license numbers, and sometimes on fog. A pitiful world.

On the other hand . . .

Three weeks before I had gone with a prostitute. She had a small apartment. Afterwards we had talked about life. She was a very pessimistic girl. She said, "It's no-fun any more. A bit of happiness and then . . . such a lot of trouble. Thanks for the fruit."

"Do you want to die?"

"The sooner the better. You can have it."

"Have what?"

"Life."

One way of looking at it . . .

But then, on that same night, we could smell gas in the little apartment, and we ran into the kitchen in a panic, naked, and saw that one of the gas jets was on. We had been boiling water for tea, and while we were in bed, the water had boiled over and put out the flame.

"Oh my God," said the girl, "just think, love, if we'd fallen asleep . . . I feel sick. It could have killed us!"

21

Before we reached the Elbe, the fog became so thick I had to slow down to thirty. Every now and then I let down the window and stuck out my head because the glass kept misting over. The fog smelled of smoke, the air smelled of water. All I could see was the stripe down the middle, sometimes not even that. There were constant signs that one lane was closed, my lane. After a while I lost my bearings completely and was afraid I'd overlooked a sign and was on the wrong highway. The uncertainty made me feel quite dizzy, although every now and then I could tell by the lights approaching that I was in the right lane.

On the Elbe Bridge, mechanics were working overtime. Their acetylene torches lit up the big tower. Beyond Coswig, I ran over a rabbit. There was the usual repulsive thud and the car skidded, as it always did, and it was after that that Julius Brummer began to talk. He hadn't said a word since Dietrich had got out. Now he said, "I threatened you a while ago, Holden. I'm sorry about that. Forgive me."

"Yes, Herr Brummer."

The fog was beginning to move. An east wind was driving it in vapor clouds across the highway. Brummer spoke deliberately, like a man dictating his will. I wondered if he was going to die soon. How strange, I thought, if he should die and I would have to remember what he had said to me that night . . .

"You've seen a lot happen since you entered my service. Bad moments . . ." He was staring at the white stripe and gradually my back began to ache. It had been a long day.

"Now a lot more is going to happen, Holden. I may need you. Can I count on you?"

I said nothing. It was 8:30. For half an hour no car had passed us and none had come toward us on the opposite lane. We were afloat in a sea of fog, as if we were the last people on earth.

"You don't know me. I'm not asking you to do anything out of friendship. No sentimentality. *I pay.* Will you help me if I pay?"

"I must know what's going on, Herr Brummer. You see, I'm just—"

"—out of jail," he said. "And that's just what I mean, Holden."

"I beg your pardon? . . ."

"Why are you just out of jail?" He answered his own question. "Because in jail you atoned. And what did you atone for? A sin committed in the past." He stuck a piece of chewing gum in his mouth and coughed. "You see, Holden, most people alive today have an inconvenient past. Some were Nazis, some were Communists. Some emigrated, some should have emigrated but didn't. Some can't believe in God anymore, others have made a mess of their marriage . . . If only there were something, some-one, who could undo all these things. The little man has

81

trouble. Families are falling apart. Everything that's been done for the children is wrong. The politicians sleep uneasily. How can anybody be expected to stand up for something he said a year ago? The men who invented the atom bomb . . . nothing tastes right to them any more. How nice it would be if one could say, 'It wasn't us, gentlemen. Other people did it . . .' "

Now it began to rain. We passed a sign. We had reached Treuenbrietzen.

"Take anyone—big people, little people . . . all of them have a past. A big past, a little past. They're afraid, they feel guilty. Do you know what all of them need, Holden?"

"What, Herr Brummer?"

"A double. By God, that would be the invention of the century! A second *I*. To take on everything one's done— the mean things, the errors, the mistakes. I should get out a patent for that one. A double for one's conscience is a soft cushion!"

22

A double . . .

I don't know if you have any idea . . . this feeling when something suddenly gets a hold on you, when it takes root in your brain, in your blood . . .

A double . . .

Somebody talks to you all day but just one sentence sticks. Maybe just a few words. And they don't let you go. Have you ever experienced it?

A double . . .

No more guilt, no more atonement. On Judgment Day you can say: I didn't do it. Somebody else did it, somebody who looks like me, speaks like me, lives as I do. But he is evil, I am good. He has to be punished, not I.

But there is no such thing as a double.

How's that?

A thing that doesn't exist is a thing, according to man, that has not yet been discovered. And the thing itself has nothing against being discovered. Such a double therefore does not *yet* exist.

I don't know if you have ever had this feeling, when an idea suddenly gets hold of you, when it takes root in your brain, in your blood . . . On that rainy night an idea was born. It was born between Treuenbrietzen and Berlin Ring, and he himself awoke it in me, he who was to become its victim—Julius Brummer.

23

Again his deliberate voice penetrated the rushing sound of the rain. Like a soft fade-out in a film, it brought me back to the present.

". . . my past, too, Holden. I'm going to be completely frank with you, not because I want your understanding. No. I'm going to pay you. But because you've got to know everything if you're to help me . . ."

A destroyed bridge. Billboards blurred in the rain. The Volkseigene Betrieb Zeiss-Jena recommend their products. Leipzig welcomes you to the Fair.

"Yes. I too have a past, and I too have no double to relieve me of it, no wicked Julius Brummer II on whom I can unload everything."

I'll have to think about it, I told myself; later, when I'm alone, I'll have to give all this a lot of thought.

"They're after me, Holden. They want to haul me into court . . ."

"Who, Herr Brummer?"

"My enemies. I'm successful, therefore I have enemies. They're trying to frame an indictment against me. They've been trying for months. Honorable citizens, respected business men, well-known people. Do you know what I've done about it?"

"What, Herr Brummer?"

"I told myself: These people too had to have a past. My theory: Everyone has a past. Cost me a lot of money, but now I've got it."

"Got what?"

"The pasts of my accusers. In photos and documents. In picture and word. And do you know where?"

"In the stolen attaché case."

"Right."

"So you *don't* have it."

"I'll get it back. You can depend on it. In Dreilinden, Checkpoint West. Herr Dietrich's friend is waiting for us. Herr Dietrich is my friend because I've given him money. Herr Dietrich's friend is my friend because Herr Dietrich has given him money. I'll get the attaché case. I've got plenty of money and I'll have many more friends, among them you, Herr Holden." His voice sank to a whisper. "Whoever owns that attaché case is the most powerful man in Düsseldorf, perhaps the most powerful man in the country. No one would dare to take him to court. There isn't a suit in the world you could bring against him. What was that? Another rabbit?"

"That was the candy, Herr Brummer. It fell off the seat."

"What candy?"

"For the children in the Zone."

24

Nine-ten P.M.

Berlin Ring.

A confusion of entrances and exits. An interchange to Frankfurt an der Oder, Küstrin, and Potsdam. Thirty kilometers maximum speed for military convoys. After Babelsberg there were new signs. Arrows pointed the way to "West Sector Berlin." Lights flew by. Now it was raining hard. The sky ahead of us was getting lighter all the time.

Checkpoint Dreilinden, brightly lit by floodlights, appeared suddenly right after a curve. There were very few cars on the road that evening, not a soul was waiting at the East checking office. I saw pictures again, read poems and slogans, and the police were friendly.

We drove on at 9:35.

A kilometer farther on, the West checkpoint loomed ahead of us, a single long barrack, with loading ramps running down the middle of the autobahn. A Berlin policeman waved us on. He wrote down our license number and was just as friendly as his colleague in the East.

"You came through Töpen?" he asked.

"Through Wartha," I told him.

At the end of the ramp stood a black Opel. Two men in raincoats were sitting in it. One of them got out and came slowly toward us, his hands in his pockets, his hat pushed down over his face.

"Everything's in order," said the friendly policeman. "Proceed."

I stepped on the gas and let the car roll toward the man in the raincoat. "There he is," said Brummer. He sounded happy. "You see how everything functions?"

"Yes, sir."

Now the man was standing beside the car. Brummer let down the window. The man was young. He leaned forward into the car. "Julius Maria Brummer?"

"Yes."

"From Düsseldorf?"

"Yes."

"We've been expecting you, Herr Brummer."

"Yes."

"Is that your chauffeur?"

"Yes."

"Good. Then he can drive the car back to Düsseldorf."

"What do you mean?" Brummer's voice was flat.

"Julius Maria Brummer," the man said slowly. "My name is Hart. I'm a police officer. I am arresting you on orders of the Düsseldorf district attorney."

The rain was drumming on the roof of the car; in the haze many lights were glittering, red and white.

Hart said, "When they found out this morning that you had left Düsseldorf, heading for West Berlin, the district attorney's office in Düsseldorf got in touch with us by teletype, asking us to hold you at the border because there was fear that you might escape."

"And what is the charge?" Brummer asked calmly.

"The charges are," replied Officer Hart, "uttering and publishing forged documents, fraudulent promotion of nonexistent corporations, speculating in letters of credit, extortion, tax evasion, and illegal dealing in foreign currencies. Please get out."

In his crumpled summer suit, Brummer got out of the car into the rainy night. In a weak voice he asked, "What are you going to do with me?"

"You will remain here until morning, at police headquarters. Then we'll fly you to Düsseldorf."

"I can't fly. I have a heart condition."

"Do you have a statement to that effect from your doctor?"

"Of course."

"Then we'll transport you on the interzone train."

The old dog howled. "Yes, Mitzili, yes . . ."

"The dog stays with the chauffeur," said Hart.

Suddenly Brummer yelled. "The animal is used to me! You can't separate us!"

"Herr Brummer, please . . . You are going to jail pending investigation."

"I'm telling you—my chauffeur can't handle the dog. She'll run away. She attacks people. I'll accept no responsibility for—"

"You can't take the dog with you."

In the dark in front of us the headlights of a car flared up for a moment and immediately died down again. I saw it, Brummer saw it. Hart didn't see it; he had his back turned. The quarrel about the dog continued.

"At least let me take the dog back to Düsseldorf!"

Again the headlights flared up and died down again, and a third time. Other people here were expecting us . . .

25

They argued about it for quite a long time, then Brummer got his way. The old dog followed him into the black Opel. I followed them, carrying Brummer's suitcase. He was sitting in the back. I put the suitcase at his feet.

"Thank you, Holden. Take a room in a hotel and drive back tomorrow." He nodded. "And don't worry. Nothing's ever as bad as it seems. Remember our talk."

"Yes, Herr Brummer."

"No further conversation," said Hart.

I said, "Good night, Herr Brummer."

The door was closed, the Opel drove away. I stood there until the red taillights had disappeared. Then I went back to the Cadillac, sat down behind the steering wheel, and waited. The rain beat on the roof of the car. Every now and then a car from the Zone drove past me. I waited eleven minutes. Then a man came forward out of the darkness at the end of the loading ramp and walked toward me. He had on black corduroy pants and a brown leather jacket, and he looked like a heavyweight wrestler. He was a very big man and he walked stooped forward a little. His brutish head rested directly on his shoulders; he had no neck, his dull blond hair was cut short, his tiny watery eyes were embedded in fat, puffy hollows. He walked in a lightly bouncing way, and he looked like a vulgarization of Julius Maria Brummer. Without a word he opened the car door and dropped on the seat beside me. I could smell the leather of his jacket and the wet material of his pants. I stared at him, he stared at me. After a long silence he said in a high, shrill voice, "Well, get going."

"Where to?"

"To Berlin, man!"

"Are you . . ."

"Sure. I'm his brother."

"Whose brother?"

"Dietrich's brother. Don't lose your cool. Everything's A-okay. Two of our comrades are taking care of the gentlemen. They got Brummer, didn't they?"

"Yes."

"Won't take long and he'll be out again. Well, for God's sake comrade, go!"

I drove off. We left the lights behind us. The wipers were flip-flopping. The giant said, "My name is Kolb."

"I thought you were—"

"I am."

"But?"

"Different fathers, young man. Different fathers."

We passed a pedestal with a rusty Soviet tank on it. Two soaking-wet soldiers were standing guard. It was the monument that had been moved from place to place again and again in Berlin. In jail I'd read an article about it. So now the tank stood here . . .

"You took an awfully long time, comrade."

"Fog."

"I know. Just the same . . . the others were here hours ago. Your name's Holden?"

"Yes."

"Been in jail."

"How do you—"

"My brother. On the phone." He sighed. "With one person it's the pokey, with another it's something else. Take a look at me. What do you suppose went wrong with me?"

"What?"

"Hernia. One false move and curtains. Do you know what I was?"

"What?"

"Ever heard of the Five Arturos?"

"Yes," I lied.

"You see. Numero uno. In all Europe. Three times in the U.S.A. I was the bottom man. A false move. Double hernia. Tough shit, no?"

We reached the Avus highway. The red lights of the RIAS-Berlin radio towers sparkled in the rain.

"Really shouldn't complain. Have a brother . . . true

blue. Supports me. Know what I mean? Well, at last he's hit the jackpot. Has it coming to him. No . . . really. There is still a God, even in our heaven. Now he's rewarding Otto for what he's done for me."

"Listen, Kolb, where are we going?"

"For God's sake, man—home. For a bit of shut-eye. Aren't you tired?"

"Yes, but . . ."

"Hasenheide."

"What's that?"

"A street in Neukölln. Pension Rosa."

"But listen . . ."

"What do you want? American Sector. Telephone in your room. That's important."

"Why?"

"Because I've got to be able to call you and tell you where you can pick up the case with the stuff."

Now there were fresh lights ahead of us. The end of the Avus. We had reached Charlottenburg. I said, "Are you sure you'll get the case back?"

"The case I don't get back doesn't exist!"

"Now, now . . ."

"Nix now now. Everything's under control. There's just one small problem: One of the three guys has shackled the case to his wrist, with a chain. And there's a lock on the chain. As I know the brothers, another one has the key."

"So?"

"Look here, you're not trying to insult me, are you? I didn't have the hernia in my fins. Is a specialty of mine. Look, the old radio tower. You know, every time I see those lights I get sentimental. No . . . I really do. I've been around, all over. Never saw anything like it. I think I speak all right now too, as if I'd been born in Berlin, not in Dresden. What do you think?"

"You're right."

"My brother couldn't stand it here. Found it too quiet. Well . . . a waiter . . . you know how it is. They like noise, confusion, crowds . . . all kinds—but me? No sir. Just look at those lights on the tower. You can eat up there, you know. I never did. Supposed to be okay."

26

My room in the Pension Rosa was as small as the one I'd occupied at the widow Meise's in Düsseldorf, and it was furnished just as poorly. But it was not damp, and there really was a telephone beside the bed. A Bible lay on a bookshelf, a brochure on how to raise small animals, and three French magazines: *Regal*, *Sensation* and *Tabor*. In *Regal* there were pictures of naked girls, in *Sensation*, naked men, in *Tabor*, both.

I went to bed and read the magazines, where I learned that rabbits were extraordinarily fertile. Between March and October they could produce four to twelve young every five weeks, the latter being capable of producing six months later, even though not full-grown for twelve months. Finally I leafed through the Bible for the story of Noah and the flood, but by that time I was too tired and didn't find it.

The telephone woke me at 2 A.M. I had fallen asleep without turning out the light. "Holden?"

"Yes."

"This is Kolb." His high-pitched voice sounded happy. "Did I wake you, comrade?"

"Yes."

"Good. We're all set. Six-thirty A.M., Tempelhof Airport. Be punctual and you'll have it."

"Do you have it?"

"Come on brother. We're not going to a fire. The guy's in his hotel, sleeping it off."

"So?"

"Man, but you're impatient. Bavarian, I'll bet."

"Yes."

"Thought so. I've just told you: Tempelhof Airport. Order coffee. I'll be there. He'll be there. He's flying at seven.

Anyway, he's booked a flight for seven. You don't have to pay any attention to me. When I go to the john, you pay and bring the car to the main entrance. Got it?"

"And if you don't go to the john?"

"You can depend on it—I'll go."

In the morning the sun was shining. It was just as hot as the day before. I drove to the airport, sat down in the restaurant and ordered coffee. Below me silvery planes were taxiing on the airfield, or waiting to be refueled. Loudspeakers were announcing departures and arrivals. I saw people walking to their planes. There was a lot going on. The restaurant began to fill up.

Kolb appeared at 6:25. He had on a double-breasted blue suit with loud white stripes, and an open white shirt. He sat down beside the entrance, paid no attention to me and I paid no attention to him. Both of us drank coffee.

At 6:40 a man came in carrying a large pigskin attaché case in his right hand. It was attached to his right wrist by a silver chain. The man was tall and slim and he was wearing horn-rimmed glasses. He looked like a professor. A blond waiter took his order at 6:42. The former bottomman of the Five Arturos was reading the *Tagesspiegel*. "Attention, Air France," said the loudspeaker. "Clipper 546 to Munich is ready to take on passengers at Gate Three. We wish you a pleasant flight."

At 6:48, a blond waiter brought the man with the horn-rimmed glasses a small pot of coffee. He was a very awkward waiter. Just before he reached the table he stumbled, the coffee pot tipped over, and its contents spilled on the grey flannel suit of the man with the horn-rimmed glasses. This was followed by quite a scene.

The man with the horn-rimmed glasses got very excited. The blond waiter apologized. Other patrons got involved and agreed that the blond waiter had been grossly negligent. The man with the horn-rimmed glasses tried to wipe his suit with a handkerchief. He didn't do very well because he could only use his left hand. The clumsy waiter recommended that he use the washroom. The man with the horn-rimmed glasses got up furiously and left the restaurant. So did Kolb. So did I . . .

The toilets were situated to the left of the entrance. As I passed the men's room I heard an ugly sound on the other side of the door. I walked through the lobby to the exit and from there to the parking lot to get the car. The gigantic radar screen was revolving slowly in the morning air.

As I drove past the glass entrance doors of the lobby, Kolb came out of one of them. He was carrying the pigskin briefcase. He got into the car and I drove off. The briefcase lay between us. The silver chain was broken. Its links were bloody. I shoved it under the seat.

"You can let me off at the Kurfürstendamm," said Kolb, drying his hands on a dirty handkerchief. There was blood on his hands too. "You have to take the Kurfürstendamm anyway if you want to get on the autobahn, and I've got to go to welfare."

"To welfare?"

"I know, now they call it Social Services Bureau. I've got to get my money."

"Won't you be early?"

"Doesn't matter. So I'll be the first in line. Don't mind waiting. I'll read the paper. What do you say to this guy, Khrushchev?" So I drove him to the end of the Kurfürstendamm, where he left me. "Was a pleasure, Holden. Was happy to be able to get the thing done so promptly. Get out of the city as fast as you can. After that you can take your time."

"Will do."

"My best to Herr Brummer. Always glad to serve him."

"I'll tell him."

"Say . . ." He was looking longingly at the box full of candy. It was still lying on the floor at the back. "Is that candy you've got there?"

"Yes."

"What are you going to do with it?"

"Nothing."

"Could I take it along? I have two boys. Crazy about candy. I don't think Herr Brummer would mind."

"I'm sure he wouldn't," I said, and he got the box out of the back. For a few seconds I could see him in the rear mirror, waving. He was standing on the curb and looked happy.

I got out of Berlin as fast as I could. On the border everything was calm again. I passed through the checkpoint without incident. Near Bruck I drove to an abandoned parking lot, stopped the car and got the briefcase out from under the seat.

It was very quiet on the parking lot so early in the morning. Cows were grazing in the distance, and I could see a windmill, its wings revolving slowly. I opened the door of the car, turned on my seat and let my legs hang over the side. In the briefcase there were many photographs and documents, letters, and photostats of documents, notarized. I looked at all the photographs, I read all the letters and documents and photostats. The sun rose in the sky; it grew warmer. Every now and then a car passed by. The cows stood in the grass, their heads lowered, grazing.

After I had read everything and looked at the photographs, I put it all back into the briefcase and shoved it under my seat again. Then I drove off. The sun was on my left now. I turned on the radio and listened to a morning concert, Station Deutschland. I thought of what Julius Brummer had said: "Whoever has that briefcase is the most powerful man in the city, perhaps the most powerful man in the country."

I didn't know how powerful the most powerful man in the city might be, nor the most powerful man in the country, but the briefcase Julius Brummer had referred to was lying under my seat now. Sometimes it slid forward and back a little, sometimes the broken silver chain tinkled, and all the time I was thinking of my mother . . .

For my mother the most beautiful day had always been Saturday, and the most beautiful time—Saturday noon. We were poor and we had debts. Still, once a week my mother's face was happy, and she'd say, "Robert dear, now we have peace and quiet until Monday morning. No bill collector, no gas bill . . . they can't even turn the electricity off this afternoon or tomorrow. So for me Saturday is the most beautiful day in the week."

I asked, "Why not Sunday, mama?"

"Because," she replied, "on Sunday I begin to dread Monday again, my precious. But on Saturday there's always that day in between."

This bit of logic impressed me as a child to such an extent that from then on I made it my own. It never left me.

93

This may also have been because all my life I never stopped being afraid—not any more of the gas or electric-light bills, but of much worse threats; no longer of debts, but of people, because people could do you harm, and did me harm . . . And the 23rd of August, 1956, the day on which I was driving Julius Brummer's Cadillac west through the Russian Zone, was a Saturday, and passing through the miserable landscape of Mark Brandenburg—because I had chosen the shorter route to Helmstedt—I thought for a long time of my mother.

The sun rose in the sky, the shadows of the meager scrub pines on the dull yellow sand grew shorter, and I thought of how this was a very special Saturday, a Saturday to end all Saturdays. But no . . . the end of all Mondays and my fear of them.

I don't know if you understand what I mean, this feeling, to have power. Until this 23rd of August, 1956, I had never had power, not in any sense of the word. And nobody I knew had any power. That was why I had tried over and over again to imagine how the powerful must feel, the great world-betrayers, the millionaires and warmongers. Actually the power I now possessed wasn't even *my* power; still I was determined to participate in it in a modest way. *I* could manage without Julius Brummer, but *he* could no longer manage without me! I felt I had every reason to hope that he was not a snob and wouldn't find it beneath him to share his secrets with his chauffeur. He didn't seem to be gaited that way. He had impressed me as a democratic man.

No, Herr Kriminal Kommissar Kehlmann from Baden-Baden, who may be the recipient of what I am writing—I don't think you know it, this feeling of power. Not real power. Not true power. Power of the kind that on the 23rd of August of last year lay under my car seat in the shape of documents and photographs. It is a heady feeling, *Herr Kommissar*. I am sure you have never felt it, just as my poor mother never did, my mother, of whom I thought on that 23rd of August between Magdeburg, Eichenbarsleben and Checkpoint Helmstedt, of whom I thought as I drove west on one of those sunny Saturday afternoons that she loved so much.

BOOK TWO

1

The wind lifted Nina Brummer's skirt as she got out of the taxi. I saw her beautiful legs. Her blond hair was flying wildly around her head. She was still so weak that she staggered as she got out, and fell against the side of the car. The driver jumped out and supported her. Then he got Nina Brummer's luggage out of the car—a Canadian natural-mink coat and a square, black jewelry case. That was all. He carried the coat and the case into the lobby of the Düsseldorf-Lohausen airport.

Nina Brummer followed him. The wind tugged at her. She was wearing a black and white checked suit, high-heeled shoes, and black gloves. Her face was white, her mouth a garish red.

I had parked the Cadillac some distance away from the entrance. I had been waiting for Nina Brummer for a quarter of an hour. I had thought I would have to wait longer; she was early. It was 6:35 P.M. on August 27, 1956. I had come back from Berlin four days before. In those four days much had happened. My head was bandaged; under my left eye the skin was still bruised; and the whole middle of my body burned as if I had undergone an operation. Yes . . . a lot had happened in those four days. I shall report about it later.

Nina Brummer disappeared through the lobby entrance. I got out and followed her. The sun was setting under wild black mountains of clouds. Around it the sky glowed sulphur yellow and copper green, violet, and scarlet. The wind was growing stronger by the minute. Signs were flapping, loose pages of newspaper fluttered around my legs, dust whirled in the air. I was limping because I was still lame from the beating I'd had to take.

In the lobby the fluorescent lighting was on, and it blended with the light of the setting sun that fell through the ceiling-to-floor windows, resulting in a cold, spectral atmosphere. There was a lot of light, but it wasn't a living light. Nothing and no one cast a shadow.

Like a voice from the region of the dead, the echoing words of a hidden loudspeaker announced: "Herr Engelsing from Vienna, just arrived on KLM, please report at the KLM office . . . Herr Engelsing from Vienna, please . . ."

The people in the lobby spoke softly. Outside the windows the dust was flying by like a veil. I stood behind a newspaper kiosk and watched Nina Brummer. She was standing at the Air France counter, checking in. Her ticket was stamped, she was given a boarding card. Above her a brass sign dangled on a chain. It read: Next flight: 20:00, AF 541 to Paris.

Nina Brummer never stopped looking around the lobby. She was expecting someone. I knew whom she was expecting and that she was waiting in vain.

The voice from the loudspeaker was distorted by static that sounded like the rustling of leaves. "Pan American Airways Clipper 231 from Hamburg. Passengers will arrive at Gate Two." I looked out onto the airfield. A four-motor plane was rolling to a stop in a whirlwind of dust. The propellers stopped turning. The mechanics bringing up the gangway were fighting the wind. Nina Brummer took her mink coat and her jewel case and walked up the broad staircase to the restaurant in the mezzanine. I followed her slowly.

The restaurant was empty. The setting sun was painting a magnificent picture on the wall: scarlet on sulphur yellow, violet on copper green. Nina Brummer sat down at a window table. The light caught her hair and it gleamed like gold. I stood in the doorway, watching her. At first she remained alone, then a waiter came and took her order, then she was alone again. She looked down at the area in front of the control tower. The passengers from the plane that had just arrived were walking toward the lobby, leaning against the wind. Fat little fuel cars buzzed up to the plane. Mechanics dragged metal hoses to the wings of the clipper.

I walked up to Nina Brummer's table. "Good evening."

There was fear in her big blue eyes. She was pale and beautiful. "Good evening," she said, in a hoarse voice.

I felt strangely let down; disappointment passed like a stab through my beaten body. "You don't recognize me?"

Her pale hands became fists and she pressed them against the black and white jacket of her suit. "I . . . no . . . who are you?"

I said nothing because the waiter was just coming back. He put a glass of cognac on the table. He looked at me curiously, then he left us. Nina Brummer whispered, "Are you . . . from the police?"

"I am the new chauffeur."

"Oh." Her hands relaxed and fell into her lap. Her nostrils quivered. Later I found out that this was a habit of hers. She could control herself very well, but not her nostrils. "I'm sorry, Herr . . ."

"Holden."

"Herr Holden. Your bandages . . . Were you in an accident?"

"In a way—yes."

"What happened?" She didn't wait for an answer, but asked, "And how do you happen to be here?"

"I knew I would find you here."

"But how is that possible? Nobody knows . . . I . . . I left the hospital secretly."

"I know."

"But how could you know?"

"I know everything," I said, and sat down.

Now the fluorescent lighting in the restaurant was turned on and outside, on the airfield, red, blue, and white lights were gleaming. In the west the horizon was rapidly turning the color of dirty ashes. Wispy black clouds scurried across the sky.

Nina Brummer's eyes lay deep in their sockets and she was very pale, but even in fear and weakness, she was beautiful. I thought of the words of the old Czech cook: "She is so beautiful, sir. Like a living angel . . ."

"Tell me," she whispered. The gold bracelets on her

99

wrists tinkled as she lifted her glass and drank. She spilled most of the cognac; the brown drops fell on the white cloth. "I'll give you a bracelet . . . I'll . . ."

"I don't want a bracelet."

". . . or money . . ."

"I don't want money."

"Then what do you want?"

"I want you to come with me."

"Are you crazy?" She laughed helplessly. Outside, the last light of the dying day was suddenly sea green, and the bones of her face glowed for a moment through her thin white skin. "Where am I supposed to go with you?"

"Home," I said. "Or back to the hospital. We'll think of some excuse. In an hour you'll be back in your bed. Nobody need know."

She pressed both hands against her temples and groaned because she couldn't grasp what I was trying to say. "What interest can you possibly have in my staying here? You say you know everything—then you must know that I want to leave my husband . . . and why."

"A lot has happened since we saw each other last. Your husband—"

"Is in jail."

"Yes . . . still."

She started, and whispered, "Still?"

"Not for long. You can't go to Paris. It would be insane. I . . . I . . ." Suddenly I said the wrong thing, because I could see her before me, naked, could see her beautiful white body that was longing with every heartbeat for someone who wasn't coming. "I . . . I won't permit it!"

"You must be out of your mind! What do you mean— you won't permit it? You are our chauffeur."

"Herr Vorm is not coming."

Now there were tears in her eyes and I felt pity for her, sincere pity, not desire any longer.

"He . . . he isn't coming?"

"No."

"I don't believe you! I sent him his ticket. He'll come. Our plane doesn't leave for another hour."

I laid something on the table.

"What's that?"

"You know what it is."

The little pale blue leaflet lay between us. Both of us looked at it. "His ticket?"

"Yes."

"How did you get it?" Now there was panic in her voice. "Has something happened to him?"

"No."

"But his ticket . . ."

"Will you please listen to me, *gnädige Frau?* Quietly? I have something to tell you."

She bit her lip, nodded, all the time looking straight at me.

"Five days ago your husband was arrested in Berlin. You know that?"

"Yes."

"Four days ago, on Saturday, I got back to Düsseldorf . . ."

2

Four days ago, on Saturday, at about 6 P.M.

I got back to Düsseldorf with the car. I took a hot bath and shaved. Then I sat down in the kitchen and ate the fine veal goulash that Mila Blehova had cooked for me. I was hungry. She knew I was coming. I had called her from Braunschweig. ("It's just eleven. I'll be with you between five and six, Frau Blehova." "Very good, Herr Holden. And please call me Mila. Everybody calls me Mila." "But then you must call me Robert." "Oh no, please. I couldn't do that." "Why not, Mila?" "You're a man, Herr Holden. And so much younger. People would talk . . .")

I had taken it easy after my return, that sunny Saturday afternoon. I had read the evening paper in the tub, I had sat at the window of my room over the garage and smoked a cigarette and looked out at the park as it slowly went under in the darkness. Then I sat in the kitchen with Mila and ate her fine goulash and drank the excellent Pilsner beer she served me. Both chambermaids and the valet had gone into town, dancing; the butler had gone to the movies.

The old dog was asleep beside the stove. So Julius Brummer had had to part with her. Mila Blehova was baking a pie. She broke two eggs into some flour, sprinkled powdered sugar on it and spread little pieces of butter over the whole thing, As she worked, she talked. "I saw my Nina this afternoon, Herr Holden. They let me see her."

"How is she?"

"Oh God, she's still weak, my little Nina, but she had rouge on her lips and she said to me, 'You see, Mila, I did it because I was so afraid something was going to happen to my husband.' " Mila Blehova began to knead the dough. Every now and then she exhaled nervously. "And I said to her, 'But Ninale, my foolish little girl, whatever got into you? The *gnädige Herr* is innocent, we know that. They're only jealous of him because he makes so much money, so they're accusing him of something he never did. Just out of meanness. They'll have to acquit him, and soon *they'll* be convicted,' and my Nina asked, 'How do you know that?' and I said, 'The *gnädige Herr* told me so himself.' "

"When?" I asked.

"Today. At noon. He came home with two gentlemen from the police, and his lawyer, to get a change of clothes and some papers, and that's when he said, 'Don't worry, Mila, the whole thing is a misunderstanding. That's all there is to it. So don't start belching again because it isn't worth it.' That's so like him—always thinking of others, never of himself."

"Yes," I said, and refilled my glass. "A wonderful man."

"Isn't he, Herr Holden! I'm so glad you feel the same way about him. As far as I'm concerned, the *gnädige Herr* is the most wonderful man in the world. So kind. So generous. And he thinks very highly of you too, Herr Holden."

She exhaled heavily. "Oh God, oh God, here I go again . . ."

Now she was rolling out the dough. "Everything's going

102

to be all right," she said cheerfully. "I'm not the least bit afraid. The *gnädige Herr* is good, that's why everything that's bad is against him. That's how I've figured it out." She spread the thin dough on a metal pie pan and started to cover it with slices of apple. "He'll like this."

"The pie is for Herr Brummer?"

"Well, of course. It's his favorite. The pastry thin and the apples thick. I asked the gentlemen from the police. They said it would be all right. I can take it to him tomorrow. I always bake a pie for him on Sunday. It's his favorite day." She smiled. "So, for a while, but just for a while, the wicked people are having it their way. Isn't that so, Herr Holden? Hitler, for instance—the whole world trembled before him, he was so powerful. But for how long? And in the end he was destroyed, with all his power, and the good thing triumphed. Or Napoleon, with all his victories—in the end they locked him up on an island. And Julius Caesar. He was certainly very powerful and still, so I hear, they stabbed him to death in the end, right in his own parliament in Rome. No, I told my Nina, in the end the good thing is always victorious. And that's why we mustn't worry about the *gnädige Herr*. Am I right?"

"Mila?"

"Yes."

"Will you do something for me?"

"Anything, Herr Holden."

I put my hand in my pocket and drew out a small key. "When I called up from Braunschweig today, I had some papers in the car, papers that prove Herr Brummer is completely innocent."

"Oh dear Jesus, I knew it! I knew it!"

"I rented a safe-deposit box in Braunschweig and put the papers in it. I'm the only one who can take them out, with this key and a code."

"But how right the *gnädige Herr* was! You *are* a good man. How lucky we were when you came to work for us!"

"I want you to take this key, Mila. Put it away carefully. Don't tell anyone that you have it. Do you know a good place to hide it?"

"I have a nephew. He lives near here. I'll take the key over to his place. This evening."

103

"Nobody can do a thing with the key, you understand? I'm the only one who can open the box. Still, I don't want to have it on me."

"As soon as the pie's done, I'll run over to my nephew's, Herr Holden."

"Thank you, Mila."

"Oh, before I forget it, somebody called up, for you. A couple of times."

"For me?"

"Yes. A friend. He said he had to speak to you."

"What was his name?"

"He didn't want to say. He sounded a little shy. He's at the Eden Bar. He said you'd know who it was if I said Eden Bar. Do you know who it is?"

I nodded, and thought of his long, silky lashes and his unfinished rhapsody.

"I may go over this evening for a minute or two. That was perfectly wonderful goulash, Mila. The best I've ever had."

"You embarrass me, Herr Holden."

"No, really—I mean it. And thanks again for looking after the key."

As she opened the oven door to check on the pie it was as if my mother were standing there, a shadowy figure against the white-tiled wall. And from far away I could hear the courageous voice of a woman who all her life had been harried by debts and tradesmen, by tax officials and the ever-recurring neccessity to put a warm meal on the table for her family. "Saturday is the loveliest day in the week . . ."

3

He looked elegant in his tuxedo, and he played marvelously, a true talent. Quite a few women had hungry expressions on their faces when they looked at him surreptitiously. A pretty fellow, this Toni Vorm.

The Eden Bar was full, not an empty table anywhere. I sat down at the horseshoe bar. A lot of candles, red velvet, and a few prostitutes. The prostitutes looked modest. There was an elderly gigolo and there were three bar girls, not exactly in their prime. I drank whiskey to celebrate this auspicious Saturday and felt tired from the trip, but not very tired. It had been a long time since I had sat at a bar and drunk whiskey.

I looked at Toni Vorm and he nodded at me across the piano, as much as to say that he'd come and talk to me as soon as he was free. I nodded in a way intended to imply that I wasn't in a hurry.

The whiskey warmed and calmed me, and I thought of a garden in which I had played in my childhood and where I had eaten cherries from a tree. We were poor, but we had had a garden for me to play in.

"Another whiskey?"

The bar girl wasn't pretty any more but she still had a good figure, a little too plump, perhaps, but since I'd got out of jail I had a weakness for slightly overweight women. She had on a black evening dress, the shoulders bare. She wore a lot of cheap jewelry, too much make-up, and her dyed red hair brushed straight back. She smiled with her lips closed. Probably had bad teeth.

"Yes," I said. "Will you have one with me?"

"Thanks." She filled my glass; she filled hers under the counter. She looked at me and smiled, still with her lips closed.

"Tea," I said.

"What do you mean?"

"You're filling your glass with tea. You couldn't possibly drink whiskey with every guest. After all, you've got to be able to balance at midnight, right?"

"You're nice," she said, and toasted me. "It *is* tea. With ice it doesn't taste bad. By the way, I have a daughter."

The lights went out; a spotlight concentrated on a black-haired girl who now walked slowly to the piano and began to undress. The band stopped playing, all except Toni Vorm.

"No, no, they can't take that away from me," the girl sang, and took off her jacket, then her skirt.

"My daughter's name is Mimi," said the bar lady. "My name is Carla."

". . . the way you wear your hat, the way you sip your tea," sang the stripper.

"Blond. Built like me. But young. Very sweet, I'm letting her study drama history."

". . . the memory of all that—no, no, they can't take that away from me . . ." Her slip. Her bra. Right stocking. Left stocking. She let a very drunk customer undo her garter belt.

"*Prost*, Carla!" I said. "My name is Robert."

"*Prost*, Robert! She's really a darling girl. Her father left us, but Mimi and I—we stick together. She auditioned yesterday, at the Stadttheater. Maybe she'll get a job some day as scenic designer."

"Hm."

"Just nineteen. You'd like her. She's sweet. Lives with me."

"Hm."

"Stay a while. We close at three. Come home with me. Mimi would love it."

The black-haired girl let her last piece of clothing fall. The spotlight went out, Toni Vorm stopped playing. When the lights went on again, the girl was gone. Toni Vorm strolled toward me. He had a break. A comic with a lot of colored balls stepped out onto the dance floor and demonstrated how comical one could be with a lot of colored balls. The guests laughed. Toni Vorm sat down beside me. Bar girl Carla withdrew.

106

"I'm glad you came, Herr Holden."

"What's up?"

"Here." He drew a small pale blue leaflet out of his pocket. "Why has she sent me this?"

I looked at the leaflet. It was a ticket, Air France to Paris, made out to Toni Vorm, booked for a flight on August 27, 20:00, from Düsseldorf-Lohausen. "Didn't you tell her I wanted nothing to do with it?"

I felt hot. "Of course I did."

"Flight to Paris. Absolute madness. And now they've locked up her old man."

"How could she possibly buy it? She's still in the hospital."

"How do I know! Must have done it by phone. Rich people have credit."

Ah yes, I thought.

"She sent the ticket to my apartment, with a note. I'm to wait for her in the airport restaurant. At seven." He leaned forward. "Let me tell you something . . . I'm getting out of here. Tomorrow morning."

"Where are you going?"

"There's an Eden Bar in Hamburg. Belongs to the same man. I've spoken to him. I'm chucking everything here."

"You're that scared?"

"Yes."

His long lashes quivered. "I don't know what part you play in this family and I couldn't care less. All I have to say is—the woman's dangerous."

"Nonsense!"

"Extremely dangerous." He waved. "Carla."

She came over to us.

"I want you to take a look at what I have here."

"A ticket. To Paris. Why?"

"And what am I doing with it?"

"You're putting it in Robert's pocket."

"And don't forget it." He slid off the bar stool. "Somebody may ask you about it any day."

The comic with the many colored balls bowed, his audience applauded. Toni Vorm said, "You'll have reason to remember me," and left us.

"Nice boy," said Carla. "Has been beside himself the

last few days. Nobody knows why. He's leaving tomorrow."

Toni Vorm sat down at the piano and began to play again. A blond girl with a friendly chimpanzee walked out onto the dance floor. The chimpanzee undressed the girl. She reminded me of Nina Brummer and I thought of Toni Vorm's warning, and I thought of how Nina Brummer looked naked.

"Your daughter is blond too?" I asked.

"Yes, pet. But she's a real blond, not like that one there."

"Can't you get away earlier?" I asked, and slipped a bill under my glass.

4

I didn't tell Nina Brummer about Carla and her daughter, Mimi, because I felt it couldn't be of any importance to her. Otherwise, though, I told her everything on that evening of August 27 as I sat opposite her in the airport restaurant, just as I have written it down here. While I spoke, it grew dark outside and the wind reached hurricane proportions. I could see the lights dancing in front of the control tower—it was like a ballet. Two planes landed while I talked, one took off. By now there were seven people in the restaurant, and one small boy.

". . . and that is how I came into possession of the ticket," I concluded. "That is how I knew I could expect you here this evening."

She looked at me silently. Her face was a white mask, but her eyes glittered feverishly. Only her eyes were alive.

"Do you believe me now?"

"No," said Nina Brummer. "I can't believe you. It *must* not be true. It would be . . . it would be too terrible."

"Let us leave."

"I have to stay."

"How much longer?"

"Until the plane leaves."

It was 7:25.

"Please believe me, it's hopeless . . ."

"I am going to wait."

"They'll call your names, both of them—his and yours."

"I am going to wait."

"Friends of yours may be here . . . friends of your husband . . ."

Now the tears were raining down her cheeks. "Can't you understand! *I don't care!* I am going to stay here. And wait."

Nervously I beckoned to the waiter and he came over to us. "A whiskey," I told him. "Double. And be quick about it." Suddenly I noticed that my hands were trembling. How strange, I thought. After all, it was Nina Brummer's fate, not mine . . .

5

I shall never forget the next half hour. I was witness to an eerie happening. A young woman aged, grew ugly; with every passing minute she withered before my eyes.

Nina Brummer turned her head away. She didn't want me to see that she was crying. But everybody could see it, everybody in the restaurant. I drank my whiskey. It tasted oily and bitter. Still, I ordered a second one.

"Doesn't the *gnädige Frau* feel well?" the waiter asked.

"Leave us alone," I said brusquely. "Everything's all right."

He went off in a huff.

"Did Toni really say that . . . that he wanted nothing more to do with me?"

"Try to understand him . . . a young man . . . afraid . . ."

"Did he say it?"

"Yes."

"Did he say, 'I'm getting out of here'?"

"I have told you everything he said."

The little boy came over to us and stared at Nina Brummer, picking his nose. "Siegfried!" cried his mother. "Come here at once!"

At 7:35 the loudspeaker announced for the first time: "Attention please. Herr Toni Vorm, Air France to Paris. Please come to the desk."

"There you are," I said.

"I don't care," she whispered.

The waiter brought my second whiskey. I was sweating. People were staring at us.

At 7:40 the raspy loudspeaker voice paged Toni Vorm again, and once more at 7:45. The voice sounded impatient and annoyed.

"Check!" I said.

The offended waiter took my money without a word. "Let's at least go downstairs, *gnädige Frau*."

"I have told him I'll meet him here. I have to wait."

"He isn't coming."

"It's only quarter to."

The loudspeaker again: "Attention please. Air France Flight 541 to Paris is ready to take on passengers at Gate Three. Ladies and gentlemen, we wish you a pleasant flight."

Seven forty-eight.

Below us the first passengers were leaving the lobby and we could see them being led across the stormswept airfield to the waiting plane.

Seven-fifty.

"Frau Nina Brummer and Herr Toni Vorm, booked on Air France Flight 541 to Paris, please go to passport and customs. The plane is waiting for you."

"Go. For heaven's sake, go," whispered Nina Brummer, "and leave me alone here."

"I am not here for any altruistic reason, Frau Brummer," I said. "I can't afford a scandal right now."

"You can't afford a scandal right now? What's that supposed to mean?"

110

"You don't know everything that happened on Saturday night. Take a look at my face."

"*What* happened?"

"Come with me and I'll tell you."

"No. I'm staying."

Seven fifty-five.

"Attention please. Herr Toni Vorm and Frau Nina Brummer, Air France Flight 541 to Paris, please come immediately to passport and customs. Your plane is about to leave!"

Suddenly she rose, swayed, and fell back on her chair. "Would you . . . please . . . help me . . ."

I supported her with my right arm, and with my left I carried her mink coat and the jewelry case. I helped her down the stairs. Everybody was watching us. In the lobby an airport official came up to us. "Are you Herr Toni Vorm?"

"Yes," I said. At this point, like her, I didn't give a damn either.

"What's wrong with the *gnädige Frau?*"

"She's ill. She can't fly. Please help us."

"Shall I call a doctor?"

"To the car," I said. "Just help us to the car. I am a doctor."

Between us we led Nina Brummer to the exit. A few people had gathered around us. Suddenly she screamed hysterically, "Toni!" and again, "Toni! Oh God . . ."

"Yes, yes," I said, and could feel the sweat trickling down my back. "Yes, darling, yes . . ."

At last I had her in the car. I gave the official money and drove off as fast as I could. The tires screeched in the curves. I could feel the wind in the steering wheel.

She didn't speak until we reached the highway, then she said, "Herr . . . Holden . . ."

"What?" By this time I was furious.

"Please drive to his apartment."

"He has left Düsseldorf!"

"I just want to see the apartment again."

"It's locked."

"I have the key."

Suddenly, wildly, she grabbed hold of me. I wasn't prepared for it and the car skidded into the left lane. I wrenched the steering wheel around. My reflex action rammed my right elbow against Nina Brummer's breast. She was thrown against the door and cried out in pain. I thought: How much longer can she take this? Any minute now she'll collapse and I can take her back to the hospital. I said, "All right. To his apartment. If you promise to be quiet."

"I'll be quiet. I'll do anything you say, Herr Holden. Just drive to his place."

"Okay," I said. "Okay."

After that she was silent until we reached the city. She sat there crying quietly. When we got into town she murmured. "Tell me what else happened. Why are you doing all this?"

I said nothing.

"You said you'd tell me."

"All right," I said. "So listen . . . I stayed for a while with . . . in this bar. It was Sunday morning and already quite light when I got home . . ."

6

It was already light when I got home that Sunday morning. The sun was shining, birds were singing in the park. The grass was still wet with dew but the flowers were already opening. I was a little drunk, not very, though. In the end mother and daughter had brewed coffee for me.

I put the car in the garage. Carla's daughter wasn't nineteen, but at least twenty-five, I decided. Perhaps she wasn't even Carla's daughter, but she *was* a real blond. I knew that now.

The chauffeur's apartment was over the garage. It consisted of one room, a walk-in closet, and a bathroom, all of which now belonged to me. I lived alone in the apartment. The villa was about two hundred meters away in the

112

park. I walked up the short staircase and was looking forward to my bed. Now I was really tired.

They were waiting for me in my room. Three of them.

I can't remember much about them except that they were big and wore hats. That I can remember. They were bigger and stronger than I was and there were three of them.

One stood behind the door, the other two were sitting on the bed. The one behind the door hit me right away as I came in, in the neck. Suddenly I was stone sober, and as I flew across the room I thought that this was what boxers called the rabbit punch. The second man kicked me in the stomach.

I collapsed. They made a mistake by beating me so brutally right from the start.

Now I was lying on the carpet. The morning sun lit up the room and the three of them worked on me for a while. I screamed, but the window was closed and I realized there was no sense in screaming, so I stopped.

Two of them picked me up and held me while the third one took everything I had on me out of my pockets and spread it on the table. At this point they hadn't beaten me bloody yet, I could see it all quite clearly, and it was then that I noticed that they still had their hats on.

"Where's the case?" said the first one.

"And don't lie!" said the second one. "We know you have it."

"You were seen," said the third one, "In Berlin. In your fucking Cadillac."

Now I noticed they they had searched the room. All drawers were open, my clothes were scattered on the floor, they had torn my grey jackets to shreds. This incensed me and I said, "I don't have it any more."

"Where is it?"

"I took it at once to a lawyer in Berlin."

"His name?"

I decided that any false name was as good as the next one and replied, "Meise." Whereupon the first one spat in my face and they went on beating me up. Two of them bent my body back over the table and the third pummeled me with his fists on my stomach and elsewhere.

I vomited bile, not much, and they changed places and

113

took turns hitting me in the stomach. In the course of which the hat of the first man fell off. They kept asking the same thing and I kept giving them the same answer: I'd given the briefcase to a lawyer in Berlin called Meise. They were sweating like pigs and knocked off for a brief rest. The first man took the car keys and went down to the garage to search the Cadillac. He came back and said, "Nix."

Then they sat me down on a chair and held onto me and hit me in the face and I began to bleed. I bled all over my suit, my white shirt, and my tie, the one with the blue diamond pattern. Then they offered me money. They showed me a wad of bills, gave me a cigarette, but they'd knocked out one of my teeth, and anyway my lips were bleeding.

More and more sunlight fell into the room, but I could only feel its warmth because the blood was running over my eyes. They smoked. I could smell it, and as they hung onto me, so that I shouldn't fall off the chair, I thought of how my father had often said that just the things one *didn't* own could give one strength. He said it to comfort my poor mother over her material needs by drawing her attention to a metaphysical happiness, but that Sunday morning I gave it a different interpretation. I thought of the fact that I no longer had the key to the safe-deposit box . . .

"Asshole!" said the first man. "Why are you making it so hard for us? What's it to you, anyway? Are you the one who's in jail?"

"Brummer's only going to get what he's got coming to him," said the second man. "So tell us where the papers are."

"I don't have them any more."

"So what's Brummer paying you?" said the third. "We'll pay more."

"He's not paying me anything."

The first man spat on me again and said, "So, my friends, there's nothing we can do but more of the same."

I won't go into what they did to me after that. It hurt terribly and they did it too fast. I can't stand a lot of pain, and minutes later it was all over with my fine resolutions.

114

I was ready to tell the three thugs to drive to Braunschweig with me and get the documents; I was ready to take their money. I was no hero and I had no desire to be one. I was ready to tell all. But I never got around to it, because I passed out. That was their mistake—they did it too fast. The last thing I remembered was the hoarse, excited barking of a dog in the park.

7

Mila Blehova was sitting beside my bed when I came to. She was wringing her hands. "Jesus, Maria, and Joseph, Herr Holden! I thought my heart would stop beating. I've been so upset." The old dog was sniffing at my blanket; she licked my hand and whimpered.

I saw that I'd been bandaged. It was very light in the room and the light hurt my eyes. My face was swollen and my body ached all over. "I heard the dog," I said.

"Yes. Our Mitzili. All of a sudden she acted crazy. She was sleeping with me. Suddenly she starts barking and whimpering and I have to take her down, into the garden, and right away she heads for the garage. She has a sixth sense, our Mitzi does. I ran after her as fast as I could, but I was too late. I saw the three murderers, the villains. Over the fence and away. Then I found you, unconscious and bleeding. I thought you were dead! I'm too old for such excitement, Herr Holden. I haven't belched that much since Hitler's war."

"They wanted the papers, Mila."

"That's what I thought."

"Who bandaged me?"

"I called Dr. Schneider. He's coming again at noon. The police were here. They're coming back at eleven."

"Good."

"And I called the *gnädige Herr's* lawyer. He said please not to tell anyone anything."

"Hm."

"And I spoke to the mason. He's going to start work to-day. Is a Sunday, but that doesn't matter. We're going to have bars put on all the windows." She had a list, and now she put on a pair of metal-rimmed spectacles. "I've put it all down. Can you listen?"

"Not much longer."

"As soon as you feel able, says the lawyer, you're to go to the prison, to the *gnädige Herr*. He's been granted permission for you. Such a mean trick." She belched with indignation.

"What's a mean trick, Mila?"

"Just think, the *gnädige Herr* asked for permission to have his dog with him, the animal is so accustomed to him, he explained to the warden. And he was ready to pay anything they asked. But they wouldn't grant permission. A canary, they said, was the most they would allow!"

"A shame!"

"And we're not to tell the *gnädige Frau* what they did to you, says the lawyer. It would excite her too much."

"Quite right."

"A good thing he told me, because about an hour ago my Nina called up."

"What did she want?"

"She was afraid the police might come and confiscate things belonging to the *gnädige Herr*—and to her."

It hurt to smile.

"She said I should bring her jewelry to her, and the receipt for the furs. We store them in the summer."

The idea that women, however passionate, never lost their sense of reality amused me. In Paris, too, one had to live on something . . .

"And documents. And letters. She wants everything. What are you laughing at, Herr Holden?"

8

The police came at eleven. I told them the three men had asked me for papers.

What papers?

No idea.

But surely I had to have some idea . . .

No. I didn't. Not the slightest. I surmised that it probably had something to do with Herr Brummer's arrest. Herr Brummer seemed to have a lot of enemies. I had been Herr Brummer's chauffeur for only a short time and therefore had no idea what it was all about.

The police were followed by the doctor. He changed the bandages and gave me a shot which made me feel very tired. I slept and dreamt of Nina. Suddenly I heard a thunderous noise. It woke me and I sat up, breathless, my heart beating wildly. For a few seconds I thought I was back in Russia and the Russian tanks were coming. Then I opened my eyes.

A bearded man, the upper part of his body naked, was looking in at the window. The window was beside my bed. It was open, and the man outside had to be floating in midair because he wasn't holding onto the sill. I have frequently feared that I was going mad. I feared it now.

The bearded man was looking at me silently. Suddenly it was very still.

"Did I wake you up with my hammering?" he asked, and stuck his head curiously into the room. The sky behind him was honey-colored.

"Who are you?"

"The mason. I'm putting bars on all the windows."

I fell back on my pillow, limp with relief. "You're standing on a ladder?"

117

He grinned and said, "What else? D'you think I have wings?"

9

"He grinned at me, and said, 'What else? D'you think I have wings?' " I said, as I stepped on the brake. We had arrived at Stresemannstrasse 31A. I pulled the key out of the ignition. "Here we are."

Nina Brummer started. She looked at the dreary front of the house, the sandstone caryatids, the shabby entrance, the crippled trees, an anguished expression on her face. Above us a street lantern swayed in the wind. The shadows of dead branches fluttered across the facade of the house and the dark windows.

"May I have my coat? I . . . I'm cold . . ."

I laid the fur coat across her shoulders. She got out at once and fell down. I helped her to her feet. Her face was dirty. I wiped it clean with my handkerchief. She was trembling, her lips were quivering.

"Take . . . me . . . upstairs."

I supported her again and we entered the dark hallway. "The . . . light . . . is . . . is on the left."

I found it, pressed the button, the hall remained dark. "It isn't working." I lit my cigarette lighter and led Nina Brummer, in her fur coat, up the creaking wooden stairs to the second floor. The faint light fell on the dirty walls, covered with mildew. Nina Brummer was heavy on my arm. Once she stopped and struggled for breath. I thought of some words by Léon Bloy that I'd read somewhere: *In the heart of man there are nooks and crannies that don't exist until suffering enters into them so that they may become valid.* As I led Nina Brummer to Toni Vorm's apartment I thought that here and now such a corner in her heart was receiving its permanent occupant.

She leaned against the wall, panting, and began to rummage in her bag. The plate with his name on it was still there, only Toni Vorm wasn't there any more. Her groping for the key made me nervous, so I pressed the bell. We could hear it ring inside, loud and hollow. She murmured, "Why did you do that?"

"And you, Madame, why are you doing all this?"

She didn't answer. She had found the key and now unlocked the door, which opened with a prolonged creaking sound. Nina Brummer walked into the apartment and turned on the light. I followed her.

The living room was empty. The furniture was gone. Newspapers and sheets of music were scattered on the floor. Two open crates, wood shavings spilling out of them. A dirty shirt. Three books. I picked one up and read the title. Marcel Proust: *À la recherche du temps perdu.*

I let the book fall. Nina Brummer was standing in the middle of the room; the light from the bare bulb in the ceiling fell on her. She looked at everything, precisely, all the time muttering words I couldn't understand. Steps dragging, shoulders sagging, she wandered off into the bathroom.

An empty tube of shaving cream, a piece of soap, a roll of toilet paper, a worn robe . . . she walked into the kitchen. Here nothing was left but the stove and, on the floor, a lot of empty bottles. I began to count the bottles. When I got to fourteen, she said in a flat voice, "And the funny thing is . . . I really loved him." She addressed the words to the sink.

"Let's go," I said.

"You don't believe me, I know. For you I'm just a rich, hysterical woman who took on a pretty boy. A pretty young boy . . ."

"You've seen everything. Now come, please."

She turned on the water, which began to flow. "And you know what's the funniest thing about it? I thought he loved me too." She laughed. "He told me I was the first love in his life, the first true love. Before me there had been no one. That's really very funny, isn't it?" She turned off the water. "How many bottles?"

"I beg your pardon . . ."

"You're counting them, aren't you?"

119

I walked up to her and turned her around and she fell against my chest and began to cry.

"I . . . I wanted to get a divorce and . . . and then we were going to get married. Did you know that he wrote a rhapsody for me?"

"We *must* go now."

"I can't . . . I must . . . I've got to sit down for a moment."

"There's nothing to sit on."

"I can't stand any longer. Oh, Mila, I feel terrible," she cried out in the voice of a miserable child.

I led her into the bathroom and sat her down on the edge of the tub. She cried for a while, then she asked for a cigarette. We smoked. We dropped the ash on the tiled floor. I told her what there still was to tell.

"I have looked at the documents and photographs. I don't know the people implicated by them, but I can judge the seriousness of the implications. Your husband is a powerful man now that he has the documents."

"But he doesn't have them. *You* have them!"

It was a curious conversation, now that I look back. Two strangers in a strange bathroom. The woman, in a mink coat, sitting on the edge of the bathtub, her chauffeur standing in front of her, and the wind outside rattling the windows . . .

I said, "That's right. I have the papers. And I intend to keep them. That's my plan."

"But . . ."

"But I shall permit Herr Brummer's lawyer to drive to Braunschweig with me and photograph the documents, in the vault," I said, complacently, a complacency I was soon to recall. "Of course I intend to keep the originals."

"No!" She pressed the palms of her hands against her temples.

"But yes. Tomorrow morning I am going to drive to Braunschweig."

"Don't do it!"

"Why not?"

With intense seriousness she replied, "My husband is an evil man."

"In spite of which you have lived with him for quite a while. Lived well."

"I didn't know *how* evil he was. When I . . . when I found out, I tried to kill myself."

Her cigarette had fallen on the floor. I stepped on it. Meanwhile she went on speaking. "Don't do it, Herr Holden. I know what will happen when my husband gets those photostats."

"What?"

"Terrible things. And nobody will be able to stop them. I know I'm saying things that can't possibly mean anything to you."

"I've been in jail," I said. "I'm forty years old. I've never had it easy. Now I'm well off. And I'm going to be still better off. Who's going to thank me if I *don't* let your husband have the photostats?"

"Other people."

"I don't care about other people."

She asked softly, "Have you ever loved anyone?"

"Let's not go into that. Where is Herr Vorm?"

"He was afraid . . . he was young. You said so yourself . . ."

I began to pace up and down. "No. I'm not taking any more risks. With your husband I know where I'm at. And you be smart. Your husband has become invincible because of what I did. Stick with us."

"I can't."

"Do you have any money? Do you have a profession? What's going to become of you if you leave your husband? A scandal. He gets a divorce. He's acquitted. You won't get a cent from him. You'll have to sell your jewelry. Piece by piece. To live. And when it's gone? I know what poverty means."

"I do too."

"So?"

"What you're saying doesn't convince me. So I'll sell my jewelry. So I'll be poor. How can I go on living with someone I hate and despise?"

"A lot of people do," I said. "It's not so difficult. And women have an easier time of it."

She shook her head, but said nothing. At that moment she was very beautiful and I was deeply moved. That was the day on which our love, our strange love, was born, on that windswept evening of August 27.

121

I said, "And now come, please."

She didn't move. She whispered, "And you . . . you were poor once too?"

"Yes."

"And why . . . why are you so worried about me?"

"You look like someone I once knew."

"Who?"

"My wife," I said softly.

Her eyes were suddenly very dark, her lips trembled as if she were going to cry again. But she didn't. She walked up to me, and in an unreal, impossible way I again had the feeling that Margit, my dead wife, was walking up to me. I stared at her. She whispered, "Where is your wife?"

"She is dead," I said tonelessly. "I murdered her."

"Why?"

"Because I loved her, and because she was unfaithful to me."

Nina's eyes were hazy. I could feel her breath. Three seconds. Five seconds. Suddenly she staggered, as if overcome by weakness.

I took her in my arms and kissed her on the mouth. She let it happen. Her mouth remained closed, and it was as if I were kissing someone dead. Her lips were cold.

Yes, that was how our love began.

We clung to each other, and it was so still, as if we were the only people in the house, perhaps in the world. In the end she looked up at me, her face white as if every drop of blood had been drained from it.

"I can't stand any more," she whispered. "Take me back to the hospital."

10

In the car she fell asleep, her head on my shoulder, and I drove carefully, so as not to waken her. Still, in a curve, she awoke for a few seconds. Before she fell asleep again she smiled at me, but she didn't recognize me.

Once she had been as poor as I had been. That helped. She was sensible and gave in at once when resistance was futile. I had sensed all this. I decided that I had driven to the airport because I had sensed all this; otherwise I wouldn't have cared what happened to her.

When we reached the Marien Hospital, we couldn't rouse her. She was on the verge of total collapse, and in a semicoma spoke crazily, called me Toni, begged for Mila.

"Herr Holden, what happened?" It was the Mother Superior Angelica Meuren, the one who every few pages signed the book in the chapel, with the strange, fervent entries. She was plump, rosy and benevolent.

I lied. "The *gnädige Frau* called me, from an espresso."

"But how did she get there?"

"She was trying to get to her husband. Worry and fear for his safety drove her out into the street, but then she didn't have the strength to do anything more."

"Of course I called the house, Herr Holden."

That was awkward.

"There was no answer."

That simplified things again.

"Mila! Help me, Mila!" Nina cried as they laid her on the stretcher.

"Be good to her," I said. "She is in a very unfortunate situation. Her husband, whom she loves above everything else, is in jail, innocent."

She looked at me silently, and I was afraid I'd gone too far. It looked as if Mother Superior Meuren was of the

123

opinion, like so many other people, that Julius Maria Brummer was finally getting what he deserved.

Meanwhile they had taken Nina upstairs. They had spread a grey blanket over her. All I could see was her blond hair. I looked after her, I even moved a few steps sideways in order to see her better. I could visualize her in all her beauty, although the grey blanket covered her almost completely; I could smell her perfume even though she was no longer there, and I thought how well it fitted together, that she had once been poor, like me. Then I could see the Mother Superior looking at me thoughtfully, and I quickly asked if the fur coat and the jewelry case could be kept at the hospital. This turned out to be possible.

"From now on we'll have nurses with Frau Brummer around the clock," the Mother Superior promised. And with a smile I didn't like, she added, "You don't have to worry about her, Herr Holden."

"Good night," I said, and wondered—is it noticeable already?

I left the hospital hurriedly. When I got home I found out why there had been no answer to the phone. "All of us had to go to the police station, Herr Holden. The girls, the butler, the valet, and I. Nothing important. Just more questions about Ninale's suicide attempt. I've been waiting up for you. Did you go to the movies?"

"Yes."

"That's good. You need a little distraction. Was it a sad picture or a funny one?"

"A funny one."

"Well, I always say, in times like these I like to see a funny picture. Heinz Rühmann. You know him?"

"Of course."

"He's my favorite. And the one with the funny nose. Fernandel. Yes, that's his name. Does your head still hurt?"

"Not any more. Could you drive to your nephew's with me tomorrow morning?"

"But of course. You want the key?"

"At seven. Or is that too early? I've got a long drive ahead of me."

"That's perfectly all right," she said. "At seven. Tonight

124

all of us are going to sleep better. They've put bars on the windows."

As a matter of fact, I did sleep well, and dreamlessly. In the morning I got the white Mercedes out of the garage and drove off with Mila. The sky was a deep blue and it was windless. It was still cool, too. The Rhine glittered in the morning light. The old dog lay between us. Mila chattered. "He's the only relative I have, still living. My sister's son. The boy . . . dear Lord, why do I still say boy? He's twenty-eight. You'll like him, Herr Holden. He's a reporter."

"Aha."

"On a local paper. He writes 'From the Police Blotter'. Suicides, anything you want. He's got a special sort of radio in his apartment. I don't understand anything about it, I'm just a stupid old woman, but he can hear about anything that happens in Düsseldorf, right away. Then he drives to wherever it's happening in his Volkswagen and takes pictures and writes about it. There it is, number fourteen."

I stopped in front of a new apartment building. The street was empty. The sun shone slanting through the trees. Mila Blehova got out. "Just wait. He said he'd come down."

I watched her walk awkwardly to the entrance and ring a bell. A window on the fifth floor opened. In her high, trembling old woman's voice she called up, "Butzel?"

"Coming," answered a voice.

Mila came back to me, followed by the dog. She stood beside the car. "He'll be right down, Herr Holden."

"What is his name?"

She giggled. "Peter Romberg. But we've always called him Butzel." She made a long "u" of it. "As far back as I can remember, he's always been Butzel."

Just then the local reporter Peter Romberg walked out of the house and into my life, and with that—at least that's how I see it today—everything became inevitable, everything that happened, is happening and is going to happen. On that early morning of August 28, Julius Maria Brummer forfeited his life. Only no one knew it at the time.

125

11

Peter Romberg was slightly built and shy, and he wore horn-rimmed glasses. His hair was a reddish blond and stood away from his head like a brush. His face was covered with freckles, and he had a big nose. He was laughing. Whenever I met Peter Romberg, he was laughing. Only in the end he didn't laugh any more.

He was wearing grey flannel slacks and a grey shirt, open at the neck. He kissed his aunt on the cheek. "Sorry, I didn't recognize you right away."

"That's all right, Butzel. This is Herr Holden."

I said "Hello," he said "Hello," and we shook hands.

"You see, I'm nearsighted. Five diopters left, six right. Blind as a bat." His teeth were irregular. Still, when he laughed, he looked sympathetic. "Thank goodness that hasn't changed since I was twenty."

Mila giggled again. "Shall I tell him, Butzel?"

"Tell me what?" I asked.

"He's only twenty-eight but he's married already, and has a little girl."

"No, really?" I was honestly astonished. "How old?"

"Six. Her name is Mickey."

"You got an early start, Herr Romberg."

"He's a good boy, Herr Holden. And he has a nice wife. He's going to have to answer to me if he ever cheats on her. I'll be after him with my rolling pin!"

"Mila!" Peter Romberg was obviously embarrassed.

"Oh, Herr Holden, you've got to meet his wife, Maria, and the little one. I'm crazy about Mickey, such a darling."

"Herr Romberg, my congratulations."

"Thanks." He laughed. "Here's the key."

I put it in my pocket.

126

He said, "You know, at first I thought Herr Brummer was a crook. Everybody does. But if there's one person on this earth I trust, it's Mila. And Mila has been saying for years that Herr Brummer is the best person in the world."

"And she's right," I said.

"You really must come and see us some time, Herr Holden."

"My pleasure, Herr Romberg."

"We don't have any decent rugs yet. My wife may be embarrassed—you know how women are—but I think the apartment's fine right now, what do you say, Mila?"

"Just fine, darling."

"And I'll show you my pictures."

"He may be my nephew," said Mila, "but I can say with a clear conscience—he takes beautiful pictures, my Butzel does."

"You know, Herr Holden—all these violent crime and police jobs—I do them for a living. But some day, when I'm independent, I'm going to do quite different things. More interesting things."

"What are you interested in, Herr Romberg?"

"Animals."

"You want to photograph animals?"

"And write about them." Now he was laughing again. "I find animals much more interesting than people."

"You must look at his pictures, Herr Holden," said Mila Blehova. "The ones of the pelicans are the most beautiful ones I've ever seen. Some day my Butzel is going to be famous. Oh, my goodness, there I go again," and she belched twice.

12

Julius Maria Brummer had put his defense in the hands of a lawyer called Zorn. That morning the lawyer drove with me to Braunschweig.

Dr. Hilmar Zorn was a very small man with the mighty head of a scholar. When he got excited or was tired, a strange thing happened to his eyes. His pupils wandered, which gave a momentary impression that he was cross-eyed. To this was added a slight speech defect and a seemingly tireless need to tug at his collar with his forefinger. He always wore colorful vests, even in hot weather, in solid colors or checked.

This morning he had me drive for half an hour at a walking pace through the quiet streets of the borough of Rungsfeld. Not until he was absolutely sure we were not being followed would he let me proceed on the autobahn. He explained, "In a situation like ours, we have to make absolutely sure we are safe in everything we undertake. Only then can we hope to succeed." He spoke very seriously. If one didn't know better, one could believe he was setting out like a crusader to defend occidental culture against warlike hordes from faraway steppes. The effect was suggestive. Anyone being defended by Dr. Zorn immediately appeared in the gentle light of someone who, perhaps, was being unjustly accused.

There was a tremendous amount of traffic on the autobahn, in both directions. Cars were driving north and south with only a few meters space between. All of us were driving at a uniform speed of a hundred kilometers. There could be no thought of passing.

It got dreadfully hot. In the end it was cooler in the car with the windows closed. The traffic didn't let up. The overheated tires sounded shrill on the hot concrete. Dr.

Zorn sat motionless beside me from 8 A.M. to 11:30. He was wearing a red vest with seven silver buttons. He didn't open any of them. His shirt was white, his tie was silver-grey, his single-breasted suit was grey. I was driving in my shirtsleeves, with the cuffs rolled up and the collar open. When the clock on the dashboard read exactly 11:30, Zorn began to speak. "You're perspiring."

I had to admit he was right.

"Take a look at me," he said. "Am I perspiring? Not in the slightest. And why not? Because I don't *want* to perspire. It's all a question of what one wants. Do you realize that without my vest on I would be much more likely to perspire? Why? Because my vest gives me poise. And poise is what counts, Herr Holden." And then, in a non sequitur, "Difficult times lie ahead."

"I beg your pardon?"

"*Bona causa triumphat*—you understand?"

"That much—yes."

"Good. Just the same. There's going to be a lot of excitement. Herr Brummer is a . . . hm . . . a symbol of the times. There's no other way to put it. A great deal of money is involved. It gives people strange ideas."

"And how am I supposed to understand that, *Herr Doktor?*"

"I can imagine that you too may have fallen victim to such strange ideas. I can imagine for instance that you think I only intend to photograph the documents in Braunschweig and leave the originals in the safe."

"That's the way I see it," I said. "You photograph, the documents remain in the safe, and I keep the key."

He sighed, looked slightly cross-eyed, and began to tug at his collar as he said, "I photograph, the documents remain in the safe, and you give me the key. Right now."

"Oh no," I said.

He clicked his tongue three times. "Then I'm afraid I see you back in Stadelheim."

"*Where?*"

"Please keep your hands on the steering wheel, Herr Holden. At the speed we're traveling it's easy to have an accident. I said Stadelheim, and I meant the Bavarian prison there. Doubtlessly you are familiar with the area. After all, you spent nine years there."

I opened the window on my side a little and breathed deeply because I was beginning to feel sick.

"Please close the window, Herr Holden. I can't stand a draft."

"There's no draft when only one window's open," I said, but I closed the window.

The little lawyer took a piece of paper out of his briefcase and put on his glasses like a schoolteacher. "Herr Holden, it is quite clear—isn't it?—that when so much is at stake, as in this *causa*, we have to clarify your role in it. You told Herr Brummer at one point that you had a textile business in Munich."

"And I did," I lied.

"You also told him that you were given a prison sentence because you fraudulently declared that business bankrupt."

"And I was given a prison sentence."

"But not for bankruptcy fraud, Herr Holden." Now the speech defect became noticeable. He said, "I m-m-must ask you for the l-l-last time to drive more carefully. According to m-m-my information, the Munich court sentenced you on April 13, 1947, to twelve years in prison for the murder of your wife, Margit." (He said "Ma-ma-margit.") "They considered the extenuating circumstances. You had been in the army for five years and a prisoner of war for two. When you came home on . . . hm . . . September 1, 1946, you f-f-found your wife . . ."

"Stop!"

". . . you f-f-found your wife in a compromising situation with the commercial artist, Leopold Hauk . . ."

"Stop, I tell you!"

". . . and with a leg broken off a chair, beat your wife, Margit Holden, née Reniewitz, in such a manner that she succumbed and died of her injuries that same night."

He went on, consulting his notes as he went along. "The jury was on your side. You won their sympathy when you stated several times that you had loved your wife very much. Such statements always make a good impression."

A blue and white sign flew by. We were fifteen hundred meters from the city of Braunschweig. The lawyer went on.

"You were a well-behaved prisoner, at least so I was informed by the prison administration. That was why you were paroled on January 11, 1956, for goo-goo-good behavior. You know, of course, that you will have to sit out the whole sentence if you break the law again." Now he was tugging at his collar.

The sweat was pouring from the roots of my hair, down my forehead. It trickled through my eyebrows and dripped down my cheeks. It ran into my mouth and tasted salty.

"You have already broken the law several times in West Berlin," said Zorn. "I can also imagine that withholding private property might make a very bad impression on your parole officer. In fact, in my mind's eye I can already see you back in your little cell."

"What do you want?"

"The key . . . Herr Holden."

One has a plan . . .

"And if I give you the key—what happens then?"

"I don't know what happens then, Herr Holden. I only know what happens if you *don't* give me the key."

Be smart . . .

"Just ahead of us, beside that gas station, there is a parking lot. You'll stop there . . ."

. . . make a second plan . . .

"Otherwise I shall be forced to bring charges against you for embezzlement, blackmail, and extortion."

. . . and neither of them work . . .

I drove to the parking lot beside the gas station and stopped. Here white and red flowers were in bloom. The lot was littered with discarded wrappers, newspaper, orange peel.

"The key," said Zorn, and tugged at his collar with his right forefinger.

I gave him the key. My hand was damp, his was dry. He said, "Don't think I can't put myself in your position. You must have suffered a lot."

"Were you in Russia?" I asked.

"At Stalingrad. You can drive on now." He tugged at his tie. "In half an hour we'll be in Braunschweig." He put the key in his vest pocket. The way he did it seemed to me graceful and deft. "I hate to see you perspiring so much, Herr Holden."

From that moment on I ceased to exist for little Dr. Zorn. He stared straight ahead, hands on knees, sitting up very straight and proper. I drove slowly because I still felt sick. I breathed deeply and after a while felt better, but I was quite incapable of formulating a single practical thought, I was so riddled with fear. It's all over, over, over, said the throbbing engine of the heavy car; over, over, over said the blood pulsating in my temples.

"Would you please drive a little faster, Herr Holden," said the little man next to me. "What I have to do in the bank will take at least two hours."

I was stronger. I could knock him out. Take the key, throw him out of the car. Drive to the bank. Yes. And then? There were telephones. He could beat me to it. Unless I killed him . . .

For God's sake, what insanity! What utter madness!

I drove faster.

"Braunschweig was a cultured city once," said Dr. Zorn. "Seventy-two percent destroyed by bombs. Burnt out and ruined . . . the most beautiful houses, the loveliest *palais*. While I'm at the bank I recommend a look at the cathedral. Twelfth century. Henry the Lionhearted is buried there."

And I did go to the cathedral, once I had established Zorn at the bank, and I looked at the Gothic saints and stood for a long time in front of the stone lions under which lay a man called Henry.

I was forty years old. If Brummer chose to bring charges against me, I would be behind bars again.

I sat down on the tomb because I felt sick. I thought of my dead wife, Margit, whom I had loved and who had been unfaithful. Now she was dead and I no longer loved her. I hadn't loved her for a long time.

A sexton passed me and said, "You can't sit there." So I got up again. Dear God, help me . . .

I stopped in the middle of the prayer because suddenly I hated myself for praying. I had tried something and it had failed. Brummer must have mistrusted me from the start and told Zorn to look into my past *before* the trip to Berlin. Pasts were a specialty of his. I should have thought of that.

And it really would have been too simple, much too simple. He was too powerful and had too much money. I had nothing. It couldn't have worked. And if I left the country? I had the car, my passport . . .

No. Impossible. If I didn't pick Zorn up at the appointed time, I was finished. If I did, I still had a small chance that Brummer might not denounce me. If I begged him to forgive me; if I was truly humble about it . . . I realized that this was one thing I had to be—humble. Then I might have a small chance. Funny that one always continues to believe in that small chance . . .

And Nina?

I couldn't think of her now. Not on top of everything else. It was all I could do to think of myself.

"Would you buy a tile, sir?" asked a thin voice.

A very old lady in a black dress was standing in front of me. Her back was hunched, and she was leaning on a cane in a way that looked tortured. Her slight body formed a semicircle. Her face was wrinkled and bloodless but her dark eyes were bright. She smiled shyly. In her left hand she was holding a cardboard box with a lot of colored pieces of paper in it. "God will reward you," she promised.

"And what will he reward me for?" I asked.

"Our cathedral needs a new roof," she explained patiently, "and a new roof needs many tiles. They're fifty pfennigs each. Will you buy one, sir?"

I gave her a mark.

"What color?"

"What do you mean?"

"What color would you like the tiles to be? It's going to

133

be a roof with many colors. Or do you want fifty pfennigs change?" Now she sounded a little breathless.

"No. And I don't care what color."

"Then I'll give you two brown ones."

She licked her finger and began to look for two brown ones in the box, in the course of which her cane fell to the ground. I picked it up. The old woman gave me two brown tickets on which there was a picture of the cathedral. Underneath it a bishop was thanking for the contribution. "Thank the dear Lord, now I can go home."

"How long have you been here?"

"Since early morning," the old woman explained. "I have to sell ten tiles every day. With your two that makes eleven for today."

"You have to? Why do you have to?"

The old lady lowered her head still farther and whispered, "I made a vow. That God should forgive me-my sin," and with that she shuffled away, back bent, head cocked to one side, smiling and friendly. The little Jehovah's Witness in Düsseldorf had smiled like that.

I wondered if the old lady had committed a mortal sin. What sort of a sin could such an old person commit anyway? But perhaps she had committed the sin in her youth. And now she was selling paper tiles to praise the Lord and satisfy the bishop.

All morning long I had been hot; now I felt chilled. So I walked out into the sunshine again. The city was stifling. The dust had a blinding effect on the light, like snow, and all things were harshly defined. I drove back to the bank.

Zorn was waiting for me at the curb, looking elegant and proper, his briefcase in his hand. I stopped, he got in and said reproachfully, "You're six minutes late."

"I had trouble finding my way back."

"Another four minutes and I'd have gone to the police."

I said nothing.

"By the way, I've rented a second box and put the key to the first box in it. I gave the second key to the bank director. He's a friend of mine. I'm telling you this so that you don't get any stupid ideas."

The air over the autobahn was steaming. For a hundred kilometers he didn't say a word, but I noticed that he was keeping a sharp eye on me, without turning his head. Finally I asked him, "Why are you watching me?"

"I'm interested," he said. "I study types. You're not a blackmailer."

"No?" I said hopefully.

"No. I'd say you were a murderer type." After that he was silent until we reached Düsseldorf. "You'll hear from me," he said as I let him off at his office building.

I was very tired and drove straight home. Mila Blehova announced, "My Ninale called up. She wants to speak to you, Herr Holden."

"Tomorrow," I told her.

"Are you hungry?"

"I don't feel well. Do you suppose there's a sleeping pill in the house?"

She brought me something; on the label it said: "Take one or two at bedtime." I took four but they did nothing for me, and I lay there and couldn't sleep and listened to the frogs croaking in the lake. I saw the sky turn lead grey, then a rosy red and finally gold. My head hurt and I was frightened. Then the sun climbed up over the trees and the frogs stopped croaking. I could hear voices in the street and the sound of bicycle bells and car horns and the faraway noises of the city. At eight o'clock the house telephone in my room rang. It was Mila.

"Herr Holden, somebody from the prison just rang up. The *gnädige Herr* wants to speak to you. He has permission for you to visit him, but it has to be before eleven. You'd better go right away."

I thought how well off some people were. For instance, the crippled old woman who after committing a sin had only to take a vow, and had nothing more to fear from God or man. Nothing more to fear . . .

14

The room was big. It was on the fourth floor of the sector where prisoners were held pending investigation, and its barred windows didn't open. That was why it was so hot in the room. It was divided from floor to ceiling by two wire-mesh walls, erected parallel to each other, a short space apart. On both sides there were tables and chairs. Between the two wire walls there was nothing.

I sat under one of the closed windows and sweated. My headache got worse. After ten minutes a door in the other half of the room opened and an officer in a black uniform came into the room. He was limping. "Herr Brummer, please," he said.

I rose.

Julius Maria Brummer walked into the other half of the room. He was wearing a white shirt and blue trousers. His shoes had no heels and the collar of his shirt was open. He wasn't wearing a tie. His round face was pale, and purple shadows lay under his watery eyes. Every now and then he lifted his left shoulder to the side of his head in an up and down and circular motion before letting it fall again. He looked as if he was trying to scratch his ear with his shoulder.

"Herr Brummer, visiting time is ten minutes," said the limping officer.

He sat down. Brummer walked up to the wire and looked at me. I stepped up to the wire on my side, but I didn't look at him.

"Look at me, Holden," said Julius Maria Brummer.

I made myself do so. I looked into the tiny, treacherous eyes of a shark, at his pale blond moustache, his ashen hamster cheeks, his low forehead, his soft mouth with the teeth of a mouse. He clung to the wire on his side and his

136

pasty face was twitching. But he said nothing. Not a word.

"Ten minutes, Herr Brummer," said the officer.

"Holden," said Brummer, his voice a whisper, almost inaudible across the wire. "My lawyer was here last night. He told me everything."

"Herr Brummer," I began, "before you go on, let me . . ."

He interrupted me. "We only have ten minutes. There are no words to express what you did . . ."

"Herr Brummer, Herr Brummer . . ."

"A few days ago you didn't even know me. You knew nothing about me. You had no reason to look after my interests. But you did." Now his voice rose. "You helped me. You know how. You took a beating on my behalf. Don't turn away. I want to look at you while I talk. Right now fate is testing me, terribly. That's why I am so deeply touched and happy to find a friend where I hadn't expected to find one."

And so I looked at him again, and with my headache causing the sight of him to flicker before my eyes, I heard him say, "You protected my property and saw to its safety in a brilliant fashion. You gave my lawyer everything, freely. And you know what touched me most, Holden? What you said when you gave him the key."

"I don't remember what I said."

"You said, 'May it help Herr Brummer. That's all I want.' Never, Holden, do you hear me? Never shall I forget it. I can't shake hands with you because I'm still a prisoner. But go to my lawyer, go right away. He is expecting you. I beg you to accept what he is going to give you out of the sincere friendship I feel for you, Holden. You're a good man."

"Herr Brummer," I said, "I only did what anyone else would have done."

He shook his big head, and a whiff of peppermint was wafted to me through the wire as he cried out, "Nobody would have done it! I wouldn't have done it! I couldn't sleep after I had to abandon you because I was positive that . . . that you'd do something quite different. You know what I mean. Yesterday was the happiest day of my life, Holden. You have restored my faith in humanity!"

"Three minutes," said the officer.

"Holden, I am going to entrust my most precious possession to you. My wife."

"But . . ."

"To whom could I entrust her who would be worthier than you?" said Julius Brummer excitedly. "Tomorrow she will leave the hospital. From then on you're to accompany her everywhere. You're not to leave her alone for a moment. You have had the bitter experience of learning what my enemies are capable of. Holden, I look upon you as my trusted friend."

"One more minute."

"I'm finished. I've said everything I wanted to say." He bowed low before me. "My respect, Holden. And my gratitude."

"Time's up."

"Please tell my wife that I love her."

"Yes, Herr Brummer. I'll be happy to tell your wife that you love her."

"And that everything's going to be all right."

"And that everything's going to be all right."

"And give Mila my love. Tell her to buy Mitzili a fine piece of meat."

He nodded and left the room. I sat down and waited for a while, until I felt better. Then I left too, but very slowly and cautiously because the floor underneath me was swaying and rolling, so were the walls around me, and I could see little dots of light in the air.

A fine piece of meat.

For his Mitzili . . .

15

"You didn't tell Herr Brummer the truth."

"Have you come to reproach me for it?" said Dr. Zorn.

Today he had on a green vest and a light brown suit.

He was sitting behind his desk, smoking a cigar. Here the windows were closed too, and clouds of blue smoke filled the room.

"Why did you protect me?"

"I'd rather not answer that," he said. The rather startling plaid of his tie was a little too colorful.

"You made inquiries about me on Herr Brummer's behalf . . ."

"No. That was my idea. Herr Brummer knows nothing about the results of my research."

"So you haven't told him anything about my past."

"Any objections, Herr Holden? Anyway, why does this excite you so much."

"Because I don't understand why you're doing it."

"To pin you down. To obligate you," he said calmly. "Besides, I can imagine that you might possibly one day be in a position to . . . hm . . . do me a favor." Now he was tugging at his collar again.

"What sort of a favor?"

"I'd rather not answer that," he said for a second time. He looked at the clock. "I'm sorry, but my next client is waiting. Would you please sign this?"

"Sign?"

"A receipt. For thirty thousand marks. You will understand, I am sure, why Herr Brummer prefers not to give you a check for the amount. Please sign, so that I can give it to you in cash."

I signed.

Zorn took the receipt, looked at it carefully, then opened the top drawer of his desk. "I hope you won't mind if I give it to you in fifty-mark bills." He counted out six hundred violet fifty-mark bills on the desk in front of me. Every now and then he licked his fingers. He arranged the bills in little heaps of one thousand marks each. "You must not put this money into any account. And as long as Herr Brummer is under arrest you must not incur any conspicuous expenses. You must promise not to change your life style in any way." He pushed a piece of paper across the desk to me. "I would like you to give me that in writing."

I gave it to him in writing by signing the prepared statement.

"During the next few days," said the little lawyer with the white mane of hair, "you will be approached by quite a few people. You will re-re-report every one of them to me and receive instructions. And now please excuse me." He rose and gave me his cool, dry hand. "By the way, did you take a look at the cathedral in Braunschweig?"

16

As I stepped outdoors, the rays of the sun struck my head like a hammer. The light hurt my eyes. This summer was beginning to be inhuman. It got hotter every day.

I took off my jacket and walked past a car dealer's, a jewelry shop and a tailor, and thought that now I could buy any car I liked, the finest watch, the best suit. That was to say—I could, but I wasn't allowed to. I had promised not to change my life style.

In accordance with my life style, I sat down in a sidewalk café and ordered a lemonade with ice. Six small tables with twelve brightly painted chairs were arranged on the sidewalk, but I was the only customer. I took out the bills and looked at them, first at the whole bundle, then one by one. So that was my reward for the fear I had felt because I had tried to blackmail somebody, and for the fact that Dr. Zorn had lied to Julius Brummer. For that I now possessed thirty thousand marks. If I hadn't tried blackmail, I would still be poor. I would also still be poor if Dr. Zorn had told Julius Brummer the truth. Two immoral actions, therefore, had had to come together for me to receive the money—one would not have sufficed. I began to understand how fortunes were made.

The waiter appeared with my lemonade and I put the money back into my pocket and drank slowly, because I didn't want to chill my stomach and become ill with so much money in my pocket. So much money . . .

The ice clinked in the glass and little drops began to condense on the outside. Lemonade is my favorite drink. When I was a little boy my mother used to make jugfuls of it, which she stored in the cellar because we didn't have an icebox. I held the glass in one hand, the other I laid on my jacket, where the money was, and thought of my mother and of a summer day long ago, which had been just as hot as this one. That was the day the bailiff came to see us to . . .

I was playing in the garden when he came, and I saw that he was very pale. He suffered terribly in the heat. Herr Kohlscheit was an old man and he had on a shiny black suit. He always carried a shabby briefcase when he came to see us, and he came often.

My mother received him and was at once very friendly. "My goodness, Herr Kohlscheit, I feel terrible, your having to come all this way in the heat to see us. It's too bad."

"My heart," said Herr Kohlscheit. "It's my heart, you know. And all the vexation. You can't imagine what I've been through today. This fellow—he tried to beat me up!"

"O heavenly day!" cried my mother.

"It's the excitement, Frau Holden. We're not so young anymore."

"Don't I know it," said my mother. "Do sit down for a moment on the porch where it's shady. And have a glass of lemonade."

"Thank you—no."

"It's ice-cold and made of real lemons, Herr Kohlscheit. *Of course* you'll have a glass. Robert dear, run down and get the jug."

"Right away, Mama. Herr Kohlscheit, please tell me what happened when the man tried to beat you up."

"Oh, you know, it's always the same thing. The police and a lot of shouting, and off they went with him; and his wife, the poor wretch, cursed me and screamed after me I should get cancer and die of it, slowly. What do you think of that, Frau Holden? And it's not my fault if the finance office sends me out and tells me: go and impound. And people think I enjoy it!"

"I'd enjoy it," I cried. "Mama, when I grow up I'm going to be a bailiff. That's an exciting profession."

"You're a child and don't know what you're talking about. Now don't interrupt when grown-ups are talking. Go and get the jug."

I ran down cellar and got the lemonade, and Herr Kohlscheit drank thirstily and said, "I'm not thanking you for the lemonade, Frau Holden, but for your kindness. And now to work." And with that, and sighing heavily, he put one of his stickers on the only valuable piece of furniture we owned, a big wardrobe from the time of the Empress Maria Theresa. "If I've got to do it," he said, "let me at least give you some advice. Pay off a few marks every now and then, just a few, and we'll never come for the wardrobe. Because just between us—we're drowning in furniture. Our warehouses are full to overflowing. We'll never get rid of the stuff."

"That's very good advice," said my mother.

When he left, Herr Kohlscheit kissed her hand. "No ill feeling?" he asked.

"But of course not," said my mother. Out on the street, the old man turned and waved and we waved back, and my mother said, "Just look, one of his socks is torn. I wouldn't be surprised if he had debts too."

"If a bailiff has debts, Mama, and can't pay them, does he have to impound his own things?" I asked, and now, so many years later, I thought of it, a glass of lemonade in one hand, the other on my jacket, just over the thirty thousand marks.

Thirty thousand marks . . . oh my God!

I finished the lemonade and paid and went to the flower shop next door. I ordered thirty red roses and said, "Please send them at once to Frau Nina Brummer. She is a patient in the Marien Hospital."

"Would you like to enclose a card, sir?"

"No."

"Who shall we put down as sender?"

"No one. Just send the flowers," I said.

Nina.

Now I could think of her again, now I felt safe. And it had nothing to do with my love for her, I decided, as I walked back to the car in the heat. In the situation I had found myself in yesterday, anyone would have thought only of himself. Or perhaps not?

I sat down on the hot leather and started the car. I thought of Nina, and felt just as unhappy as I had felt carefree moments ago. Perhaps it wasn't love, or certainly not a good love. Otherwise I would have thought of her yesterday, first and foremost of her. I probably only wanted to sleep with her.

But then why did I feel so guilty? Why did it depress me to think of her? Why did I feel so unsure? I wanted her to trust me. Wasn't that love—when one wanted the other person to trust one? '

When I stopped at a red light, a newspaper boy came up to the car, the *Mittagsblatt* in his hand. I bought one. The headline ran across four columns: BRUMMER DECLARES HE IS INNOCENT!

The car behind me tooted. The traffic light had turned green. I drove on and wondered if Nina would realize right away who had sent the flowers, and suddenly I thought I could smell her perfume, yes, quite clearly.

Perhaps it was love . . .

17

My steps echoed as I walked into the hall of the villa. The windows were closed, the curtains drawn to keep out the heat. It was dark and cool in the house, and it smelled of wax. On a table in front of the fireplace lay a lot of letters.

"Mila?"

No answer.

I went into the kitchen. It was immaculate. A tap was dripping. In the silence it sounded loud.

"Mila?"

I could hear the dog whining. The second door in the kitchen, which led to Mila's room, was pushed open and the old boxer walked into the kitchen. Half blind and helpless, she bumped into the stove as usual, whimpered a little and rubbed her misshapen body against my trousers.

"Come on in, Herr Holden," I heard Mila call out.

I had never been in her room. It was small; the one window had a view of the park. A rocking chair stood in front of it. On a table next to it there were photographs of Nina—large ones, small ones, at least a dozen. Nina as a little girl in a short dress, a bow in her hair; Nina as a teenager, as a young woman on horseback . . .

The old cook was lying on a white iron bedstead, a picture of a Madonna hung above it. Her face was grey and shiny, her lips were blue. She was holding both hands pressed against her chest. She had on a black dress, as usual, old-fashioned laced shoes and her white apron. Her cap had slipped a little, but it was still on her head.

"For God's sake, Mila, what happened?"

"It's nothing, Herr Holden. Don't get excited. I'll be all right in a minute. It's my thyroid. It happens sometimes."

"You need a doctor!"

"Mercy no! I've taken my drops. In an hour I'll be perfectly all right. It only happened because I got so excited a while ago."

"About what?"

"Herr Holden, they're all gone—the butler, the valet, the maids, the gardener. They all left together. We're alone in the house."

The dog whimpered.

"And of course our Mitzi, the poor old thing."

"What do you mean—gone? Where did they go?"

"They just went. Packed their things and left. The gardener put them up to it. Told them the servants in the neighborhood were talking about it, and that they just couldn't stay, with the *gnä' Herr* in jail." She swallowed hard, the sweat was running down her kind old face. "What a hassle, Herr Holden! I threatened them. I said they'd be sued if they left without giving notice, but they only laughed at me. Said they didn't care. Let us sue, they said. Nothing could happen to them with the *gnä' Herr* in jail because . . . because he's a crook. One of . . . of the big profiteers. That's when I got my attack, but I'm already beginning to feel better."

I sat down on the rocking chair and looked at the photographs. The old cook looked at me tensely. "But you're not going to leave us, are you, Herr Holden?"

"No," I said, and went on looking at the photographs.

"I knew it. You'll stick to the *gnädige Herr*."

"Yes," I said, and looked at the photographs.

"Tomorrow my Nina comes home. I'll cook a fine meal for the three of us. And until the *gnä' Herr* has been acquitted, we'll hire a cleaning woman. Is all we need anyway, isn't that right, Mitzili?"

The old boxer whimpered.

"Aren't you glad too, Herr Holden, that the *gnädige Frau* is coming home?"

I nodded and looked hastily out into the garden because I couldn't bear the sight of the photographs any longer. A ripe, yellow apple fell from one of the old trees. I saw it fall and roll downhill to the glittering lake.

18

"Thank you for the roses," said Nina Brummer.

She was sitting on the side of her bed in the hospital. One of the hospital employees was carrying her luggage down to the car. We were alone. Nina was wearing a white linen dress that morning. Vivid blue, red, yellow and green flowers were painted on it, obviously by hand. She was very pale and very beautiful. She looked at me as she spoke, friendly and a little worried.

"How did you know they were from me?" I was standing in front of her, my cap in my hand.

"Because there wasn't a card, no sender, nothing." She looked at the flowers standing in a vase on the window sill. "Herr Holden, I have to make something clear to you before we go home. It isn't easy to find the right words, because I don't want to hurt you. You worried about me;

you helped me . . ." She moved her head and the sunlight fell on her hair, making it glisten. "Yes, you were a great help, and I am grateful to you. I don't have many friends left. I would be happy if you would remain my friend. But I must beg you not to send me any more red roses."

I looked at her; she avoided my eyes and began to walk up and down the room. Not far off the little chapel bell began to ring. Her linen dress clung to her body, her red shoes had thin high heels. A slight flush passed across her cheeks as she said, "I beg you to be sensible."

"I am."

Now she looked at me suddenly, and her big blue eyes darkened, became almost black. It fascinated me. At that moment she was as beautiful as a young innocent girl. "Would you say it was sensible to tell a woman you love her when you've only just met her and don't know anything about her?"

"I know enough about you," I said. "I don't want to know any more. Besides, being sensible and love have nothing to do with each other."

"But with me they have, Herr Holden. You know what I've just gone through. I intend to be sensible from now on and never love anyone again. Never. I can't."

"You can learn," I said. "There's no hurry."

"And if I learn to love again, Herr Holden—what then?"

"Then I shall ask you to get a divorce and take up life with me."

"But only a few days ago you pleaded with me not to leave my husband!"

"A few days ago I had no money."

"That was a very unfortunate answer, Herr Holden." Now she was trembling. "I can imagine where you got that money."

"Things didn't go quite as you may be thinking," I said.

"I don't want to know how they went. My husband has the documents, yes?"

"Yes."

"That's all I want to know. You know that I wanted to die when I found out what my husband was accused of. In the meantime you have managed to make money with it.

146

That's your private business. But I must insist that you also respect my private life, otherwise . . ."

"Otherwise?"

"Otherwise I must ask you to look for another job."

"That puts me in a dilemma," I said. "Now that I have accepted the money, I can't leave. Now they need me. As for respecting your private life, *gnädige Frau* . . ."

"I used the wrong words. Excuse me. It . . . it is difficult for me . . ." Then, like a child who hopes to overwhelm her teacher with a sudden idea, she cried, "You say you love me. Then for the sake of that love, leave me in peace!"

"I don't feel that it is any concern of yours that I love you."

She smiled. "So we don't have to talk about it any more."

"Certainly not, if you don't wish it."

"You're nice, Herr Holden." Impulsively she stretched out her hand. I grasped it.

"And may I consider this a peace treaty?" she asked.

"On the contrary," I replied. "It is a declaration of war!"

"Herr Holden!"

"Don't be afraid, *gnädige Frau*. It will be a very gentle war. Because surely you realize that neither of us has behaved very respectably. You haven't, I haven't. We're both in the same boat. So we've got to get along with each other."

She wasn't smiling any longer. She turned away abruptly and walked toward the door. "Will you please take my jewel case."

I didn't move.

At the door she turned. "Well?" and tried to look at me arrogantly because both of us knew that the jewel case was the first test of strength.

"And the roses?" I asked.

"I can't go home with thirty red roses, Herr Holden. Don't be naïve."

"Not with thirty, but with one."

"With one would be even worse. Think of the servants."

"The servants have left. Nobody is at home but Mila."

"I asked you to carry my jewel case."

"Yes," I said, "I heard you."

A few seconds passed as we looked at each other. Nina's pupils darkened again and I could feel my heart beating. As a child on the way to school I had played games like this. If I only need four steps to the lamppost without stepping on a crack in the sidewalk, then I won't be called on in arithmetic. On that summer day I played a different game. If Nina takes a rose, she will love me one day.

Six seconds, seven, eight. Then slowly, very slowly, she walked over to the vase on the sill. Her face was the color of the rose as she broke it off just below the blossom and laid it on the gold, platinum, and gems in the jewel case. The lock made a clicking sound as she closed the lid. I looked at her once more and felt that the incident had excited her. Her lips were parted, her eyes half closed.

"Now will you take the case?"

"Yes," I said. "Now I will."

Twenty-nine roses stayed in the room, but what did that matter? The one she had taken home was worth all the rest.

On the stairs, as we passed the saints in their niches, I noticed that I was sweating. She walked down ahead of me on her high heels, in her tight-fitting flowered dress. I looked at her hair; her perfume was wafted up to me; I saw her slender wrists, her delicate ankles. Once she turned around and looked at me arrogantly.

I smiled.

Whereupon she turned her back on me abruptly and her heels beat an angry tattoo across the floor of the hall, and my heart beat in time with them.

19

The rose bed gleamed red in the sunshine, the iris stood blue and white, yellow and blue, white and yellow in the green grass. Birds were singing in the old trees, a woodpecker was rat-tat-tatting busily, and dragonflies were flitting over the silvery lake. As I carried Nina's luggage across the gravel path to the house, I thought of the rainy night when I had walked across this gravel path for the first time. Strange people had been milling around, police cars parked on the grass, and in the villa there had been a smell of gas. To me it seemed as if years lay between that night and this morning.

We were a short distance from the villa when the front door opened and a little girl emerged and came to a standstill under the ostentatious letters J and B, a very little girl in a light blue dress. She held a bunch of white carnations in her little hands, gazed at us seriously and nervously licked her lips, after which she looked pleadingly into the darkness of the open door. Behind it I could hear voices.

The little girl nodded heroically and ran toward us. She stumbled once and almost fell, but she caught herself in time and reached us quite out of breath. "Mickey, darling," cried Nina, her arms spread wide, and as soon as I heard the name it came to me who the child probably was—the daughter of Mila Blehova's only relative, the police reporter, Peter Romberg.

"Welcome home, *Tante*," Mickey cried gaily. She had evidently been told to present Nina with the carnations, and for the moment had every intention of doing so. But then something unexpected happened. Mickey stood still. All of us stood still. The little girl had black eyes and now they became enormous. She looked at me sharply, and I

149

looked back at her with some embarrassment. Mickey's
skin was like silk and her hair was very fine and cut short.

"This is Herr Holden," Nina explained. "You don't
know him yet, but you'll be driving with him often."

"How do you do, Herr Holden," Mickey said solemnly.

"How do you do, Mickey."

The child broke into a smile, shyly at first, then more
courageously, until in the end she was laughing, her mouth
wide open, and I could see her irregular little teeth. Now,
still laughing, she walked up to me and held out the carnations. "For you, Herr Holden," after which she turned to
Nina, curtsied and said, obviously coached, "We're so
happy to have you back with us, *Tante* Nina."

Just then there was a cry and Mila Blehova came running out of the house. She was followed by Peter Romberg
and the lawyer, Dr. Zorn, who today was wearing a brown
suit with a yellow checked vest. While the two men
laughed, Mila was crying desperately, "Jesus, Maria, and
Joseph, Mickey, what *are* you doing? The carnations aren't
for Herr Holden. They're for the *gnädige Frau*. We just
told you!"

"But I'd rather give them to Herr Holden," said
Mickey.

I stood there like an idiot, holding the carnations,
Nina's luggage on the ground beside me. Now even she
was laughing.

"But why do you want to give him the flowers?" Mila
was wringing her hands while nearsighted, freckled Peter
Romberg took pictures of us.

"Because I like him," said Mickey. She came up to me.
"Will you play with me, Herr Holden?"

"Sure I will."

"You've got to ask me cities. I know a lot of them.
Even the capital of Poland . . . Warsaw."

"You've made a conquest, Herr Holden," said Nina.

"One conquest, yes," I said, and Nina turned away
quickly and embraced Mila.

"My dear old Mila!"

"Oh, *gnä' Frau*, please don't be angry with the child."

"You can ask me about animals too," said Mickey.

"My heartiest congratulations on your recovery." Dr.
Zorn bowed low. His white hair stood like the seed head

150

of a faded dandelion around his head. "And the very best wishes from your husband. I'm to tell you he is with you in his thoughts every minute."

"Papa!" cried Mickey. "You've got to take a picture of me and Herr Holden."

Peter Romberg knelt in the grass and Mickey hooked her arm in mine like a grown woman and both of us laughed into the camera. We stood surrounded by flowers, in the sunshine, and no one had any idea what terror, what a hideous nightmare this picture was going to serve soon . . . very soon.

20

In the hall there were flowers in vases, in pots, in baskets and little bowls. The flowers had come from Brummer and other people. I took the luggage upstairs and Dr. Zorn retired at once with Nina. "I have important things to discuss with you, *gnädige Frau*."

"I don't need you any more, Herr Holden," said Nina, cold as a fish. So I went to the kitchen. Peter Romberg was just leaving. He had to go to his office.

Mickey began to complain. "Oh Papa, please leave me here. I want to play with Herr Holden."

"Herr Holden is busy. You mustn't bother him."

"But he promised me. Do I bother you, Herr Holden?"

"Leave her here," I said. "It's perfectly all right. I did promise her. She can help me wash the car."

"Yippee!!!"

Mila shook her head. "I can't believe it, Herr Holden. She's always so shy, won't talk to a soul. But with you . . ."

"Come on, Herr Holden. Let's wash the car."

So I got the Cadillac out of the garage and drove it under a big chestnut tree. Here it was cooler. The Mercedes was still parked on the street, in front of the entrance. I put on overalls and told Mickey, "First of all, take off that nice dress and your shoes and stockings, or I'll be in trouble with your mother if you go home all dirty."

So Mickey took off everything except her pink underpants. Her body was white, her little shoulder blades stuck out, and on her left shoulder she had a birthmark.

I let her hose down the Cadillac. More fun! Because of course every now and then she missed the big car and "accidentally" sprayed me, and every time she did I was horribly startled and declared I'd have a heart attack, and Mickey laughed until she nearly choked. Then we soaped down the car, and while we did that Mickey showed off her learning. "Ask me about an iceberg."

"What about an iceberg?"

"Nine tenths under water, only one tenth above the water. That's why ships run into them."

"No!"

"Ask me some more. About cities and countries."

"What is the capital of Austria?"

"Vienna."

"Good."

"More."

"Who was Adolf Hitler?"

She looked at me sadly.

"Never heard of him?"

With the irritation of an expert who doesn't know the answer, she said, "One can't know everything." And then, with the curiosity of a child, "Who *was* Adolf Hitler?"

Yes, who was Adolf Hitler?

I began to think how to explain him to a child, but I didn't get far because suddenly, out on the street, there was a crash. Metal against metal, glass splintering on stone.

Mickey's reaction was one of unmitigated delight. "Herr Holden, Herr Holden, somebody's run into you!"

We ran to the park gate. A blue BMW had run into Brummer's white Mercedes. The hood of the BMW was imbedded in the trunk of the Mercedes. No sign of any other car on the street in the midday heat. A young woman was standing beside the two cars . . . what am I saying? A young girl, practically still high-school age. She had on a red linen dress with white trim, red shoes, and red gloves. Her hair was black and cut youthfully, her skin was very white, her big mouth was red. I found her beautiful, but it was the type of beauty that made you think of a youth of poverty and denial. She looked crushed. I got the impression that she'd been yelled at and knocked around a lot. A beauty from a basement home.

I had to look twice because I couldn't believe my eyes. She was so young, couldn't have been more than twenty, but—no doubt about it—she was pregnant. Beautifully built, with an unmistakably protruding stomach.

"How could this possibly have happened?" I asked.

The girl said nothing. She stared at me, and I began to feel uncomfortable. I had never seen such fear in any eyes, or . . . no. It wasn't fear. It was . . . dammit all, it was tragedy! Now I had the word. Her eyes were tragic, everything about the girl was tragic.

"Oh my," said Mickey. "That's going to cost you something!"

The girl closed her eyes. Her lips were twitching. She clung to the BMW.

"Mickey, go back into the park. Go on."

She left us, disgusted, and took up a stand close to the fence so as not to miss a word of our conversation. I said to the young girl, "Take it easy. Your insurance will pay the damage."

She swayed.

"Shall I get you a glass of water?"

"I'm all right." Her smile was distorted, it made her look more tragic than ever. "I . . . suddenly I felt dizzy. I couldn't see clearly. That's how it must have happened. I'm . . ."

"Yes. I can see. Go and sit down in your car. I'll call the police."

The next thing she was clutching me with both hands and her words hissed in my face. "No! Not the police!"

I tried to free myself but couldn't. In her panic she was extraordinarily strong. "Not the police!" she repeated.

"Now look here—I'm a chauffeur. The Mercedes doesn't belong to me."

"Herr Holden!" cried Mickey. "Do you want me to get *Tante* Mila?"

The strange girl let go of me. She said, "The BMW doesn't belong to me either."

"Did you steal it?" Mickey cried delightedly.

"It belongs to a friend of mine."

"What's his name?"

"Herbert Schwertfeger," she whispered. I'd heard the name somewhere, but couldn't remember where and when.

"And what's your name? Speak up."

The black-haired girl replied so loudly that even Mickey could hear her. "My name is Hilde Lutz. I live on Reginastrasse 31."

"Have you any identification on you?"

She shook her head.

"Nothing?"

"No. And I . . . I don't have a driver's license."

I don't know, Herr Kriminal Kommissar Kehlmann . . . just to mention you for whom I am filling all these pages, because I do think it is fitting for me to remind myself occasionally why I am reporting all this and to what end it is leading . . . I don't know, Herr Kriminal Kommissar Kehlmann of Baden-Baden, whether your profession ever permits you, occasionally, to feel pity for someone. I don't know whether you were born rich or poor. Don't tell me that doesn't make a difference. The fact that this pregnant young girl, Hilde Lutz, had doubtlessly been born poor, this fact, *Herr Kommissar*, aroused pity in me. Her poverty, *Herr Kommissar*, united us. Wealth divides, its effect is exclusive. That was something I had learned in connection with Herr Brummer and his beautiful, arrogant wife. Wealth withdraws man from his surroundings. The rich are secure, yet at the same time separated from bad-smelling crowds in buses and subways; they are enclosed, creatures apart in their luxurious cars and guarded villas, in their sleepers on trains and their luxury cabins on ships, secure but isolated. Perhaps I would have felt no pity if the Mercedes had been mine and the BMW hers. I hope you understand what I'm driving at, *Herr Kommissar*. If you don't, then just add what I did to the long list of my other crimes.

I said to Hilde Lutz, "What sort of a mess do you think you're getting me into? If I don't call the police, who's going to pay the damage?"

"My friend will pay. Herr Schwertfeger."

"I don't even know where he lives."

"And we don't even know if that's your right name, Hilde Lutz!" cried Mickey. She'd got the name all right. At the time it didn't mean anything to me. Today, as I write these lines, it means everything. Because everything would have turned out differently and could have ended without disaster if Mickey hadn't understood the name.

Hilde Lutz said, "Please let's drive to my apartment. I'll show you my papers. We'll call Herr Schwertfeger and he'll attend to everything."

"I've just told you, it's not my Mercedes."

"Please!"

Her face was ashen.

"All right," I said, with the highly decent intention, *Herr Kriminal Kommissar*, to help this poor girl. As you read on, you will begin to have second thoughts, as I did, about the desirability of highly decent intentions.

"Oh, I do thank you. You'll be back in half an hour."

"All right, Mickey, tell *Tante* Mila what's happened."

"Don't go with her, Herr Holden. I'm scared."

"You don't have to be scared. You're staying here."

"I'm not afraid for me, Herr Holden. I'm afraid for you!" she cried, and her big black eyes were huge, and the ribs on her tiny chest were heaving with her excited breathing. "Stay! Stay here!"

But I didn't stay. I drove off with Hilde Lutz toward Reginastrasse 31, and with that into evil, darkness, horror . . .

21

"Come in," said Hilde Lutz.

She lived in a studio apartment overlooking the roofs of the city, in a modern building. We had gone up nine floors in the elevator. The room I walked into seemed very large. It was warm and light. The furniture was modern, there was a couch with colored pillows and a grand piano. A dark radio stood on the light linoleum floor; no rug yet. A few books, two maps, a modern painting with sharp aggressive shapes. It was a beautiful apartment, but by no means completely furnished. The owner had apparently run out of money, or whoever had financed the interior decoration had suddenly decided to economize. Pretty young girls with helpless expressions often lived in apartments like this. They have a boyfriend, but no money and no profession. The boyfriend has the profession and the money. The young girls live on love and hope . . . Frequently the boyfriend is married.

While Hilde Lutz began to rummage through a drawer in the desk, I walked out onto the balcony and looked down. The cars moving along the Reginastrasse looked small. A silver blimp floated in the sunny sky. "Drink Underberg" was printed on its rear.

"Herr Holden?"

Hilde Lutz was standing beside the piano. I could hear her teeth chattering. "You . . . you wanted to see a document," she said. "Here it is," and she laid something down on the piano.

"I . . . I'll call my friend," with which she disappeared. I walked over to the piano. What I found was the photostate of a document. I read:

> From: The Commander of the Security Police and the SD Weissruthenien.
> To: Staff Reichsführer SS.
> Secret Document Nr. 102/22/43. Under seal.
> Minsk, July 20, 1943.
> On Tuesday, July 20, 1943, at approximately 5 P.M. I arrested the 80 Jews employed by the High Commissioner of Weissruthenien and transported them for special treatment. Those with gold fillings were first taken to the specialists for such cases, as ordered . . .

That was how it began, and it went on for a whole typewritten page, single-spaced. At the end the amount of ammunition was given: ninety-five rounds. A few of the eighty Jews apparently didn't die at once. The document was signed: *Herbert Schwertfeger, SS Obersturmbann-führer*.

I sat down on the chair in front of the piano and read the whole thing through again, and began to understand everything. Just as I had reached this point, a door opened and a man of about fifty came into the room. He was short, his face was red, and he was exceptionally elegantly dressed. In fact I couldn't remember ever having seen anyone more elegant. His light brown suede shoes, the matching socks, the sand-colored summer suit, his off-white shirt, silk tie—it all matched so beautifully. He wore his grey hair combed back, cut short, and parted meticulously. His blue eyes looked fearlessly out into the world. His lips were thin. You would have been impressed at once by the serious intentions of this man, *Herr Kriminal Kommissar*.

A white silk handkerchief was stuck neatly in the breast pocket of his jacket. He brought a refreshing odor of *eau de cologne* into the room with him. In spite of his small stature, he held himself very straight. Without doubt a highly respectable citizen who was devoted to the classics and Bach. He said in a pleasant voice, "Good day, Herr Holden."

I rose and replied, "Herr Schwertfeger, if I am not mistaken," whereupon he held out his hand and shook mine, and succeeded because I didn't react fast enough.

I looked at the photostat, undoubtedly made by Dr. Zorn, and read again, to give myself strength, the passage in which a two-year-old Jewish child was described as having had its head bashed in against a tree trunk. And as I read I could smell the fine scent of *eau de cologne*, so pleasant on this hot day.

I looked up. "Of course I would never have come here if I had known what your friend's purpose was."

"My friend," he said, in the same pleasant, becalming tone, "had no purpose but to carry out my wishes."

"So she rammed into the Mercedes on purpose. Are you prepared to pay for the damages or do I have to go to the police?"

"Of course I'll pay. Let's not waste any time on that. It's unimportant."

"Not for me. I think the repair will cost anywhere between two and three hundred marks."

He laid three one-hundred-mark bills on the piano and asked, "Were you in the army?"

"Yes."

"Where?"

"In Russia," I said. "But let's not go into that or I may vomit."

"I was in Russia too," he said.

"Yes. As I have just read."

"War is war, Herr Holden. I was an officer. I was given orders. I obeyed them as I had sworn I would. Am I supposed to answer for what I did today, thirteen years later, on the instigation of a bastard who has no idea of how things were then?" Now he was off. "Do you think it was easy for me to obey orders like that? German men, Herr Holden, were not created for things like that."

"And the child whose head was smashed against a tree?"

"The man was drunk. I had to feed them *schnapps* or they wouldn't have carried out my orders." He patted his lips with his handkerchief, shifted his tie. "One doesn't have one's eyes everywhere. One turns away for a moment and the thing has happened. Of course I shot the man. And now, Herr Holden, let's get down to business."

"Good afternoon," I said, but he didn't let me go.

"Listen to me. You are the man who brought this piece of shit," he looked at the photostat as if it had been a repulsive reptile, "in from the East."

I looked at the photostat too. It was preferable to looking at Herr Schwertfeger, and I read the paragraph in which the *SS Obersturmbannführer* regretted that among the eighty Jews there had been an unwelcome predominance of women. Meanwhile he was saying, "Thirteen years have passed. We've worked like dogs. We have rebuilt what was ruined, and then a bastard like this comes along and wants to destroy everything."

"Talk to Dr. Zorn. I presume he was the one who sent you this. I've had nothing to do with it."

"You have a lot to do with it. Let me finish. Is this sort

158

of thing to go on forever—hatred and revenge? Is there going to be no end to it? In my opinion the time has come to forget the past."

"Dr. Zorn," I said. "He's the person you've got to talk to about it. I'm not your man."

"Herr Holden . . . I don't want to talk about the flourishing business I have succeeded in building up by the sweat of my brow, in these thirteen years, built up out of ashes and ruins. No. Not about that. And not about the fact that I employ fourteen hundred people. And not about my family . . ."

"Ah," I said. "You have a family."

"My wife is dead," he said, "but I have many relatives and I look after them. I have two grown sons. One is studying law, the other is a doctor. But I'm not going to talk about them."

I listened attentively because I was curious to know what he had on his mind. "Herr Holden, your employer is a profiteer who belongs behind bars. He has damaged me to the extent of over half a million marks. He has hurt others more. He has broken his word, he has lied and deceived us and taken advantage of us financially. Let's stick to the facts: Herr Brummer belongs in jail. Surely it must still be possible to call for justice when the right is on one's side!"

"So what are you so excited about? You have called for justice."

"And what happens? He comes with this document. He wants to silence me. He wants me to withdraw charges. He wants my submission. You are a normal human being, Herr Holden. I want your verdict: Is this admissable? Here I stand"—he stretched out his left arm—"a man who did his duty, who obeyed orders for which he must answer with his conscience. And here"—he stretched out his right arm—"Herr Brummer, a common crook, the worst type of blackmailer, a bastard . . . yes, I'll repeat that—a bastard. And you hesitate for a moment with your decision as to what side you're on?"

"I'm not hesitating at all. I'm with Herr Brummer."

He stuck his hands in his trouser pockets and looked at me, and began to whistle. I said nothing. Finally he spoke.

"Very well, then." He took a small piece of paper out of his breast pocket and laid it down beside the document.

"Here is a check for a hundred thousand marks. The only thing lacking is my signature. I don't know how much you are getting from Herr Brummer, but I don't imagine it's as much as that. Get me the original of this document and I'll sign the check. Come on man, be smart."

"I can't get you the original. It's in a safe-deposit box."

"With a hundred thousand marks, you'll find a way. Don't be an ass. Split with the lawyer. Do whatever you damn please. I want your answer by this evening. Hilde will call you. That is all." Now he spoke harshly, like a man who had no problems. "And I won't take no for an answer."

I could imagine how he had spoken to his men in Minsk.

"Listen to me—"

"Good day," he said, and left the room.

I was alone.

The check without his signature lay beside the photostat with his signature. On the check I read the words, "One hundred thousand," on the photostat the words "special treatment." Then I read the words, "Pay to the order of . . ." and the words "an unwelcome predominance of women." Then Hilde Lutz walked into the room and we stared at each other. I discovered suddenly that there were little liver spots on her flesh. She had to sit down. She said, "He's gone."

Pay to the order of . . .

"I'm to call you. Tonight, at seven."

One hundred thousand marks. Pay to the account of . . .

"I'm in my sixth month. I didn't know anything about his past. I swear I didn't . . ."

"How old are you?"

"Nineteen. He found me working in an espresso. He's always been good to me."

"Why doesn't he marry you?"

"He's embarrassed. He's afraid of his sons, of his whole family. He's thirty years older. That's why I was so happy when I found out I was pregnant. He's crazy about children. He's always said, 'If you get pregnant, I'll marry you.' "

"He'll never marry you."

She began to cry. "He won't marry me if they lock him up."

"He won't marry you anyway."

"He will! He will! He promised me. He loves children."

... with its head against a tree trunk ...

Poor Hilde Lutz. It wasn't her fault.

"You've got to see to it that he doesn't go to jail, Herr Holden. Please, please, please! Take the money!"

"You've got to think of yourself, Fräulein Lutz. Now you've got something on him. Let him pay for it, pay well, and then get out of here."

"You mean I should blackmail him?"

"Everybody blackmails everybody in this little world of ours. You're crazy if you don't do it, with the child coming, and unmarried, and no assistance of any kind. Get what you can out of him and hurry up about it."

She was trembling. "Don't say another word. I love him. I don't want to know what he's done. I . . . I love him more than life itself!"

... ammunition rounds used: 95 ...

22

At one minute before seven the phone rang.

I was in the kitchen, eating what Mila had cooked for me. She had just joined me after serving Nina, who was eating by herself, upstairs. Since she had come home she had avoided Mila and me.

"Just when I sit down," Mila grumbled.

She got up and walked over to the white telephone on the wall. Lately she walked laboriously and slightly bent.

161

"Must have water in my feet . . . Yes? Yes, he's here *gnä' Frau.*" She gestured to me. "Just a minute."

The intercom system in the Brummer house was a little complicated. When one called, it rang first on the main phone, which you could unplug and carry from room to room. From this main phone you could connect to other phones, as for instance the one in the kitchen.

I walked over to the phone and heard Nina's voice. "It's for you, Herr Holden. A lady. She doesn't want to give her name."

"Please excuse the disturbance, *gnädige Frau*," I said, but she didn't reply, and I could hear the click as she hung up the receiver. And then the desperate voice I had dreaded, "Good evening, Herr Holden. You know who is speaking?"

"Yes. I'm sorry, but the answer is no."

Silence. Nothing but static in the open line.

"But . . . but then what shall I do?"

"I told you what to do."

"And the child? Please . . ."

"I have to hang up now."

"Please, please don't hang up!"

I laid the white receiver back on its cradle and went back to the table. I went on eating but suddenly it didn't taste like anything any more. The beer, too, was tasteless. Mila Blehova looked at me and suddenly she laughed softly. "What do you say to that, Mitzili? He's here only two weeks and already he's turning girls' heads!"

I said nothing and ate.

Mila was still amused. "Isn't a bad looking fellow, is he, Mitzili? A good looking man. Bless my soul, but if I were young I'd try my luck with him, hihihi!" She patted my hand affectionately and the telephone on the wall rang again. This time I answered it myself.

Nina's voice was sharper. "The lady, Herr Holden . . ."

"Really, *gnädige Frau*, I'm terribly sorry . . ." But there was the thin desperate voice again. "Don't hang up, Herr Holden, please. I've spoken to him. If it's a question of money . . ."

"No," I said. "No, no, no! I can't do it. Can't you grasp that? I can't do anything about it. And don't call again!" I hung up. I was sweating. If things went on like this . . .

"I'll bet she's young," said Mila, with the curiosity of an old woman.

"What? . . . Yes. Nineteen."

"It's really crazy . . . the way they'll throw themselves at a man nowadays." Mila threw the dog a piece of meat, drank some beer, and wiped her mouth with the back of her hand. "Well, when I think back, I was pretty wild myself when I was young. Oh my, yes . . . when I think of the Kleinseite in Prague . . . the evenings along the Moldau . . . but my goodness, Herr Holden, I wasn't that bad. She's really making a nuisance of herself, if you ask me. But of course, there are so few men since the war . . ."

The phone rang again.

I answered it.

"Herr Holden!"

"*Gnädige Frau?*"

"Come upstairs, to my room!"

"Right away, *gnädige Frau.*"

"And now you're in trouble with my Nina," Mila said sympathetically. "It's really the limit, what girls like that will do."

I put on my brown jacket and adjusted my tie.

Nina Brummer's room lay in the east wing. It was furnished in white and gold, Empire style. Chairs and tables rested on gracefully swung legs, there was a secretary by the window, a narrow cupboard. The bed was large, a wide French bed that dominated the room. The wallpaper was striped white and gold. A door opened into a huge bathroom. A chandelier was burning although it wasn't really dark yet, and the boughs of the trees outside were stirred by the wind.

Nina sat in front of a huge mirror. She had on a black silk robe and matching slippers. The electric light glittered on her blond hair. As we talked she changed the position of her legs three times, but during our entire conversation she never moved her head. I stood behind her in the doorway and she spoke into the mirror. She did everything she could to make the conversation humiliating for me. She seemed to be extremely irritated. Her nostrils were quivering. On the vanity table in front of her, between perfume bottles, powder boxes and hairbrush, stood the white main telephone, and as I walked in, it rang again.

163

Nina said into the mirror, "That's the fourth time, Herr Holden. I told the lady when she called the third time that this was not your telephone."

The phone was still ringing.

"What do you propose to do, Herr Holden?"

"Please pick up the receiver and put it down again."

She did as I told her. Now there was silence in the room. She crossed her legs for the first time. Every time she crossed her legs it became obvious that she was in the process of changing.

I could see in the mirror that it was her intention to humiliate me. "Was that a private call?"

"No."

"I thought so."

Her eyes were dark. I could see them darken in the mirror, and I was suddenly overcome with the crazy desire to walk up to her and tear the silk robe off her shoulders and throw her on the bed. But of course I remained standing in the doorway and heard her say, "It was the girl who ran into the Mercedes this morning, wasn't it?"

"Yes, *gnädige Frau*."

"What does she want from you?"

I was silent. I looked at her legs and smelled her perfume.

She said icily, "For heaven's sake, don't think for a moment that your private life interests me. But I have the feeling there is a lot more to this than your private life. Why am I not told what's going on, Holden? Can't you realize that it is intolerable for me to see my chauffeur intruding into my affairs and those of my husband and . . ."

"I am not intruding," I said, and now I was furious. "I was forced . . ."

The telephone rang again.

"I can see that," said Nina. She lifted the receiver and let it fall again. "How long do you suppose this is going to go on?"

"I don't know. I hope not much longer."

"I demand that you tell me this minute what happened today."

"I have already told you, *gnädige Frau*, that Herr Schwertfeger gave me three hundred marks for the repair of the car."

"That isn't all."

"I'm sorry. Dr. Zorn forbade me to tell you anything more than that."

Now her eyes were almost closed. She crossed her legs for the third time. Slowly, very slowly. I had never seen her angry before. Now I saw her angry. Her lips were parted, her breasts rose and fell.

"He forbade it?"

"Yes."

"So he doesn't trust me."

"I can't be a judge of that. I would advise you to speak to Dr. Zorn personally about it."

The telephone rang again. Between clenched teeth Nina said, "This is unbearable." Again she went through the procedure of lifting the receiver and putting it down again, and the phone was silent. It was that simple to silence the cries for help of a poor creature. Now Nina was breathing heavily. "Holden, you are my employee. I pay you on the first of every month. Is that clear?"

"That is clear, *gnädige Frau*."

"Then I am ordering you to tell me what happened today. Forget Zorn's orders."

"I can't do that."

"You can. I pay him too."

"Herr Brummer pays him," I said, "and the attorney pays me. I'm sorry, *gnädige Frau*. Please don't ask me any more. For your own safety it's better that you know nothing."

After that we looked at each other in the mirror without saying a word. In the end she said, "Very well. I thought we were going to get along, Holden. In spite of what you have done and what I have done. All right. I know where I'm at. From now on I shall consider you my enemy."

"I am very unhappy that——"

"Don't interrupt when I'm speaking. Anyway I must ask you not to speak to me unless spoken to. I know this is your first position as chauffeur and I can't expect you to behave like one, but it's time you learned. Don't look at me like that. I forbid you to look at me like that. Get the car out of the garage. I'm driving into the city in half an hour. Did you hear me? If so, why are you still standing there? Can't you see that I'm in the middle of changing?

165

Have you gone crazy, Holden? I want to make it quite clear that I have no intention of putting up with your shameless behavior. I don't care what you know about me. I know a thing or two about you that would interest my husband. There, I can see that's shut you up. So . . . in half an hour. And Holden . . ."

"*Gnädige Frau?*"

"You're to wear civilian clothes only in your free time. Otherwise you're to appear in uniform."

I thought . . . walk up to her, tear the robe off her shoulders, throw her on the bed . . .

I said, "Yes, *gnädige Frau.*"

And the telephone hadn't rung again. That, at least was something.

23

"Sonnenblickstrasse 67," said Nina Brummer. She got into the back of the Cadillac; I held the door open for her and she looked past me as she got in. She was wearing her mink coat, a silver evening dress, and silver satin shoes. I closed the door, got behind the steering wheel, and drove off. When we reached Cecilienallee, Nina said, "You're driving too fast."

She was right. I was still furious. Now I eased up on the gas pedal. I could see her pale face in the rear-view mirror. Every now and then, in the reflection of the lights whizzing by, her hair gleamed gold for seconds. It is a picture that has remained with me to this day. If I close my eyes I can see her at once. I tried to catch her eye; she noticed it and turned her head away.

At the Sonnenblickstrasse I helped her out. She said, "You're doing the right thing to help me out. You're doing the wrong thing when you grasp my hand to do so. You should hold out your hand so that I can grasp it, if I wish to."

I said nothing.

"Pick me up at eleven. Go to a movie if you like."

Again I said nothing, only bowed slightly. I waited until she had disappeared in the garden of the villa, then I walked to a nearby phone booth and called Peter Romberg and asked if I might come over to see them. "I'm not far away. But please tell me if it's not convenient."

"Not at all! We'll be delighted!"

It was a beautiful evening. The city was cooling off after a hot day and a lot of people were out on the streets, strolling, window shopping. In an espresso I bought a box of chocolates for Mickey.

When I got to the Rombergs, Mickey's mother was just giving her a bath. "Mama, mama!" she screamed. "Shut the door so Herr Holden can't see me!"

"Don't be silly, Mickey. Herr Holden has seen a naked little girl before in his life."

"But I'm embarrassed."

Romberg introduced me to his wife, a small, slight woman with brown hair and brown almond-shaped eyes. Like her husband, she wore glasses. She wasn't exactly pretty but somehow very pleasant. On entering the apartment one felt at once: A happy family lives here.

So as not to be forgotten in the bathroom, Mickey had begun to sing. "I feel so lonely, my heart is heavy, I hear the songs of Mexico . . . Mama!"

"What is it?"

"Open the door."

"You just told me to close it."

"Only a crack. I want to hear what you're saying."

"You don't have to hear everything," said Frau Romberg, and opened the door a crack. No doubt about it—Mickey was in command! While she splashed around in the tub, her parents showed me the apartment—three rooms, modern furniture. In the first room there was a desk covered with photos and papers, cameras, films, books. A police monitor stood in a corner. It was turned on and I could hear it humming.

"Police monitor. So that I can get going right away whenever anything happens."

167

In the next room a radio was playing dance music. "We just bought it, Herr Holden. Look at that tuning system. And it's paid for!"

In the bathroom Mickey was singing again. It wasn't exactly a quiet family. They seemed completely impervious to noise! I had to admire a new standing lamp in the kitchen, a new refrigerator ("That's still on installment") and in the little foyer a wall clothes rack, prettily screened in flowered chintz. "That was Peter's birthday present," said Frau Romberg. "But there's still an awful lot missing."

"Slowly but surely," said Peter Romberg proudly, and gave his wife a kiss, and she blushed like a young girl.

"If he goes on working as well as he does now, Herr Holden, they're going to give him steady employment. As an *editor!*"

"The gentlemen are worried that somebody'll snatch me away," explained Peter Romberg, and the two looked at each other, in love and united in their endeavors, full of admiration for each other, neither of them beautiful, but both with friendly eyes behind their glittering glasses.

"Düssel five. Düssel five." A man's voice from the monitor in Peter's office. "Goethestrasse-Elfenstrasse. Collision. Street car and LKW."

"Düssel five. Roger," said another voice. Then the monitor started humming again. "Well, Herr Romberg?" I said.

"I don't bother about anything trivial like that. Come on, let's have a drink and I'll show you my photos."

"I'll be with you in a second," said Frau Romberg. "I just want to get Mickey to bed," and she disappeared into the bathroom, which was followed almost immediately by shrill cries of protest: "But mama, you *can't* be that mean! With Herr Holden here!"

Romberg looked at me and we laughed. "Nice child," I said.

He got a bottle of cognac and glasses and we sat down in his office. Huge enlargements of photographs—all animals—hung on the walls. "We adore Mickey," he said, "if only she wasn't such a fabricator."

"What do you mean?"

"Oh, she does it to impress, tells the most fantastic stories—a wolf escaped from the zoo, her friend Linda's

168

mother is an American millionairess, I'm a German millionaire, she has asthma . . ."

"I did the same thing."

"I'm sure not that bad, Herr Holden. Did the policeman on the corner ever tell you you didn't have to do your homework?"

"Düssel five. Düssel five. We need a wrecker. The LKW is rammed into the street car. We can't free the intersection."

"Düssel five. We're sending the wrecker. Anybody hurt?"

"Nobody hurt. Only a mess of glass."

"You see," said Peter. "Small potatoes. I can always tell."

Mickey came into the room. She had on brightly colored slippers and a long blue nightgown. She gave me her hand and curtsied and began to speak very fast, evidently scared to death that somebody would interrupt her! "Good evening, Herr Holden. I know who Hitler is now. I looked him up in my child's encyclopedia. He was a terrible person. It says in the encyclopedia that he had people tortured and killed and that he started a war and ruined a lot of countries." She drew a deep breath or she would have choked, and recited from memory, "He fled from the responsibility for the debacle by committing suicide. He left behind him a Germany devastated, divided and helpless as never before in its history." She finished, exhausted with her mental efforts, "And with all that he started life as a *painter!*"

I gave her the box of chocolates and received a wet kiss. "Oh papa, mama, look! With nuts, and all different fillings. May I eat one of the nut ones now, please, please!"

"In bed."

"Herr Holden, is the Mercedes all right again?"

"I said in bed," said Frau Romberg. "One chocolate and to sleep," and she dragged Mickey off with her. In the doorway of her room Mickey turned and waved to me and I waved back, and I saw her framed by many colored toys, all animals—a giraffe, a rabbit, lambs, poodles, dogs and cats, and a monkey.

We drank cognac and smoked, the police monitor hummed, and Romberg showed me his animal pictures

169

and I felt very much at home. I didn't even think of Nina. We took off our jackets, loosened our ties, and Romberg talked about his pictures. I liked the swans best. He had caught them taking off and coming down on a lake.

"Sometimes they weigh as much as twenty kilos. Just imagine the strength the creature has to have to get off the water! Needs a twenty-to-thirty-meter runway! And then he only gets up in the air by using every ounce of muscular power he has. If you started to compare the flight of a swan with that of a plane, you'd find out that the swan shouldn't be flying at all! As a plane he'd be too heavy!" His face was aglow now; he was talking about something that had captivated him. I thought how everything we enjoy makes us beautiful.

"I'd be so happy if Peter could do nothing else but pictures like that," said Frau Romberg softly.

"Just be patient a little longer, darling, until we've paid off everything we owe," he said, and stroked her rough, houseworn hands. "Then I'll find somebody to finance me."

"For what?"

"I want to publish animal books, under my own imprint. Look how successful Bernatzik's been. And Trimeck. Everybody is interested in animals. I'm sure there's money in it. All you need is the capital to start."

"Düssel two. Düssel two," said the voice in the loudspeaker. "Proceed to Reginastrasse 31. Reginastrasse 31. We have a report of a woman jumped out of a window . . ."

It didn't register right away. I asked, "How much capital would you need?"

"Oh . . . I'd say about ten thousand. Fifteen thousand. I could get the rest from the bank. Why? Do you know anybody?"

"Yes," I said. "There's a chance. Not right now but perhaps in a month or two."

"Oh Peter! Wouldn't that be wonderful?"

"Yes . . . wonderful," he said, grinning happily as he rose. "Herr Holden, please stay until I get back. I'll be as quick as I can."

"Where are you going?"

"To Reginastrasse. A woman's jumped out of the window. Didn't you hear?" I pulled myself together and managed to say calmly, "Reginastrasse? What number?"

"Thirty-one. Why?"

"I was just wondering . . . So, hurry up and get there, Herr Romberg."

"Probably nothing to it. Jealousy, or something like that. But where there's smoke there's usually fire. Better than a dumb street-car collision."

Then he was gone, and the monitor went on humming, and I saw Frau Romberg and heard what she had to say, smiling and all excited now, but I couldn't grasp any of it. Because all the time I was thinking, although I knew better and couldn't even hope . . . let it be some other woman. Not her. She's too young. And she's innocent. Not her. Not her. *Not her* . . .

Frau Romberg's voice reached me. You have no idea what it would mean to Peter, Herr Holden. His own imprint. His own pictures. No more free-lance jobs for a pittance. No more working day and night."

I nodded.

"And you really think there's a chance?"

I nodded.

"Düssel two. Düssel two," said the voice. "Have you got to Reginastrasse?"

Static in the loudspeaker, then a different voice. "Here Düssel two. It's a mess. She jumped from the ninth floor."

No. No. No.

". . . a young girl. As I just said—a mess."

"Dead?"

"You've got to be kidding! I said ninth floor. Send an ambulance. And a coupla cops. We can't handle the crowd. The press boys are here too."

"'What's the woman's name?" He said *Frau*.

"She isn't a *Frau*. She's a *Fräulein*. And pregnant. According to neighbors. Probably the motive. Lutz is her name. Hilde Lutz."

"Spell it."

It spilled out of the loudspeaker, drop by drop: "H, Henry. I, Isidor. L, Ludwig. D, Dora. E. Eric. Next word. L, Ludwig. U, Ulrich. T, Theodore. Z, Zeppelin . . ."

The door of Mickey's room flew open. She stood in the

doorway, her eyes enormous, her little hands clutched to her chest. "Herr Holden!"

"What *are* you doing? Back into bed with you!" cried her mother.

Mickey came rushing up to me. "But we *know* her!"

"Know whom?"

"Hilde Lutz. The one who jumped out of the window!"

"Why aren't you asleep? Why do you lie awake for hours listening to us grown-ups?"

"The voices were so loud, mama. Herr Holden, why don't you say anything? Say something! Hilde Lutz—she's the one who ran into the Mercedes!"

"Mickey, now I'm really angry. Go back to bed at once!"

Mickey's lips quivered. "But I know her, mama, I really do."

"Mickey!"

"Herr Holden, say something! Tell mama it's true!"

I said, "You've got things wrong, Mickey. The woman you mean was Olga Fürst. Yes . . . that was her name—Olga Fürst."

"There you are!"

For a moment Mickey said nothing, then, with wide, uncomprehending eyes she said softly, "Why are you letting me down like this? It's mean of you. And for no reason. You, whom I love . . ."

"And now go," said Frau Romberg, pushing the child gently in front of her.

Mickey began to cry, quietly, and walked slowly into her room. She closed the door without a sound. I took my glass in both hands and drank, but I spilled half of it.

"You must excuse her, Herr Holden. We have quite a problem with the child . . . just to get attention . . ."

24

At 11 P.M. I was at Sonnenblickstrasse 67. At 11:15 Nina appeared and I opened the door for her and held out my hand in case Frau Brummer should decide to take it as support when she got in, but she decided not to take it, and I drove off, not too fast, and didn't speak until spoken to and wasn't spoken to.

Now the streets were empty. Nina thought her thoughts and I thought mine. I thought: Poor stupid Hilde Lutz. Why didn't you listen to me? You should have done as I told you. Herr Brummer had the right idea. With a man's past one can control his present. And his future. A great idea, greater than you, Hilde Lutz. And greater than me. For an idea like that none of us is big enough. Those are all wicked pasts that we brought to light, by our united efforts—Herr Brummer, Herr Dietrich in his black slicker, his powerful brother, Kolb, little Dr. Zorn, and myself. Blood, a lot of blood and evil besmirches these pasts, lies and betrayals, treachery and murder. With these pasts we have thrown light on evil happenings and they will continue to breed evil. Because it is quite clear: Evil cannot be forgotten until there has been atonement. And who is to atone for so much evil?

No one.

Poor, stupid Hilde Lutz.

Now Herr Schwertfeger doesn't have to marry you any more. Maybe you've done him a favor. What will he do now? Say nothing? That's all Dr. Zorn asked of me and it's all he's going to ask of everyone concerned. And if everyone concerned says nothing, nothing will happen to any of them, and the evil will live on, unatoned. Poor Hilde Lutz.

You are dead. Eighty Jews in Minsk are dead. But Herr

Brummer and Herr Schwertfeger live on. The living can act, the dead are finally silenced. Which is a good thing for the living. They will certainly be able to come to an understanding among themselves. And nobody is left to accuse them. Not a soul.

Farewell, poor stupid Hilde Lutz. You couldn't see what the score was. But I can . . .

25

During the next four days, *Herr Kriminal Kommissar*, the following gentlemen got in touch with me through middlemen: Joachim von Butzkow, Otto Gegner, Ludwig Marwede and Leopold Rothschuh. I am sure the names are familiar to you, since the gentlemen are prominent industrialists from Düsseldorf, Frankfurt am Main and Stuttgart. Why did they contact me?

I found out during these four days and also that: One of the gentlemen had hired the men who had beaten me up on the 23rd of August in an effort to get out of me where the documents were. I was unable to find out which of the four men it was, but I did find out that he had told the others about it. In this way they had come to the conclusion that I might be willing and in a position to help them, if not under the pressure of a beating, then perhaps through the medium of money. However, they were mistaken also in this respect. I immediately reported each contact to Dr. Zorn and rejected every bribe, which I didn't find very difficult because I couldn't see any chance of ever coming into possession of the original documents again.

The past crimes for which the four feared punishment in the present were different:

Herr Joachim von Butzkow, as Chief Justice of his province during the Third Reich, had occasionally been overzealous in his verdicts and had been responsible for the death of fourteen German citizens.

Herr Otto Gegner had made his fortune during the years 1945 to 1947 in American cigarettes. The cigarettes were unloaded in Greek ports, far away from any possible interference by American authorities, and were transported to Austria and Germany by truck through various Soviet satellite countries. The transport was manned by Red Army soldiers. Herr Otto Gegner repaid·this friendly gesture by betraying to the Soviets, in West Berlin and Vienna, the political activists they were seeking.

At the time, these kidnappings on the open streets, in which the victim, who had been pointed out by an informer, was assaulted by "persons unknown" and shoved into a car, usually a black limousine, had attracted a lot of attention, but all efforts by the Austrian and German authorities to come up with any German or Austrian accomplices had been futile.

Herr Ludwig Marwede was a homosexual. Some of his much too young "friends" had contributed letters and photographs.

Herr Leopold Rothschuh's real name was Heinrich Gotthart and he was on a Polish blacklist of people to be extradited and stand trial for crimes committed while Wehrwirtschaftsführer, or military organizer in the so-called Warthegau, 1941 to 1944. The documents in Zorn's safekeeping accused him of kidnapping, sadism, murder, and the theft of art objects.

The four gentlemen were extremely well off. With the exception of Herr Marwede, they had families, and their homes were focal points of the best society. Their children went to private schools.

On September fourteenth, Dr. Zorn called me. He said he wanted to talk to me. I was told to be at his office at noon, and at the appointed time I was sitting in the windowless waiting room of his office.

The door opened and Dr. Hilmar Zorn ushered out a visitor. Today the lawyer was wearing a blue suit and a pearl grey vest, with the same contrasting trim as his jacket. His visitor had on a grey pin-striped suit, a white shirt, and a black tie. Herbert Schwertfeger looked as elegant as ever. I was so astounded to see him here that I greeted him, which at once infuriated me.

Herbert Schwertfeger had considerably more poise than I did. He didn't greet me, he wasn't in the least surprised to see me; on the contrary, he behaved as if he'd never laid eyes on me in his life. His fearless blue eyes looked through me. He had to lean very slightly over me to get his hat off the hook, and as he did so he said, "Excuse me," as one apologizes formally to a stranger. It occurred to me that the black tie he was wearing might be a sign of mourning.

"Good day, *Herr Doktor*," he said.

"My pleasure, Herr Schwertfeger."

My pleasure, Herr Schwertfeger?

The door closed, and Dr. Zorn came over to me, rubbing his hands. "Greetings, my good fellow. Come in."

In his office the window was closed as usual and the air was blue with cigar smoke. "Aren't you feeling well?"

"That was Herr Schwertfeger!"

"Yes. Why? Do you smoke? No? But you don't mind if I do? Good." He snipped off the tip of his cigar, smiled gently, and I could see that he intended to face the latest events with the nonchalance of a good actor.

"My dear friend, I see you're surprised. What about? That Herr Schwertfeger has retained me as a lawyer?"

"You are his lawyer?"

"I am. As of today." He ran his fingers through his mane of white hair. A seal ring gleamed on his finger.

"Just a minute," I said. "You can't represent Herr Brummer *and* Herr Schwertfeger."

"I couldn't until yesterday because the two were adversaries. That changed today." He laughed triumphantly and seemed overcome with admiration for what he had accomplished. I was equally overcome. "On the contrary—as of today they are allies." But he was tugging gently at his tie. "Herr Schwertfeger has just spent two hours with me. I found him deeply shocked—first of all by the totally unexpected death of someone he loved, but also because he had come very close to becoming involved in a colossal conspiracy against Herr Brummer."

"A conspiracy . . . aha!" I said idiotically.

"You are a novice in such things. Let me explain

176

briefly. Together with some other gentlemen, Herr Schwertfeger brought serious charges against Herr Brummer because, until yesterday, he was convinced that Herr Brummer was guilty of them. Now he has suddenly found out that he was the victim of misinformation and highly irregular accounting."

"That must have come suddenly."

"It did. Without realizing it, he had for months been playing into the hands of one of Herr Brummer's most powerful enemies, who had succeeded in convincing him, and others, of criminal behavior on Herr Brummer's part. However, the scales have fallen from Herr Schwertfeger's eyes." He got excited and began to stammer. "Now he knows who the true c-c-culprits are. That is why he has decided to stand by Herr Brummer in his struggle against the banker, Liebling. Of course that's sensational news. Unbeatable. This evening, at seven P.M., we are holding a press conference at the Breidenbacher Hof. Herr Schwertfeger has deposited with me all the documents we need to expose Liebling."

"*Bona causa triumphat,*" I said.

"Let's hope so."

"I don't understand one thing," I said. "All Herr Brummer's incriminating witnesses can't have a shady past. They can't *all* be blackmailed."

"D. . . d . . . don't use that w-w-word, Herr Holden, please." He shook his head disapprovingly and tugged at his collar.

"I mean, there've got to be a few *decent* people left in this country. This is crazy!"

"There are a lot of d-d-decent people in this country, Herr Holden. But it looks as if Herr Brummer didn't do business with them, let us say thank God. It seems that he developed his theory of the usefulness of a shady past at a very early stage in his career, right after the collapse of Germany. Of course we do have a few inconvenient witnesses who have nothing we can hold against them. Fortunately they are not important ones. If we can topple Liebling, we are saved. And with that I have come to the point."

"I beg your pardon."

177

"Has Liebling approached you personally, or through a middleman?"

"I never heard of the man in my life."

The expression in his scholarly eyes became treacherous. "I shall find out if you are lying, Herr Holden, and you know what will happen then. How much did Liebling offer you?"

I rose. "I don't have to put up with this sort of thing."

"Sit down," he said, in a loud voice.

"Not until you have apologized."

We glared at each other, then he nodded. "I apologize."

I sat down.

Zorn said, "T-t-try to understand my excitement, Herr Holden. Lothar Liebling is the only one who is determined to go through with it. I have sent him the photostats that incriminate him. The others have promised to play along with us, but Liebling has let me know that he intends to testify against Herr Brummer, withholding nothing, regardless of any consequences to himself. You can see, the man is a character."

"Like Herr Schwertfeger."

"Herr Schwertfeger will submit evidence that Lothar Liebling was the driving force behind the conspiracy against Herr Brummer."

"Won't that be difficult to prove?"

"Yes. But not impossible, if we all stand together. One thing, however, would make things very difficult, and that's why I've asked you to come here, Herr Holden. Think carefully. I have also asked Herr Brummer to think carefully. But neither of us could come to any conclusion. What can it possibly be that makes Lothar Liebling so adamant? What proof does he have? What is he staking it all on?"

"I have no idea."

"Not so fast! We *have* to find the answer. It's a matter of life or death. Liebling must *not* have a leg to stand on, he must *not* know more than we do, he must *not* be stronger than the rest of us put together."

"I understand, but I still have no idea—"

"Is it possible that on the way from Berlin to Braunschweig you lost some documents?"

I didn't answer.

"You know what I mean when I say 'lost.' "

I remained calm. "If I had kept any of the documents I would not be sitting in front of you now, letting myself be insulted."

"A good answer," he said. "It's convincing." He cleared his throat. "That leaves Frau Brummer."

"What about her?" I asked too loudly.

He smiled sadly. "She has complained about you. Yes, don't look so surprised. I have been told that you don't treat the *gnädige Frau* with the proper respect. For instance, you refused to answer her questions."

"In accordance with your instructions."

"I admire your sense of duty, Herr Holden. It is quite evident that you were a long-time soldier and a long time in jail. I shall be delighted when Frau Brummer complains again. She also complains about me."

"About you?"

Since I had seen Herr Schwertfeger here I felt like a babbling idiot; now I was behaving like one.

"Yes. To Herr Brummer. I am in an embarrassing situation. Herr Brummer demands top security for his wife. He loves her; she is his most precious possession. Which is why he has forbidden me to tell her anything. He doesn't want her involved. This desire to protect her above everything else was born out of love. But Frau Brummer? You see how she reacts."

What was all this leading up to?—I asked myself stupidly.

"And so it goes. Herr Brummer orders that you accompany his wife everywhere. Result: Frau Brummer complains that she has no freedom of movement. Or: Herr Brummer orders me to place all personal documents, valuables, and jewelry belonging to his wife in a safe-deposit box. Result: Frau Brummer complains that she c-c-can't wear her jewelry. Herr Holden, do you think Frau Brummer could possibly be in touch with Lothar Liebling?"

He spoke the last sentence with no transition, without changing his voice. Thank God, I thought . . . so that was what it was all leading up to. My brain started to function again.

"That's a terrible accusation," I began, but he stopped me with a derogatory wave of the hand.

179

"Only a question, nothing else. I am Herr Brummer's lawyer. I am to restore his freedom and his good name. For that it is necessary for me to eliminate Liebling as a menace. But to whom can I turn if I want information about Frau Brummer? Ask her? . . . Well then, ask Herr Brummer? He loves his wife; his information would be worthless. Which leaves you. You are uncommitted. You have been told to accompany Frau Brummer everywhere. I want you to report to me immediately if you notice anything out of the ordinary. And don't say you can't do that. You've accepted plenty of money . . ."

"I didn't say I couldn't do it."

He rose and held out his hand. "Thank you very much."

"Not at all," I said, and thought how the little lawyer couldn't have chosen a worse accomplice. A quarter of an hour ago he and his kind had seemed like supermen to me. Now I had a quite different opinion of the gentlemen. My self-confidence returned, and my assurance.

Everything comes back to square one, I thought. I am still a member of the company. My situation is improved, my position is stronger. Yes, that's what I thought. Idiot. Blind, vain, doomed idiot!

26

That day there was a terrible thunderstorm. I remember the storm because I remember the day so well. I don't think I shall ever forget it. At first it passed back and forth across Düsseldorf without really breaking. The sky was black, the light sulphur-yellow because of the dust which sudden gusts of wind blew, cloudlike, into the oppressive air. But not a drop of rain, no thunder, no lightning. The streets were dark and hot. In some shops they had turned on the lights as early as three o'clock. Even the wind was hot; and everybody was tense.

At 3:30 P.M. I was to pick up Nina at a friend's house in the Dellbrückstrasse. On the way there I turned on the radio. I had let down the window on my side and the hot, dry wind swept across my face. The high-pitched voice of a woman was speaking as if to children: "It was dark, and when they reached the bridge the older brother let his younger brother go on ahead, as the devil had advised, and when they were in the middle of the bridge, he struck his younger brother a blow so that he fell off the bridge and was dead. Then the older brother buried his younger brother in the sand under the bridge and took his treasure of gold from him, because that was what the devil had told him to do, and he took the treasure to the king, whereupon the king gave him his daughter in marriage . . ."

I had to stop for a red light. Yellow dust swirled around the car. It grew darker and darker as the light began to fail. I thought how in German fairy tales there was so much murder and lying, betrayal and fear, as there was in life . . .

The light turned green and I drove on.

". . . But since nothing is hidden before God, it so happened that a shepherd was driving his herd across the bridge many years later, and saw a little white bone lying in the sand below, and thought it would make a good mouthpiece for his horn. So he climbed down and picked it up and carved a mouthpiece out of it . . ."

The street lights were turned on. People began to hurry. The whole street seemed unnerved. That was the way it had been in the cities before the sirens had begun to wail . . .

". . . And when the shepherd blew on it for the first time, to his great astonishment the little bone mouthpiece began to sing:

> 'Oh little shepherd, you blow
> On my bone, on my bone.
> 'Twas my brother who killed me
> And buried me here,
> All alone, all alone.

181

For the gold, for the gold
and the king's pretty daughter . . .'

" 'What an extraordinary mouthpiece,' said the shepherd. 'It can sing! I must take it to the king.' "

A patrol car came speeding up behind me, its siren screaming, its blue emergency light revolving. I could see it in the rear-view mirror and drew up sharply at the curb. The car whizzed past me. I drove on, the wind blowing dust in my face, and I could feel my eyes beginning to smart. And still the storm didn't break.

". . . And when the shepherd came before the king, the little mouthpiece began to sing again, and the king understood, and had the earth underneath the bridge dug up, and the skeleton of the younger brother was found. The wicked brother couldn't deny what he had done, and they sewed him into a sack and drowned him alive. But the bones of the murdered brother were laid to rest in a beautiful grave in the churchyard. And that's how the story ends, my children. The wicked brother allied himself with the devil because of the gold. He trusted the devil and ate and drank with him. But whoever eats with the devil should have a long spoon."

Three seconds of silence, then a man's voice: "Radio North-West Germany, Hamburg. You have just heard the Children's Hour. The fairy tale, 'The Singing Bone', was read by Ingeborg Lechner."

At that moment the first flash of lightning lit up the sky. It blinded me so that I had to close my eyes and step hard on the brake. The thunder followed almost immediately, dry and explosive, like nearby shots. A woman screamed. And then the rain came pouring down, at last, and the light turned green.

27

She was wearing a red, light wool dress that day, and she was waiting for me in the doorway when I drove up. I got out of the car, opened the door for her, and she ran as fast as she could in the driving rain, but the few steps sufficed. As she fell onto the back seat, the red wool dress already clung to her body like a wet bathing suit, and the rain was running down my collar.

"Straight home," she said. She was breathing heavily.

You couldn't see ten meters ahead. Now the lightning was flashing uninterruptedly and the thunder rolled with a loud hollow sound. All pedestrians had disappeared from the streets, but the cars were standing bumper to bumper at every intersection. Many drivers were blowing their horns. The rain was drumming on the roof of the car; it fell in silver streaks through the eerie green aquarium light of a day that had died.

"I said something, Holden."

"I'm sorry. I didn't hear it."

"You're to drive faster."

"I can't drive faster."

"But I'm afraid of the storm."

I said nothing. She was cowering in a corner, her eyes closed, her hands over her ears. I could see her in the mirror. I felt sorry for her, but I couldn't drive faster. Impossible.

Just the same, I got to Cecilienallee in twenty minutes. Over the river the rain looked like a compact block of cement, with fog brewing around it. Here the storm had broken big branches off the trees. They lay in the street with the water pouring over them, down to the Rhine. The drains were stopped up with earth, leaves, flowers, grass; the sidewalks were impassable. And still the storm went on and the light remained sulphur-green. We had arrived at the villa and I was about to turn in the driveway when I heard her scream, "Stop here!"

I stepped on the brake and the heavy car skidded slightly and stopped in front of the big oak tree beside the entrance. A man was standing under it. Nina had already spotted him; I only saw him now. It was Toni Vorm. The storm must have taken him by surprise because he wasn't wearing a coat, only grey flannel trousers, light sandals, a blue jacket, and a white, open shirt. The tree had protected him to some extent from the rain. He was very pale. His beautiful black eyes with the silky lashes were glittering. It took him three steps, his broad shoulders and slim hips moving like a cat, to reach the car. Nina threw open the door. "Toni!"

He fell on the seat beside her and slammed the door. I turned around. Nina's expression was enigmatic. I couldn't fathom what she was thinking. Her hand was on her heart. She whispered, "What are you doing here?"

The young man with the black curly hair and beautiful, expressive hands said, "I called up. I was told you'd be back in an hour. So I waited here. Good day, Herr Holden."

"Good day, Herr Vorm."

In Munich I had had a neighbor. He owned a dog, a friendly animal with floppy ears. My neighbor, whose wife made him miserable, made his dog's life miserable. He whipped the dog, kicked it, took away its food from under its nose, gave the animal orders and beat him before he could fulfill them. In the end he bought a choke collar for the dog. That was when I took him to task about it, and he said, "That's something you don't understand, Herr Holden. I'm training Rex to hunt, that's why he has to learn to obey, on the double. He knows what I'm doing, don't you, Rex?" Spoken to in such a gentle voice, the dog cocked his head to one side, barked happily, and wagged his tail, and his eyes were filled with an expression of love and submission, of boundless admiration and devotion to the man who maltreated him. It was quite apparent that if there was one person in the world for whom this animal would let himself be torn apart, then it was my neighbor.

184

Now I saw the same expression in Nina Brummer's eyes as she looked at Toni Vorm.

"What happened?" she whispered.

"Not here."

"You can't come to the house. Mila . . ."

Vorm said, "Drive on, Herr Holden."

I did nothing.

Nina screamed, as if beside herself, "Didn't you hear? You're to drive on!"

Vorm said tactfully, "We're all nervous." There was lightning over the water, followed immediately by thunder. "Please," in the same diplomatic tone, "drive away from here, Herr Holden."

I sat motionless, staring at both of them.

"If you don't want to drive, Herr Holden, get out! Herr Vorm will drive."

The dog's eyes, I thought, whipped and kicked . . .

"Where do you want me to drive?"

"Down to the Rhine," said Vorm.

So I drove down to the Rhine. In the mirror I could see how Nina looked at him, how he looked at her. Nobody spoke, the rain drummed on the roof of the car, the lightning flashed, the thunder crashed. Once Nina's hand slid across the seat, a few centimeters to his hand, but his hand didn't move. He just looked at her sentimentally, as if trying to evoke mutual memories.

What did he want? Why had he come back? It infuriated me that neither of them spoke, that I wasn't going to find out what he was after.

"There!" said Vorm.

A small inn loomed ahead of us, with a beer garden. Tables under the trees, chairs propped against them. The rain poured down them to the sodden ground.

"I can't go in there," said Nina. "We often buy beer and soda here. The people who deliver would recognize me."

"Herr Holden will go in," said Vorm. "Please."

I shook my head. Nina looked at me with murder in her eyes. "You will go, Herr Holden. At once!"

I shook my head.

"Have you gone crazy, Herr Holden? What's got into you?"

185

"I'm not going."

She flung open the door and jumped out into the rain. In seconds I was standing beside her, grabbing her shoulders, and she staggered back. The rain stung like hail on our faces. "And if they recognize you?"

"I don't care. I don't give a damn about anything."

Toni Vorm had stayed in the car. He was watching our struggle anxiously.

"You'll wreck everything!" I yelled. "Everything!"

Nina freed herself and slapped my face as hard as she could, and ran stumbling in the direction of the tavern, and I thought: if anyone sees us—and caught up with her, and said softly, "All right. I'll leave you alone."

She ran back to the car. I heard the door slam. Now the two were alone and I was out in the rain . . .

The tavern was empty. A fat woman was sitting behind the bar, reading the paper; a cat was purring in her lap. There were no covers on the table. A bare light bulb was burning where the fat woman was sitting. Otherwise there was no light. I took off my jacket and sat down at a window, and there was the Cadillac, standing in the green light of the storm. I couldn't see the two people sitting inside, nobody could. It was too dark. But I knew they were sitting there . . .

The fat woman came up to me. She had a friendly face. "Some weather, isn't it."

I saw the Cadillac standing outside.

"Something to drink?"

"A cognac, yes."

"With a chaser, maybe?"

"Yes. Beer."

She shuffled away, and the fat orange cat came purring up to me, and I saw the Cadillac standing outside . . .

28

She struck me . . . she struck me.

There are things I can still put up with. She has done all of them. Up to now. But now she has struck me. That's something she shouldn't have done. Because it's too much.

"A chaser? A cognac?"

"A double."

"A double. Yes, sir."

My wife struck me. When I came into the room, she struck me in the face. That was when I did it. Everything began to revolve around me. The same thing was happening to me now. The blood was throbbing in my temples, as it had then . . .

"Another double? Yes, sir."

I had to close my eyes because everything was turning around me and the blood was throbbing, throbbing in my head. She struck me . . . The car was standing outside.

I don't want to look at it. I must not look at it.

Outside everything was revolving too, in green streaks of rain. And the car in the middle of it. They're sitting in it and talking, and I don't know what they're talking about. She's looking at him with those watery faithful dog's eyes, at the beautiful young man with whom she's done it in bed, naked and panting. He has come back, her body is longing for his and they'll do it again . . . They'll do it again . . .

No.

No?

I shall prevent it.

Idiot! How do you propose to prevent it?

I prevented something once and got twelve years for it. And Margit was dead. But she couldn't be unfaithful to me any more. I'll do it again. And this time I won't go to prison for it.

Calm down. I have to calm down.

No, I don't. Not any more. There has to be an end to it. To all of it. It's all too much for me. I can't cope with it any more. I'll finish it off, myself and the two of them.

I'll go back to them. I'm stronger than Pretty Boy. I'm more courageous. Margit is only a woman. No. Not Margit. That was . . . that was a long time ago. Her name is Nina. Margit . . . Nina. I won't pay any attention to them. I'll drive off without saying a word. It's still raining. It will look like an accident. They'll fall upon me, of course, and try to make me stop. But they'll be sitting behind me. You can't do much to a person when you're sitting behind him. Half a kilometer, and the road runs parallel to the Rhine. The river comes up to the street. I know the place. A lot of warning signs there because the water's very deep. I turn the wheel sharply, the car shoots across the road. They scream. They want to get out of the coffin that's taking them down, down . . . but it's too late. Water pours in through the open window. They cling to each other, I cling to the wheel. Margit and Toni. Nina and Toni . . .

I lay money on the table and put on my wet jacket. I walk slowly because now it makes no difference how wet I get. Ten steps to the Cadillac, standing there in the green light of the storm, massive and dark. And the car seems to sway before my eyes, like everything else.

I stagger up to the car from behind so that they don't see me. It's important that they don't see me. Five steps, and I slip. Fall. Get up again. The blood is pounding in my head. Margit and Nina . . . Margit and Nina . . .

Three more steps.

Why is the light still so green? The water will be too. Fish and plants will accompany us. At night it will be dark and cold, but we won't be cold any more. Her beautiful body will rot and there'll be algae and little fishes in her beautiful hair . . .

One more step.

I think: She struck me, and that finished everything.

I tore open the car door and got in behind the wheel. And I felt Nina's hand on my shoulder and heard her sob, "Holden! Thank God, Holden—you've come back!"

29

"Holden! Thank God, Holden—you've come back!"

I took my foot off the gas pedal and turned around, slowly, because my body felt sluggish; and Nina fell back in her seat in her damp wool dress, her eyes brimming with tears, her hands trembling. Toni Vorm was sitting beside her, and now I was looking at him. He immediately threw his arm up to protect his face. "If you lay a hand on me, I'll jump out of the car and scream for help."

I opened the window on my side and breathed deep, and passed my hand over my face and said, slurring as if drunk—which I was—"Who's going to lay a hand on you, Herr Vorm? Who's going to lay a hand on you?"

On the Rhine a ship's horn was blowing. The storm was letting up, only the rain was coming down, hard as ever.

"You bastard!" said Nina. "You bloody bastard!"

Vorm's answer was a shrug.

"What's happened?" I asked, and had to think that but for these few minutes' interruption, all three of us wouldn't have been in a position to talk any more.

Nina was curled up, a heap of misery, her blond hair tumbling over her knees, which her crumpled dress now exposed. "He's blackmailing me," she said.

I told myself I'd better be very careful. I was on the verge of losing control myself. Breathe evenly, speak slowly, I told myself, don't do anything rash.

Toni Vorm speaking: "Herr Holden, since you know all about our relationship, I am asking for your understanding."

Nina laughed hysterically.

It was so dark, I couldn't see their faces. Fog came creeping across the road from the river, the green light had turned grey. Now it died altogether. The street lights glowed dimly in the mist. And again a foghorn blaring over the Rhine.

Toni Vorm spoke to the accompaniment of the drumming of the rain on the roof of the car and Nina's weak sobs. "Put yourself in my place, Herr Holden. I move to Hamburg only to find out that I *don't* have the job at the Eden Bar."

"Why not?"

"The proprietor here just wanted to get rid of me. In Hamburg he already has a pianist with a three-year contract. So I'm out on the street. I'd no sooner registered when I had the tax people on my neck. I owe back taxes in Düsseldorf. I can't pay them. I can't buy food. I'm living in a boarding house in a room I haven't paid for. I don't even have a piano to work on. My rhapsody . . . you remember, Herr Holden? I'd almost finished it—"

Nina laughed again.

I put on the emergency brake and took the key out of the ignition. I didn't want any surprises. Above all, I didn't want to drive into the Rhine any more, and certainly not by mistake. People are funny . . .

Now that I had grasped the fact that Nina despised and hated this pretty boy, I suddenly loved the life I had been ready to throw away moments ago, loved it passionately! I had wanted to take that life? Idiot!

Life was full of hope, life suddenly promised everything I had always longed for.

Toni Vorm said, "Nina—"

"Don't call me Nina!"

"Frau Brummer is unfair. We loved each other. I only came back once more because we loved each other."

I thought: the guy's got nerve . . .

"Why did you come back?"

"Have you ever been poor?"

"Yes."

"Then you'll understand. I had nothing but debts in Hamburg. One creditor after the other. Somebody must have talked, because suddenly there was a rumor in the city."

"What sort of a rumor?"

"That I had had an affair with Frau Brummer . . . I'm

190

not allowed to say Nina any more . . . Not very pleasant."

"You're a beast! A beast!"

"Every day the rumors got louder. Vorm and Brummer. I was scared. I didn't want to start anything with Herr Brummer. That's understandable, isn't it?"

"Go on," I said. The young man had nerve . . .

"I wanted to emigrate. To Canada. As far away as possible. But I didn't have any money. And then this fellow came to me. Held. That was his name. He said straight out that I had a certain letter from Nina. Somebody must have seen you when you brought me that letter—"

"That's ridiculous!"

"Nobody saw you," Nina groaned. "He's a bastard! A cheap blackmailer!"

"Let him talk, *gnädige Frau*," I said, and something in the way I said it must have aroused his suspicion, the suspicion of a rat.

"If you lay one hand on me, I'll jump out of the car!"

"I am not going to touch you. Go on."

"This man offered me money for the letter."

Nina said tonelessly, "In the letter I wrote why I had tried to take my life. I wrote that in a moment of despair my husband had told me what he had done . . ."

"That was in the letter?" I asked, horrified.

"Yes."

"You wrote that your husband had confessed everything to you?"

"Not everything, but enough. I was crazy . . ."

At last I understood. I asked Toni Vorm—a mere shadow now in the dark recess of the car, "Was the man buying the letter for Herr Lothar Liebling?"

Astounded, Toni Vorm asked, "How do you know that?"

"How much did he offer you?"

"Twenty thousand. He said Herr Brummer had brought pressure against Herr Liebling, who now had to do what he could to save himself. A letter in which Frau Brummer more or less corroborated her husband's guilt, in his own words, would have a pretty damning effect in court—"

"Shit!" I said. "Liebling knew you had that letter? He's clairvoyant maybe?"

"I—"

"You offered him the letter."

"No!"

"Then why didn't you burn it long ago?"

"Stop, Herr Holden." Nina sounded exhausted. "It's useless. He wants money."

Vorm wrung his hands. He was taking his role very seriously. "I'm desperate. I don't want to give Liebling the letter. That's why I'm here."

"Why?"

"He wants me to give him the money," said Nina.

"Only because I need it so desperately. It doesn't make any difference to you. You're rich—"

"Don't say another word!"

"Yes," I said. "I think you'd better shut up." After which all three of us were silent for a while. Then I asked, "Where is the letter?"

"In my suitcase. Checked at the station. I don't have the ticket on me."

"Oh God," Nina said softly. "Oh my God . . . And for you I wanted to . . ." She covered her face with her hands.

"My situation is desperate," he said again, stubbornly this time, as if insisting on something he had a right to.

"You'd better pay him," I told Nina.

"I don't have any money."

"Sell some of your jewelry."

"The lawyer has my jewelry," she said, and I remembered what Zorn had told me.

"You have friends," said Vorm. "Borrow the money."

"Twenty thousand marks?" I said. "Are you crazy?"

"That's what Liebling has offered. Call him up and find out for yourself."

Nina said, "It's no use. I can't raise half of it. Do whatever you like. Just get out."

"Stop!" I said. "What about your husband? What about the trial?"

"Herr Holden is being sensible, Nina."

"Shut up!" I yelled, and at once his arm was up, protecting his face.

Nina said, "Get out. I can't stand the sight of you an-

192

other minute. Give me a little time, a few hours. I'll see what I can do."

"My train leaves at midnight," said Vorm. "I've got to take it. Liebling will only wait until tomorrow noon. I'm staying at the Pension Elite."

He got out of the car and walked through the rain to the tavern. We watched him go. The storm was moving south, the sky was growing lighter. Nina said, "Forgive me."

I nodded.

"Forgive me for striking you. Forgive me for everything, Herr Holden. I'm more sorry than I can say."

I nodded.

30

At home, she went to her room. I went to the kitchen, where Mila was baking an apple pie for Herr Brummer again. I watched her, and every now and then I heard the telephone click. It clicked every time Nina dialed another number.

"My, but my Nina's making a lot of calls," Mila said lovingly, and lovingly she piled slices of apple on the thin pie crust. "It's probably because of the press conference this evening. I heard all about it this morning on the radio. There's been a sensational turn of events. Wonderful! It's just as I told you, Herr Holden. We don't have to worry about the *gnä' Herr*. In the end the good thing always wins."

I went to my room and lay down on my bed and thought about a lot of things. At night I had supper with Mila in the kitchen. The phone was still clicking. Once it rang. Nina's voice sounded tired. "Please don't go to bed, Herr Holden. I may need you."

So I played canasta with Mila, and because only two of

us were playing we had to hold a lot of cards in our hand, and I thought of other things, and lost. At ten we heard the evening news. Not a word about the press conference. "It's too early," said Mila. "Well now, Herr Holden, do you want to risk another game?"

"No," I said. "I must get some fresh air or I'll fall asleep."

It was warm in the park. Frogs—it sounded like hundreds of them—were croaking at the edge of the lake. The sky was clear. I could see the stars. I walked up and down on the gravel path between the villa and the street, and smoked. The air was clean after the storm. I breathed deep and felt at peace with myself. I had felt just like that when they had sentenced me, when at last everything was settled. Everything was settled now, too, I thought.

I went back into the house and up the stairs to the first floor, past the peasant Breughel, the Fragonard trees and Tintoretto's Suzanna. Nina was sitting at a table by the window, her head in her hands, the telephone in front of her. Every light in the room was turned on, the white-gold furniture looked bright. Nina had on a sand-colored skirt and a soft yellow pullover. No makeup. Her lips were grey, there were dark circles under her eyes. "What is it, Herr Holden?"

"Please don't consider this impertinent but—have you been able to raise the money?"

"Four thousand marks. I'm waiting for another answer. But it's only ten-thirty." She went on, "I can only ask my women friends, none of the men. It's a lot of money. My friends are doing their best, but who has that much money available? Perhaps—"

The phone rang. She answered at once. "Yes, Elli?" Then she listened. "Well, it can't be helped. For heaven's sake, of course I understand. And I'm grateful for your efforts . . . Oh no, no, it isn't all that important. Bye now," and she hung up. "Four thousand," she said, "and that's it."

A window was open, the frogs were croaking loudly. The night wind stirred the curtains and I could see all things with astonishing clarity—the gold rose petals on the wallpaper, Nina's little ears under her blond hair, the

194

little black mole on her left cheek, as I said, "I have the rest."

She shook her head.

"Yes," I said. "You have to think of yourself now."

"It's your money."

"I got it for some dirty business, why shouldn't I spend it on some dirty business?"

She was silent.

I said, "I love you. I don't want anything to happen to you."

"How can you love me after . . . after all the things I've done to you?"

"I don't know," I said, "but I do."

She walked over to the open window, her back turned to me, and said, "At first I hoped you'd come, Herr Holden. I admit it. When one is afraid, one becomes unscrupulous and immoral, isn't that so? I . . . I thought you would ask for something in return."

"And would you have given it to me?"

"Yes," she said simply. "Because then it would have been a business transaction and I would have known that you didn't love me."

"But I'm not going to ask for anything."

"That means you want a lot more."

"I could ask for it if it was something one could ask for. The way things are, I can only hope for it."

She turned around. Her eyes were very dark again. "No," she said. "I can't possibly take money from you."

31

At 11:30 we were at the Düsseldorf Hauptbahnhof, in the big drafty checkroom. Hundreds of suitcases and trunks were piled high on wooden shelves. There was a smell of smoke, people with tired faces, a child crying because it wanted to sleep. A couple was sitting on a bench, leaning against each other, supporting each other, drunk. Nina had on a light mohair coat and flat brown shoes. She still wore no makeup. She stood very close to me.

At 11:35 Toni Vorm appeared, the collar of his soft blue coat turned up, his hat down low over his forehead. When Nina saw him, she moaned, "I can't . . . I can't . . ."

"You have to," I told her. "I don't know if he'll give me the right letter."

Meanwhile Vorm went up to one of the clerks and gave him the ticket for his suitcase. Three quarters of an hour earlier Nina had called him at his pension and said she would meet him here. We saw him get his suitcase and hand it to a porter. Then he came over to us. Now he didn't waste any more time on phony niceties. His train left in twenty minutes and there was business to attend to.

"We'll go to the restaurant," he said.

We said nothing.

We walked behind the huge porter—Vorm had chosen a tall, burly fellow—down the long passage that led under the tracks to the restaurant. The air was abominable, the room was full of smoke, and there was a sickly stale smell of beer and food. A lot of people were being waited on by tired waitresses. Vorm said, "Here," and the porter put down the suitcase. Vorm paid the man and he left.

Vorm had chosen a table near the entrance. A policeman was sitting at the table next to it, drinking Coca-Cola.

Nina's face was expressionless. She had cried herself out.

"Where is the money?" asked Vorm.

"You're getting it from me," I said. "But not twenty thousand. Ten thousand, and that's it."

"Twenty thousand. That's what I can get from Liebling. I'm sorry, but I need the money."

"Fifteen thousand."

"No."

"Come on," I said to Nina.

We got up and walked toward the exit. Vorm said softly, "Agreed."

So we went back to the table and sat down again. He opened his suitcase and took out the letter. "Is that it?" I asked Nina.

196

Nina nodded, after Vorm had taken the letter out of its envelope and held both items up like a magician producing rabbits out of a hat. Yes, it was the letter. I recognized Nina's trembly, spiderweb writing on the envelope.

I took a roll of bills out of my pocket, the violet fifty-mark bills I had received from Dr. Zorn. I began to count, and with every bill I felt a stab between my shoulders, as if someone were sticking pins into me there, three hundred of them . . .

The money piled up in front of the pretty young man. He was counting right along with me, his lips moving silently. When I got past two hundred, the policeman at the next table grinned and said, "It should happen to me!" Vorm gave him a cheerful smile and I went on counting to three hundred, keeping a sharp eye on the letter lying between us. We both put out our hands together, he for the money, I for the letter.

"Attention!" said the loudspeaker. "The Hamburg express, stopping at Bielefeld and Hannover, will leave in five minutes from Platform 13. We wish you a pleasant trip."

Vorm pocketed the money and got up. I got up too.

"Sit down," he said softly, and turning to the policeman, "Officer, would you be so good as to tell my friends how to get to the Kreuzstrasse from here?"

"I'll be glad to." The policeman moved his chair closer.

"Thanks very much," said Toni Vorm. He bowed to Nina, who looked away. Then he walked hurriedly to the exit. It wasn't possible to overpower him somewhere in the dark outside. The policeman was at my side and now launched into an elaborate explanation. "So . . . let's say this glass of beer is the station. You exit here, and you're on the Wilhelmplatz. You walk straight ahead until you get to Bismarckstrasse. Three blocks on Bismarckstrasse, then turn left . . ."

Toni Vorm had reached the exit. The ploy with the policeman was a clever move. The light reflected for a moment off the revolving door, then he was gone. And my money with him.

32

"I've got to have a drink," said Nina.

We had walked out onto the deserted plaza in front of the station. She swayed suddenly and grasped my arm. "I've got to have a drink, right away. I . . . I feel simply terrible. I want to throw up every time I think of him."

"Don't think of him."

"I've got to have a drink. Then I'll be able to sleep and won't have to think of him any more." She leaned against me and began to cry. Above her head I could see the empty plaza and the puddles of rain water, with the street lights reflected in them. She sobbed, and I heard her say, "I'll give it back to you. I'll manage somehow. All of it. Oh, what a beast he is . . ."

A prostitute, her full lips brightly rouged, walked past, swinging her bag, and shook her finger at me. "Bad boy! Don't upset mama!"

I laid my lips on Nina's hair and looked out at the empty plaza, at the many puddles, with the lights reflected in them.

33

That night we pub-crawled, from one place to another. Never to any of the good ones. Nina would have been recognized there. Wherever we went, we drank whiskey.

Nina couldn't stand it anywhere for too long. She got restless and we would move on again. "I can't breathe in here," she'd say. "Let's go." Or, "This music's driving me crazy. You can't hear yourself think." And so I accompanied her through the city. We were a strange pair: she with no makeup on, in her flat shoes, sweater and skirt, and I in my chauffeur's uniform. A lot of people stared at us, especially when Nina wept, as she did every now and then. Then she said, "Take off that pin, Holden."

So I took off the pin with the gold letters J and B, and left my chauffeur's cap in the car before we went into the next bar. It was a small place, in the heart of the city. Candles were burning on the tables; there was no electricity. A man was playing the piano. And this time I was a guest in a blue suit, white shirt, and blue tie, just like everybody else. "This is nice," said Nina. "We'll stay here." By now she was a little tipsy, but she wasn't tired.

Only girls were waiting at the bar.

"Whiskey," I said.

"She's a pretty girl, Holden."

"Yes."

"She's interested in you."

"No."

"Yes, she is. Don't you like her?"

"No."

"Oh . . . Holden . . ."

The whiskey came. "You're pretty," Nina told the girl. "What's your name?"

"Lily, *gnädige Frau.*"

"That's a pretty name."

"Thank you, *gnädige Frau.*"

I said to Nina, "Don't you think it's time we went home?"

She took my hand. "I'm afraid to go home, and be alone in my room. No, no—not yet. I'm not drunk, really I'm not. I . . . I'm just beginning to feel better. You know something . . . I'm glad it happened. I mean it. I still thought of him and longed for him. Now that's over."

"Really?"

"Really."

"I love you."

"So you do want something."

"Yes," I said, "of course."

"You're honest."

By now I wasn't quite sober any more either. "We belong together, you and I. Some day you'll realize it. But there's no hurry. I can wait."

"How long?"

"For you—very long."

"There are so many pretty girls, Holden. Look at Lily."

"I want you."

"Crazy. That's what it is, what we're talking about . . . crazy." But her hand remained on mine, and now she was looking at me so intently, I felt hot suddenly. "Now *you* have the letter," she said.

I took it out of my pocket and said, "I'd like to read it."

She blushed like a young girl. "No!" Then she saw the expression on my face and said softly, "All right. Read it."

"Now I don't want to any more."

I held the letter over the candle. It burned with a bright yellow flame, curling and browning at the edges. I waited until it was all burnt, then I dropped the charred remains into an ash tray and crushed them with my swizzler. "And don't write any more letters."

"Not to you, either?"

"Not to anybody. Because all people are capable of doing evil."

"Have you loved many women in your life?"

"Not many."

"Holden?"

"Yes?"

"There have been quite a lot of men in my life."

"Do you want another drink?"

"Oh, Holden, you're nice."

"I'm in love," I said. "That makes things easier."

34

We stayed in the candlelit bar. The pianist asked if there were any songs we'd like him to play. Nina chose the song from *Moulin Rouge*, and asked if I would like to dance with her.

"I don't dance well."

"I don't believe it."

"But it's true."

"Come on," said Nina.

It was three o'clock in the morning, and besides us there were only four couples left. We were the only ones dancing. "You should never wear makeup," I told her. "You're so much more beautiful without it. When I saw you for the first time, you didn't have any makeup on, and I fell in love with you then and there."

"When was that?"

"You don't know anything about it. You were lying unconscious, on a hospital bed, and I saw you through the window of the door to your room."

"No!" She was horrified.

"The doctor was giving you an injection, directly into the heart."

"You saw me *naked?*"

"Yes."

". . . Whenever we kiss," sang the pianist, "I worry and wonder . . ."

"I must have looked hideous."

"Yes," I said. "Hideous."

". . . Your lips may be near, but where is your heart? . . ." sang the piano player, and we were circling slowly.

"Holden."

"Yes?"

"Did you see my birthmark?"

"What birthmark?"

"Under my left . . . on the left side of my body. It's so ugly. I've tried to have it removed. It's at least as big as the nail on my little finger. You *must* have seen it."

"I have a birthmark on the calf of my left leg."

"Oh . . . Holden . . ."

"I think you're over it."

"Yes. Maybe. I'd like to put on some lipstick."

"Please don't."

"I have a lipstick with me."

"But I don't want you to."

"Your parents were poor, weren't they?"

"Yes."

"Mine too."

"I know." I stepped clumsily on her foot. "I'm sorry. You see, I really can't dance."

"It was my fault. Come on, let's have another drink."

35

So we had another drink, and she asked, "Aren't you surprised that I'm not drunk yet?"

I nodded.

"When I'm unhappy, I never get drunk."

"I wish you were horribly drunk."

She laughed.

An old woman came up to us with a basket of flowers, and Nina said, "No."

"Oh yes," I said, and bought a single rose.

Pretty Lily brought a glass and cut the rose shorter and put it in water. "Do you still have the other one?" I asked.

Nina laughed. "Do you know where it is now? In a bank vault. The lawyer has taken all my jewelry. Remember?"

"Now you're laughing again," I told her.

The bar closed at five. When we walked out into the street, the sun was shining. The sky was still pale, but it was already very warm. As we drove to the Rhine we saw women selling newspapers and boys delivering milk. Nina sat beside me and held my rose in her hand. We had the windows down, and the air was marvelous after the storm. Not until we reached the river did she speak. Then she said, "I don't want to go home."

"You have to."

"I don't want to be alone. When I'm alone I'll begin thinking of it all again. Have breakfast with me."

"Now?"

"I have an idea. Drive up the river. I saw a boat there once, somewhere. It's a place to eat. A sign said 'Open twenty-four hours.' "

The highway was still wet, and heavy drops fell from the trees onto the roof of the car. The birds were singing. A quarter of an hour later we reached the boat. It was painted white and had a glassed-in superstructure that was equipped like an espresso. A few tables with checked covers and chairs painted red stood on the deck. We boarded the boat on a narrow gangplank, and sat down in the sun. A hatch opened and an old man appeared. He was dressed all in white—shirt, apron, pants—and his hair was white; so was the stubble on his unshaven cheeks. He was wearing spectacles and he looked amused.

"Morning, sir. Morning, young lady." He came up to us, looked us over and said, "In love and all in. Don't I know it. Need something to put you back on your feet." He didn't let us get a word in but settled on the breakfast menu himself. "Coffee, bread and butter, three eggs each, fried with plenty of ham. Orange juice for a starter. Will do wonders for you, ma'am. Let an old man tell you what's good for you." With which he disappeared down the hatch again and we could hear him bustling around in the kitchen.

"He looks like Hemingway," I said.

"Have you read his books?"

"All of them."

We said in unison, "For whom the bell tolls . . ."

I asked, "Do you like love stories?"

"Yes, very much," and she looked out across the water.

The river was one solid silver band from shore to shore. Gulls swooped low, flapping their wings very slowly. They looked elegant. A tug, hauling three barges, glided by. We could hear the chug-chug of its engine. Black smoke rose diagonally from its funnel. Our boat rolled almost imperceptibly in its backwash. The mooring ropes creaked.

I put my hand on Nina's and we sat like that until the old man brought our breakfast. The coffee smelled good, the eggs and ham were still sizzling in their little copper pans. The orange juice was ice-cold. The bread was dark and fresh, and caraway seeds were baked in the crust. The pats of butter had little drops of ice water on them. We ate as if starved, and now we looked at each other and smiled. The old man came with a fresh pot of coffee and filled up our cups again, and he was smiling too.

"Are you all alone here?" asked Nina.

"I have two helpers," he said. "They go home in the evening. I'm alone here at night, yes."

"But when do you sleep?"

"I don't sleep very much. A half hour or so now and then. I can't sleep since Dresden . . ."

"You were there when . . ."

"Yes. And since then I'm alone. Took my whole family. I was lucky. But since then I can't sleep. So I bought this boat. It's a good boat. All sorts of interesting people come here, evenings. And I like being on the water. I always think, if it should burn again . . . you know." He shuffled off.

"Holden?"

"Yes."

"What's going to become of us?"

"I don't know."

"But it's all insane, absolutely insane . . ."

"You have such beautiful skin . . . When we're finally living together, I'm not going to let you use any makeup."

We got home around six o'clock. On the steps in front of the entrance lay the morning paper. The headline read: *Sensational Development in the Brummer Case. Herbert Schwertfeger Admits Conspiracy.*

36

September 15.

"Herr Holden? Zorn speaking. I am referring to our last conversation. I asked you to do something for us. You know what?"

"I know what."

"The business has meanwhile been settled to our satisfaction. The gentleman I mentioned to you has thought better of it."

"I'm glad to hear that."

"I still don't see quite clearly what could have happened, but after all, it's how things end that counts, isn't it? You may consider the instructions I gave you as carried out."

"Very good."

"One more thing. Tomorrow you will be asked to call on Dr. Lofting."

"Who is that?"

"The public prosecutor. The latest events seem to have confused him. He has some questions he wants to ask you."

"Understandable."

"Exactly. You must answer his questions truthfully, Herr Holden."

"Of course."

"You must tell him everything you know. You understand me?"

"I understand you, *Herr Doktor*. I must tell the public prosecutor everything I know."

37

"I don't know anything," I said. "I'm sorry, but I don't know anything."

The curtains in Dr. Lofting's room were drawn to keep out the heat. It was cool and dark in the room. Shelves full of books lined the walls. Dr. Lofting, tall and slim, sat opposite me in an old-fashioned armchair. He spoke softly, had a pale face and big mournful eyes with heavy black bags under them. He looked like someone who worked at night, and his mouth was the soft, delicately curved mouth of an artist or a passionate lover, and that was what he was—a passionate lover of justice.

He said, very quietly, "I know you are lying."

I shook my head.

"Everybody concerned is lying," said Lofting. A pile of files, at least half a meter high, lay in front of him. He laid his long-fingered, nicotine-stained hand on it. "All this is incriminating material against Herr Brummer. He is guilty. You know that just as well as I do."

"I don't know anything of the sort. I know nothing."

He went on speaking softly. "Herr Brummer has done things which are punishable by law. Many people have furnished evidence against him in this room: Herr Schwertfeger, Herr Liebling, Herr von Butzkow—to mention a few. Now they are withdrawing everything they have said, every one of them, one by one."

I hunched my shoulders and let them fall again.

"Herr Holden, I have been working here for twenty-five years. Believe me, sooner or later, justice triumphs. Sometimes it takes a long time, but it never takes too long. That doesn't happen, Herr Holden. In the end it simply boils down to the cunning of common sense. In the last analysis, crime does *not* pay."

I thought that here Dr. Lofting and Mila Blehova were of the same opinion. I said, "I don't know what you're trying to tell me."

"I know you don't know. You don't know anything, Herr Holden. You have decided to side with injustice and to know nothing."

"I must protest. You . . ."

"No," he said quietly. "You don't have to protest, Herr Holden. Not to me. I can see through you. I can see through everything in this case. There is nothing we can do about it. Not yet, Herr Holden. But the day will come when we shall be able to do something about it, of that I am sure. And it will be in my lifetime. Injustice is being served here, and that sort of thing can't last. Don't rejoice if it looks as if Herr Brummer is coming out of this victorious. Because he won't come out of it victorious. He will be judged. One day."

"I am sorry, *Herr Doktor*, but I can't help you. And I really don't understand half of what you're telling me."

"You were in prison."

"And I was pardoned. You have no right to hold my past against me."

"I am not holding your past against you. I am appealing to your judgment. Don't continue on the path you are on now. You still have a chance. If you testify, I have the power to protect you."

"I have nothing to testify."

"Herr Holden, what happened on the twenty-second of August on the way to Berlin?"

"Nothing. It was hot."

"What happened to you in Berlin, after Herr Brummer's arrest?"

"Nothing. I spent the night in Berlin and came back the next day."

"Do you know a man called Kolb?"

"No."

He showed me a photograph of the powerful Saxon.

"Never saw him."

"Who beat you up in your room?"

"Strangers."

"Why?"

"They thought I had some documents . . ."

207

"What documents?"

"I don't know."

"Were they documents with which Herr Brummer intended to blackmail his enemies?"

"I don't know."

"Are you prepared to repeat what you have just told me under oath?"

"Of course."

"You may go, Herr Holden. You are unteachable."

I stood up and bowed. At the door I turned around and saw the public prosecutor bury his pale face in his hands with a motion of exhaustion, of resignation and disgust, and it was dark in his room, and cool.

38

September 17.

"Herr Holden? Zorn speaking. It is twelve-thirty. Drive to the airport. You will find a ticket at the Pan Am desk. For you. To Berlin. Your plane leaves at three P.M."

"The *gnädige Frau* . . ."

". . . has been informed. By me. In Berlin you will stay at the Hotel am Zoo. A room has been reserved for you."

"And?"

"And nothing. You fly to Berlin and return tomorrow on the one o'clock plane. I want you to go to as many bars as possible, and spend as much as possible. We will reimburse you, of course. Take a girl along. Attract attention. Spend lavishly. That is all."

39

When I said good-bye to Nina, she said quickly, "I'll take you to the airport." Then she blushed. "But that's impossible! What am I talking about?"

"It would make me very happy."

She thought it over seriously. "If anybody sees us, I can say I went with you so as to bring the car back. Why are you looking at me like that?"

"You're willing to lie for me?"

"Please. Don't say anything. I'm coming with you and we're not going to talk about it."

In the car Nina sat beside me. "What's the purpose of this trip, anyway?"

"The court isn't satisfied with the Berlin story. But there's nothing more to be got out of that. I imagine Zorn wants to mislead the investigation. That's why I'm supposed to act in a way that attracts attention, go to bars . . ."

"With a girl?"

"That's what he said."

"Do you know a girl in Berlin?"

"No."

"So what will you do?"

"I'll go to the bars alone and drink with whatever girls are there."

"There are a lot of pretty girls in Berlin."

"I'll go alone."

"What sort of a conversation is this anyway? What business of mine is it what you do in Berlin? Have a good time, Herr Holden."

"I shall go alone and I shall think of you."

"Please. We were not going to talk about it."

"*You* were not going to talk about it. I shall think of you. I shall think of you all the time."

We said good-bye in front of the airport building. Nina drove off, and I stood in the bright sunlight and waved. She must have been watching me in the mirror because she waved back until the car disappeared around a curve. I walked into the lobby and picked up my ticket. I had plenty of time, so I sat down on the terrace and ordered coffee and watched the planes taking off and landing. Everybody looked happy because the weather was so beautiful, and everybody was friendly.

I drank my coffee and supported my chin with my right hand because it still smelled a little of Nina's perfume. From our farewell. I closed my eyes and could see her in her various dresses, laughing, running, listening to me, being serious with me, and in my thoughts did everything I wanted to do with her.

"Attention! Pan American Airways, Flight 312 to Berlin. All passengers come to the desk, please."

A pretty stewardess stood at the Pan Am desk, waiting for all the passengers to assemble. Then she said, "Ladies and gentlemen, we regret to have to inform you that Flight 312 to Berlin will be delayed three hours because of necessary repairs. Anyone who would like to go back to the city can do so in our bus. Flight 312 to Berlin will leave at six P.M. Thank you."

A few people were annoyed, but most of the passengers took it good-naturedly, and with a few of these I took the bus back to the city. I walked around for a while, looked in shop windows, then I took a taxi to the Rhine. All the time I thought of Nina and again and again I raised my right hand to my lips, but the scent was fading. I drove to the white boat. I thought I'd sit in the sun for a while and watch the river, because I had time and because I am sentimental.

"Wait for me," I told the driver as I got out. And then my heart began to beat wildly, because I saw the red and black Cadillac parked under an old tree.

On the boat deck a few people were sitting at the tables, chatting gaily. I saw Nina at once. She was sitting at the rear of the boat, her back turned on the people, her chin on her hands, staring out at the river. I walked over to her. When she heard my steps she turned around and when she saw me she clutched her heart. Her mouth opened, but she couldn't seem to speak. I sat down and explained that the plane departure was delayed and she put a trembling hand to her mouth.

"I . . . I was so terribly startled when I saw you. I thought your plane must have crashed and you were dead. It . . . it was eerie. Suddenly you were standing there . . . I . . . I'm all right now."

Her eyes were dark again. The river glistened in the sunlight and today there were many ships on the Rhine.

I said, "You're here."

"Yes."

"I thought of you all the time."

"Don't."

I bent forward and kissed her hand.

"Please . . . please don't."

I straightened up.

"When does your plane leave?"

"At six."

"Now it's four. If I take you to the airport, we have a whole hour."

"You want to drive me to the airport *again?*"

She nodded.

So I sent the taxi away, and when I got back to Nina, there was the old man in the white pants and white shirt. He was unshaven again, and he recognized me at once.

"Just a minute, sir. The drinks will be right along."

Nina said softly, "I ordered something to drink. Just think, the old man has whiskey. And a refrigerator."

"Good," I said. "We'll drink whiskey with soda and ice, and the ice cubes will tinkle and the glasses will haze over and we'll sit in the sun and gaze at each other for one whole hour."

"It's crazy."

"What's crazy?"

"Everything that's happening. The plane. The whiskey. Everything!"

40

Berlin was a bore. At passport control I saw how right my
theory had been as to the purpose of my trip. The officer
put my passport down, looked at me sharply, then at the
passport again, and seemed to hesitate.

"Is anything wrong?"

"Oh no. Not at all. Thank you very much," he said, a
little too friendly. I walked on and a few steps later turned
around and saw him pick up the phone. Dr. Lofting certainly was keeping an eye on me! Not that it would do
him much good.

I went to four bars. In the fourth I invited a redhead to
join me and spent a lot of money, which wasn't difficult
because she took me for a rich businessman from the West
and wanted champagne, French champagne. She was very
astonished when I took her home at one o'clock. Didn't I
feel well, she wanted to know, and I said I didn't, and she
said she was sorry. At 1:30 I was in bed, and next day I
flew back to Düsseldorf. During the whole flight I wondered if Nina would be there to meet me. As we were
landing, I felt pessimistic about it, and when I saw her I
was overjoyed.

We didn't speak until we were seated in the car; then
she said, "I never behaved like this in my whole life."

"Behaved how?"

"So . . . so illogically. I had no intention of picking you
up. I thought you'd only get the wrong idea if I did . . ."

"What wrong idea?"

"A very wrong idea. But then I told myself, he's so nice.
He helped you. We're two grown-ups. Why shouldn't I
pick him up?"

"Quite right, *gnädige Frau!*"

"There's really nothing wrong about it, is there?"

"Absolutely nothing," I said. "It's the most natural thing in the world for a lady to pick up her chauffeur when he returns from a trip."

"Now you're being fresh." She was laughing.

"May I add something?"

"No."

"Sorry."

"So what is it?"

"Please don't see a reason *not* to fall in love with me in the fact that I gave you money."

It was the wrong thing to say. She didn't answer, and for three days she was formal, unapproachable, and aloof. I asked myself how long things could go on like this. I couldn't make her out. Perhaps she was really only grateful to me for having given her the money and had felt it her duty to be nice to me. For a while. But then why *had* she come to the airport? And above all, why had she driven out to our boat, dammit all?

I became increasingly nervous. Then came the 29th of September, and things began to happen fast. It started with Peter Romberg asking me to come and visit them again one evening after supper. I asked Nina for the evening off and bought a box of chocolates again for Mickey, and flowers for Frau Romberg.

Mickey was already in bed when I got there. She accepted the box of chocolates gravely. "Thank you."

"What's the matter, Mickey?"

"Nothing."

"You're looking at me so funnily. Almost as if you were angry with me."

"You must be mistaken, Herr Holden. I am not angry with you." But she quite obviously was. Her black hair tumbled over her thin little shoulders, her little hands lay folded on the bedspread, and she looked at me sullenly as she said, "Besides, I'm not allowed to talk about it."

"Well, well now," I said.

Peter Romberg, who was standing beside me, took my arm and led me to his office. Frau Romberg shut all the doors and sat down with us. The monitor was humming. Romberg turned the volume up. "So that she can't hear," he explained.

"She's going to listen anyway," said Frau Romberg.

"I know," he said. "But she won't be able to understand us."

"What on earth has happened?" I asked.

The two looked at each other, and behind their strong glasses the expression in their friendly eyes was one of embarrassment. "Let's have a cognac first," said Romberg.

So we had a drink and the monitor reported a brawl in a tavern near the cathedral and Düssel seven was sent out to restore order.

"It's a strange story," said Romberg. "Please don't take offense."

"For heaven's sake," I said, because by now I was nervous, "go ahead and tell me, whatever it is."

"Well then, come over here to my desk," said Romberg, and I went and stood beside him. Seven photographs lay side by side on a space that had been cleared for them. Six showed various women, old and young. The seventh was the one of Mickey and me in the park of Brummer's villa. It was the one Peter Romberg had taken the day of Nina's return from the hospital. We were laughing. We stood between beds of flowers with the sun shining on us, and Mickey had hooked her arm through mine.

Of the women in the other six photos, I recognized one, and as I did I felt cold and sticky, and slowly, horribly, the old fear came stealing up on me. I didn't know yet why I was frightened or what I was afraid of. It was just there suddenly, the old fear, creeping over me.

"Do you know any of these women, Herr Holden?"

"No," I lied.

"Well, then I can't understand the whole thing," said Frau Romberg, in a tone of complete bewilderment. Her husband said nothing. He looked at me thoughtfully. And I looked at the photographs, especially the one of the woman I knew—pretty, stupid, young Hilde Lutz. There she stood, in a fur coat, without a hat, and she was laughing. It was a photograph that had been handled a lot. Romberg must have picked it up somewhere. He was a reporter. It was his profession to find things.

"You're *sure* you know none of these women?"

"No. Who are they?"

Frau Romberg sighed. "Herr Holden, you will recall how angry I was with Mickey the last time you were here . . ."

I nodded, and it irritated me terribly to feel Romberg watching me intently, with cool, scientific interest. It was the way a scholar might eye a strange phenomenon that he can't explain—yet. And I, the phenomenon, knew damn well that I wasn't inexplicable at all. While the police voice promised Düssel seven that they'd get an ambulance and a doctor because the brawl at the inn near the cathedral had resulted in two injured, Frau Romberg was saying, "At the time the monitor said that a young woman had jumped out of the window . . . what was her name, now?"

This was a little too obvious, I thought, and I said, "I don't remember the name."

"Hilde Lutz," said Romberg, who was now sitting where I couldn't see him.

"Maybe. As I said, I don't remember any more."

"Peter drove there, and Mickey came running in suddenly and declared she had seen this Hilde Lutz, remember?"

"That's right," I said, playing the man who dimly recalls something. "This Hilde Lutz was the girl who was supposed to have run into our Mercedes."

The fear. The fear. Not for myself this time; I was afraid something might happen to these good people, and to her, to the child. They didn't know what treacherous, insecure ground they were standing on, a dark quagmire . . . I said, "Yes, now I remember. Mickey must have got things mixed up. The woman who ran into the Mercedes was called Fürst. Olga Fürst." A good thing that I remembered the name.

A good thing?

"When Peter came home, I told him the story, and he had a serious talk with Mickey. He told her she simply had to stop making up these wild stories. But she cried and cried; we couldn't calm her. No, no, no, she screamed, the woman's name was Hilde Lutz. More tears. We talked to her again, but there simply was no shaking her. She got so excited, she threw up. She was so upset. It's been a problem for us, Herr Holden, a real problem."

"Düssel eleven and Düssel twenty-five . . . Night watchman reports suspicious noises in Warehouse Storm, Tegetthofstrasse, corner Wieland . . ."

215

"For days it was dreadful. Such tension. There'd never been anything like it between us. We've always been so happy together. We gave her every possible chance to excuse herself for having made up the story. It was no use. Then yesterday, my husband tried this." She stopped, looked down at the floor.

I turned around and looked at her husband. He filled up our glasses again and began to speak haltingly, as if honestly in despair over the situation. "You say you don't know any of these women."

"No."

"This one is Hilde Lutz." He pointed her out.

"The one who jumped out of the window?" I went on playing the idiot.

"Yes."

"Where did you get the photo?"

"A detective gave it to me. He got it for me when we didn't know what to do about Mickey. For God's sake, don't think I was spying!"

"Who could possibly think anything like that?" I said, and answered myself: it was just what I was thinking.

"But I had to get this thing with Mickey cleared up. So I took this photo of the Lutz girl and laid it between the pictures of five other women, as you can see. Then I called Mickey into the room. I said, 'You declare that you saw Hilde Lutz. All right, so tell me if there's a picture of her here, among these six women.' Without any hesitation, Mickey pointed one out. It was the right one, Herr Holden."

Now both of them were looking at me.

I said nothing. The monitor hummed, and I hoped the thing would say something, but it didn't.

"How do you explain that, Herr Holden?" asked Frau Romberg.

"I can't explain it."

"But there *has* to be an explanation. Miracles don't happen!"

"No," I said. "Miracles don't happen," and thought: Forget the whole thing. Don't give it another thought. Let the dead rest in peace. Don't go hunting in the dark. But this man was a reporter. It was his job to hunt in the dark. And if he hunted long enough . . .

216

Little Dr. Zorn had erected a gigantic scaffolding. Intrigue and counterintrigue. Witnesses and counterwitnesses. He had thought of everything. The only thing he hadn't thought of was a child's offended sense of fairness. A small child now endangered the whole powerful structure, the high-and-mighty plans, Brummer's freedom, the future of all of us. A small child.

"Herr Holden, I get the impression that you are very unhappy because you are not telling us the truth."

I rose. "I must go."

"Why?"

"Because I can't answer your question."

"Herr Holden," said Peter Romberg. "I went to the registration office. There are twenty-two women in Düsseldorf called Fürst. Only two are called Olga. I visited both of them. One is seventy-five and a cripple; the other is a model. On that particular day she was in Rome."

"I like you," I said. "I like you all very much. Listen to me. Forget the whole thing. Don't think of it any more. You'll get into trouble, big trouble, if you don't. Believe me!"

They looked at me, then they looked at each other, and in the end Frau Romberg said, and her tone was motherly, "We won't talk about it any more, but please stay."

With an indifference that didn't sound sincere, Romberg said, "The whole thing is so stupid. I have some new pictures to show you, Herr Holden. *Prosit!*"

"*Prosit*, Herr Holden," said his wife.

I sat down again. Over my head the two looked at each other, seriously and sadly. They didn't think I could see them but I could, in the big mirror hanging on the wall behind them. "*Prosit!*" I said hoarsely.

It was pointless. All three of us tried hard, but it was no use. The conversation was tortured, the atmosphere filled with distrust. Soon it became unbearable. I left half an hour later. No one asked me to stay.

41

"Holden!"

I had almost reached the garage when I heard Nina's voice. She was silhouetted against the window of her lighted room. I walked across the grass to the villa. She said softly, "Come up."

There were no lights in the house, but there was a moon, and I walked up the creaking stairs by its light. Nina was sitting on the side of her bed when I walked in. She had on a long red gown, a black robe over it. An ashtray stood on a small table beside her. It was full to the brim.

"Sit down."

I sat down.

"Dr. Zorn just called. He was very excited. He congratulated me."

"What for?"

"They are letting my husband come home, on five hundred thousand marks bail."

My mouth went dry, my hands were suddenly ice-cold.

"When?"

"Tomorrow, noon."

I said nothing. What was there to say?

"Now you've got what you wanted."

It was just what I was thinking—I had it all right, but I didn't want it. She was wrong about that.

"I begged you not to let him have the documents."

"I was in a bind. I couldn't—no," I interrupted myself. "You're right. I didn't have to give him the documents. Of course there would have been consequences if I had refused, and I didn't want to accept them. I wanted to be free."

"And money."

"And money—yes."

We looked at each other, and we spoke to each other like enemies. Where was the trust there had been between us, the intimacy? We had laughed together, we had felt as one about so many things, our relationship had grown deeper, and now it was all over. Never happened.

"When he comes home, Holden, he will be invincible. You don't know him. You don't know what he's like when he feels powerful and invulnerable. You will now."

"That's something we have to accept. People like him *are* invincible."

"Because of you, Holden! Because of you! You're the one who made him invincible. It's your fault, your guilt, and you can't free yourself of that!"

"What do you mean—guilt? And what is freedom anyway? Just once . . . just once I wanted a share of the big money."

She said softly, "And I'm no better. I married him without love. To have money. For beautiful clothes, furs, jewels. I'm not trying to talk myself out of it. You and I, people like us, we're the ones who made him invincible. And are therefore just as guilty as he."

"What's going to happen? What are you going to do?"

"I don't know yet."

"You don't know?"

"No. Let's not fool ourselves. You've given yourself up to him. For me that decision still lies ahead. Leave me alone now, Holden."

"Good night," I said unhappily.

"Good night." Then she did the worst thing she could have done—she gave me her hand, as if we were comrades now, not lovers. Comrades in the same boat, the boat of the damned. Her hand was dry and cool.

That night I couldn't sleep. From my bed, through my window, I could see her window. The lights never went out. Twice I saw her silhouette as she looked out into the park. At about three I managed to fall asleep, only to wake up again at four, bathed in sweat. The sun was up but the lights in Nina's room were still burning. The birds were singing and I thought of the boat, the boat of the damned.

42

Reporters were swarming outside the park long before noon. Three policemen were stationed at the gate to prevent any reporters from entering. Men from the weekly newsreel and a TV team were setting up cameras. They laid cables to the sound trucks. They were cheerful and very busy about it. Curious people stared into the park through the iron fence, children among them.

At 2:30 I left with the Cadillac. As I passed through the gate I was photographed and greeted with ironic cries. "Going to get the *Herr Direktor* from his vacation?"

I did what Dr. Zorn had told me to do on the phone. I proceeded to the police station and picked up the plainclothesman who was to see that Brummer's return home took place without incident. The man was waiting for me on the street. He sat beside me and said nothing. Now I drove into the city to pick up Dr. Zorn. He was wearing a black suit and a grass-green vest. He seemed very nervous, like someone who fears that his audacious plan might be foiled at the last moment by somebody's stupidity. When we reached the jail, he got out and spoke to the two officers on duty at the entrance. They opened the gate and directed me into a dismal courtyard. About thirty men were waiting for us. I saw cameras again, broadcasting equipment, microphones, cables. The men were standing around, smoking, bored. They looked as if they had been waiting for quite some time.

The day was cloudy. There was little light in the courtyard, which was probably why the camermen had brought along floodlights. The silent plainclothesman and Dr. Zorn left me, and I spotted Peter Romberg among the reporters. I nodded in a friendly fashion; he bowed slightly, seriously, but made no move toward me.

"Romberg!" I called out to him.

This attracted attention to him, which he quite obviously didn't like, so he came over to me, embarrassed and aloof. "Hello."

"Why didn't you come over?"

"I didn't know whether you'd want me to."

"But that's nonsense!" I said helplessly. "Haven't you forgotten the whole thing yet?"

He shook his head. "You're a decent man, Herr Holden, and I think you know the game that's being played here."

"The game? . . ."

"I've come across something. A clue. I don't see very much yet, at any rate not clearly. But I see a little. You are being loyal to Herr Brummer because of Mila. That's why you won't tell me everything you know. But I'll get to the bottom of it. I'll find out the truth."

"You're crazy," I said bitterly. "What concern is the truth to you?"

"The truth is everyone's concern, Herr Holden."

At that moment the floodlights were turned on and the gloomy courtyard lit up like a film studio. At the barred windows the faces of the curious became visible, ghostly white—convicts and wardens, the convicted and their jailers, all of them staring at the three men who now walked out of a narrow steel door into the courtyard and came to a stop, side by side: little Dr. Zorn, the taciturn plainclothesman, and Julius Maria Brummer.

"Just a minute!" cried Zorn, and raised his hand. He gave Brummer a large pair of dark glasses, and Brummer put them on. There he stood—massive and fat, his ashen face swollen, the lips of his tiny mouth grey. The floodlights were reflected in his rosy bald head. He was wearing a blue suit, a white shirt, a silver tie. He didn't say a word. Zorn cried out nervously, "You may take pictures."

Cameras whirred, Leica shutters clicked, there were flashes. In front of the narrow steel door, the following drama now took place: Zorn and Brummer shook hands. Zorn laughed. The plainclothesman managed an embarrassed smile. Brummer remained expressionless.

Unreal . . . the way he stood there, a flat colossus of a man, usually such a ridiculous sight. Now he looked like revenge incarnate: *I have come to get even with all of you ...*

The cameras whirred. A man with a microphone stepped forward. Suddenly it was very quiet in the courtyard. The man began to speak.

"Herr Brummer, on behalf of my colleagues from the press, radio, television, and the weekly newsreel, I have been delegated to ask you a few questions."

Brummer's little mouth tightened. Disdainfully he gestured to his lawyer, who said, "Herr Brummer does not intend to answer any questions. I must ask you to address all questions to me. I am his attorney. I can give you five minutes."

"We want Brummer to speak!" someone yelled.

"We have very little time." Zorn's voice was icy.

"Herr Doktor Zorn," said the man with the microphone. "Does the release of your client mean that the case against him has been dismissed?"

"The case has not been dismissed. Not yet. However the incriminating evidence has been so weakened that the court can no longer justify keeping my client under arrest."

"May we deduce from the fact that you are also representing the industrialist Schwertfeger, that both clients now have common interests?"

"That may not be deduced. I am an attorney. I have many clients."

Somebody laughed.

The little lawyer, tugging at his collar, said, "We are going to file libel suits against nine daily papers, a well-known illustrated magazine, and two radio stations because they have publicized items about my client that are untrue and slanderous. Further suits may follow."

"How did it come about that the incriminating evidence against Herr Brummer was so suddenly and so quickly reduced to such a minimum as to make Herr Brummer's release possible?"

"No comment."

Somebody had come up to me. Public Prosecutor Dr. Lofting. He stood beside me, thin and a little stooped, his hands in the pockets of his creased suit, pale and sad. The bags under his eyes were darker than ever. I bowed silently, he did the same. We were standing in the dark, behind the floodlights and cameras.

"Was it an unbiased investigation and have you no complaints as to its conduct?"

"Absolutely none. In the name of my client and on my own behalf I would like to thank Public Prosecutor Dr. Lofting for his fair, irreproachable, and considerate handling of the investigation. I would l-l-like to say that in this case the public prosecutor was faced with an extremely difficult task. I'm sorry, gentlemen, but the five minutes are up. Our car, please."

"Good-bye," I said to Lofting.

"*Auf Wiedersehen*," he said quietly. "Because we shall meet again, Herr Holden. You can depend on it."

I inched the car into the glaring light toward the three men. I stopped, got out of the car and opened the door. Standing very straight, massive and powerful, Julius Maria Brummer stood before me and shook my hand, vigorously and long. I could feel the nausea rising up to my throat, but even worse than the nausea was the fear. I thought of Nina's words. The man had truly become invincible, through me . . . through me . . .

A reporter took a flash picture, so close that it blinded me momentarily and I had to close my eyes. When I opened them again I could see Peter Romberg making his way back through the crowd.

Now the three men got into the car. I was the last to get in. The cameras followed us, the floodlights were caught in my rear-view mirror and again I was momentarily blinded. But now they also lit up Dr. Lofting. We were moving slowly past him. He was smiling, and I had to turn away from that smile because I couldn't bear it.

43

"Everything all right at home, Holden?"

"Yes, Herr Brummer."

We were driving through the city. I was glad that Brummer was sitting in the back. This way he couldn't see my face. At this point I wasn't exactly in control of my expression.

"My wife all right?"

"Yes, sir."

"Mila, and my old Mitzi?"

"Everybody's fine, Herr Brummer."

I had never heard him speak like this—imperiously, demandingly, mercilessly. Officers spoke like that, the big brass. What this voice ordered had to be obeyed, unequivocally, not because the speaker of this voice was so powerful, but because what stood behind him was.

"A lot of work for you in the near future, Holden."

"Yes, sir."

"Berlin. Hamburg. Frankfurt. Vienna. We'll be on the go."

"Yes, Herr Brummer."

Yes, *Herr General*. Oh dear God in heaven . . .

Dr. Zorn said, "Herr Holden has behaved impeccably in every respect. I would like to thank him."

"I would too," said Brummer. "Sincerely and with all my heart. I shall never forget it."

The taciturn plainclothesman looked at me sadly out of the corners of his eyes, but he said nothing.

We got to the Rhine and I proceeded north. The weather got worse. It became windy and there was fog over the water. In front of the entrance to the villa, the cameras were rolling as we approached, floodlights, flashguns. I could only inch forward because so many reporters came up close to photograph inside the car. Finally the three policemen pushed everyone away, the gates were closed behind us, and we drove silently over the gravel driveway to the entrance of the villa.

On his tiny feet, as gracefully as a dancing balloon in spite of his huge body, Julius Maria Brummer walked up the steps. In the hallway, which I was the last to enter, the old boxer came barking to meet him, jumped up at him again and again, licked his hands and let out yowls of joy. "Mitzili, my old Mitzili . . ."

Mila came into the hall. She was dressed all in black and was very pale. Brummer embraced her and kissed her on the cheek. Mila raised her hand and made the sign of the cross on Brummer's forehead.

Nina came down the stairs.

Brummer took off his dark glasses and went to meet her. They met on the stairs, halfway up, and looked into each other's eyes for what seemed to me an eternity. Nina had on a green summer dress and green high-heeled shoes. She was heavily made-up and looked exhausted.

Julius Brummer placed one arm around her waist and together they walked up the stairs and disappeared in the dark passage that led to their rooms.

"Must forgive me if I weep, gentlemen," sobbed Mila. "But this is the happiest day of my life."

44

The next eight days were the worst days of my life. I saw Nina, but I couldn't speak to her. I drove her to various places, but he was always with her. I tried to catch her eye, but she looked away. She didn't speak to me, only he did. She looked wretched. When she smiled you could see that she had put on too much makeup. Her skin was flaky.

I was kept busy. Brummer was on the go all the time—

conferences, visits to ministries, the courthouse, and, of course, Zorn. He asked for me at the strangest times, once at four o'clock in the morning. He had to go to the General Post Office to mail a letter, himself, personally—it was that important.

I didn't care when he called me because those were nights when I lay awake. Evidently one didn't have to have experienced Dresden to be unable to sleep. A lot of other things could destroy one's sleep. I lay on my bed and looked across the park at Nina's window. Sometimes the lights were turned out early, but often they were on for a long time; sometimes they were turned off early, then turned on again, and I always thought of one thing because his bedroom was next to hers.

A new butler, a new gardener, and two new maids were engaged during these days, but I saw very little of them because I was on the go all the time. On the third evening Brummer gave a party. Thirty people were invited. Brummer had chosen them carefully. They were all prominent people. I stood in the park as the cars drove up, one after the other. It was a warm evening. Brummer and Nina received their guests at the front door. She was wearing a silver lamé evening dress, a lot of jewelry, and an orchid. He had on a dark blue tuxedo and a red cummerbund. It was like a court reception. Car after car drove up, one couple after the other got out and greeted their host and hostess. It was a party given out of spite, out of Brummer's self-assertiveness, a social demonstration of strength, because of course everything was photographed. Let the press see who accepted his invitations only three days after his release from jail. Let everybody in the whole country see!

In the kitchen a cook and three waiters had been hired for the evening. The new maids were helping. The kitchen looked like a battlefield. Brummer had ordered the following menu: malossol caviar, turtle soup, *poularde de Bruxelles* with a variety of salads, cheese, coffee, and so on. And champagne with every course. Mila, who was directing this incredible hubbub, smiled at me radiantly as I entered. Her face was glistening with sweat. "Did you ever see such a wonderful party, Herr Holden? Like in the good old days. Bless my soul, but I feel wonderful! Here, have a glass." She poured champagne for me and I could see she was a little tipsy. "Caviar for everybody, as much as they can eat! That's what the *gnä' Herr* said. And champagne!"

I counted six one-pound cans of caviar on ice. Nobody could have counted the bottles of champagne. They were even piled up in Mila's room.

Nina came in. The servants greeted her; so did I.

"Is everything under control, Mila?"

"Give us a half hour, *gnä' Frau*, and everything will be ready."

One look . . . just one look . . .

"Then the martinis can be served now."

She left. She hadn't looked at me. Not once.

I went out into the street and joined the chauffeurs who were standing around their cars, smoking, but they didn't seem to trust me and I wasn't able to get a conversation going. I went to my room. Every window in the villa was brilliantly lit, several were open, I could hear laughter and voices, and again and again I thought I could hear Nina's voice. In the end I was beside myself with helpless jealousy and fury.

Then, at about ten, the phone rang. Perhaps somebody wasn't feeling well, I thought, and I was going to be asked to take him home, but it wasn't Brummer, it was Mila. She said, "You're to put on your blue suit and come over."

"My blue suit? Why? . . ." but she had already hung up. I changed and walked over to the kitchen.

One of the waiters, in tails, wearing white gloves, said to me seriously, "Please follow me." He walked ahead of me into the hall. On the first floor I again could hear laughter and voices, but we remained on the ground floor. The waiter opened a paneled door and led me into a small dining room which I had never seen before. The walls and ceiling were dark wood. Candles flickered on the table, which was covered with a white damask cloth and set with fine silver and china; otherwise there was no light. Mila Blehova's white hair shone in the candlelight. She had on a black silk dress with a white lace collar, a brooch, a ring, and a garnet bracelet, and she was beaming at me. "For us, Herr Holden, just for us!" she said in her coarse

Czech dialect. "The *gnä' Herr* wants us to have a fine evening too. You can serve now, Herr Koller."

I sat down. Mila was dewy-eyed with joy. "I didn't know a thing about it, Herr Holden. The waiters prepared it all, on his orders, as a surprise for us! That's the *gnä' Herr* for you. What a good man! And a true socialist!"

The waiter came and went. He poured champagne, brought caviar. Mila plopped a huge amount of the shiny black roe onto her plate. "More lemon, Herr Koller, please. That little bit will never be enough." So Herr Koller brought more lemon and Mila ate gluttonously. "No, no toast. I'll eat it with a spoon. If I had a lot of money, I'd eat nothing but caviar. I could eat every bit of it! Herr Koller?"

"Yes."

"Don't stand around so stiff and formal. Help yourself to a glass."

"Thanks. Very good of you."

Seated in front of the dark paneling, Mila looked like an old duchess painted by an English court painter. Her false teeth sparkled when she spoke. "Today the *gnä' Herr* talked to me about the future, my future. When I'm old. The belching doesn't get any better, and I just can't do much of anything any more in the heat. I can still work, but it won't be much longer. You can bring us the consommé now, Herr Koller."

Herr Koller bowed and went off.

"Look at the dope! Bowing to me! Well, as I was saying, the *gnä' Herr* asked if he should buy a little apartment for me, and he'd give me an allowance every month, you know, till I'm ten feet under the ground. But I said no, I'd rather stay with my Nina and my old Mitzi, and with him. And what do you think he said? I should pick out a room for myself in the house and I could live right along with them, without having to do any work, like an old mother. Oh, but this is a day of joy for me!"

"I'm happy for you, Mila."

"I know you are. If there's anyone who doesn't begrudge me my happinesss, it's you, Herr Holden. There . . . here comes the turtle soup. And after that the *poularde*. Dear Mother of God, am I ever hungry!"

45

The fourth day. The fifth. The sixth.

I couldn't speak to Nina. Whenever I saw her, Brummer was with her. At night I took sleeping pills. They didn't work. I bought cognac. That gave me a few hours sleep, but then I was awake again and looking across the park at her window. Was the light burning in her room or was it out? Either way was dreadful.

On the seventh day I decided I'd give notice. I would promise Brummer to keep our secret. I would tell him that I intended to go into business for myself with the money he had given me. He didn't need me any more.

I had to forget Nina, fast. If I didn't, there would be a catastrophe. I had thought it would all be much too easy. It *was* crazy. Nina had been right. Why should she love me, how could she love a person she scarcely knew? Insane. Absolutely insane. I had to disappear. Nina was only a woman. Brummer seemed on the verge of rehabilitation. She had wanted to leave him for Toni Vorm, but she had loved Toni Vorm. Why should she leave Brummer for a man she *didn't* love?

On the eighth day it rained heavily. At 8:30 I drove Brummer into the city, to his huge office building. "Oh yes, Holden, before I forget. We drive to Munich tomorrow. Have the car lubed and the oil changed."

"Yes, sir."

"And drive back to the house and pick up my wife. She has to go somewhere. I won't need you again this morning."

"Yes, Herr Brummer."

Nina.

Now I would see her. Alone. And speak to her alone for the first time in all these days. I was overjoyed at the very thought of seeing her again, of being alone with her, even if only in this big, cold car, in the morning, in the rain.

She was wearing the black and white checked suit and black alligator shoes. A bag to match. A little black hat, worn atilt on her blond hair. The new butler brought her to the car under the protection of a big umbrella. She didn't say anything in his presence. She sat in the back and was silent until we reached the street. Then she said shyly, "Drive to the boat," and blushed. "Only for a minute, Holden. But I must talk to you."

"And I have to talk to you! Have to!"

"Not while you're driving."

"No," I said. "You're right. Not while I'm driving." And it really would have been impossible. I was much too excited. I had trouble keeping the car on the road.

Nina . . . Nina . . . Nina . . .

This time we went into the glassed-in cabin. We were the only guests. The rain was pounding on the deck. The old unshaven man appeared, rubbing his hands. "The young lovers!"

We ordered coffee and he disappeared. The Rhine was grey, like the sky and the air. The rain splashed a carpet of tiny spouts of water over the river and the boat moved gently. It was very quiet, and we looked at each other.

"I have told my husband that I intend to leave him."

"No!"

"Yes. Last night." She spoke slowly and calmly, like someone who has finally come to a decision. "These last days have been terrible."

"For me too."

"You said once that one could live with someone whom one despised, and that in this respect women had an easier time of it. You were wrong."

The rain drummed on the roof of the cabin. I looked at her and grew happier with every breath I took, with every beat of my heart. "He . . . he has become inhuman. He looks upon himself as a god, and everyone is subordinate to him. The party, Holden . . . if you could have seen the people! How they flattered him, how they fawned on him, the compliments I got . . ."

"It's the money. All that money."

"I don't want any part of it, not any more. It's gruesome, Holden, that's what it is. He lives as if nothing had happened. The crimes he has confessed to me—they never existed! He doesn't play the innocent, Holden. He *is* innocent! In his own mind he is innocent. That's what I told him."

"What?"

"Everything I've just told you. I asked him for a divorce. I don't want any money from him, not a penny. I'm young, I can work, we have no children—thank God. I told him that if he wanted it, I would take the blame in court."

"And he?"

The old man from Dresden, sleepless and unshaven, brought our coffee, and we waited until he was gone.

"And he?" I repeated.

"He was wonderful."

"Wonderful?"

"Suddenly I felt sorry for him. He was so generous. You know, I may really be the only person in the world that he loves. He . . . he said he could understand me. Then he wept in my arms. We talked for a long time . . ."

I saw the light. I thought it was something quite different.

"He said it was terrible for him, but he could understand me. He didn't want to hold me against my will, but I should please give him time, a little time. He's going to Munich tomorrow. I'm to give him that much time, until he comes back. Oh Holden, I'm so happy that I told him. It was the only thing to do."

"And when he lets you go—what will you do?"

"I don't know yet. Work. Live my own life. Start all over again from the beginning."

"And what about me? About us?"

"I don't know. All I know is that I don't want to lie any more. Perhaps someday we'll love each other, but then I want it to be a love everyone can know about. A clean love. Without meanness and deceit. I don't ever want to feel dirty again. I don't want to feel like a whore any more. Holden, it means everything to me that you should understand me. I want to be *decent*. That's more important to me right now than love."

"And because it's more important to you, you're sitting here now and telling me all this?"

"I don't understand." She looked at me, startled, then knew at once how I meant it, and reddened. I put my arm around her. "Don't," she whispered.

I kissed her. She protested, but not for long. Suddenly she took my face between both hands and pressed her body against mine and responded to my kiss with a wildness and passion I had never experienced in my life. Her little black hat fell off. The boat rocked gently beneath us, we clung to each other as if we were drowning and I realized suddenly that all we had left in the world was each other.

46

Düsseldorf. Cologne. Bonn. Frankfurt. Mannheim, Karlsruhe.

So far everything had gone smoothly. It rained steadily but the visibility was adequate. Brummer called Düsseldorf from Cologne and Mannheim. It was Zorn's number every time. We reached Pforzheim just as night was falling. Here, in the south, the coming of autumn was more noticeable. It was early this year. It was only the beginning of October but in the woods the leaves were already turning yellow, brown, and red. The meadows looked faded, and along the river bank hundreds of autumn crocus were in bloom. They were burning potato stalks in the fields and the rain kept the fires smoldering.

At about five the fog came creeping in out of the woods, thin at first, then in light puffs, then clouds of it. The sky grew black, the rain never stopped, the fog flowed sluggishly across the highway.

"We'll stop for coffee and then drive through to Munich," said Brummer. He was very calm that day. I remember admiring him. If he was suffering because of his wife's decision, he certainly had himself under control. He spoke very little, and I was sure he was thinking of Nina. I was thinking of her all the time.

At Service Area Pforzheim, the lame old dog, who had been lying between us, jumped clumsily out of the car and barked at a cat. We walked to the restaurant through the rain. Here it was warm. Four truckers were playing cards. A jukebox was blaring. The waitress was pretty.

"Two espressos and one call to Düsseldorf."

Again Brummer talked to Dr. Zorn. I drank my coffee and looked out at the rain. When Nina was free, we would leave Düsseldorf. Perhaps we'd move to Munich. Or Hamburg. Or Vienna. So many cities to choose from. We were too old for children, we'd stay alone. Together. An apartment first, then perhaps a small house. I still had some money left, for a starter . . .

Brummer came back. "Nasty business."

"Has something happened?"

"Yes. Let's go."

In the car he lit a cigar. Clumsily. The fog was moving now. An east wind was driving it across the highway. I had to let down the window on my side because the glass kept steaming over. The fog smelled of smoke, and the rain smelled like rotting leaves. Fallen leaves were scattered all over the road. In the woods around Stuttgart, all I could see was the white stripe down the middle of the road, sometimes not even that. I slowed down to thirty. The dog fell asleep. She twitched in her sleep, sometimes she growled. Perhaps she was dreaming of cats.

"Do you know Peter Romberg?" Brummer spoke with his cigar in his mouth. Every now and then the ash glowed.

"Yes."

"That little girl of his . . . do you know her too?"

"Yes."

"Happy family, no? They're supposed to be crazy about the child."

"That's right."

"Would do anything for her, right?"

"They give in to her on pretty much everything."

"That wasn't what I meant. I meant they'd do anything

that was asked of them if the child were endangered. What do you say?"

Now I was driving twenty. The woods receded. On our left, on shadowy hillsides, there were suddenly a lot of lights. It had to be Stuttgart. We saw the lights for a moment only, through a hole in the fog, then they were swallowed up again, shrouded in a milky mist.

"I don't know what you mean, Herr Brummer."

"You know very well what I mean. Why didn't you tell Zorn about it? It was your duty to do so. Absolutely!" He sounded teary, like an offended child.

"How do you know . . ."

"Zorn. I just spoke to him. A lot of people work for him, he has connections everywhere. This fellow Romberg is going around talking off the top of his head. About his little girl. Hilde Lutz. The Mercedes. And now tell me what really happened."

So I told him the whole story. He smoked and listened. In the end he said, again in that high-pitched querulous voice, "And all that you kept to yourself?"

"I didn't think it was important," I lied.

"Not important?" He laughed. It sounded like the grunting of a pig. "If Romberg succeeds in proving that on that day you were in this Lutz girl's apartment, if the public prosecutor finds out about that . . . good God! Zorn has everything sewed up, my whole case, absolutely foolproof. And now this shit. Can we buy Romberg?"

"I don't think so."

"What proof does he have?"

"Mickey. She swears she heard the name Lutz."

"Can we claim she wasn't with you on that day?"

"No."

"Why not?"

"Your wife, Mila, and Romberg saw us."

"Romberg doesn't count. He's their prize witness. Mila and my wife will swear to the opposite."

"Romberg took a picture of Mickey and me."

"Where is it?"

"He has it."

"You have to get us that photo. And the negative."

"He won't give it to me."

"You got us into this fucking mess. It's up to you—"

234

"I didn't get you into this—"

"Don't contradict me. You'll get that photo, and the negative. And if he refuses to give them up—okay. You say he adores the child, so . . . something will happen to the child."

"Herr Brummer."

"What?"

"I want to give notice."

He took the cigar out of his mouth and stared at me.

"I . . . I've done everything I possibly could for you. You've paid me for it. I want to start a new life for myself. I'm sure you can understand that. I . . ."

He began to laugh, a chuckle at first, then his fat body shook, shook finally with loud laughter. His breath came out of his little mouth like a wheeze, he gasped for breath asthmatically, like a pig, a fat treacherous pig. The dog woke up and whined.

"Be quiet, Mitzili." He was snorting as he said, "A case of nerves, eh? Too much excitement. I can understand it. We're human, after all. Take my wife." The fat pig laughed again. "My Nina. God knows, if there's one person on this earth who loves me, it's my Nina. And she's completely disoriented. It's all been too much for her. Actually asked me to give her a divorce. Can you imagine that? Incredible, isn't it? I mean, the fact that I can talk about it like this. Why don't you say something?"

"It's the fog, Herr Brummer. I have to concentrate on what I'm doing."

"Yes, by all means, Holden, concentrate on what you're doing." He was still grunting and laughing. "I mentioned my wife as an example of the fact that right now neither of you seem to be in command of your decisions. She wants a divorce. You want to give notice. One might almost come to the conclusion that you got together on it!" He grunted again. "Nothing but nerves. I'm sending Nina south for a rest. I wasn't in the least upset when she came to me with this monstrous idea. I didn't take her seriously for a moment. Told her I could understand her. What else could I say? Was going a bit too far, though. Right now I have more serious troubles. I won't give her a divorce. Nothing could persuade me. I need her. Best wife in the world. But right now—nerves shot. Like you, Holden. That's why I can't take you seriously either."

"But I beg you to do so, Herr Brummer. I want to leave your service."

"And go back to jail?" he asked, snorting cheerfully. "What are you doing, Holden? For God's sake be careful! We almost went off the road."

"You know why I went to jail?"

"But of course."

"Since when?"

"Known it for a long time. Why?"

My lips were stuck together. I said heavily, "Zorn said you didn't know."

"Good old Zorn."

"But you gave me thirty thousand marks as a reward for—"

"That's what *you* think."

"What do you mean?"

"Holden, do you think we're idiots?" Now his voice was querulous again. "Did you sign a receipt for the money? Yes or no."

"Yes."

"Just as I expected. You're no better than I am, Holden. But what would have happened if I'd sent you back to jail at the time? I'd have had one collaborator less, that's all. A valuable collaborator, to be sure, who went on to do me more valuable service. That's why I didn't do anything about it."

Now we were afloat in the fog. I slowed down to ten. During the last half hour we hadn't met a car.

"And how smart that was! Because you see, Holden, if you really try to leave me now, then we'll accuse you of blackmailing us for thirty thousand marks. To get certain documents from us. You can, of course, have all sorts of things to say on your own behalf, but proof? You can't prove a thing. You don't have the documents any more, but we, Holden, we still have your signature on that receipt."

Suddenly I heard a whirring sound, static, and a woman's voice, speaking as if to children. "The wicked brother allied himself with the devil because of the gold.

236

He . . . ate and drank with him. But whoever eats with the devil should have a long spoon."

"When you accepted the money, you asked Dr. Zorn what you were getting it for. He said that perhaps one day he would ask *you* to do *him* a favor."

. . . he ate and drank with him . . . His caviar. His champagne. His poularde *with the various salads . . .*

"Today he is asking you to do him this favor. He is asking you to obtain the photo of you and Mickey from Peter Romberg. And the negative."

"I can't do it. I won't—"

"You have to and you will."

"Let me go, Herr Brummer. Take the money. I don't have all of it any more, but take the rest."

"I don't want the money. I have plenty of money. You will stay, just as my poor wife will stay. Neither of you know what's good for you."

"How long . . . how much longer are you going to force me to stay with you?"

"As long as I need you, Holden. Don't be childish. Are you badly off? No. So that's that."

. . . but whoever eats with the devil . . .

I ran over an animal. The usual sickening thud, the car skidded a little, the old dog yelped.

"What was that?"

"A rabbit."

. . . should have a long spoon.

BOOK THREE

in the doorway, looking pale and frightened. Her brown hair fell in a disorderly fashion over her forehead. She wasn't wearing her glasses and her eyes watered from

1

Déjà vu . . .

I've seen it all. I've heard it all. I've experienced it all.
Do you know this strange feeling of *déjà vu*, Herr Kriminal Kommissar Kehlmann, for whom I am patiently filling
these pages? You go for a walk, early in the morning, in a
small spa. The streets are empty. A duck in the sunlight.
A white house with flowering cress in a window box. A
ladder leaning against the house. A girl, blond, wearing a
shawl. You ask her the way to the baths. And suddenly
you feel that you've asked the girl just that, you've seen
the duck, the ladder, the flowering cress before, and you
know the way to the baths before the girl tells you. Have
you ever had this feeling, *Herr Kriminal Kommissar?*

On that foggy night in October, on the autobahn, between Stuttgart and Ulm, I ran over a rabbit. And something registered in my brain, in my memory.

Déjà vu . . .

I had run over a rabbit before, on a foggy night, on the
autobahn. That had been along the Elbe, just after
Coswig, on the way to Berlin. At a time when Nina was in
the hospital, fighting for her life. A few hours before they
arrested Brummer.

Déjà entendu . . .

You throw a coin into a vending machine, press the
right button, and get your change back. I drive over a rabbit, and suddenly I remember everything Julius Brummer
said on that day . . .

"Take anyone—big people, little people . . . all of them

241

have a past. A big past, a little past. They're afraid, they feel guilty. Do you know what all of them need, Holden? . . ."

Words spoken in the fog, weeks ago, along the Elbe, just beyond Coswig. Now I hear them again, weeks later, again in the fog, just after Stuttgart, on the way to Ulm . . .

"A double. By God, that would be the invention of the century. A second *I*. To take on everything one's done . . . I should get out a patent for that one!"

A double . . .

I don't know if you've ever had this feeling, *Herr Kriminal Kommissar* Kehlmann, when something gets a hold on you, when it takes root in your brain, in your blood . . .

A double . . .

He won't let Nina go. He won't let me go. More tragedies will happen. We'll never find the way to each other. Never.

A double . . .

". . . I won't give her a divorce. Nothing could persuade me. I need her. Best wife in the world . . ."

And if Herr Brummer were to die suddenly? He has a weak heart. He wears a gold disc around his pale, puffy neck . . . My double does it, not I.

No guilt. No atonement.

"God Almighty, I didn't do it," I shall say on Judgment Day. "Someone else committed this crime, someone who looks like me, speaks like me, lives like me. But he is evil and I am good. He is the one who has to be punished. He, not I."

But I don't have a double. A second *I* doesn't exist.

Wait a minute . . .

A thing that doesn't exist is a thing that has not yet been discovered. The thing itself has nothing against being discovered. Such a double therefore does not *yet* exist . . .

I don't know if you have ever had this feeling, *Herr Kriminal Kommissar*. An idea suddenly gets hold of you, takes root in your brain, in your blood . . .

Julius Maria Brummer formulated this idea in the fog between Coswig and Berlin Ring. In the fog, weeks later, between Stuttgart and Ulm, it began to take shape in my brain. He himself gave birth to it, he who was now to be its victim—Julius Maria Brummer.

2

It is difficult, *Herr Kommissar*, to create one's own double, but it is by no means impossible. One has to think realistically when one is about to create an unreal, grisly phantom. One has to think clearly if the phantom is to be convincing. Above all one has to contend with the opposition of most people against this incomprehensible, metaphysical phenomenon; it is therefore wise to proceed in a mathematical fashion. Every phase of the procedure has to be thought through and prepared precisely. Never should the shadow of a doubt arise as to the reality of what seems to be unreal and inexplicable. One can only bring disorder into the thinking capacities of others when one's own line of thought is in order. It is difficult to create a double for oneself, *Herr Kriminal Kommissar*, but it is by no means impossible.

After I had decided, on that foggy night, to kill Julius Maria Brummer without giving any court of law the possibility to punish me for it, I went ahead with my plan without a moment's hesitation. Three difficulties had to be reckoned with if I was to succeed in this perfect crime.

First:—It was essential that I continue to live the life I had been living in a way that attracted no attention whatsoever, that is to say I had to continue to appear completely subservient to Brummer.

Second—and this was the most difficult of all:—I had to convince Nina that I was resigned to things as they were. Here, of course, there was the danger that she would despise me for it, but there were no two ways about it—what I intended to do I had to do alone. I dared not have an accomplice.

The third thing was really the easiest:—the creation of an imaginary double.

3

In order to make this report generally comprehensible, *Herr Kriminal Kommissar*, and to demonstrate with what a simple system I was working, I would like to tell first about the incident at the gas station. I think you will then be in a position to perceive the basis of my undertaking: the rational dissemination of an irrational terror.

The incident at the gas station began on a Wednesday, after our return from Munich. I know it was a Wednesday, because I had the afternoon off, and I needed a free afternoon for what I had in mind.

I left my room a little after 4 P.M. Brummer's three cars were in the garage, and the garage door was always open on Wednesday afternoon, in case Nina Brummer wanted to use one of the cars. The keys were in the ignition, the car papers in the glove compartment.

I hadn't seen Nina since our return. As I walked over to the villa, I looked up at the second floor and got the feeling that the curtain at one of the windows had just been pushed aside and let fall again. But of course I could have been mistaken. It was cool on this October day, the leaves on the trees had turned brown, red, and orange, and down by the lake a few birds were cawing. They sounded loud in the stillness of the afternoon, and the sky was grey.

I went into the kitchen and said good-bye to the old Czech cook because it was important that she see me before I left.

"Don't wait supper for me, Mila. I'll eat in the city."

I was wearing a grey suit, a white shirt, and a blue tie, and I went into the kitchen also because I wanted Mila to see what I was wearing.

The foliage in Cecilienallee had changed color too. A

thin layer of fog lay over the Rhine. A tug was chug-chugging upstream with its load. I could smell its black smoke, which was being pushed down to the water by the oppressive air.

At Hofgarten I took a bus and drove to the city. In a department store near the station I bought two suits, one brown, the other black with pin stripes, both from the rack. I also bought a green tie with black spots and a grey tie with black stripes. I bought the cheapest of everything because I did not intend to wear these suits and ties very often. Finally I bought the cheapest suitcase I could find and packed everything in it. Then I walked to the station and checked the suitcase in the baggage room. They gave me a blue ticket with a number on it. By now it was 5:30. The rush hour had begun, people were hurrying home from businesses and factories. Car horns were blowing impatiently, street cars jangled, and all intersections were jammed. I took a taxi back to the Rhine. At the Kleverstrasse-Schwerinstrasse intersection I had the man stop, and got out.

I hope it is clear to you, Herr Kriminal Kommissar Kehlmann, that I am telling this in such detail so that you may recognize the element of shock in this first incident, because the same shock mechanism formed the basis of all future incidents.

I now walked slowly to the little movie house, three blocks north on the Lützowstrasse. On that particular Wednesday they were playing a French crime film I had already seen, *The Devils*. It was important that I go to a film I had already seen, because I could count later on being asked what it was about. In my grey suit, white shirt and blue tie I walked into the lobby of the small movie house and bought a loge seat. It was already dark in the auditorium; they were running the commercials. An usherette stood at the entrance door. She was young, pretty, and had red hair. I gave her a smile and turned slightly, so that the little daylight outside fell on me and she could see me clearly. "Hi, honey. How about a little fun, just the two of us?"

She pursed her lips in a studied Brigitte Bardot pout, threw back her head, puffed up her breasts and walked ahead of me without a word, into the dark auditorium.

245

Her flashlight lit up rows of empty seats. I caught up with her, laid a hand on her round hips and whispered, "Come on. Be a sport."

She stopped, slapped my hand, pointed with her flashlight and said, "In here."

"Okay," I said. "Have it your own way. Could have been a hell of an evening."

"You're just the guy I've been waiting for," said he little usherette, and off she went.

The commercials were followed by the newsreel. After the newsreel, the lights went on. I looked around for the exit and saw it, on the right side, behind a red velvet curtain. Then I looked at the redhead, still standing at the door, waved, and she turned her back on me. The lights went out and the feature began. I waited until the title and credits were over, then I took off my shoes and, crouching, in my stocking feet, walked to the end of the empty row and to the exit. Behind the red curtain there was a dark passage with moldy walls. It opened out onto a courtyard and from there to the street. And the best thing about it was that one could get back into the movie house the same way.

Now it was 6:26. The next performance began at 8:15. The feature would probably be over around eight. I had an hour and a half. Not much. I ran down Cecilienallee. It was already dark because of the bad weather, something to be thankful for. At the villa there was light in a few windows, and as I walked into the park (the gate had a concealed electric lock) I could hear the old dog bark. The next few minutes were tricky. I had to get the Cadillac out of the garage. Nothing disastrous about it if anyone saw me; I would say I was taking the car to have the oil changed. But it would mean that I'd have to forget what I'd just built up so carefully.

But nobody saw me. The car rolled silently out into the street. I closed the gate and drove off as fast as I dared. Every minute in the Cadillac brought me a minute closer to my goal, but also closer to the possibility of a last-minute disaster. Because if someone saw me returning, I could forget the whole thing too.

In the city the traffic was still heavy and moving slowly. At the station there was, of course, nowhere to park. I left the Cadillac under a No Parking sign and ran to the baggage room. If a cop put a ticket under my windshield wiper, I could pay the two mark fine in the course of the evening at any police station. Then there would be no record of the violation and I wouldn't have to show any identification.

At the baggage room I retrieved my cheap suitcase and ran back to the car. No ticket. I was lucky. I hoped I was lucky. I thought of Nina, but then thought quickly of something else. Right now I had to be calm and in control of what lay ahead. I must not think of Nina. Not now.

I drove back to the Rhine. By now it was quite dark. In an empty side street I took off my grey suit and put on the cheap brown one, I changed my blue tie for the green one with the black spots. I roughed up my hair, threw the suitcase and my suit in the back and drove off again. Seven-ten. I had fifty minutes left. The most difficult part lay ahead.

4

I drove to the gas station on Lützowstrasse, where I got gas regularly. I stopped beside one of the red pumps and remained behind the wheel, under the neon lights. A young man was sitting in the brightly lit glass booth. His name was Paul. He knew me. I think he liked me. He often told me about his motorbike. It wasn't his yet, he was saving up for it, but he talked about it as if he'd owned it for years. Hilfreich was his second name. He had acne and probably not much luck with girls. Now he came over to the car in his white mechanic's coat, grinning. "Good evening, Herr Holden."

"Good evening, Paul." We shook hands. There was an exceptionally large pimple on the left side of his forehead. "Fill it up."

"Okay."

He hauled the hose out of the pump and unscrewed the gas tank cap. The motor in the pump began to hum, the gasoline flowed into the tank, the liter and mark numbers revolved rapidly. I sat quietly behind the wheel and waited. I was sorry about what I was going to have to do to Paul, but I had no choice. I thought of Peter Romberg, of Mickey, of Nina. And of myself. None of us could live in peace until Julius Maria Brummer was dead. There was no other way. But I felt sorry for Paul Hilfreich.

The pump clicked. The tank was full. Paul came to the window and asked cheerfully. "Oil okay?"

"Yes." Seven-fourteen.

"Tires?"

"Okay too."

"Battery?"

"Everything's in order," I said irritably. I was sweating again.

"Then it's twenty-four marks thirty, Herr Holden."

"Charge it to Herr Brummer."

"Sorry, Herr Holden, but I can't do that any more."

"Why not?" I asked, although I knew very well that he couldn't do it any more, and why.

"Herr Brummer doesn't have a charge account with us any more since he . . . since he came home. He wants all bills paid in cash. But you know that, Herr Holden."

"Dammit, of course I do," I said, and slapped my forehead, pretending to be annoyed with myself. "But now I'm in a bind. I don't have a cent on me. Can I sign for it?"

"But of course." Paul laughed. "You can pay next time."

"Thanks, Paul."

"You're welcome. Have a good trip."

In the mirror I could see him waving as I drove off. Seven-sixteen. And Mickey was a little safer. And I had moved a step farther on my way to Nina. And Julius Brummer had moved a step farther on the way to his death.

I stopped in another quiet street, changed again, and threw the cheap brown suit and green tie into the suitcase. Then I drove back to the station, parked under the No Parking sign again, ran to the baggage room and for the

248

second time that day deposited the suitcase there. With the blue ticket in my hand. I ran back to the car. Seven thirty-one. In half an hour I had to be back in my seat in the movie house . . . in half an hour, or it had all been for nothing. I got behind the wheel, I stepped on the starter. I stepped on it a second time. A third time. The car wouldn't start.

5

I did everything I could think of. I pulled out the choke, I pushed the gas pedal all the way down, I turned the ignition off, turned it on again—the car wouldn't start.

I began to pray as I tried this and that, and my hands were sweating so, they slipped off everything. As I prayed I thought that God wouldn't listen to me because it was murder I was planning, plain, evil murder. But no. It was a necessary, a decent murder. But was there such a thing as a decent murder, I asked myself, as I tried choke, gas pedal, choke again. No. There was no such thing. So I stopped praying and began to curse instead, and the car started.

I drove back to the Rhine. The streets were empty now and I managed to get there in eight minutes. At 7:46 I stopped, headlights off, in front of Julius Brummer's beautiful villa. I jumped out of the car and opened the wrought-iron gate. Now the lights were on in all the rooms; where the curtains were drawn, it shone through the cracks. I drove the Cadillac across the gravel driveway to the garage as quietly as I could. I had stuck a match between the closed doors before I left; when I opened the door, the match fell down. So nobody had been here in the meantime. Or had somebody been here and noticed the match and jammed it back between the door?

I was exhausted. I couldn't breathe. My head ached,

and red circles were revolving before my eyes. Back into the car. The car into the garage. The garage door closed. Across the gravel driveway, back to the gate. Again I heard the old dog bark. Then I saw Mila's silhouette in the lighted kitchen window, and as I opened the gate with trembling hands I could hear her quavering voice: "Is anybody there?"

I ran into a dark alley. It didn't matter if Mila had seen a shadow that looked like mine. No. It didn't matter . . .

I ran to the little movie house. My heart was pounding, my head felt like bursting, and it was 7:51 . . . 7:52 . . . 7:53 . . . I reached the courtyard behind the auditorium and took off my shoes. Then I saw the two. They were standing directly in front of the movie exit, kissing. Two young people in love. There they stood, she with her arms around him, and now she took his face between both hands.

I flattened myself against the moldy wall. The two didn't stop kissing. He said something, she kissed him again, and they were standing directly in front of the exit . . .

Go away, I told them wordlessly. Go away, go away, go away . . .

But they went right on necking, and a cat ran across the yard, meowing.

Seven fifty-six. Seven fifty-seven.

"No," said the girl. "I can't."

"Yes you can," said the man. "If you love me, you can. Or don't you love me?"

"But I never did it," said the girl.

"If you don't want to, then say so," said the man.

"But I do want to," said the girl. "I do."

He laid one arm around her shoulders, and now they were coming toward me. I flattened myself deeper into the shadow and they walked past me without seeing me, and the girl said, "You'll be the first."

I ran across the courtyard in my stocking feet, and through the narrow passage. The dirty red curtain touched my face as I passed through it. The film was still running . . .

I slipped back into my seat, flattened down my hair, wiped the sweat out of my eyes, and tried to breathe more slowly. On the canvas the good were just being rewarded and the evil punished and justice was triumphing in spite of all obstacles. Dramatic finale music, and the lights went on. The redheaded usherette came into the auditorium and called out, "Exit right!" She showed the few people the way out, in the course of which she came upon me again, and I said, "No go? You're sure?" She threw back her head and said to the dirty curtain, "The guys in this country really have a nerve. I've just about had it!" So that she would be sure not to forget me, I patted her on the hips again, and she slapped my hand again, but by now she was laughing.

I walked home slowly. I wasn't in a hurry any more. I strolled along the Rhine and saw the lights on the other side and a ship gliding over the dark water. The people on board were singing, and someone was playing the concertina. I breathed in the smoky, autumnal air and looked forward to the summer that would follow this winter, because Julius Brummer would not live to see it. It would be a beautiful summer for little Mickey and her father, and for Nina and me. All would be well when Julius Brummer was dead.

Suddenly I was very tired. My legs ached as I walked up the spiral staircase to my small apartment over the garage. I had locked the entrance door. Now I opened it. On the floor lay a letter. Somebody must have slid it under the door. When I saw Nina's handwriting, my heart beat fast. I tore open the envelope. A sheet of paper fell out. I picked it up and read, "I must speak to you. My husband is going to the lawyer tomorrow afternoon. Be at the boat at 3:30."

I sat down on my bed and held the letter up to my face because I hoped it had caught some of her perfume, but it smelled only of paper, and I thought how Nina was writing letters again. I looked out of my window, across at hers. She was standing behind the curtain. I could see her silhouette. She must have been waiting for me. Now she moved, and the light went out in her room. I turned out the light in mine, and this action on both our parts seemed to join us with a profound tenderness. It was as if the dark descended upon us like the warm cover of a bed in which we were lying together, our arms around each other, protecting each other, united in the night.

251

6

She was wearing flat, black shoes, a black raincoat, and a black scarf around her head, with her blond hair flowing from under it. The weather was uncertain. It had already rained hard twice, but now the sun was shining again. The east wind was driving ragged grey clouds across the pale blue sky. The shadows they cast sailed across the water.

I was at the little boat restaurant punctually at 3:30. Nina was already there. She was standing on the street, partially hidden by an old chestnut tree. I had left Brummer at Dr. Zorn's. I was to pick him up at five.

One hour . . . only one hour, yet to me it seemed like a promise of eternity when I saw Nina through the windshield, running toward me. I opened the right door and she flung herself down on the seat beside me. She was breathing hard; the wind had given her color. She had never looked more beautiful.

"We've got to get away from here!"

"But why?" I could smell her perfume, the scent of her hair. Desire threatened to overwhelm me. She said, "I'm afraid."

"Of what?"

"Of him!" she screamed. "Of him!" And then, "For God's sake, *go!*"

I drove off. She sat there and didn't look at me, and the shadows the clouds made glided across the water, across the highway and across us. I drove for ten minutes, then Nina said, "Here."

I stopped. Sparsely wooded meadowland lay below the highway in both directions. Here the Rhine was some distance away from the road and on the land between there were shrubs, their foliage turned orange, gnarled willows,

252

high reeds, and overgrown paths leading to a wooded area. "Drive the car off the road," said Nina.

I drove to a thicket at the edge of the woods and parked it under an old tree. Here you couldn't see it from the road. Nina got out and walked into the thicket. She walked so fast, I had a hard time following her. Branches hit me in the face, I stumbled over roots and slipped in little puddles of swamp water. Nina walked on and on into the wood, which grew denser, the trees higher. Frogs were croaking and a few crows flew away above us, cawing. On the highway I could hear a car speeding by, its tires humming.

In a small clearing, Nina stopped. Gigantic old trees rose all around us, the sand, algae and grasses of recent floodwaters still visible on their white-washed trunks. It was twilight in the clearing. You could hear the river rushing by. There was a smell of rotting wood. Nina was watching me approach. Her nostrils were quivering, her eyes were glistening, so were her lips. I embraced her, and she moaned softly. I took her face in both hands and she threw her arms around me and clung to me, and as we kissed I thought of the young people at the exit door of the little movie house. Innocents . . .

Nina closed her eyes but I kept mine open, and I could see her white skin, her silky lashes and golden hair, so near . . . and the shadows of the clouds passed over us and we were happy. Then she pushed me away and her face was hard, her voice was harsh, and she said, "He won't give me a divorce."

"I know," I said, and tried to take her hand, but she stepped back until the trunk of a tree stopped her. "You know? How do you know?"

"He told me. On the way to Munich. He also refused to let me go."

She stuck both hands in her pockets and spoke to me as if I had been her worst enemy. "And you? What did you do?"

"Nothing."

I couldn't tell her what I had done in the meantime. She was not to know. And if she despised me for it, if she hated me . . . *she must not know.*

"Nothing?" she repeated coolly. "Well, that's just great.

253

You do nothing, you say nothing, you leave me without news. I have to write to you, and you . . ." (now she was no longer using the intimate *Du*) "you profess to love me?" She was breathing hard.

"Nina, I . . ."

"Don't call me Nina. You have no right to call me Nina. You've lied to me, you've deceived me. Nothing's real about you . . . nothing!"

I moved toward her and wanted to draw her to me, but she shouted, "Stay where you are! I thought it was your intention to give notice, Herr Holden. I thought you wanted to go away with me, Herr Holden, and live with me. In poverty, if necessary."

"I can't leave him. He knows too much about me."

"What does he know? What?"

"That I wanted to blackmail him. That I was in jail. That I'll have to go back to jail if he reports me. He has me in his power. *He* has deceived you, not I. I don't want to go back to jail."

"And I?" Now she was pale. She pressed both fists against her breasts. "And I? He comes to me every night. He was never more gentle. He longs for me, so he says. And he comes every night and doesn't go away. He sleeps with me. In my bed!"

"Don't!"

"Why? Is listening to it worse? Would you like to hear what he does? What he calls me? What he says? You don't want to hear it, do you?"

"No!" I shouted.

"Well," she whispered, "that's beautiful. Shout at me. *That* takes courage. How courageous you are, Herr Holden! And so clever. Such big plans, so much good advice. And now? What do you advise me to do now?"

"You've got to be sensible. I'll think of something . . ." My voice sounded far away. "We mustn't do anything hasty."

"Right. Nothing hasty." Her eyes were black, her face was a mask of disdain. "We have time. Let him come again, today, tomorrow, the day after tomorrow. To his dear little Nina who delights him, whom he adores!" Now she was shouting. "Last night, when you came home, you saw me standing at the window, didn't you? Well, I wasn't alone. He was with me. It was he who turned out the light, not I!"

I didn't dare to tell her anything. I had to listen to her every reproach, endure all her scorn . . . I said nothing.

She went on in a quiet, venomous tone that was more unbearable than her shouting. "You're a coward. A sentimental, phony coward. I remind you of your wife, and that's it. What you call love is nothing but your guilty conscience."

Again I said nothing, and I could hear the river rushing by, the birds screeching. "And I trusted you," she was saying in that same tone of quiet scorn. "I relied on you. My God, I have more respect for *him!* He at least gets what he wants. He's a man!" She held her face between both hands and stared at me as if I had been a stranger.

I turned around without a word and began to walk back along the narrow path, through the underbrush, and the branches struck me in the face again and scratched me. Five steps . . . seven . . . then I heard her cry, "Holden!"

Eight steps, nine, ten . . .

"Holden! Please . . . come back."

But I didn't go back. I walked to the car, got behind the wheel and drove toward the highway. As I turned the car around, I saw her. She was stumbling out of the wood; her scarf had slipped down over her shoulders, her coat was open. She stretched out her arms, pleadingly. "Please . . ."

I stepped on the gas. The heavy car lurched up onto the highway, skidded, then shot forward. I sat crouched over the steering wheel and watched the speedometer needle swing to the right, and saw the road with the old trees flying toward me, saw the birds skimming over the water, ragged clouds in the sky, a ship in the distance. I didn't see Nina any more. I didn't turn around to look. I couldn't. I didn't have the strength.

7

That happened on Thursday.

On Friday the terror began, the terror I had thought up and set in motion . . .

At eleven I drove Julius Brummer and his beautiful wife into the city. No one spoke. The two sat in the back. I could see them in the mirror. Nina looked wretched. There were deep shadows under her eyes and she had put on much too much makeup. Julius Brummer had folded his little fingers over his stomach. Sometimes he puckered his lips and whistled. When he wasn't looking at his wife, he was looking at me, either at my back or at my face in the mirror. Something seemed to have put him in a good mood because once he laughed out loud. And I thought: every night, every night . . .

When we got to Lützowstrasse, I heard him say, "Have the tire checked here, Holden."

"Yes, Herr Brummer," I replied. The right front tire of the Cadillac had too little air. Brummer had noticed it as we left. It had too little air because I had let some out the night before.

The gas station was ahead of us. I let the car roll up to the air pump. Paul came running out. "Good morning, everybody," he said cheerfully. He was wearing a band-aid over the big pimple on his forehead. A new one was brewing on the tip of his nose.

"The right front tire needs air," I said.

Paul ran off and got the gauge. He knelt down, unscrewed the cap and in a few minutes had the tire filled again.

"Thanks, Paul," I said, and gave him twenty pfennigs.

He reddened. "Oh . . . Herr Holden . . ."

All ready to drive off, I said, "Yes?"

His face got redder. He was terribly embarrassed. His dirty little hands opened and closed nervously. He lowered his head and his voice. "I wouldn't mention it, but the boss balanced the books yesterday and I had to give him the money. Could you please pay me back?"

"Pay you back? For what?" I asked, begging him for forgiveness in my mind and thinking how all this was happening to save the life of an innocent child, a child that couldn't defend herself.

"But you remember, Herr Holden . . ." Now Paul's voice was so low, you could barely understand him. "Twenty-four marks thirty. Please don't be mad, but it's only because I have to pay an installment on the bike, latest tomorrow . . ."

Brummer's irritated voice from the back. "What's the matter with the boy?"

I turned around. Brummer's eyes glittered suspiciously. Nina was looking at me too, wearily, sadly.

"No idea, Herr Brummer. I don't know what he wants."

Brummer rolled down the window on his side and pointed a rosy finger at Paul. "You . . . what's your name?"

"Paul."

"Does my chauffeur owe you money, Paul?"

"Yes," said Paul.

"No," said I.

We spoke simultaneously. Then we stared at each other. Paul's mouth was open. "B-b-but, Herr Holden!"

"But what?" I said. "Come on, Paul. Pull yourself together. Have I ever left owing you money since we don't charge any more?"

"No. Never—"

"So there you are!"

"—until the day before yesterday. You said you didn't have any money on you. For God's sake, you *must* remember it!"

Now I let my hands fall from the steering wheel, my shoulders sag, and counted to seven. I would have counted further, but when I got to seven, I heard Brummer's voice. "So what's going on, Holden?"

I turned around again. "Herr Brummer, I've known

257

Paul ever since I've been working for you. The boy's honest. There must be some misunderstanding. I—"

"Stop all this nonsense, Holden. Did you get gas here the day before yesterday? Yes or no?"

"If I got gas here, I'd say so. What reason would I have not to say so?"

The boy was white as a sheet now; even his pimples had paled. "Oh God, Herr Holden, but you *were* here! You talked to me. We shook hands. I'm not crazy!"

"And I'm not crazy either. *I was not here!*"

The owner of the gas station, a lanky, wounded veteran called Merz, came over. Merz had lost an arm in the war. "What's wrong, Herr Brummer?"

Grunting, Brummer got out of the car. So did I. As I did so, I turned and saw Nina. Her eyes were filled with fear. Without making a sound, her lips formed a word. I looked away quickly.

Now the four of us were standing beside the red and black Cadillac. The wind was driving rustling leaves over the lot. Suddenly Paul started to bawl. The tears ran over his poor, acne-scarred skin into his mouth. He licked them away and shook his head and looked stupefied. Brummer explained the situation. Merz was a decent fellow and wasn't easily impressed by anyone. "Herr Brummer, I'll vouch for any of my employees. The kid's honest. He doesn't lie."

Now it was my turn to get excited. "Look here, Herr Merz. Are you trying to say *I'm* lying?"

"I'm not trying to say anything," was the cool reply.

With the canny logic that had made millions for him, Brummer shouted, "But one of the two *has* to be lying!"

I had my back turned to the car, but still I could feel Nina's eyes on me. I said to Paul, "When was I supposed to be here? Come on, tell me. This whole dumb thing isn't my fault. So . . . when was I here?"

Paul sobbed, "The day before yesterday. Around quarter to seven."

I said to Brummer, "But that's when I was at the movies."

"Herr Holden, Herr Holden, I don't want the twenty-four marks thirty any more. I'll pay for the gas. *Just say you were here!*"

"Come on, Paul. This is getting us nowhere. *I was not here!*"

There was silence. Brummer whistled again. Then he spat and rubbed out the spittle with his foot. Then he turned to the boy. Whipping up and down on his little feet, he said, "All right now, let's see. My Cadillac was here the day before yesterday, shortly before seven."

"Yes, Herr Brummer."

"And my chauffeur bought gas."

"I was in the movies!"

"Be quiet, Holden. Go on, Paul. What was my chauffeur wearing?"

"I don't know any more . . . yes, I do. He had on a brown suit and a green tie, and a white shirt."

"I don't own a brown suit!" I yelled.

"Don't get excited, Holden. Nobody's going to do anything to you."

"I must insist that this thing is cleared up right away."

"You don't have to insist," said Brummer. "I am interested in just that, myself." He took his fat wallet out of his pocket and counted out thirty marks. "Let's settle the money end of it first. Here. The rest is for Paul."

"I don't want your money, Herr Brummer," the boy cried in despair. "I want you to believe me!"

"Yes, yes. Calm down, boy. Of course I believe you." He turned to Merz. "May I use your phone?"

Merz led Brummer over to the booth. He turned around once and glared at me. He was convinced that I was lying. Everybody was convinced I was lying, thank God.

"Paul!"

It was Nina's voice. I turned around. She had moved over to the open window and was smiling encouragingly at the boy, who was trembling with excitement. "Are you *sure* it was Herr Holden?" she asked. "Couldn't it have been some other man?"

"It *was* Herr Holden! I swear by the life of my mother!"

She looked at me. I shook my head. Paul screamed. "I don't care if Herr Merz fires me! I'll say it again and again! *You were here!*"

Moving lightly on tiptoe, Brummer came back. The wind blew dry leaves against his black, sharply creased pants. He was whistling again. He stopped in front of me and whistled in my face for what seemed quite a long time. Then he said, "Home."

"But you wanted to—"

"Didn't you hear me? I said home!"

Then we played the game: who can stare at whom longest, and I lost and opened the car door for him. I got in behind the wheel and saw Nina's wide eyes in the mirror and looked to one side into Paul's tragic eyes and thought that I'd done quite a lot of damage for a starter. But then I saw Julius Brummer in the mirror, and the sight of him gave me a lift. Because he wasn't whistling any more; he wasn't humming; he wasn't laughing. He sat there pale and disturbed, and he was afraid. Only he didn't know yet of what. Soon he would know.

8

"Please remain available," said Brummer.

He got out of the car and began to walk toward the villa. After a few steps he turned around and barked at his wife, "Come on! What are you waiting for?" Nina had stopped in front of me and was staring at me as if she had never seen me before. Now she started and obediently followed her husband.

I looked after them until both had disappeared, then I went to my room over the garage, got out a bottle of cognac and drank a swig, but only one. I sat down beside my window and waited. Half an hour later, Dr. Zorn arrived. I saw him and Brummer walking up and down beside the lake. The little lawyer had on a light blue suit. His white hair glistened in the pale light of the October sun. From time to time Brummer stopped and gestured vehemently. The little lawyer calmed him down and they went on walking beside the water, through the autumn leaves and autumn crocus and rotting grass. Finally they drove off quite suddenly in Zorn's car.

An hour later my phone rang. It was Mila Blehova. "Your lunch is ready, Herr Holden."

"I'll be right over."

In the kitchen, Mila had laid the table for the two of us. The blind old dog whimpered when I walked in. "Hush, Mitzili."

But Mitzi didn't hush and refused to calm down. She sniffed at my trousers and whimpered and barked. I shoved her aside, but she kept coming back. She was whimpering as if she were afraid of something. In the end Mila let her out into the garden. "Why are you such a nuisance today? Wish I knew what was wrong with you."

She sat down with me. "I think all of us are going crazy. Looks like I've cooked for nothing. My Nina doesn't want to eat, the *gnä' Herr*? No. Isn't hungry. All we need now is for you to say you're not hungry."

"But I am hungry."

"Well, thank goodness for that. At least one of us. Meatballs. Help yourself, and take plenty." She swallowed as if it hurt. "I'm belching again. You know, Herr Holden, it's an awful thing to say because I love my Nina so much and I'm devoted to the *gnä' Herr*, as you know, but with all the excitement lately, I do think sometimes . . . I wouldn't mind being on my own. With my thyroid . . . I just can't take it. Something's happened *again*."

"What makes you think that?"

"My Ninale cried, the *gnä' Herr* yelled at her. They won't tell me a thing. Why? Because they don't want to upset me. As if hearing them going on like that didn't upset me! You know what?"

"What?"

"I'd like to be on my own. I really would." She belched again, and the pain brought the tears to her eyes. She pushed her plate away. "It's just too stupid! Now *I* can't eat! Oh dear Jesus . . . and things used to run so smoothly, so peacefully."

The house phone rang.

"I'll answer it, Mila. Don't get up."

I picked up the receiver while Mila groaned, and there

261

was his voice again, brutish yet fearful at the same time. "Get over here to my office."

"Right away, Herr Brummer."

"And now your meatballs will get cold," said Mila. "What sort of a life is this, anyway?"

Between kitchen and hall there was a short passage with doors at either end. With both of them closed one found oneself in a dark, windowless area. The minute the kitchen door swung to behind me I could smell Nina's perfume. Then she had thrown her arms around me, and her lips were on mine. I couldn't see her, I could only feel her body. She kissed me. "Forgive me," she said. "For yesterday."

This was madness. At any moment one of the doors might open. Mila could come in, the butler, one of the maids, Brummer. Nina's beloved voice in the dark. "I'm so frightened. What's going on?"

"I don't know."

"When can I see you?"

"Tomorrow. On the boat. At three."

"I'll be there."

She slipped out of my arms, the kitchen door opened and closed and I was alone in the dark. Her scent remained with me.

I walked out into the hall and looked in a mirror and wiped some lipstick off my mouth. Then I walked to Brummer's office, knocked on the door and opened it. I saw Brummer, I saw Zorn, and I saw six strange men.

9

The six men were all about my size and looked my age. They stood in a row in front of a window. The room was large, bookshelves lined the walls. Brummer read a lot. He suffered from the *idée fixe* that he was uneducated.

Near the fireplace there was a desk. On it stood a large photograph of Nina. When I saw it I suddenly felt hot. I had never been in this room before. The photograph showed Nina in a tight-fitting bathing suit, on the beach, waving and laughing. It was the same photograph I had seen in Toni Vorm's apartment.

Brummer and Zorn were standing side by side. The little lawyer was straightening out the fringe of the Persian carpet with his foot. I bowed to him.

"Good day. Please go and stand over there, Herr Holden. Between the second and third men from the left."

So I went and stood between the second and third men from the left, who continued to stare straight ahead, like all the rest. The little lawyer . . . today he had on a silver-grey vest with small orange squares . . . went over to a wainscot door and the red-haired usherette walked into the room. She was all dressed up and seemed very excited. She was wearing a skin-tight black silk suit which she proceeded to model provocatively. She could hardly walk in her very high-heeled shoes. Her jacket was cut low and her red hair tumbled loose over her shoulders. She looked at all of us, standing at the window, giggled nervously and reddened. "Yes," she said. "He's there."

"Which one is he?" asked Zorn, tugging at his collar.

"The third one from the left," said the girl.

"Are you sure?"

"Quite sure. May I say something? He was fresh, I must admit, but he made a nice impression. I don't think he's done anything bad."

"All right, all right," said Zorn. "Here's twenty marks for your trouble. Don't worry about it. The whole thing's a joke."

"Oh."

"Yes. We made a bet about something."

"I see."

Zorn paid the men too, nonchalantly and disdainfully. He gave me nothing. "Thank you, gentlemen. You may go. Through the hall, then left. The door is open."

The men left silently, the redhead looked at me once more, curiously, then she left too. Brummer sat down on the desk, his short legs dangling; Zorn sat down in a leather armchair.

"Herr Holden," said the lawyer, clipping off the tip of a cigar. "I t-t-take it you've had thoughts of your own about what just t-t-took place."

I was delighted to hear him stammer. I looked at the photograph on the desk and thought of Nina's soft lips. "Yes," I said.

"And with wh-wh-what results?"

I turned to Brummer, who was swinging his legs and pulling at his blond moustache. "If you believe the boy and not me, then I repeat my request that you accept my notice, Herr Brummer."

"That would suit you, wouldn't it?" he replied, snorting. "You stay with me or you go back to jail."

"Then I shall bring charges."

"Against whom?"

"Against the boy. He's lying."

"I don't think he's lying," said Brummer.

"Then I shall report the man who used your Cadillac the other day and bought gas at the Lützow garage."

"You're not going to do that either," said Brummer.

"And what's to stop me?"

"I'll stop you. If you report anything, I'll do the same. Is that clear?"

I said nothing.

"Of course we are convinced, Herr Holden," said the little lawyer, "that it was you who bought gas at the Lützow station. What we don't know is why you are denying it."

"I was in the movies. The girl recognized me."

"Now listen to me. Herr Brummer and I were in a m-m-movie house a while ago." He tugged at his collar. "In the daytime." He blew great clouds of smoke into the air. "When the lights went out, I left. Half an hour later I came back. I used the exit. Herr Brummer didn't notice it. The usher didn't either. If this is your alibi, Herr Holden, I f-f-feel sorry for you."

I thought: but you can only stammer that you feel sorry for me. I said, "And why on earth should I try to create such an alibi? Why should I drive the car to a garage where they know me? Why should I deliberately put myself in the position I am in now?"

"Perhaps because this position suits you," said the little

lawyer. "You're a man who's always making plans. Once you wanted to blackmail us. Then you wanted to give notice. Always fresh plans, Herr Holden, always fresh plans . . ." And he and Brummer looked at each other and laughed heartily, and winked at each other as if they had an amusing secret . . .

10

In the afternoon I drove to the station again. This time I found a place to park. It was 3:15. Brummer and Zorn had gone to the prosecutor's office; I was to pick them up at six. So I had a lot of time for what I intended to do. I went to the baggage room, got my suitcase, went to the washroom and changed into the brown suit and green tie. I put the suitcase in the car. I took a taxi and told the driver to drive north as far as Frauenlobweg. As we drove, I looked to see if anyone was following us, but I could see no one. I took a second taxi to Artusstrasse. Here I went to an optician and bought a pair of dark glasses. In another shop I bought a white, blind man's cane. I had them wrap the cane. I took a third taxi to Recklinghauserstrasse, and all the time I watched to see if anyone was following me.

At Recklinghauserstrasse I got out and waited until the taxi had disappeared. Then I stepped into the hallway of a house, put on the dark glasses and unwrapped the white cane. I stuffed the paper in my pocket. After that I walked slowly, tapping on the sidewalk with the cane, around the corner into Hattingerstrasse. Now I had to cross the street. An old woman helped me. "God bless you," I said.

In moments of contemplation and inner calm, Julius Brummer supported charitable institutions. He donated money to hospitals, orphanages, and an infantile-paralysis association. In the Hattingerstrasse he had financed a rehabilitation center for the blind. Beside the entrance of the grey, dilapidated building you could read: Julius Maria Brummer Foundation for the Blind. First floor.

I walked into the entrance hall. It smelled of cabbage and rancid fat. Somewhere a child screamed, a radio was turned on loud, and some of the windows in the hallway were boarded up. Julius Brummer hadn't exactly chosen the finest house for his charitable efforts, nor the cleanest. But what did it matter? The blind couldn't see the dirt; all they could do was smell it.

On the first floor there was a dirty door that didn't close properly. It opened onto a dirty waiting room with the view of a dismal courtyard. A photograph of the philanthropist hung on one wall. Underneath it the inscription: *To lose hope is the only sin. Julius Maria Brummer.*

I thought of the fact that the blind couldn't see Julius Maria Brummer's face and couldn't read his advice to them, and what a pity that was.

I walked into the next room, which was just as dirty as the first. Here, too, there was a photograph of Brummer, but no quote. There was a table, a few chairs, a typewriter. Cans of floor wax, woven baskets and sandals, clotheslines, blankets, and other things the blind make to sell lay on the floor. A young girl sat behind the typewriter. She was wearing a black skirt, a white blouse, and a gold belt. Her bra lifted her ample bosom to an aggressively protruding bastion and around her hips her skirt looked ready to burst its zipper. She was made up like a nightclub star, she even had false eyelashes, and her nails were lacquered gold. Her mouth was a flaming red. For whom, I wondered? For whom all this here? A few horseflies were buzzing against the closed windows. It didn't seem to bother the girl. I tapped my way up to her, greeted her humbly, and she responded to my greeting with a hearty "Welcome!" I noticed suddenly that she had a harelip. The blind couldn't see it, I thought, which was probably why . . .

"My name," I said, and couldn't help being amused, "is Zorn. Hilmar Zorn. I haven't been living in Düsseldorf very long. I come from Berlin, where I took a typing course. I've been told you have a similar course here."

"That's right," said the girl with the harelip. She came

266

up to me and shook my hand vigorously. Her eyes were shining. She must have been about twenty-five, and she reeked to high heaven of cheap scent.

"I suppose you belong to an Association for the Blind, Herr Zorn?"

"Of course."

"How old are you, Herr Zorn?" At last she let go my hand, but she remained standing in front of me, and the tip of her red tongue flicked constantly across her harelip.

"Forty-four."

"Do you want to register now?"

"Perhaps I could find out first how you operate here?"

"Are you married, Herr Zorn?"

"No."

"There are a lot of unmarried men here," said the girl. "By the way, my name is Licht. Grete Licht."

"Pleased to meet you. Have you been working here for a long time, Frau Licht?"

"Fräulein," she said. "Ever since it was founded. Before that I worked for a motion picture company. I left because the guys were so fresh. Here all the men are polite." She hooked her arm in mine and pressed it close. "I like polite men. If anyone gets fresh with me, he'll soon find out where he can go. Come on, I'll show you where the workroom is."

"Don't you get lonely, working here?"

"Never. You can't imagine the stories I hear! You know . . . I'm not saying this just to be nice, but when I get married I might very well marry a blind man. Not because of the pension, truly not because of that. But the blind . . . they're different. They're loyal. And attentive. Real gentlemen!" said Grete Licht with the harelip.

In the next room there were a lot of tables. The windows were closed, there was a smell of disinfectant. Fifteen blind men were working in this room, two on raffia rugs and doormats, others knitting. In front of the windows there were five old typewriters. The men working at them were looking straight ahead, their mouths open. They were wearing dark glasses. The girl with the harelip led me up to a machine that wasn't being used and settled me down in a chair in front of it. She led me to the typewriter by the hand, and with her hand showed me where the paper lay.

"The teacher's gone home. There are different exercises every day. Sometimes you have to write something you've memorized from dictation, or a composition of your own. You can learn other things here too. Would you like me to dictate something to you?"

"No, thank you. I'd like to practice a little first. See if I still can." I inserted a sheet of paper in the typewriter, feeling my way. She laid a hand on my shoulder and said to the blind man sitting on my right, "Herr Sauer, you'll give Herr Zorn any help he may need, won't you?"

Sauer looked like a man about my age. "Be glad to, Fräulein Grete," he said, and went on typing.

The girl with the harelip left. On her way out she laid her hand on the shoulders of two other men, and they turned in her direction and looked at her with their dead eyes and smiled happily.

I began to type. I typed the alphabet, making a few mistakes and ragged margins, then I typed numbers from one to ten. I typed the Lord's Prayer. It was a very old typewriter. Julius Brummer hadn't spent a fortune here. I could read the composition Herr Sauer was writing. "What makes people happy?" was the title. I read, "Peopld are mad hoppy wen they hev anoder persone who love him. I loav my wife. My wif cheet. 3 & - ? I hev none it fer weegs. I folllo her in tadi and herd her taling with him. It cos a lt of moni but sje fifnt notise it and I kpow now tha my wif is upfathful to me."

He was doing all right . . .

I took my sheet of paper out of the machine and inserted a fresh one, and while the blind wove baskets and wrote compositions about the happiness of man, I wrote on the miserable paper of the Julius Maria Brummer Foundation for the Blind:

You know that I exist. I look like your chauffeur. That's too bad for you. And too bad for your chauffeur. If you don't do as I say, I shall kill you. Your chauffeur will go to prison for it. Your chauffeur, not I. Because we, you and I, don't know each other and I have no motive for killing you. I am only doing what my employer tells me to do. Your chauffeur knows you. He has plenty of reasons to kill you. Any court will recognize that.

I succeeded in taking your Cadillac out of the garage, and passing as your chauffeur; I bought gas. There will be many other things I will be able to do. You will do as I say, or you will die. My employer wants to see you where you belong: in jail. You are trying to get the reporter Romberg to relinquish a photograph. You will stop every effort in this respect immediately. I shall kill you if you don't do as I say. And your chauffeur will go to jail for it. Your chauffeur, not I.

Then I wrote the address on a cheap green envelope I had bought on my way here.

"You write first-rate," said Herr Sauer.

"Could be worse."

"Say, could you possibly lend me five marks? I'll repay you, word of honor."

I said nothing.

"Please. I owe the money to a taxi driver. He won't drive me again until I've paid him. So much depends on his driving me tonight."

11

"Did he try to borrow money from you?" asked Grete Licht. I had spent an hour at the typewriter, writing all sorts of things, which I left beside the machine.

"Who?" I asked.

"Herr Sauer. He tries it on everybody."

"I gave him five marks."

"He's driving himself crazy. Some women have all the luck. You should see the old witch. Older than he is, fat

269

and ugly. But he borrows money for a taxi to follow her around. The driver tells him who she's meeting and where. Then he cries on my shoulder." She came up to me and took my hand again. "Will you come back?"

"Of course I'll come back."

"That'll be nice," said Grete Licht, and pressed my hand to her ample bosom.

In the hallway I took off my dark glasses and wrapped up my cane again. In the Hattingerstrasse I hailed a taxi and drove to the station. I changed, and put the glasses and the cane in the suitcase with my other things, and checked it again.

I mailed the letter to Brummer at the main post office. Five forty-five. I drove to the prosecutor's office. At ten minutes past six little Dr. Zorn came out. "We're going to be here at least two hours more." At the time it didn't occur to me that other people also needed an alibi.

"Good night, *Herr Doktor*," I said, and drove to the Rhine. When I got to the gates of the villa I could see they were open, and that a woman was standing between them, and my heart began to beat wildly. I stopped. Nina was out of breath. "Thank God you're here! I've been waiting for ages."

"What's happened?"

The wind blew her blond hair into her mouth. "Mickey . . ."

"What's happened to her?" An icy hand was reaching for my heart.

"We must go to the Rombergs. Mickey has disappeared."

12

The fog crept up from the Rhine, the air was damp, the sky was dark. I drove so slowly that the trees on Cecilien-allee came forward singly into the rays of the headlights. Nina said, "Romberg called Mila. The child had classes until one. At three her parents started looking for her. Poor Mila. She got so excited, she had to lie down. The doctor's with her now."

I made a left turn and the car drove silently westward, up Parkstrasse. "Robert?"

"Yes?"

"Has . . . has my husband anything to do with this?"

I said, "Do you remember the day you came home from the hospital? Romberg took pictures of all of us; one of Mickey and me. Your husband wants that picture."

"But why?"

"That was the day Herr Schwertfeger's girlfriend jumped out of a ninth-floor window. She was the girl who ran her car into our Mercedes. Mickey saw her and heard her name. Hilde Lutz. With that photo, and with Mickey, Romberg can prove that a connection exists between Hilde Lutz, your husband and Herr Schwertfeger."

"And you think that he . . . that he intends to black-mail Romberg with the child?"

"I know that is his intention."

She pressed her hands against her temples and groaned. "It's your fault! You let him have the documents."

I braked so hard that Nina was thrown forward. Her forehead hit the dashboard and she cried out. I tried to grasp her, but she jumped out of the car. I followed her to the apartment house where the Rombergs lived. We took the elevator to the third floor. Nina rang the bell, we could hear steps, the door was flung open. Maria Romberg stood

271

in the doorway, looking pale and frightened. Her brown hair fell in a disorderly fashion over her forehead. She wasn't wearing her glasses and her eyes were red from weeping. Behind her I could see into Mickey's room with the empty bed and the bright toy animals—cat, monkey, lamb, dog . . .

Frau Romberg saw us but she said nothing. Nina said, "Have you heard anything?"

Maria Romberg shook her head.

"May we come in?"

"Who is it?" Peter Romberg's voice, coming from his office. Almost at once he was there. His face was so pale his freckles looked blue. His red hair stood away from his head, more unkempt than ever. His voice was filled with hatred. "Shut the door, Maria."

She tried to close the door, but I put one foot against it and said, "Just a minute. I must speak to you."

Romberg was so enraged, he could barely say the two words, "Get out!"

"But for God's sake," said Nina, "it isn't our fault that Mickey has disappeared."

Romberg pointed at me. "Ask him whose fault it is. I'm sorry for you, Frau Brummer. You were always good to us."

From his office we could hear the police monitor: "Düssel seven . . . Düssel seven . . . Proceed to Heysestrasse. A drunken brawl. Düssel seven . . . Düssel seven . . ."

I said, "Romberg, for God's sake come to your senses! Do you want to wait until they kill your daughter?"

Maria Romberg screamed.

"I told you to stay out of it. I told you to forget all about it! Why didn't you do as I told you?"

"You're capable of every crime in the book, aren't you, Holden?"

"I want to help you, Romberg. Give me the photo . . ."

". . . and I get Mickey back. Just what I figured."

"You damn fool! Then give the photo to the prosecutor! *Do something with it!*"

"I'm going to do something with it! You can depend on that! My paper will do something, just as soon as we have enough evidence. The prosecutor! That would suit you, wouldn't it? Plenty of evidence went to the prosecutor, and what happened? Herr Brummer is free! An honorable man!" He lowered his voice but it was still filled with hatred. "When we get going, millions are going to hear about it, millions of *decent* people, and then we'll see what happens to your fine boss! And to you!"

"And Mickey? What's going to happen to her? Does that fucking photo mean more to you than the life of your child?"

He stepped up close to me. "If any harm comes to Mickey," he hissed, "then God help all of you."

"You're crazy! By then it'll be too late!"

"We thought you were our friend . . . "

"I am your friend!" I screamed.

"You're a louse! That's what you are! A fucking liar!"

"Herr Romberg!" Nina cried.

The door of the apartment opposite opened. A fat man stood in the doorway, his suspenders dangling. "Anything wrong, Herr Romberg? Who are these people? Do you want to call the police?"

"Yes," said Romberg. "Please call the police."

I grasped Nina's hand and forced her to follow me down the stairs. I heard the fat man ask, "Who were they?" and Romberg answer, "Scum!" Then I heard both doors close.

I didn't let Nina's hand go until we reached the car. I got behind the wheel. The street was deserted, the wind was driving the leaves across the pavement. Their rustling was the only sound in the stillness.

"Do you . . . do you have a cigarette?"

We smoked.

"It's not all your fault," she said. "I'm just as much to blame."

"Nonsense!"

She shook her head. "When a crime is committed, not only those who commit it are guilty, but those who let it happen."

"Platitudes. He is strong, we are weak. He has money, we have none. It's my fault. I could have prevented it. Without the documents he would have been powerless, he would have been convicted. Today he laughs at us."

She was silent and I could hear the night wind sighing

and the dead leaves rustling. Suddenly she whispered, "Robert?"

"Yes?"

"I think, just now, I have begun to love you."

"Nina . . ."

"I mean it. At first I couldn't stand you; then I was afraid of you. But now, when you touch me . . . it was never like that before. Now I know—I have begun to love you."

"Why?"

"Because you said it was your fault. Because you let Romberg insult you. You're not as clever as he is, not so cunning. You're no match for him. Robert, you're not courageous."

"No," I said. "I'm not courageous."

She put her arms around me and kissed me softly on the cheek. I said, "What if somebody sees us?"

"Coward," she said, and kissed me on the mouth. "I don't know what's going to happen, Robert. But I promise you, when it's all over, and if we survive, and if you and I are ever free, I shall be a good wife to you, Robert."

She kissed me again, and above her golden hair I looked out onto the deserted street and thought of a poem I'd read in prison, a long time ago: "Coward, take the hand of a coward . . ."

I sat up so suddenly, I startled Nina. "What is it?" Then she saw what I saw—a little black-haired girl in a red coat, coming up the street wearily, leaning against the wind, a school satchel strapped to her back.

Nina jumped out of the car, and I opened the window so that I could hear what they said. "Mickey, darling! Whatever have you been up to? Where have you been?"

"Who's that in the car?"

"Herr Holden."

"I don't like him."

"Why?"

"He doesn't tell the truth."

"Mickey, where have you been?"

"Well, there were these two men outside school and I asked them what the time was because I wanted to know if I could stay out and play a little longer with my friend, but it was too late, and they said they'd take me home. They had a beautiful car."

"But Mickey, you know you've been told *never* to go with strangers!"

"I know. But it was so late. So I went with them. And then their car broke down and we had to wait."

"Where?"

"In a big house. I don't know where it was, but they gave me lemonade and some coloring books . . . "

"But what about your parents? Didn't you think of them?"

"Of course I did. One of the men said he'd call them right away. Oh, *Tante* Nina, didn't he call?"

"No, Mickey. He didn't."

"Well, I can't understand that. They were so nice. They gave me suckers and now, when they brought me home, one of them called my father, from the booth at the corner. I saw him do it."

"Up you go now, straight home!"

"Well, of course, Tante Nina. Where else should I go?"

Nina walked with her to the entrance of the house, then she came back to me and I drove off.

"I must report my husband to the police."

"Nonsense!"

"He'll have the child murdered. He'll stop at nothing. That call from the booth . . . can you imagine what the man told Romberg? If he doesn't give up the photo, Mickey will disappear again, and this time forever!"

"Can you prove that your husband had anything to do with it? Right now he's with Lofting, been with him for hours."

"But we can't just sit back and let him kill the child!"

"The child won't be killed. Romberg will give up the photo. He's not an idiot," I said, and didn't believe a word of it. Neither did she.

A sudden gust of wind blew through the treetops of Cecilienallee, and I saw choppy little waves on the Rhine. The dry leaves danced a ghostly ballet.

A car was parked in front of the villa. I drove into the garage. Nina didn't get out until I did. It was dark in the garage and I bumped against her and threw my arms around her. We clung to each other, her cheek against

275

mine and we listened to the wind whistling outside and the creaking of a large branch.

"Tomorrow at three," Nina whispered. "He has to go to court again. You'll have time. I'll take a taxi."

"I'll be there."

"I'll be thinking of it, Robert. Until tomorrow at three. I'll be thinking of nothing else."

"Neither will I."

"Don't look across at my window any more."

"I have to."

"When . . . when the light goes out, think of me," she whispered. "I'll think of you too, the whole time."

I kissed her hand. She said, "I love you."

"Because I'm a coward?"

"Goodnight, coward."

She walked away quickly. I was about to follow her, but as I was closing the garage door, I heard a voice. Dr. Zorn. "Good evening, *gnädige Frau*."

He was standing on the gravel path, five meters away, a small, thin silhouette. "We heard the car. Herr Brummer asked me to meet you. He wants to speak to you." He pointed a finger at me. "You too, Holden."

The three of us walked to the villa. Once, as we walked, Nina touched my hand. Dr. Zorn said, "We're going to have a storm."

Neither of us said anything.

"What did you say, *gnädige Frau?*"

"I didn't say anything."

"Oh, I'm sorry. It's difficult to hear above the wind."

13

Julius Maria Brummer was sitting on the edge of Mila's bed as we walked into the little room behind the kitchen. The old cook was lying on her back, her breathing shallow and rapid. She looked dreadful. Her face was grey and glistening with sweat, her lips were blue, her hands were clutching her stomach. She had taken out her dentures. They lay immersed in a glass of water.

Julius Brummer was wiping the old woman's forehead gently with a white silk handkerchief. He gave the impression of a son deeply concerned about his mother.

"There they are!" Mila tried to sit up. Gasping, she cried, "Any news of the child, *gnä' Frau*? Have they found her?"

"Mickey is back home, Mila." Nina hurried over to the bed. She stroked Mila's sunken cheeks. "She got home ten minutes ago. Herr Holden and I saw her."

Mila sank back on her pillows. She was crying and laughing. In between she kept trying to swallow; it sounded as if she were choking, and she kept her hands pressed to her stomach. "Is she all right?" she gasped. "Nothing's happened to her?"

"Not a thing, Mila." Nina looked at her husband and addressed him in a loud voice as she went on. "Two men took her with them in a car. They were going to take her home. Then the car broke down. It took so long to repair it."

"Jesus Maria, but I've told Mickey over and over again she's not ever to go with strangers. What do you think of that, *gnä' Herr*? Such a big girl and so stupid. Well, she doesn't have that from me."

Julius Brummer's expression was sentimental. He said softly, "Children will be children. Let us thank God that everything is all right." Just as sentimentally he looked up at Nina. "And thank you, darling."

"For what?" Nina's voice cracked. You could barely understand what she was saying.

"That you took her straight back to her parents." He leaned forward and kissed her hand. "I am sure they must have been grateful for your help."

"Very grateful," said Nina. Her eyes narrowed to slits and she looked at him with an expression of revulsion, but he only smiled and nodded.

"You see . . ." Then he turned to me. "And my thanks to you, Herr Holden. It's good to know one can depend on you."

There was a small noise behind my back. I turned. Dr. Zorn was picking up one of the many photographs of Nina that had fallen off the table by the window.

"Clumsy of me. I bumped into it." And Dr. Zorn smiled amiably and looked pleased.

Suddenly Mila was fighting for breath. She groaned.

"My poor darling," whispered Nina, bending over her.

"I'm really feeling better. It's the excitement. I'll be able to do the venison roast tomorrow, *gnä' Frau.*"

"I won't hear of it!"

"But of course I will. We've got venison roast for the dinner party, remember? Tomorrow I'll be as fit as a fiddle, *gnä' Frau,* you'll see."

Brummer got up and crossed his arms behind his back. His voice was melodious. "What you need, old lady, is a rest. And right away!"

"But I can't leave . . . "

"And why not? If anyone deserves a vacation, it's you."

"No, it's you, *gnä' Herr.*"

"I'm younger. You can't compare the two of us. You've had more than enough excitement here lately. Things just can't go on like this."

"But Merciful Mother in Heaven, where shall I go?"

"Now you listen to me, my good old Mila. You've been with us eleven years. You've served us faithfully, cooked for us, looked after us. You've become ill in my house . . ."

"No, I haven't."

"Yes, you have." He looked up at the lithograph of the Madonna over the bed. "I feel guilty, very guilty."

"Go on, *gnä' Herr* . . . begging your pardon, but you're talking nonsense!"

"No I'm not, and you're only saying so because you're the best person in the world. I know that at heart you'd like to live a more peaceful life."

"Well, yes, perhaps, but not right now!"

"But yes, right now! I have that little house in Schliersee. Mila. I intend to give it to you."

"Please, *gnä' Herr,* please don't talk like that or I'll start belching again."

"Mila, the house is yours. With everything in it. I go on paying your wages, you can visit us whenever you like, but first Holden will drive you down there. And you stay until

278

you feel perfectly well again. Is that clear? I'll write and tell Dr. Schneider to look after you."

"Oh *gnä' Frau,* please tell the *gnä' Herr* that . . . that this is crazy! He shouldn't throw his money around like that, with all he's so rich. I'm not worth it!"

"You're worth it, and a lot more, and you deserve it more than anyone else," said Brummer, and wiped the sweat from her brow again. She grabbed his rosy hand and kissed it.

"No, no!" he protested.

Mila wiped away her tears, but fresh ones kept coming. With her rheumatic fingers, with their broken down nails, she rubbed her eyes. "Ach, *gnä' Frau,* bless my soul, but don't you have the best husband in the world?"

Nina looked at her husband. He was smiling happily. Dr. Zorn was smiling happily. I was smiling happily. "Yes," said Nina, and now she was smiling happily too. "The best husband in the world."

14

My letter arrived in the morning mail. I was in the hall when the haughty new butler separated the letters from the magazines and newspapers the mailman had brought. There it was, the letter I had written with the blind . . .

The new butler put it together with all the rest on a tray and carried it into Brummer's office. The heavy upholstered door closed behind him. Now I had to wait for what was to happen next.

Nothing happened.

Nine o'clock. Nine-thirty. Ten. Ten-thirty.

Nothing happened.

I went to the garage, got out the Cadillac and washed it. I washed the Mercedes. Eleven-thirty. Nothing. I went up to my room. It wasn't good that I had to drink something

279

in the morning to calm down, with everything only just beginning . . .

Just a slug. No more. But after one swallow my hands were trembling so, I spilled most of what I'd poured out and had to take another. And another.

I went back to the garage, took out the third car and washed it. Now it was twelve. At 12:15, Dr. Zorn arrived. He waved genially as he walked past me. At 12:30 the butler appeared and said that Herr Brummer wished to speak to me.

I put on my jacket and walked over to the villa. In Brummer's office the old dog came waddling over to me and rubbed against my knee. Zorn was standing by the window, Brummer was sitting at his desk, and my letter was lying directly in front of him.

"You wanted to see me, Herr Brummer?"

"Yes. I wanted to see you." He looked at me, then he looked at Zorn, then both of them looked at me, then at the letter. It was a cold day, the central heating wasn't on yet, and, although I had felt cold a while before, I was sweating now.

"The dog," said Brummer.

"I beg your pardon?"

"The dog wants to go out. Take her for a walk around the lake." Then he put a piece of chewing gum in his mouth and began to whistle.

"Come on, Mitzili," I said.

It was 12:45.

15

At 2:30 I drove Brummer to the public prosecutor's office. He wanted to hear the news and I had turned on the radio at his request. We heard what was going on in Algiers,

London, and Little Rock. Also what was going on in Germany . . .

"Bonn. In today's session of parliament an opposition party member asked the following question: What steps is the government planning to take in connection with the fact that the case against the Düsseldorf financier, Julius Maria Brummer, the date for which had already been set, had to be postponed because all key prosecution witnesses recanted their expected testimony for no apparent reason? Does the government know that Brummer has been released on five hundred thousand marks bail in spite of the fact that—"

"Turn the mother-fucker off," said Julius Maria Brummer.

I turned off the radio. He hummed and whistled. He said, "Pick up my wife at five. She's at the dressmaker's. Take her home. I don't need you till six."

"Yes, Herr Brummer."

As he got out of the car, he stopped to ask, "Can you type?"

"Yes, sir."

"Well?"

"So-so."

"Well then, at six." And he walked into the building.

It was 2:45. I drove to Grüntorweg. I left the car there and took a taxi to the Rhine. About a kilometer from the restaurant I paid the driver. He turned the car and drove back to the city. I walked along the path beside the river and looked out onto the water, which was roughed up with little waves.

Nina was standing in the shade of the chestnut tree again. When she saw me she began to walk toward me. She had on beige pants and flat beige shoes, a short fur jacket and dark glasses. Around her blond hair she wore a dark scarf. Quite a distance lay between us. First we walked slowly, then faster, in the end we were running. She took my hand and together we strolled upriver. We didn't speak.

The floating restaurant was empty, the deck had been cleared. The old man who looked like Hemingway was on his knees, scrubbing the deck. He didn't notice us. The river path was hidden every now and then by leafy trees. Gulls were circling over the river.

We reached the place where the wooded meadowland began. As she had done before, Nina walked ahead of me into the warm, sandy thicket where the grasses and algae of the last floodwater still clung to the trees. In a clearing Nina stopped and waited for me.

Her lips tasted salty, her breath smelled of fresh milk. We sat down side by side on a small strip of grass and held hands. It was windless and sheltered in the clearing, and above our heads, in the crowns of the old willows, the autumn wind was murmuring. I thought how I would never want another woman, and how happy we would be once I had killed Julius Brummer. And I thought how strange it was that I should think like this when there was so much about Nina that I didn't know. Actually I didn't know much more than that it made me happy when she held my hand. Like in school, I thought . . .

"What are you thinking of?"

"That we're behaving like school children."

"I've never behaved like this."

"Neither have I."

"Not even with your wife?"

"No."

"Sure?"

"Sure."

"But you loved your wife."

"Differently."

"You say she looked like me."

"But she wasn't like you."

"What was she like? Tell me. I want to know."

"Why?"

"Because I'm jealous of her."

"She's dead."

"But I look like her. Perhaps you only love me because I look like her."

"Silly . . . "

"Perhaps you don't love me at all. Perhaps you still love her. Actually I'm very unhappy because I look like your dead wife."

I kissed her, and she sank back onto the grass, on her back, and I was lying on her I opened her fur jacket and stroked her breasts, which rose and fell with her breathing, and her eyes grew misty and her hands played with her hair. I heard the gull screeching and a steamer coming closer slowly, very slowly. My hands moved inside her sweater.

"Robert?"

"Yes?"

"Did you write the letter?"

16

I took my hand away from her soft flesh and sat up, but she remained flat on her back and looked at me, troubled and sad.

"What letter?"

"Don't lie to me. All the men I have known lied to me. I couldn't bear it if you did too."

"I haven't the slightest idea what you're talking about."

"Please, Robert."

"I haven't written any letter."

"Swear it?"

"I swear it."

"By our love?"

"By our love."

"We shall never be happy, we shall never be one, if you're lying."

"Of course not," I said. What else could I say?

She looked at me. The sky and the old willow branches were reflected in her eyes. The steamer came closer. Tuc-tuctuc went the engine. Nina sat up.

"What nice eyes you have. Such nice lying eyes."

I looked at her and was silent.

"It's so easy to lie, Robert. The other person has no defense. That's why it's so cowardly."

"I'm not lying."

The steamer moved on. We looked into each other's eyes and I think it was my love that made it possible to endure her gaze. I think, in the end, it was my love that convinced her. She said, "I believe you. But then things are even worse," and suddenly she was in my arms again.

"Tell me what happened," I said.

She told about the mysterious letter Brummer had received, and its content. He had read the letter to her and had asked her if she could possibly imagine that I had written it, and why.

"And what did you say?" I asked, holding her in my arms, stroking her hair.

"I said I couldn't possibly imagine your writing it." She clung to me. "Robert, I'm crazy. All of us are crazy."

"So you can imagine my writing it."

"Only that you did it, but I can't imagine why. I . . . I thought perhaps you had some sort of plan . . . for the two of us . . . so that we could live together at last . . . some insane idea . . ."

"I don't have a plan," I said, stroking her hair. "And your husband? What does he think?"

Her answer filled me with a wild joy. "He's afraid, Robert. All of a sudden, he's afraid."

17

Suddenly you are afraid, Julius Brummer, fat bastard with millions. Suddenly you are afraid. And this is only the beginning, Julius Brummer, the beginning of a long journey we are going to take together, you and I, into an unreal world of terror, from which there will be no escape, not for you. Only I shall emerge again into the bright light of a rational world. And then I shall live with Nina to the end of my days and never be parted from her, and a little child will be safe again.

As I thought all these things, Nina was saying, "They've been trying to find the machine the letter was written on."

"And have they found it?"

"She shook her head. "Not yet." And after a short silence, "Robert?"

"Yes?"

"Tell me . . . what does the letter mean?"

"You know what it means."

"But things like that only happen in movies and novels."

"He doesn't have to be a double," I said. "A man who looks a lot like me would be enough. There are look-alikes. Once I walked into the lobby of a hotel in Munich. I was to meet someone there. The desk clerk waved me over and gave me a lot of mail. It was what had come since the last time I had stayed at the hotel, said he. But I had never stayed at the hotel. I had never heard of the person to whom the letters were addressed. I gave them back. The desk clerk apologized. The letters simply belonged to a man who looked like me. Things like that happen—not only in novels."

Nina sat up suddenly and looked at me searchingly. "What's the matter?" I asked.

"You talk about it so calmly, so sensibly. Doesn't it frighten you?"

"It frightened me before any of you. Ever since the incident at the gas station I've realized what was going on."

"What?"

"That they've found a man who looks like me."

"Who?"

"Your husband has many enemies. I don't know which one of them it is. Liebling, perhaps. Or it may be Herr von Butzkow. One of the men whom your husband is blackmailing with the documents. The one who doesn't intend to take it, who wants to revenge himself. Through me."

"Through you?"

"Of course. The man who looks like me can do whatever he likes. It will always look as if I had done it."

She whispered, "He can do whatever . . . you mean *anything?*"

"Yes. Anything."

"And . . ."

"Yes. And murder. If he murders your husband, it will look as if I did it. I have a motive. Your husband is blackmailing me. And I love you."

"Oh God!"

Slowly she sank back onto my raincoat, which I had spread out for her. She lay still, her hair flattened out around her head like a fan, her lips parted, her eyes veiled. "Robert . . . I'm terribly in love with you. I've never experienced anything like it, not with any man. When you look at me the way you're looking at me now, I feel dizzy. It's so sweet . . . to have you look at me like this . . . but we will never get together . . . never. Something will happen. Something terrible . . . "

"No!"

"When two people love each other truly, something terrible always happens. One of them dies. Or there's war and they're separated. Something will happen. You'll see. They won't let us be happy."

"I shall defend myself against this man."

"How?"

"I'll find a way."

"You're only trying to calm me. You're just as afraid as I am."

"Yes. That's true."

"And I love you for it. Let your hand lie there. Don't move it. It makes me happy." I bent over her and kissed her. Then I laid my head on her breast and heard her say, "I want to be your wife. Now. Right away. I want you to be my man, Robert."

I sat up. She looked into my eyes. "Yes. Please, please. Do it. Please do it. I know they will separate us. Something will happen, but before it happens, I want to have been your woman."

"I love you," I said. Our hands began to move in unison, our breath was joined and what we said came of its own accord. Her body was more beautiful than the body of any woman I had ever seen, her tenderness was sweeter than anything I had ever experienced with any woman, and I shall never forget what she said in this hour.

Another tug came up the river, its engine chugging, and gulls circled screeching in the sky above us. Nina wasn't at all like Margit, my dead wife, there was no resemblance whatsoever between them. Crazy, that I had ever thought there was.

"Am I good for you?" she whispered. "Am I the way you want me to be?"

"You are beautiful, my love . . . beautiful."

The tug moved closer, its engine louder, and I could hear the water lapping against the shore. Nina cried out once. And I felt as if my life was streaming away with the river's current. At that moment I would have liked to die.

The sound of the tug grew fainter. I heard Nina whisper, "If we could die together, *now* . . . that would be wonderful . . ."

18

I don't know if you have ever experienced anything like it, Herr Kriminal Kommissar Kehlmann, whether you have ever desired a woman for a long time, yearned for her for a long time. At first it is rarely beautiful. With most people it gets to be beautiful only later. With us it was beautiful right from the start.

Night was falling when we left the clearing, fog was creeping up from the river, the clouds were dark grey, the air was blue, and it smelled of autumn. Leaves were scattered over the highway. We walked slowly, holding hands, and we kept looking at each other. Sometimes we stopped to kiss, but these were different kisses now.

"I'm desperate," she said. "Absolutely desperate. I can't remember ever having felt like this in my whole life."

"I'll find a way. Give me time. Just a little more time."

"You've said that before."

We had reached the Hofgarten and the Rhine Terrace. "Tonight I have to talk to him again . . . have to see him again. How am I supposed to bear it—now?"

"Just a little more time."

She looked at me. Her eyes flickered. "You *do* have a plan."

"No."

"Give me a little hope, Robert. You *are* planning something, something I don't understand. I don't want to know what it is, only *that there is something!* Robert, it will keep me alive!"

And my heart ached as I said to her, "I don't have any plan, Nina. Not yet. Go home. It's almost six. I must pick up your husband on time or he may get suspicious."

"And you have nothing to do with the letter?"

I didn't dare to confide in her, I didn't dare to involve her in any way. What I intended to do, I had to do alone. And I begged her forgiveness in my thoughts, for the fact that I could give her so little when she had given me so much, as I shook my head and kissed her hand, and said, "Go home, dear heart. Go home now." And she walked away, her shoulders sagging, her steps tired.

The evening business traffic had begun. Buses stopped at the Hofgarten, one after the other. A lot of people got out. I had arrived here for the first time on one of those buses, a long time ago. Among the people getting off there were many couples. They walked past me arm in arm and looked at each other lovingly, and chattered and laughed. I watched Nina walking away down Cecilienallee without turning around. To see her wandering off like that, alone, was the saddest thing I had ever experienced. I suppose this was because I had just been so very happy.

I stopped a taxi, got in and told the driver, "Grüntorweg," where the Cadillac was parked. I drove to the prosecutor's office as fast as I could. I got there at ten past six. Too late. Brummer was already waiting for me on the street. He looked at me sharply as I opened the door for him. "You're late, Holden."

"I'm sorry, Herr Brummer. The *gnädige Frau* wasn't ready when I got to the dressmaker."

"Wasn't ready?" He grunted and pursed his rosy little mouth in a smile. "Had to wait, I suppose."

"Yes sir."

He shook his head as he got in. "Women!" he said.

I closed the door and drove off. The streetlights were on. This year autumn was early.

"It's high time," I could hear Brummer say from behind me.

"I beg your pardon?"

"I said it was high time my wife got away from here. Her nerves are shot. And then to have to wait all that time at the dressmaker . . . To hell with Düsseldorf! She'll get a good rest in Majorca, come back her old self again."

I managed to control the car and stop without a jolt at a red light.

"Got her ticket this afternoon. She flies the day after to-morrow. She needs a thorough change and rest after all she's been through. Dr. Zorn has given me the name of an excellent hotel down there. Says it's the best time of the year. German tourists gone, weather perfect. I think she should stay a month or two. What do you think, Holden?"

"I'm sure you're right, sir," I said, and could feel the sweat running down my collar.

"Perhaps longer. We'll see. I'll go down myself for Christmas. Stay over New Year. Have a few good days coming to me. By the way, Holden, I forgot to tell you—tomorrow's the day you drive Mila to her new home . . ."

"Mila?"

"The old dear's packing already. Tomorrow you drive her to Schliersee." His thick voice seemed to be oozing out of a mountain of cotton. "Holden! What's the matter with you? The light's green!"

19

Mila Blehova walked through the entire house; she went once more from room to room. The evening before she had said good-bye to the Rombergs, now she was saying good-bye to the house in which she had worked for so many years. She had on a black dress and a black coat, and a black hat was perched on her white hair. Every now and then she stroked a piece of furniture with her worn red hands; sometimes she just stood still and her eyes had that faraway look old people sometimes have when they are reliving the past.

Nina and I were with her. It was impossible to say a word to Nina. Brummer seemed to take pleasure in being constantly in and out, watching us as if we had been strange animals. Nina looked ghastly. There were dark shadows under her eyes. She had obviously made no effort with her hair and makeup. Since our hour by the river I had had no opportunity to speak to her, and it was clear now that I wouldn't have a chance to do so before she left for Majorca. I kept having to tell myself that everything I had succeeded in accomplishing so far would be in vain if I betrayed myself now.

We went from room to room with Mila Blehova, up to the second floor and down into the kitchen. All her worldly possessions were packed in three large suitcases. They stood in the kitchen. Mila Blehova stroked the stove, the refrigerator. "There's still a lot of beer, *gnä' Frau,*" she said. "Should be enough till the new woman comes. Be sure to tell her that the refrigerator freezes everything if you put it over five. And the electric iron's got to be fixed. I got a shock again last week. Almost threw me across the kitchen."

"Yes, Mila, yes," said Nina. She could barely speak, and there were tears in her eyes.

"But why are you crying, Ninale? Jesus, Maria, and Joseph! I'll be coming back to see you soon."

"You may come whenever you feel like it, my good old Mila," said Brummer, watching his wife all the time with almost clinical fascination. "Any time you feel like it."

"Gnä' Frau is going away herself," Mila said consolingly. "So she couldn't see me, even if I was here!"

"That's right, Mila." Brummer rubbed his hands. "What a sensible woman you are. I'm sending all my women away."

He was sending all his women away . . . yes . . .

Julius Maria Brummer was proceeding cautiously. Too much was at stake for him in this last round of his

290

struggle. He was clearing the decks. He was sending everyone away whose criticism he feared, whose respect he didn't want to lose. He was making a lot of room for himself, to spread himself out for the last round.

I picked up two of Mila's suitcases, but she stopped me. "Just a minute!"

"What for?"

"We've all got to sit down for one minute before I go. So that we may all be in good health when we meet again. That's what we always did at home."

. . . at home . . .

While we sat out Mila's minute on the hard kitchen chairs, Mila with her hands folded in prayer, I thought that all I had "at home" was Nina, and that on the following day she was flying to Majorca. What had taken place beside the river only made our separation worse. But then I thought that this separation was probably the best thing that could have happened to me and my plans. Because for me, too, much was at stake in this last round of the struggle; I too needed a cleared deck and a lot of room to cope with Julius Maria Brummer and the end I had in store for him.

As I was thinking these things, Mila Blehova was praying aloud, softly. "Almighty God, bless and protect those who are traveling and those who are staying behind. Bless and protect my little Nina, the *gnädige Herr*, Herr Holden, our Mitzili, my Butzel and his wife, and little Mickey. Let your blessing accompany them wherever they go and whatever they do, and may those who love each other meet again. Amen."

She opened her eyes and with a gentle smile said, "So . . . now we can go."

I carried her suitcases through the autumnal park. So many leaves were scattered over the lawn, the flower beds had faded, the blossoms were rotting on the ground. There was a drizzly rain, dark clouds in the sky, and it was cold. The old dog waddled behind the old cook, whimpering. Mila bent down and stroked her. Brummer was beside himself with admiration over the dog's behavior. "She knows you're leaving, Mila. She can feel it, just like a human being." He too leaned forward to pat the dog. It was the first and only moment he took his eyes off Nina and

291

me. Nina whispered, "Hotel Ritz." I whispered, "I'll call. Tomorrow night." Then the moment had passed. Brummer straightened up and embraced Mila. Her white hair rested against his gold watchchain. He kissed her on the cheek; she made the sign of the cross on his forehead. Then she embraced Nina, and then she broke down and sobbed. "Too stupid! Now *I* have to start crying. The good Lord will look after you, my Ninale. I'm coming back. I'm coming back soon. I'm coming back very soon!" She stroked Nina's face with her worn hands. Brummer cried briskly, "But now, that's it! In you get or you'll catch cold before we get you out of here, my good old Mila!"

So the old cook from Prague got into the ostentatious Cadillac, still weeping, and I bowed to Nina and said, "I hope you have a good restful time in Majorca, *gnädige Frau.*"

"I hope so too, Herr Holden. Take care of yourself."

"Thank you, *gnädige Frau,*" I said, and thought of our afternoon by the river and knew that she was thinking of it too, and it gave me strength. Brummer said, "Take your time, Holden. You don't have to be back until the day after tomorrow, evening. Give Mila a hand when you get to Schliersee. Help her settle in a bit."

"Very good, sir," I said, and thought with satisfaction of what Brummer would experience, the day after tomorrow, when I got back . . .

20

We drove off. Brummer and Nina waved. Mila waved back. I looked in the mirror and saw Nina once more, the last time for a long time.

It was raining everywhere—in Frankfurt, Mannheim, Heidelberg. We drove through forests with bare black trees, across misty plateaus with dark harvested acres, past meadows of faded grass; and blackbirds, hundreds of them, were scattered across fields and farmland, or perched in the bare branches of the trees. Sometimes a few flew up in the air, but they never flew very high or far.

Mila Blehova soon calmed down. We had only just left Düsseldorf behind us when she said, "Of course it's always terrible to say good-bye after so many years together, but I'll be going back. And I'll be honest with you, Herr Holden, it was all too much for me, these last months. I'm really quite happy that I'm going to be on my own in Schliersee. And it won't do my Ninale any harm to get away from everything for a while."

"You're right, Mila."

"Even if the *gnädige Herr* does do everything in the world for her. She couldn't ask for a better husband."

There was a big bag on the floor at her feet. In it there were sandwiches and candy, cookies and bicarbonate of soda, a drinking cup and a bottle of soda water. When Mila wasn't talking about "home" she was nibbling a cookie or taking bicarb, "for the belching," or she was sucking candy. She was incessantly busy. In Frankfurt she invited me to a lavish lunch. In spite of cookies and candy, she was hungry.

After lunch she told stories about when she was a young girl. She talked only about the faraway past and she talked all day. As a young girl, Mila had been a member of Sokol, the national Czech association of gymnasts. In 1920 she had gone with them to a huge rally in Vienna. She could recall every detail of that experience—the festivities, the flags, the pretty young girls all in white, the tents, the torches and the acrobatics. And the songs! In her high, thin old voice she sang one of them for me on that rainy day on the autobahn, then she translated the text for me. It was all about freedom and comradeship.

In the end she fell asleep, sagging sideways and snoring softly. As I drove south, through woods, fields and farmland, through the pouring rain, with the wipers flailing back and forth, I thought of Nina and our afternoon beside the river and of what lay ahead for me.

We got to Schliersee around midnight. It was raining in Bavaria too. The lake was shrouded in fog and as I got

Mila's suitcases out of the trunk I could hear the whistle of a train on the opposite side of the lake and the clanking rhythm of its wheels.

Brummer's summer house had a big garden and was situated on the lake shore, on the outskirts of the village of Schliersee. It was furnished in Bavarian style. The caretaker's name was Jacob Gottholmseder, and he greeted us cheerfully. He was wearing a green loden suit with deerhorn buttons, a red vest, and a silver watchchain with silver coins dangling from it. Herr Gottholmseder was small, fat and genial. He had lit every stove in the house and reserved a room for me at a nearby hotel.

Mila was very tired. Between Stuttgart and Munich she had drunk a little cognac ("for my heart . . . so's I stay awake . . .") which was also packed in her enormous bag, in a small flask. By now she was a little tipsy. She embraced me before she went up the wooden staircase to the second floor. "Thanks for driving me down, Herr Holden. Sleep well. I'll see you tomorrow. I'll fix you a good breakfast."

I drove through the rain to the hotel where the room had been reserved for me, took a bath and went to bed. The long drive had tired me too. My shoulders and neck ached. I lay on my back and listened to the rain, the whistle of the trains, and the rhythm of their wheels on the other side of the lake. Then I fell asleep and in my dreams I was with Nina, Brummer was dead, and we were happy and in love.

Next day a weak autumn sun was shining. I drove the Cadillac to a nearby garage and had the car serviced. Then I breakfasted with jolly Herr Gottholmseder, who had bought white sausages for us. After his coffee he drank beer with his sausages. It was a long breakfast . . .

Herr Gottholmseder had been a gymnast in his youth too, a Bavarian gymnast, naturally, and he also knew a lot of songs. In the course of the morning, he sang some of them. One song began with a eulogy on the Bavarian scene: *On the mountains lives freedom, on the mountains things are true, There where all the castles stand, of our good King Ludwig Two!*

I helped Mila unpack. Herr Gottholmseder, a widower and eleven years in Brummer's service, occupied two rooms on the first floor. Mila fixed herself up comfortably on the second. Her bedroom faced the garden; beyond it lay the blue lake, and beyond the lake, the jolly little mountain trains passed by with fat white puffs of smoke. Like toys.

Mila had packed all her pictures of Nina in a shoe box. I opened it and took out the pictures and stood them up on a small table beside Mila's bed. In the afternoon I went to the village and, from a barber called Schoisswohl, bought a large razor. It was the old-fashioned kind with a bone handle into which the long thin blade could be folded back. It was just the kind of razor I needed for what I intended to do, and I wanted to buy it as far away from Düsseldorf as possible. Toward evening I went back to my hotel and put through a call to Palma de Mallorca, Hotel Ritz. I waited three hours and drank cognac while I waited. Then I changed the call to "emergency" and waited another hour. At last I was called to the phone.

The small booth was beside the main desk. First I heard a lot of static, then a Spanish voice told me to speak. I could barely understand the voice that answered. I asked for Señora Nina Brummer. More static. Then I heard Nina's voice, but so far away, I wondered if I was only imagining it. "Hello . . . yes?"

"Nina! Can you hear me?"

"Hello . . . hello . . . "

"Can you hear me?"

"Hello . . . this is Nina Brummer speaking. Who is it?"

"Nina!" I screamed, the sweat running down my forehead, into my eyes. "Can you hear me?"

"Hello . . . hello . . . this is Nina Brummer . . . "

The German operator tuned in. "Can't you understand the person you're calling?"

"The person I'm calling can't understand me! What sort of shitty connection is this anyway? I've been waiting for hours!"

"Please don't talk to me like that, sir. It's not my fault. The connection goes through Spain. I'll try to get you a better one."

She tried. Another half hour passed, and I sat in the hotel lobby and drank cognac and it began to rain again. It rained a lot in Bavaria, the tired desk clerk told me. It had

rained through the entire October Festival. Then I was
called to the phone again, and it crackled and whistled
and popped in the receiver, and again I heard Nina's nervous voice and she couldn't hear me. I tried two more
times, but it was no use. I couldn't get a decent connection. In the end I was drunk and gave up.

21

I left at 7 A.M. Mila and Herr Gottholmseder stood in
front of the house and waved, and I waved back until the
road curved. Mila had kissed me on the cheek too and
made the sign of the cross on my forehead, and Herr Gottholmseder had said, "Don't worry about us, Herr Holden.
We two old people will make a fine life for ourselves
down here. One day I'll cook, next day Frau Blehova.
We've known each other for a long time and we're good
friends. In the evening we'll listen to the radio or go to a
movie. We have two movie houses in Schliersee now."

I stopped at the Main Station in Munich and sent Nina
a telegram. I had to consider the fact that strangers would
read it, so I wrote, "Call impossible yesterday. Will try
again today same time."

At the autobahn exit to Stuttgart I bought a few bottles
of Coca-Cola in one store, in another two ham rolls. In
the first store I declared—which wasn't true—that the
salesgirl had short-changed me by forty pfennigs and
raised hell, so that everybody would be sure to remember
me. That was at 8:15 A.M. I drove off and kept up a
steady 120-kilometer speed. I stopped only for gas. When
I was hungry I ate while driving, when I was thirsty I
drank while driving. I was in a hurry. I had to make up
the time I needed for my next move in Düsseldorf.

After Heidelberg it began to rain again, and it rained
again in Mannheim and Frankfurt. In Düsseldorf, where it

was also raining, I drove to the station. I got my cheap suitcase out of the baggage room and went to the washroom, still wearing my chauffeur's uniform. When I left the washroom I was wearing a black pinstripe suit, a white shirt and a silver-gray tie. I put the suitcase on the floor in the back of the Cadillac. Then I went to a phone booth and dialed Brummer's number. The haughty new butler answered. With my hand over the receiver, my fingers spread, and in a disguised voice I said, "This is attorney Dettelheim's office. Dr. Dettelheim would like to speak to Herr Brummer."

"Sorry, Herr Brummer is not at home."

I had anticipated and hoped this would be the case because I knew Brummer had an appointment with Public Prosecutor Dr. Lofting on his calendar for today. But there was something else I wanted to know. "When do you expect him home?"

The butler's arrogant voice answered, "Probably not before eight P.M."

"Thank you."

I hung up. The station clock read 6:34. I took a taxi to Hofgarten and asked the driver to wait. What I had to do now was dangerous, but it had to be done. I walked quickly up Cecilienallee, where nearly all the leaves were gone from the trees. The Bavarian razor was in my pocket, and under my jacket, pressed against my body with my left arm, I was carrying the jack handle from the Cadillac. I had taken it along because with the razor alone I couldn't do what had to be done.

The blind old dog came yapping up to me through the park. She sniffed at my trousers. They were trousers she didn't recognize. I walked quickly up to the villa and rang the bell. The haughty new butler opened the door. His name was Richard. He was tall and thin, his hair was grey and cut short, his face was narrow and long. His upper lip curled naturally and his eyebrows were usually raised ironically. He was wearing a green apron and was evidently in the process of cleaning the silver, which was spread out on a table in the hall.

"Back already?"

"No, but I will be in a minute," I said, and walked down the passage that led to Brummer's office.

297

"*Very* funny," said Richard. He didn't like me.

"I drove straight to the prosecutor's office from the autobahn and told Herr Brummer I was back. He sent me here to look for a couple of letters on his desk and bring them to him. Dr. Dettelheim needs them."

"Yes," said Richard. "His office called."

As I opened the door to Brummer's office I turned around and saw that Richard had gone back to his silver. That suited me. But even if he had had second thoughts and followed me, it wouldn't have mattered. I had the jack handle and whatever I did would be blamed on my double. I didn't like Richard either.

22

The door to Brummer's office was a double door, both sections thickly padded, and it was absolutely soundproof. This was of course a great advantage. I had to work fast. I started with the two Persian carpets. With the razor I cut them up into many pieces, which took quite a bit of doing. Then I took the valuable oil paintings down from the wall, tore the canvas and smashed the gold frames easily with the jack handle. I slashed the drapes and tore them down from their rods, I slashed the leather upholstery of the armchairs down to the springs and the stuffing poured out. I lifted the radio high and dropped it. Two blows with the jack handle demolished it. A glass case with fragile antique ornaments stood by the window. I was surprised at how easy it was to wreck it and its contents. I took books off the shelves at random and tore them. I also tore up all the papers on Brummer's desk. I smashed Nina's picture and a Jewish menorah, and finally poured ink over the havoc I had created. The results were overwhelming. I could be satisfied. It looked as if a madman had run amok in a delirium of destruction.

Seven-five. I went back into the hall, where Richard was still cleaning silver. "Found what you were looking for?"

"Yes," I replied. "Tell the new cook to have dinner ready for Herr Brummer at eight."

He said nothing. He never gave a last reply. It was a habit of his. Perhaps he thought it was elegant.

I walked through the twilit park to the street and along the Rhine to the Hofgarten, where I got into my waiting cab and drove to the station. I changed, checked my suitcase again, and left the station in my chauffeur's uniform with the gold letters J and B, and wearing my chauffeur's visor cap.

Now I took my time. I had put the razor in the suitcase, the jack handle back in the Cadillac. Slowly I drove the dusty car to the Rhine. When I got to the villa I purposely made a lot of noise opening the gate, raced the motor once more in the garage and slammed the garage door behind me. By now it was 8:15 and the night was dark. The lights were on in every room in the house. I walked up to it. A wind had sprung up and was soughing in the trees and an old branch creaked as I passed, as if it was about to break. I hadn't even reached the front door when it was thrown open. Richard was standing in the doorway. His face was white, his hands were trembling, so was his voice, and he wasn't the least bit haughty any more. "Herr Holden. . . ."

"Yes? What?"

"Is it really you, Herr Holden?" He looked at me as if he were seeing a ghost.

"Of course it's me. What's the matter with you, Richard? Are you drunk?"

There was no arrogance now in his long face, and his eyebrows were not raised ironically. The man was scared to death, and that was good, that was wonderful!

His voice cracked as he said, "But . . . but where have you come from?"

"From Schliersee. What's going on here? Where is Herr Brummer."

"In . . . in his office."

I had to go up to him to pass him and he shrank from me. That's fine, I thought. That's great!

"You're to go to him at once."

299

So I walked down the short passage to Brummer's office again, and removed my cap as I entered. The desk lamp wasn't on because I'd broken it. It was lying on the cut-up carpet, its parchment shade smeared with ink. Julius Brummer was sitting on the arm of one of the chairs, the seat and back of which I had ripped open. I could see that he was holding himself upright with great difficulty. The bright ceiling light shone mercilessly on his sweaty, bald head, his blue lips, the dark circles under his eyes. He was panting. His breathing was shallow and wheezy. There he sat, arms dangling at his side, looking up at me amid the wreckage of splintered wood, scraps of carpeting, broken antiques, destroyed books and pictures, and torn paper. As I entered I started a greeting but didn't finish, instead I said, "Oh my God!"

Brummer said nothing but continued to look up at me, wheezing with every breath, and since the drapes were on the floor, torn to shreds, I could see both of us mirrored in the window pane, and beyond the glass, the black backdrop of the nocturnal park outside, restless in the wind, with its creaking branches and rustling boughs. "Herr Brummer!" I cried, with a hasty look that took in all the insane ruination, "don't tell me it's happened again—" and interrupted myself, and said nothing more.

He spoke with difficulty, and as he spoke his body seemed to deflate. "When did you get back to Düsseldorf?"

"Just now. I drove here direct from the autobahn. Herr Brummer, you've got to lie down!"

I hurried over to him but he kicked me away with his little foot. "Don't touch me! The butler will swear that you've been here before. You told him there were papers you had to get for me. You . . . you did this. I'll . . . I'll . . . " He had to pause, his breath rattling. "I shall hold you responsible. Dr. Zorn . . . Dr. Zorn has been informed. You . . . you think you can get away with this insane plan of yours . . . you think we believe your story of the man who looks like you . . . but we don't, Holden . . . we don't . . ."

I walked to the door.

"Stop!"

I didn't stop. I said, "This is too much, Herr Brummer.

I'm not putting up with it any longer, and I don't give a damn for the consequences. I'm going to call the police."

"You are not going to call the police!"

"But I am," I said, my hand on the door handle. "This is a madhouse!"

I heard a dull thud. I turned around, and there he lay amid broken glass and splintered wood, on the ruined carpet, with his head in a pool of ink. There he lay, on his back, his fat body hideously contorted, his legs at grotesque angles, his hands pressed to his chest. He face was blue, his lips were black, and his black tongue lolled out of a corner of his open mouth.

I went back and knelt down beside him and slowly, mechanically, removed his tie. Then I unbuttoned his vest and shirt and saw the little gold disc that hung from a thin gold chain around his fat neck. I knew that disc; I had seen it before, on a hot summer day on the autobahn, in the Zone, at Hermsdorfer Kreuz. Mechanically I groped in the right hand pocket of his jacket and took out the little box with the transparent red capsules. And then I knelt motionlessly beside the motionless man and looked at him, the red capsule in my hand, and read what was inscribed on the little gold disc: *I am having a heart attack. Please look in the right-hand pocket of my jacket and put one of the capsules you will find there in my mouth. Thank you. Julius Brummer.*

So you are having a heart attack, Herr Brummer. And what is one supposed to do? One is supposed to look in the right hand pocket of your jacket and put one of the capsules found there in your mouth. That's what one is supposed to do. And you are saying thank you in advance, Herr Brummer. You convey your thanks engraved in gold. That's the least you can do, Herr Brummer. Because if one fulfills your wish and puts one of these capsules in your mouth, then, Herr Brummer, you will start breathing again. Your face will lose that hideous color and your tongue will go back where it belongs, namely in your mouth. You'll come to and button your shirt as modestly as a young girl, and you'll go on living, Herr Brummer. If one fulfills your gold engraved request.

And yet . . . what will happen then? Nothing very pleasant. Nothing very pleasant for a lot of people . . .

Therefore . . . would fulfilling your request be the smart thing to do, Herr Brummer, lying here in front of me as if struck by lightning?

I don't think so.

And yet . . . if one does not fulfill your request, then, in a few minutes, you will be dead. The only two living creatures still glad that you are alive are an old dog and an old cook. Isn't that just a little too few when one consider how many people are terrified by your living presence?

I am having a heart attack . . .

Well, yes . . . And?

It's bad news for you, Herr Brummer, but for whom else is it bad news? Who will weep at your grave? Little Mickey will go to school without fear and play the games little girls play, without fear. Nina will return home from Majorca, unafraid. All we have to do is wait a little, two or three minutes. That's a very short time when one considers how long we have already waited, and when one takes into account that we had expected to have to wait much longer . . .

The door behind me opened. I turned around. Richard came in. He didn't see Brummer at once because he was lying behind the chair. He began to say, "Dr. Zorn is here and—" Then he saw Brummer, saw me, and screamed. Behind him the little white-haired lawyer appeared. Quickly I punctured the red capsule with my nail and shoved it into Brummer's mouth. Gently I closed his mouth.

"Is he dead?" cried Zorn, sinking to his knees beside me.

Julius Brummer's fat breast rose as he took his first feeble breath.

"No," I said. "He's alive."

"Thank God!" cried the lawyer. The butler lowered his head silently.

"Yes," I said. "Thank God."

23

A bell rang. On a little opaque glass pane, some letters and numbers lighted up: *748: Booth 11.*

It was near midnight. For half an hour I had been sitting on a long bench in front of a row of phone booths in the lobby of the Düsseldorf Main Post Office. I had put through an emergency call to Majorca for which I had had to pay thirty marks in advance, and had received the number 748. So now I stood up and went to Booth 11. Only two tired men were left on the bench.

I picked up the receiver and heard a girl's voice, "We are ready with your call to Majorca."

This time the connection was absolutely clear. Another girl's voice said, "Hotel Ritz. To whom do you wish to speak?"

"Señora Nina Brummer, please."

"One moment."

There was a click in the wire, then, "Here is Señora Brummer . . . "

It was as if she were standing beside me in the booth, I could hear her so clearly. "Nina!"

"Robert!" I could hear her breathing. "I've been waiting for hours. I'm going crazy. I thought something had happened—"

"Something has happened. Your husband has had a heart attack, the most serious one yet . . . "

"Oh God, is he? . . . "

"No. He's alive. They operated for two hours."

Then neither of us spoke. The current in the open wire hummed. After a while I said, "Dr. Zorn has forbidden me to tell you about it. He wants it kept secret. I had to give him my word that I wouldn't tell you."

"But why?"

"It's . . . it's all connected with this . . . this man. He turned up again and destroyed the office at the villa. Smashed everything. That was why your husband had the heart attack."

"I'm coming home at once!"

"You can't! It's impossible!"

"But I'm so afraid. I want to be with you. Or at least near you!"

"That's absolutely insane. Nobody must know that I've told you. You've got to stay down there, Nina. I'll call again. I'll write every day. But you've got to stay down there!"

"Robert . . . "

"Yes?"

"What do the doctors say? Will he pull through?"

"Yes."

"But . . . perhaps they're wrong. Doctors can be wrong."

"I'll call you at once if anything happens. Now I've got to get back to the hospital. Zorn is there. He only let me go when I swore I'd be back in an hour."

"Robert . . . do you still think of it?"

"Of course I do, beloved."

"I think of it all the time. All day. And at night I dream about it."

"Have a drink. Whiskey."

"I've been doing that all evening."

"Have one more."

"It's raining here. I'm standing at the window and I can see the rain."

"It's raining here too."

"Is there a window where you're talking?"

I looked at the wall of the booth and at the phone box where a small light was signaling: "Overtime. Please report at the desk when finished." I said, "Yes, there's a window. I can see the rain too."

"Look at the rain. That's what I'm doing. It's all we have."

"Soon we'll be together forever," I said.

"*Leb wohl*, Robert. Call again soon."

"Tomorrow, dear heart. Until tomorrow."

"Maybe he'll die . . ."

"Maybe."

Then I was standing at the desk, paying for the over-time, and then I walked out into the street. I took off my cap and bared my head to the rain and let it run down my face. The rain gave me a hundred little kisses, and it was raining in Majorca too.

24

Julius Maria Brummer did not die that night. He didn't die at all, although it took quite some time before the doctors could finally say he would survive. It took them ten days. For ten days Julius Brummer hovered between life and death. In those ten days I wrote Nina ten letters and she wrote ten letters to me: *Herrn Robert Holden, General Delivery, Main Post Office, Düsseldorf.* Three times I called her. I always told her the same thing—that I loved her and that his condition remained unchanged. No worse, no better.

"Yesterday I did something terrible. I prayed that he die."

"I've been praying for it all the time."

But God didn't answer our prayer. On the eleventh day I had to tell Nina, "The doctors say the crisis is past. He's no longer critical. It will take a long time for him to recover, but he will recover."

That was the night I got drunk. I sat by the window of my room and looked across at the dark villa. It was raining hard and I drank for hours. At last I fell asleep in my chair. When I woke up it was daylight, but it was still raining.

I was called to Dr. Zorn. The little lawyer looked bad. He coughed, tugged at his collar and stammered a lot. I thought with satisfaction that we were all gradually doing each other in, one after the other, but there was no joy in my satisfaction.

"Herr Holden, I spoke to Herr Brummer today. For five minutes. You won't be allowed to v-v-visit him for some time. That's why he asked me to give you a message."

"Yes?"

"He wants to apologize for what he said to you before ... before he collapsed. He was terribly excited."

"Does that mean that he finally believes me?"

"Yes. Yes ... that's what it means. All of us ... " He tugged at his collar; he seemed to be weighing every word carefully. " ... all of us must resign ourselves to the fact that a person exists who looks almost exactly like you. And that Herr Brummer's enemies are determined to ter-ter-terror-terror [Good work!—I thought]-terrorize Herr Brummer with this man."

Was this to be taken seriously, or was he putting on an act? Was the little lawyer telling the truth or was he lying to me as he had lied before? Hard to tell.

"And you intend to bring charges against this man?" I asked.

"No."

"Why not?"

"The case against Herr Brummer has not been dismissed—yet. Can you imagine what a scandal it would create if we were to bring such charges? If the press were to get wind of it? That's just what the boys are waiting for. No, no charges, under any circumstances. Not until the case has been dismissed. *Then* we'll call in the police. But not until then." The little lawyer ran his fingers through his mane of white hair. "And that is why Herr Brummer is asking you to say nothing about this latest incident, especially not to his wife."

"Frau Brummer is in Majorca."

He looked at me, absolutely expressionless, and said, "She might possibly write to you. Or call you up."

"*Me?*"

"To find out how things are at home. In case she does, Herr Brummer wants you to say that everything at home is all right."

I said, "Don't you think Frau Brummer will begin to suspect something when she doesn't hear from her husband?"

"But she will hear from him."

306

"I beg your pardon?"

"He can write to her. At first he'll dictate the letters. Besides, he can call her up any time he likes. He has a te-te-telephone beside his bed."

25

"Düsseldorf . . . we are ready with your call to Majorca."

"Hello . . . hello . . . Hotel Ritz."

"Señora Brummer, please."

"One moment . . . "

"This is Señora Brummer."

"Nina!"

"Robert! I've been waiting and waiting for your call!"

"I couldn't get to the post office sooner. I was with Zorn and . . . "

"My husband called this afternoon."

I said nothing.

"Did you hear me? My husband called!"

"Yes. I expected it."

"He . . . he was pretending to be speaking from his office. He was pretending to be perfectly all right! He . . . he told me how much he is in love with me. He could barely talk. I could hear him panting, his breathing was terrible, but when I asked him if he was ill he said no, no, it was just a poor connection and he'd come up the stairs too fast. Robert, he's going to call again tomorrow! He's going to call every day! I'll go crazy! I can't stand it any more . . . his voice . . . your voice . . . "

"Shall I stop calling?"

"No! Heavens, no! But things can't go on like this. It's getting worse all the time."

"Dearest, just give me a little more time."

"You *do* have a plan. Tell me that you have a plan.
307

Anything! Just tell me or I'll go to pieces. Tell me you're going to do *something!*"

"I am going to do something. It will all end. Soon."

26

Schliersee. December 5.
Dear Herr Holden,

At last I have time to write to you. I've been so busy getting settled and it took me quite a while to get used to everything. But now even Herr Gottholm-seder says the house has *never* been so clean and cozy!

I get along very well with him, and he likes my cooking. In return for what I do for him, he chops wood for me and lights the ovens. At first we went to the movies some evenings but now, what do you think's happened? The good *gnädige Herr* has given us a television set! I was so touched, I cried! He really is an angel! I pray for him every day, that he should be vindicated in this wicked case.

The set has been installed and now we watch television every evening. We've bought a pair of rabbits. Herr Gottholmseder built the hutches. I have received letters from the *gnädige Herr* and from my Ninale. They both write that they are well. And how are you, Herr Holden? *Ach,* I often get lonesome for Düsseldorf and all of you. But I'm very happy here too, and so grateful.

I think I'll be coming to visit all of you for Christmas. It's very cold here. How is it in Düsseldorf? On the Schliersberg there's a little snow already. Please write to me, Herr Holden, and take care of yourself.

Sincerely and affectionately, your

Emilie Blehova

27

A day before Christmas, Brummer asked me to come and see him. He had a room in the park section of an elegant private hospital, a large room, furnished with antiques and decorated in discreet colors, like a private bedroom. He was sitting up in bed as I came in and looked at me, his expression mellow.

His face was the color of grey chalk, his hamster cheeks were slack, and between his pale lips I could see his yellow, mousy teeth. He had on red and gold striped pajamas, half open, exposing his blond hairy chest and white flesh. A big table stood beside his bed, covered with files, letters, books, two telephones, a radio and a tape recorder. It was late afternoon. A strong east wind was blowing outside, shaking the bare branches of the trees. A large *Advent* wreath with four fat candles stood beside the window.

Brummer said softly, "Holden, I'm glad to see you again."

"Good evening, Herr Brummer."

"Dr. Zorn told you that I beg you to forgive me?"

"Yes, Herr Brummer."

"And do you forgive me?"

"Yes, Herr Brummer."

"That makes me very happy, Holden. No, I really mean it. Perhaps you can't understand, but when one has stood on the brink of death, as I have, then one wants to receive . . . and give . . . trust, love, kindness." He spoke in a singsong voice, and softly, very softly. "Tomorrow is Christmas, Herr Holden, a day of peace. Light the candles on the *Advent* wreath. Let us look at the warm lights and feel peace in our hearts."

So I walked over to the window, lit the yellow candles and sat down beside his bed. Brummer folded his rosy little hands and gazed at the wreath. His bald head glowed. He was still breathing with difficulty. His mighty chest rose and fell unevenly.

"I have had time to think things over, Holden. This attack was a warning I can't afford to ignore. What's the use of working oneself to death? How much longer will I live? Well . . . there you are. No. When I get out of here, I don't intend to fight any more. I have plenty of money. All I need. Let the others wear themselves out. We're going to travel, Holden. A lot. I'm going to buy a house on the Riviera. When the weather gets bad here, that's where we'll go."

"And what are you going to do about the man who looks like me?"

"Don't worry about him. We'll get him. And bring charges against him. We only have to wait until the case has been dismissed."

"And how long is that going to take?"

"Are you afraid of this man?"

"Yes."

"You shouldn't be. If anybody should be afraid of him, it's me. And I am not afraid. Not in the least. Take this envelope. There's money in it. My Christmas presents to you and the rest of the staff. Take a few days off. Have a good time. I'm sending all of them my best wishes, through you."

"Thank you."

"And how is my Mitzili?"

"She's fine."

"My wife is very well too, Holden. She sends you greetings."

"Thank you."

"I've spoken to her. I told her I didn't feel up to the trip to Majorca, not right now. She understood. Said she wanted to come home, but I talked her out of it. A man who doesn't feel fit is only a burden to his wife. She agreed with me. Wonderful woman, isn't she?"

"Yes, Herr Brummer. She certainly is."

"And now you'd better go, Holden. I'm not supposed to do a lot of talking yet. Merry Christmas, Holden."

"And to you too, Herr Brummer . . . a Merry Christmas."

I pocketed the envelope, shook hands with him, and walked through a long white passage and down a wide staircase to the exit. The Cadillac was standing under a street light. I opened the door and sat down behind the wheel. Then I heard his voice. "Good evening, Herr Holden," said Public Prosecutor Dr. Lofting.

28

There he was, seated behind me, tall and slim. The rays of the street light fell on his pale face with the big mournful eyes, which today looked more mournful than ever.

"How did you get into the car?"

"I called at the house. I was told you were visiting Herr Brummer. So I drove here. It was cold out on the street, and you hadn't locked the car."

"What do you want?"

"I want to show you something."

"I don't have time."

"It's important."

"For whom?"

"For you. Will you come with me?"

"Where to?"

"To another hospital."

"*What?*"

"Start driving. I'll show you the way."

So I drove off and he directed me through the city, and a quarter of an hour later we stopped in front of an ugly old hospital.

"I'll go ahead," said Dr. Lofting, after exchanging a few words with a nurse. Again I walked along a long white passage. We turned a corner and I could hear children's voices. They were singing "Silent Night."

"Here," said the Public Prosecutor with the face of a

311

man who worked nights. He opened a door and let me enter.

The room was small. The window looked out onto a shaft. A large bed stood beside it. The light of a blue lamp fell on it, fell on the inert body of little Mickey Romberg. Her head was bandaged, the upper part of her body was in a cast, a little blood had dried on her lips. She looked dead. She looked terribly small. All I could see of her face was her mouth, her nose and her closed eyes. She was breathing unevenly.

I felt so nauseated, I thought I would vomit. I walked over to the window and breathed in the damp evening air, breathed as deeply as I could.

" . . . all is calm, all is bright . . . " sang the children's voices.

The nausea passed. I turned around. Dr. Lofting said, "She won't wake up. She has been given an injection."

"What . . . what happened?"

"She was run over."

"When?"

"This afternoon. She was at a Christmas party. Her mother was going to pick her up. Lately the child has been escorted wherever she had to go. And picked up. You know why, Herr Holden?"

I said nothing.

". . . Holy Infant, so tender and mild . . ."

"Do you know why?"

"Yes."

"Her mother was late because she was detained by an anonymous phone call. Witnesses say the child was standing on the curb, watching for her mother, when a black Mercedes ran into her, with two wheels on the curb. She was thrown ten meters in the air. The car didn't stop."

"The license number?"

"The car didn't have a license number, Herr Holden," said Dr. Lofting.

" . . . Sleep in heavenly pea-eace, slee-eep in heavenly peace . . ." sang the children. Then a concertina played, and the sweet young voices began the second verse.

"Will she pull through?" I asked Lofting, my eyes on the restlessly breathing child who lay, tiny and lost, in the big bed with the unreal, blue, fairy-tale light on her.

312

"Concussion, broken ribs, contusions. But she's not critical. She'll pull through. You know the child?"

"Yes."

"And her parents?"

"Yes."

"Herr Holden, do you believe this was an ordinary accident?"

I said nothing.

"Do you believe there is a connection between this accident and Herr Brummer?"

I said nothing.

"Will you talk now, Herr Holden? Will you finally tell us what you know?"

I said nothing and my eyes were still on poor little Mickey.

"You won't talk?"

"I have nothing to say."

"You're a liar."

"You can call me what you like."

"I'll call you a goddamn liar and a goddamn coward."

"Whatever you like," I said. "It makes no difference."

I looked at him and saw the tears well up in his dark eyes. He said, and his voice was trembling, "Just the same, Herr Holden, you will not triumph. Good-bye, Herr Holden, sleep well . . . if you can. And have a very happy holiday."

He left the room quickly.

I sat down on the edge of Mickey's bed and listened to her weak breathing and heard her moan and saw the dried blood on her little mouth. Nearby, the children were singing the third verse of "Silent Night."

29

"Herr Holden?"

"Yes."

"Zorn speaking. I have just been informed that Dr. Lofting took you to see little Mickey Romberg."

"Yes."

"That was a dreadful accident. And just before Christmas."

"Yes."

"I'm sure you were dreadfully upset."

"Yes."

"Did Dr. Lofting take advantage of your distress and try to get information out of you?"

"Yes."

"Did you give him any in-in-information?"

"No."

"Good. Because half an hour ago Herr Romberg came to see me. The father of the child."

"What did he want?"

"He brought me the photograph, Herr Holden, and the negative. You know what photograph I mean?"

"Yes."

"Herr Romberg suggested that his daughter's accident had something to do with the photograph. Ridiculous, of course. I tried to talk him out of it. However, he didn't want the photograph any more. He . . . he gave the impression of being exhausted. I hope the child's condition improves rapidly. I've sent flowers to the hospital, and toys . . . Do you hear me, Holden?"

"I hear you."

"Well then, Merry Christmas, Herr Holden. Have a happy holiday."

30

I didn't tell Nina about Mickey's accident the next time I called her, and I didn't mention it in the next letter I wrote. I tried to visit the child, but was told by the man in the booth at the gate, "Sorry, sir, but that isn't possible."

"Why not?"

"I have strict instructions from the parents of the child and from the police to let nobody visit her."

"May I ask what her condition is?"

"Improved."

As I walked out into the street again, I met Peter Romberg and his wife. I greeted them, but they walked past me without a sign of recognition. He looked straight ahead but Maria looked at me, and I could see the tears glistening behind her glasses. The expression on her face was one of despair and resignation, and of crushing vulnerability. In 1938 I had seen Jewish women in Vienna, cleaning the streets with dilute muriatic acid, while so-called Aryans stood watching them, grinning. Those Jewish women had looked like Frau Romberg. And the woman in Berlin, who had given birth to her child in a crowded cellar during an air raid, with two hundred people watching her. In Russia the peasant women seeing their houses burned to the ground had looked like that. All these women had had the same expression. But in Peter Romberg's face I could read nothing but hatred. I could feel it, even though he didn't look at me.

I called the man in the booth every day to find out how Mickey was getting along and was told every time that her condition was improving. "She ought to go away somewhere, to recuperate, somewhere south, where it's warm, but of course her mother would have to go with her, and I don't think there's a lot of money there . . . "

That was the day I went to the bank. After Brummer had been released on bail, he had given me permission to open a bank account, which I had done. Today I went up to one of the tellers and said, "Good morning. I would like to withdraw five thousand marks from my account."

The teller took his little pad of withdrawal forms and filled one out for five thousand marks. He asked for my account number and I gave it to him—371 874—and he filled that in. Then he pushed the little pad over to me for my signature. I signed: *Robert Holden.*

I signed a little differently than usual, but not noticeably different. The signature I gave the teller that morning was *very much like* my real signature. Now he tore the form off the pad and stuck half a label on the back; the other half he gave to me. Both parts had the same number: 56 745. I thanked him and walked to the other side of the hall where the tellers were cashiering. Above their desks hung a large sign on which the numbers that lighted up kept changing. When the cashiers received the withdrawal slip from the bookkeeping department, they pressed a button and notified the customer by means of the numbers on the board. I waited six minutes, then my number appeared: 56 745: Cashier 5.

I went to Cashier 5 and smiled. He smiled at me and asked:

"How would you like it?"

"In one-hundred mark bills."

He counted out fifty one hundred mark bills; I pocketed the money and left the bank. I have forgotten to say that of course I had changed into my cheap black suit in the station washroom before going to the bank. Now I went back to the station, changed again, and checked the suitcase. Then I went to the post office and filled out a money order form for five thousand marks. The addressee was Peter Romberg. As sender I wrote a name I made up and the number of a nonexistent street.

On the following morning I received a debit slip, stating that I had personally withdrawn five thousand marks the day before, whereupon I called Dr. Zorn and said that I had to speak to him at once.

"I'm very busy. Won't tomorrow do?"

"No. I must see you at once."

"Is it about . . . about him?"

"Yes."

"You may come right away."

31

The debit slip lay between us on Zorn's desk. I pointed out, "It says here that I was at the bank yesterday and withdrew five thousand marks. I was *not* at the bank!" I yelled. "And I did *not* withdraw five thousand marks!"

"Don't shout! Calm down!"

"What do you mean—calm down? It's my money! The man can do it again. Who knows, he may be at the bank right now!"

"He evidently knows your account number."

"Evidently."

"And can forge your signature."

"You're very bright today, *Herr Doktor*," I said. "I don't give a damn whether Herr Brummer notifies the police or not, as long as what this lunatic does concerns *him*. But now *I'm* involved, and *I* demand that the police be notified!"

"Impossible!"

"Then come with me to the bank. Right now. And ask how this could possibly happen. What the man looked like, how he behaved. I want to know."

"Doesn't come into question."

"Why not?"

"Because the bank would notify the police at once."

"So how do I get my money back?"

He looked at me silently for a moment, then he got up. "Wait a m-m-minute," he said, and left the room. He came back five minutes later. He was very nervous. "Herr Holden, I c-c-called Herr Brummer. We will make it up to you. I'll write out a check for you, for five thousand marks, on the condition that you say nothing about this whole business to anyone."

"And if it happens again?"

"It won't happen again. I'll go to the bank with you, right away. We'll change your account. From now on all checks and withdrawal slips must carry your signature *and mine.*"

It was that simple to get Julius Maria Brummer to pay for Mickey Romberg's convalescence, and a little more . . .

This incident with the bank apparently had a bad effect on Brummer's recovery, because he had to stay on in the hospital. Around the middle of January we had a lot of snow. It fell day and night, thick white flakes, and the land sank farther and farther down under a massive blanket of snow. Train schedules were affected, many roads were closed to automobile traffic, flights were cancelled.

Mail to Majorca was at a standstill, and I called Nina more frequently. She was unhappy and tense. "I want to come home, Robert. How long am I supposed to stay down here? Whenever I talk to him about it he has some new excuse. Too much to do, has to go away, doesn't feel well. I want to come home!"

"You have to wait, Nina."

"But is there any use to *any* of this?"

"Please trust me."

"I love you, Robert. I trust you. But it's unbearable!"

On the twentieth of February, Julius Maria Brummer was released from the hospital. I brought him home, swathed in warm blankets. He had to stay in his room for five days; then, the doctor said, I could walk with him in the park, a half-hour in the morning, a half-hour in the afternoon. He had lost a lot of weight, his suits hung on him loosely, he looked like a scarecrow. With the cautious steps of an old man he walked on the cleared paths, pale and unsteady, leaning heavily on me. We were walking along the shore of the frozen lake when he said, "Just spoke to my wife, Holden. She's coming home tomorrow. We'll meet her at the airport."

My heart ached as I said, "Yes, Herr Brummer."

"I finally told her what really happened. So she doesn't faint dead away when she sees me. Of course she was terribly upset, but I told her I was perfectly all right again, and that seemed to calm her down. By the way, Holden, in two or three days we're going to Baden-Baden. I have to take the cure."

32

"Attention, please!" said the loudspeaker. "West German Airlines. Flight from Palma de Mallorca arriving . . . "

I was sitting with Brummer in the restaurant of the Düsseldorf airport. He had refused to take off his heavy fur coat although it was very warm in the dining room. He was cold all the time.

Far away, a four-motor plane appeared out of a low grey cloud ceiling and began its descent over the snowy airfield. Like a dark shadow it landed on the runway, shooting forward and spewing clouds of silvery snow on either side of its wheels. It was a dreary day. While the plane circled and came taxiing slowly toward us, I thought of a stormy night last summer, when I had sat here with Nina, waiting for Toni Vorm, who never came. Later, on the same night, I had kissed her for the first time. So much had happened since then, much too much. And now she was coming back. The silver plane taxiing toward us was bringing her back to me.

To me?

Not to me. Not yet. But now she wouldn't have much longer to wait until we could finally be together forever, without fear.

"Come on," said Brummer. "Give me a hand."

So I led the mighty man with the dark glasses down to the lobby and up to the arrival barrier. I propped him against it, my victim, whom I had at least got to the point where he couldn't walk anymore without help. I gave

319

Brummer the red roses I had been carrying until now so that he could present them to his wife.

One after another the passengers from Palma de Mallorca came through the gate, smiling, laughing, cheerful. They waved and shouted loud greetings to friends. A merry flight. And then Nina came. She was wearing the grey Persian lamb coat that had been sent to her, high-heeled black shoes, no jewelry, no head-covering. Her blond hair fell wide and open over the collar of her coat. She was deeply tanned and my heart beat fast when I saw that she was wearing no makeup.

During this last summer, only so recently passed yet seemingly so long ago, I had told her over and over again how I loved her beautiful skin and that when we were finally together I wouldn't let her use makeup. And now, on the morning of her return, she was wearing no makeup and that meant, of course: *I love you.*

Brummer embraced Nina and kissed her on both cheeks. Over his shoulder she looked at me. Her eyes were glittering feverishly. We hadn't seen each other for ninety-three days, hadn't touched each other in all that time. Her eyes were shining. I knew what she was thinking of and I was thinking the same thing. The blood was pounding in my temples, and I longed for her with every inch of my body, and in her eyes I could see she felt the same way.

Brummer handed her the roses and asked if she'd had a good flight. "Excellent," she said aloud, and, "Hello, Herr Holden."

I bowed low, my cap in my hand. "Good day, *gnädige Frau*. I'm very happy to see you back."

"I'm happy to be back too, Herr Holden. Although I should be very angry with you for not having called to tell me what my husband was going through."

"I forbade him to tell you," Brummer explained, his breathing short.

"Just the same—it was his duty to let me know," Nina said seriously.

Now we were looking at each other openly because she had addressed me directly, on purpose, and suddenly I could see her before me as she had been that afternoon by the river—naked. My hands were trembling so, I folded them behind my back so that Brummer might not notice.

320

We couldn't seem to look away from each other. I felt hot and I drew a deep breath as I realized what we were doing, Nina and I . . . we were making love with our eyes.

I heard Brummer groan. He swayed a little. I sprang forward, but he shook his head. "It's . . . it's nothing." He was fighting desperately for control; it was quite obvious that he was feeling ill. His lips were blue. "I'm . . . I'm just a little dizzy." He was smiling at Nina, a grimace. "The excitement . . . the joy . . . You get the luggage, Holden. We'll . . . we'll go to the car."

"Yes, Herr Brummer," I said, and gave Nina a final kiss with my eyes. Then I waited for her luggage to appear, and carried it to the Cadillac, which was parked just outside the entrance. We drove home. On the way Brummer told Nina of his intention to go to Baden-Baden in two or three days. Now he was watching her so closely that we couldn't make love in the rear-view mirror.

"Could you be ready in three days?"

"Of course," she said, and even if it was only her voice I could hear, it was as if we were making love. It was because we hadn't seen each other for such a long time and because we longed for each other so much—that was why her voice affected me just as much as her eyes did. When I helped her out of the car I felt something like an electric shock and I saw that she felt it too, because suddenly her tanned face reddened. Richard appeared and helped with the luggage. Together we carried everything into the house behind Nina, who walked up the stairs ahead of us, slowly, her hips swaying a little.

That was the last I saw of Nina before we left for Baden-Baden. In those three days, Brummer never left her side. He had to go to bed right away after our return from the airport, and he insisted that Nina remain with him. He was very weak, so I didn't mind that she had to be with him constantly. It didn't upset me because I knew that from now on, everything was going to happen fast.

On the afternoon of the day before we were to leave, I got my suitcase out of the baggage room. This time I also used the white cane and the dark glasses, and I drove once more to the Julius Maria Brummer Foundation for the Blind.

Grete Licht, the girl with the harelip, too much makeup

and the provocative bra, was delighted to see me. "You haven't been here for ages, Herr . . . "

"Zorn," I said, tapping my way across the dirty office between baskets, doormats, and floor wax.

"Zorn. Of course. I remember the name. Where have you been all this time? You never came back."

"I was away," I said. "And then I was ill."

She grasped my hand and held it to her ample bosom, and as she smiled, her hare-lip separated. "Do you want to type today?"

"Yes, please."

So Grete Licht led me into the next room where it smelled of disinfectant and a lot of blind people were working—knitting, weaving, and at the window five of the old typewriters were being used by five men who looked straight ahead, their mouths open. Jealous Herr Sauer, whose wife was unfaithful to him and who owed me five marks, was among them.

I greeted him. He said he didn't remember me, but perhaps he just didn't want to give me back the five marks. After Grete Licht had left, I inserted a sheet of paper in the machine, and wrote as follows:

> You paid no attention to my letter. On your orders a terrible crime was committed against a little girl. As an experiment, I tried defrauding your chauffeur, Holden, of money. He didn't report it. Without doubt under pressure from you. This proves that you are trying to prevent charges from being brought against me, out of fear that it might influence the investigation still pending against you. But there will be no further investigation, Herr Brummer. You are going to Baden-Baden, and in Baden-Baden you are going to die. In Baden-Baden I shall kill you.
>
> Your chauffeur will go to jail for it, not I. Because you and I don't know each other and I have no motive. I only do what my employer tells me to do. Your chauffeur knows you. He has reason enough to kill you. Any court will recognize that. I am sorry for your chauffeur, but there is nothing I can do about it. We are ready. You may therefore expect to die in Baden-Baden.

I took the letter out of the typewriter, put it into a cheap envelope, and wrote Julius Brummer's name on it, and the address of the hotel in Baden-Baden where he expected to stay. I mailed the letter at the main post office. Then I changed again, put everything back into the cheap suitcase, checked it, and drove home. Now, I thought, everything was set for the last act of the drama, and again—but this time for the last time—everything turned out quite differently.

33

The roads through the Black Forest had been cleared, but in the woods the snow was still piled high. We passed cribs with the deer feeding. They were so hungry they had come to feed in broad daylight. Some came to the edge of the highway, and we saw a lot of young deer, floundering and almost lost in the high drifts.

It was very quiet in Baden-Baden. Many of the hotels were closed. There were few cars. I drove along Lichtentalerallee, past the gambling casino, and along the Oos River. Here in the valley it was warmer than in Düsseldorf, and there was much less snow. It looked as if it would soon be spring in Baden-Baden.

The hotel where Brummer had reserved a suite stood in a park, away from the street. I stopped at the entrance; bellboys hurried forward to take the luggage. I drove the car to the parking lot and hurried back to the hotel because I wanted to be there when Brummer got the letter. I wanted to see his reaction. I arrived just in time, but there was no reaction.

He tore open the envelope, took out the letter and read it hastily. But this time not a muscle in his pasty face moved; he didn't breathe faster and his eyes remained inscrutable behind his dark glasses. As he walked behind

Nina to the elevator, he told the desk clerk, "Please connect me immediately with Düsseldorf," and he gave Dr. Zorn's telephone number.

"Right away, *Herr Präsident,*" said the desk clerk, in his dress suit with the gold keys emblem on his lapel. I don't know why, but from then on everyone in Baden-Baden addressed Julius Brummer as *"Herr Präsident."* Perhaps it was the thing to do in such elegant resorts.

I cleared my throat loudly. Brummer turned around on the threshold of the elevator door, which the bellboy was holding open for him, and stared at me as if he had forgotten me completely. "Oh, Holden . . . that's right. I don't need you now. You have a room in the Glockenspiel Hotel. Take a nap, if you like. You may report at five."

"Yes, Herr Brummer." I bowed to Nina, who was already in the elevator. She said, *"Auf Wiedersehen."*

Brummer looked at her sharply. "What did you say? Oh . . . that's right. So until five, Holden."

The bellboy closed the door, the elevator hummed on its way up. I took my suitcase, which was still standing in the lobby, and walked through the snowy park and down the street to the Glockenspiel Hotel. A room on the second floor had been reserved for me; it looked out on a quiet garden. It was a large room, furnished in old-fashioned style. The whole house was old-fashioned and dark. It belonged to two old ladies who ran it very privately, more like a boardinghouse. I was given—besides the key to my room—a key to the front door, because there was no desk clerk and no doorman, and nobody seemed to care when you came or went, or what visitors you received.

I undressed and washed, then I lay down on the large wooden bed, in my robe, and began to think. I was sure that Brummer would now tell Zorn to notify the police. The letter, with its definite deaththreat, was something that could not be ignored. And a police investigation was just what I wanted. It would make things more difficult for me, but it would also make things a lot safer. I *needed* a police investigation. The police had to know about all these strange events *before* Brummer was murdered. Because when he was murdered, the police must already have been informed and grown used to the fact that there was a man running around Germany who looked like me.

324

Half an hour later the sun came out from behind the clouds and my room was suddenly very bright. The snow on the roof began to melt. I could hear it dripping. The noise made me sleepy. I closed my eyes and fell asleep and dreamt that Nina was with me. In my dream she kissed me. Suddenly I woke up, and she *was* there, and was really kissing me, and her hands were on my shoulders.

"Nina!"

"Sh!" she whispered. "Softly, my beloved."

Her hair fell over my face. She kissed me again. I could smell her perfume, the scent of her skin. I threw my arms around her and she sank down on top of me. Outside, the sun was shining, the snow was melting drop by drop on the wooden floor of some balcony or other, and through her blond hair I could see the blue sky.

"I couldn't stand it any longer," she whispered. "I had to come or I'd have gone crazy."

"Did anybody see you?"

"Just a girl out in the hall. I asked her which was your room."

"We're taking a terrible risk."

"I don't care, Robert. If I can't be alone with you for a while, I'll die!"

"Where is your husband?"

"In the hotel. The spa doctor is giving him a thorough examination. It'll take at least an hour." She clung to me, I felt her body moving against mine . . .

"The door . . . "

"I locked it," she whispered. And then it was like the swift current of a river again, as it had been long ago, by the Rhine, under the old trees. I had no idea that it would be the last time for a long, long time.

34

Dr. Hilmar Zorn arrived in Baden-Baden next morning. I picked him up at the Oos station. With him were two serious, unobtrusively dressed men. They looked sturdy and intelligent. Dr. Zorn introduced us. Their names were Jung and Elfin. He didn't say who the two were or why they had come with him to Baden-Baden. On the way to the hotel, nobody spoke. Zorn had himself announced and went up in the elevator with the two men, after asking me to wait in the lobby.

There was no doubt about it, I decided—the men were from the police, so things were going the way I wanted. I walked up and down the lobby. It was pleasantly warm; the snow was melting fast, in the park it was already quite thin. Ten minutes later I was called to Brummer's room. He was occupying a suite on the second floor and was receiving us in a big red salon. Nina was there. She was sitting on a frail rococo chair near the window and bowed her head slightly when I entered. Her eyes were shining and I knew she was thinking of yesterday, as I was. But she looked very serious and pale.

"Holden," said Brummer, who was wearing a black and gold robe and was seated in front of the fireplace. "You have been introduced to the two gentlemen?"

"Yes sir," I said, and looked at the two men who were seated beside Zorn on a Recamier sofa, intelligent and alert.

"The gentlemen are policemen," said Brummer, "or I should say they *were* policemen. Now they are running a private detective agency."

This startled me, something I hoped nobody noticed. "Dr. Zorn has known the gentlemen for some time. He has complete confidence in them. They are going to stay with us."

"To stay with us?" I repeated idiotically, just for something to say, so that no one would notice how confused I was. I needed time. I had to give this surprising turn of events some thought. So *again* Brummer hadn't notified the police . . .

"You will be interested to know, Herr Holden, that our unknown friend has written again. He threatens to murder me, here in Baden-Baden. You will understand I am sure that under the circumstances I feel it is necessary to hire some protection—"

"The police—"

"Shut up about the police, dammit all!" he said, loud and furiously. "I don't want to hear another word about the police. You know damn well why I'm not calling them in at this time. And what's more—these gentlemen are in a position to do a lot more for me. With the police I'm just one case among many. With these gentlemen I am their exclusive client."

I said nothing.

Zorn said, "The gentlemen will stay here, in the hotel. Neither Herr nor Frau Brummer will make a move without one of them."

I drew a deep breath.

"What's the matter?" Brummer asked quickly.

"I beg your pardon?"

"Did you say something?"

"I cleared my throat, that's all."

"Very well. You may go. I don't need you, Holden."

35

The next four weeks were pure hell. I couldn't see Nina alone, not for a single moment, nor speak to her. Whenever I saw her one of the detectives was with her. They went for walks with her, shopped with her, dined with her.

I began to get the impression that they were paying more attention to her than to Brummer, but of course that was absurd. They simply took their job seriously.

Days went by. It got warmer. The snow was gone. We had an early spring. I drove Brummer and Nina through the Black Forest to Herrenalb, to Wildbad. Wherever we went, one of the detectives went with us. Compared with these four weeks in Baden-Baden, the time in Majorca had been paradise. Then I had been able to write to Nina, to talk to her, all of which was impossible now. The two detectives destroyed any possibility of communication between us. We could still look at each other, but only for the briefest moments and always with the fear of being caught.

Something had to happen soon; I couldn't stand things as they were much longer. Brummer's condition was obviously improving. That at least made me happier because when he was back to normal again he was to take walks, according to the doctor, long walks in the woods. And I knew Baden-Baden; I knew all the surrounding woods and every path in them.

There was one walk that led to a small cave, along the edge of a precipice. That was where it was to happen. I didn't have to accompany him on those walks. I would therefore have the opportunity to act. I was quite sure that Brummer would take this walk as soon as he felt well enough. The cave was famous, everybody went to see it when visiting Baden-Baden, and Brummer had even mentioned it himself.

So March went by. Now it was very warm in Baden-Baden. The gently wooded valley absorbed the spring sunshine into its dark, fruitful earth. It was hard to believe that only four weeks before, snow had covered the ground.

On the afternoon of April 6, 1957, I drove Brummer and Detective Elfin to the Oos station. Brummer was expecting a visitor; I didn't know whom. We walked up and down the covered platform and waited for the Düsseldorf express, which was fifteen minutes late. When it finally came, I saw who was visiting Brummer. He got out of a first class compartment, looking serious, short, red-faced, and as dapper as ever. He had on a dark blue single-breasted suit, blue socks, blue suede shoes, a white shirt, and a silk tie discreetly striped in silver and old rose. And as usual, Herbert Schwertfeger, top-ranking industrialist in Düsseldorf in the year 1957 and SS Obersturmbannführer in Minsk in 1943, smelled refreshingly of *eau de cologne*.

He shook hands with his colleague, Brummer, and looked him sharply in the eye. He gave me a short nod and bowed slightly to Elfin. Then he walked with his springy step down the brick platform beside Brummer while I carried his suitcase and asked myself: Why has he come? Why has he come?

I got my answer almost immediately. As soon as we were seated in the Cadillac and I began to drive—Brummer and Schwertfeger were sitting in the back, Detective Elfin beside me, stone-faced—Brummer said with a hearty laugh, "By the way, for your information, Schwertfeger, Elfin is carrying a revolver in a shoulder holster."

"A revolver?" I heard Schwertfeger say.

"He's a detective, I'd have you know. Had to hire him. Surprising, isn't it? You'll meet a second gentleman whose duty it also is to guard me. I've been threatened."

"By whom?"

"I'll tell you all about it."

"But look here, if anybody's threatening you, why don't you take it to the police?"

"Not until the investigation's over. Until then I'll manage with these two fellows."

"Well," said Schwertfeger, in the harsh voice of someone accustomed to giving orders, "then it looks to me as if you've taken on a lifetime job, Herr Elfin."

The detective smiled mechanically.

I heard Brummer say in an uncertain voice, "What do you mean? You wrote that all was going well. I thought—"

"That's what I thought. But not so, my dear Brummer. Lofting is being difficult."

"And the investigation?"

"We can't count on it being dropped in the near future. I'll tell you all about it when we get to the hotel."

We can't count on it being dropped in the near future . . .

Now I knew why Herr Schwertfeger had come. But now I also knew something else, namely that *I* would have to bring charges if everything was not to be in vain—the cave, the precipice, the letters—everything. I had hesitated long enough. The time had come to act.

36

So many flowers were in bloom in Baden-Baden on this 7th day of April 1957—yellow, blue, white. I saw primula, cowslips, crocus, and violets on the banks of the sleepily murmuring Oos River as I drove the heavy Cadillac through the Lichtentalerallee. Everybody on the street looked friendly. The women were smiling, there was a slight air of mystery about them. They were wearing light, bright dresses. Quite a few wore dashing hats. I saw a lot of dashing hats that morning as I drove to the police station.

The men were wearing grey, light brown, light and dark blue suits; most of them had left their coats at home. The men looked at the women and took their time about it. They weren't in a hurry. Nobody was in a hurry on this spring day in Baden-Baden except myself. I was driven by my hatred. As I drove to the police station I was driven by the invisible inaudible clockwork I had set in motion.

At the police station I spoke to the officer on duty, and then to you, Herr Kriminal Kommissar Kehlmann, in your pleasant room on the second floor, to you for whom I have been patiently filling these pages for months now. I gave you my name and the name of my employer, and I told you I wanted to file a complaint. You were wearing grey flannel trousers and a beige sport jacket, brown loafers, and a green tie, and you asked me what I wanted to report. I had given the answer to this question of yours a great deal of thought. I had learned it by heart so long and so precisely that the words I now spoke seemed quite strange and senseless, without meaning. I told you, looking straight into your blue eyes, "I want to report a theft, criminal slander, breach of peace, and embezzlement," whereupon you asked quietly, "Is your report directed against anyone specific?"

"Yes," I said, just as quietly, "against one man."

"Not bad—for one man," you said.

"That isn't all," I went on. "In a short time this man will also commit a murder."

Then you looked at me for a long time without saying a word. I had known all along that at this point you would take just such a hard, long look at me, you or whoever would be listening to me. I let you stare at me, my own face expressionless, and began to count. One, two, . . . I got as far as seven. I had expected to get to ten.

You asked, "Are you filing this report against an unknown person?"

"No."

"You know the man's name?"

"Yes."

"And what is his name, Herr Holden?"

I thought of how I hated Julius Brummer more than I could possibly ever love anyone. I thought of my determination to bring about his death. I said, "The man's name is Robert Holden."

Whereupon, *Herr Kommissar*, you looked at the initials on my lapel. I gave you time. I had known that at this point you would need time, you or whoever was receiving my report. I began to count again. I counted to four. I had expected to get to seven or eight. You said, "Your name is Robert Holden and you want to bring charges against Robert Holden?"

"Yes, *Herr Kommissar*."

A heavy truck drove by on the street below. I could hear the gears grinding as the driver put them in reverse. You asked, "Is there a second Robert Holden?"

I had also given the answer to this question a lot of thought. I said, "No, there is no second Robert Holden."

"In other words you want to bring charges against yourself."

"Yes, *Herr Kommissar*." I said politely. "That's what I want to do."

37

You listened to me attentively after that, Herr Kriminal Kommissar Kehlmann, you listened to me for three whole hours, then you told me to go back to my hotel and wait. You forbade me to leave Baden-Baden without notifying you. You said you would proceed with an investigation.

Actually it would have been your duty to hold me, but the story I told you wasn't all that simple. It was an extraordinarily complicated story, this tale of a mysterious unknown. That was why you didn't dare to hold me at this point. You sent me home after promising to see what you could do about this mysterious man who looked so much like me, this eerie phantom who was threatening to murder Julius Brummer.

So I went back to my room in the Glockenspiel Hotel. There I sat, shaking with fear, my hands ice cold, my head bursting, and I kept thinking, thinking . . . always the same thing. Had you believed my story? Had I told it convincingly? Did you believe that this double of mine existed?

If you didn't believe me, I was lost. Then it had all been for nothing—the caution, the smart thinking, the careful preparation.

But would you have accepted my story and let me go if you *hadn't* believed me? Not likely. Therefore you believed me . . .

But *did* you believe me? Perhaps you let me go just because you didn't believe me, to make me feel secure, to be able to watch me for days, weeks, perhaps months . . .

I had to calm down. No rashness, not at this point. I had to think in an orderly fashion. Writing it all down like this was supposed to help me to collect myself and think clearly. Only in that way could I hope to cope with the last difficult steps I had to take.

There were two possibilities for the future of these pages. On the one hand, what I had embarked on could succeed. In that case the world would be minus a villain and I could breathe freely again and be safe. In that case I would keep what I'd written to myself and read it from time to time in order to realize again that in a world of dispirited judges and bribed witnesses there still existed a kind of incorruptible justice that had chosen me as its tool. On the other hand, what I had embarked on could fail. In that case, Herr Kriminal Kommissar Kehlmann, you were to consider this manuscript my confession.

38

I wrote for a long time on that seventh day of April, and I went on writing on the eighth and ninth. I kept wondering how much I would be able to get down on paper before Julius Brummer began to take his walks. Since Herr Schwertfeger's visit his condition had worsened again. I thought of Nina as I wrote, and of our strange love, which was so often tragic and so rarely happy. I thought of what would happen when Brummer found out that I had gone to the police. And suddenly I realized that it was all absolutely insane, what I intended to do. I looked at myself in the mirror, horrified. I was going to kill a human being . . . something I had done once before. But now . . . it was *insane! I couldn't do it! Never!*

A knock on the door. "Come in."

The friendly maid came in. Her name was Rosie, and she spoke in a strong Swabian dialect. "There is a gentleman downstairs who wants to speak to you."

"Who is it?"

"He didn't say. You're please to come down."

So I put on my jacket, put what I'd written away, and went downstairs without suspecting anything. I had taken the Cadillac to be serviced and asked the mechanic to see if the transmission was in order and to let me know. It was probably the mechanic, I thought. The people here did good work and were very conscientious.

It wasn't the mechanic.

It was you, *Herr Kriminal Kommissar.*

"Good day, Herr Holden," you said.

"Good day, *Herr Kommissar,*" I replied. "What brings you here? Have you found out something?"

You answered calmly, "An hour ago Herr Brummer was murdered."

"Murdered?" I thought I would choke over the word. Then everything began to circle around me—the stuffed bear, the old-fashioned furniture, the family pictures, the whole lobby.

"Yes. Poisoned," you said in your quiet way. "Herr Holden, I am arresting you on suspicion of murdering Julius Maria Brummer."

Epilogue

1

Two days after Julius Maria Brummer's death, his dog died. I found out from Chief Kehlmann. Brummer's old Mitzi was dead. She died a more peaceful death than her master; she simply fell asleep. They buried her in Baden-Baden, in the hotel park. Julius Brummer's body was transferred to Düsseldorf after the medical examiner had released the body.

At my first hearing in Baden-Baden, I found out how Brummer had died. He had been working in the bedroom of his suite. Nina had gone out with Detective Elfin. Detective Jung was next door, in Brummer's salon, playing solitaire. He heard Brummer groan and after that a dull thud, and hurried into the bedroom. Brummer had collapsed beside his bed. He was in the throes of a serious heart attack. Jung unbuttoned Brummer's shirt, saw the gold disc, and did what the inscription told him to do. He took a new, unopened box of the heart medicine out of Brummer's pocket and put one of the soft red gelatine capsules in Brummer's mouth after piercing it with his nail. At once he could smell the strong almond odor of prussic acid. Horrified, Jung realized what Brummer had just swallowed, but it was too late. Brummer's heavy body was shaken by a convulsion, then he was dead.

"When did you exchange the capsules?" asked Kehlmann.

I was sitting in his pleasant office again, with the thick carpet and the picture of a wild hunting scene on the wall, but this time I wasn't sitting there as a free man, come to file a complaint; this time I was under suspicion of murder and had been led out of my cell by a police officer.

"I did not murder Brummer."

"Where did you get the poison?"

"I never had any poison."

"So you don't want to give us a confession."

"I have nothing to confess."

"I think you have. A lot."

"But not the murder. I did not murder Brummer. I didn't do it!"

He got up and went into the next room, and when he came back I suddenly felt hot all over. He was carrying the cheap fiber suitcase that I had kept in the baggage room of the Düsseldorf Main Station. He put it down on the table and opened it. Both suits were in it, the ties, the white cane, the dark glasses.

"Do you recognize these things?"

"No."

"They don't belong to you?"

"No."

"After your arrest we searched your room in the Glockenspiel Hotel. We found what you had been writing, and a blue ticket. With the blue ticket we were given this suitcase at the Düsseldorf Main Station. But it isn't yours?"

The ticket . . . of course I would have destroyed it, burnt it, but later, when I had really murdered Brummer. I couldn't have expected that I would be arrested *before* committing the crime.

"I lied. It *is* my suitcase."

"So you played your own double."

"Yes . . . yes . . . "

"And you were lying when you came to see me on April 7th to file a complaint."

"Yes . . . That is—"

"Why did you create a double for yourself?"

"So as to have an alibi . . . "

"When Brummer was murdered."

"No—yes—"

"So you *did* intend to murder him."

"No—I mean, yes—*but I didn't murder him!* Somebody got there ahead of me."

336

"You're lying again."

"I'm telling the truth. You've *got* to believe me. I'll tell you everything . . . "

"You can tell what you have to say to Dr. Lofting," he said coldly.

"Lofting? Why Lofting?"

"From today on you are under arrest pending investigation. Prosecutor Lofting is assuming jurisdiction."

2

"Have a seat, Herr Holden," Dr. Lofting said softly.

The curtains in his room were drawn to keep out the heat. It was cool and dark and I saw the shelves on the wall again, filled with books. So much had happened since I had seen them last. Dr. Lofting sat opposite me in his old-fashioned armchair. His face was pale, his big eyes looked sad. He sat motionless, his hands folded under his chin, Dr. Lofting, passionate lover of justice. "How was the trip?" he asked, as I sat down.

"You know what the trip was like. Was I handcuffed on your orders?"

"Yes."

"Why?"

"To prevent your escape."

"I did not murder Julius Brummer."

"Herr Holden." He spoke softly, slowly; he sounded depressed. "I told you once that sooner or later justice always triumphs. Sometimes it takes longer, but it never takes too long. In the end evil never wins out. Herr Brummer is dead. He has atoned. You are under arrest. Confess what you have done, because you too must atone. You can't escape us any more. Under the circumstances it would be senseless to lie."

I managed to control myself. I said calmly, "I cannot confess to a murder I did not commit."

"Why did you create a double if you had no intention of murdering him?"

"I didn't say I had no intention to murder him; I said I *didn't* murder him."

He looked at me silently for a long time, and the black bags hung like grapes under his clever eyes. "You love Frau Brummer," he said finally, without any particular stress on the words.

"What makes you say that?"

"Frau Brummer wanted to divorce her husband because of you, but her husband wouldn't let her go."

"I know nothing about that."

"But I do."

"How?"

"Frau Brummer told me. Yesterday."

"How is she? May I see her?"

"You may see no one, and you may talk to no one. You may receive no letters from her nor write to her. Not until you have confessed."

"I am innocent."

"You are not innocent, Herr Holden, not on many counts, even if you did not kill Herr Brummer. Because even if you didn't kill him, you certainly intended to. If somebody hadn't got there ahead of you, you would have killed him."

"No! That isn't true. Just before they arrested me, on that very afternoon, I suddenly realized that I didn't have the strength to go through with it."

"You would have landed in this office anyway. Your creation of a double suffers from one logical error. If you really had a double, and this double had really been given the assignment to kill Herr Brummer, then such a man would never had done anything before the murder to attract attention to himself. On the contrary, he would have remained invisible to the end, because only then could he have been sure that all suspicion would fall on *you*, not on himself. But what did your double do? He behaved like an actor. Look—here I am again, yes—I exist. Would that have been his behavior? Never! Who could possibly have behaved like that but *you?*"

He is right, I thought in my confusion . . . he is right. Nina . . . he wouldn't let her visit me, I couldn't see her until I had confessed. But if I confessed, I was lost. I couldn't confess. It would be a lie. But if I lied, he would let Nina come to see me.

And then? What then?

I had to pull myself together. I had to calm down.

"I can't go on. Call Dr. Zorn."

"Dr. Zorn has refused to take your case."

"Herr Doktor . . . I will tell you everything, the whole truth. I will hide nothing. It will take a long time, but you will hear everything."

"It doesn't matter how long it takes," he said softly, "as long as it is the truth."

"I started to write my story. What I have written was in my hotel room. It was confiscated. Have you read it?"

"Yes."

"Then you know how I came to be in Brummer's service."

"I know what you have written about it."

"So hear the rest," I said, and I began to speak, struggling to be calm and controlled about it. I told him everything, I concealed nothing. I spoke for two hours, on the next day the same, and on the following day. It took me four days to tell the whole story, and it was the truth. When I was finally silent, he was silent too, looking down at his desk. In the end I couldn't stand his silence any longer, and I asked, "Do you believe me?"

Seriously and mercilessly, like an angel on Judgment Day, Dr. Lofting moved his head slowly from right to left and from left to right. And it was dark in his room, and cool.

3

Dear Herr Holden,

My God, but it is all so terrible, what's happened to you and the poor *gnädige Herr*. I am beside myself and I still can't believe it's happened, not even after all this time. This murderer, this wicked murderer. Who could possibly have done it? When I read about it in the paper I got right onto the train and came here to Düsseldorf, to my Ninale. She is brokenhearted and cries day and night. And the funeral of the *gnädige Herr* was terrible, even though there were a lot of flowers and so many people. My Ninale fainted at the grave. She's better now. But she wants to be alone. She insists that I go back to Schliersee. She wanted to tell you that _____

_____

_____

_____because, dear Herr Holden, I believe firmly that you are *absolutely* innocent. Think of what I've always said: the good thing will triumph. They will find the wicked man who murdered the *gnädige Herr*. For your consolation and support I am copying a psalm out of my prayer book:

"Haste thee O God to deliver me; make haste to help me, O Lord. Let them be ashamed and confounded that seek after my soul; let them be turned backward and put to confusion that wish me evil. Let them for their reward be soon brought to shame; that cry over me. There! There! But let all those that seek thee be joyful and glad in thee; and let all such as delight in thy salvation say always, The Lord be praised."

Dear Herr Holden, I shall pray for you every day, that they should find you innocent and let you go free. Meanwhile be brave. This dreadful time will pass.

Your very unhappy and sincerely devoted,

Emilie Blehova

4

But Nina wasn't allowed to write to me and she wasn't allowed to visit me, not even for the few minutes I had once been permitted to visit Brummer in this miserable jail. First I had to confess, said Dr. Lofting. First I had to confess . . .

The weeks passed by. It was summer, and hot in my cell. In Dr. Lofting's office it remained cool and dark; still I preferred to sit in my hot cell rather than in his cool office. I dreaded every interrogation. I could say what I liked—he shook his head. I could tell him whatever I liked, he always came back with the question: "Where did you get the poison? Who sold it to you, Herr Holden?"

So as not to go out of my mind, I appealed to the prison administration to return what I had written to me and to permit me to continue with it. I was given permission, and began to write daily from nine to twelve, and evenings from seven until the lights were turned out at nine-thirty, except when I was being interrogated.

It got hotter and hotter. In July I wrote in my cell naked. The sweat ran down my body. Sometimes a thunderstorm cooled things off, but that didn't happen often. I wrote on and on. It was my therapy against madness, my protection against Dr. Lofting shaking his head. And they wouldn't let Nina see me, not until I had confessed . . .

In the four months following my arrest in Baden-Baden,

I wrote all that you are reading on these pages, Herr Dr. Lofting and Herr Kriminal Kommissar Kehlmann. Every now and then the pages were taken from me, then returned to me. It was clear that they were taken from me for you to read, Herr Kriminal Kommissar Kehlmann and Herr Dr. Lofting.

During these four months I was dressed in the suits that had been packed in the cheap fiber suitcase, and I was confronted by Paul from the gas station, by the pretty usherette from the movie house on the Lützowstrasse, and by Grete Licht from Julius Maria Brummer's Foundation for the Blind. For Fräulein Licht I was given my dark glasses and the white cane. One after the other Dr. Lofting had found all witnesses, and all of them recognized me. Again and again Dr. Lofting sent me back from his cool room to my hot cell, and I wrote on and on. In the end, in a miserable way, I was quite content with what I was doing. Writing it all down was a comfort, and helped me during these months. And they wouldn't let me see Nina . . . they wouldn't let me see Nina . . .

Once I received a postcard. It was a colored picture of the Gardasee, and on the other side, in a child's handwriting, the words:

> Dear Uncle Holden, How are you? I am well. We hav been in Dsenzano for three weks. I am brone. Vati and Mami are her to. We swim a lot. It is veri hot. Dont be angry becos I behave so funni. Mami has tol me everthin. It was a mesunerstaning. Many lovin gretings and kises from yur Mickey.

Underneath was written:

> Our thoughts are with you. Maria and Peter Romberg.

So they had forgiven me.

And they too believed that I had murdered Julius Brummer.

5

In August there were terrible storms. I was taken to Dr.
Lofting for interrogation twice a week. He asked a lot of
questions, and some of them I didn't understand. He
looked frailer than ever, but I wasn't looking too well either. Whenever I was taken to be shaved or have my hair
cut, and could look into a mirror, I felt sick. My cheeks
were sunken, my eyes were dull, my hair was lifeless. My
color was a dirty grey and my lips were bloodless. Every
day I had to walk for an hour around and around the
yard, and breathe deeply, so that I might remain well for
the trial and verdict. I didn't mind these hours outdoors,
but I was always glad to get back to my cell and my writing.

At first I dreamt of Nina every night and my dreams
woke me, and the lying awake that followed was worse
than the interrogations. But in August I didn't dream any
more, and when I couldn't sleep I waited patiently for the
dawn, when I would be able to go back to my writing.

In early September I suddenly became very calm. I had
decided to resign myself to my fate. In a sense Dr. Lofting
was right when he accused me of having murdered Julius
Brummer. Because, in a sense, I was his murderer. I had
decided to kill Brummer and the decision was what counted, not the execution. A murder planned was just as great
a crime as a murder committed. I could not go unpun-
ished; I had to atone. Not only for the planned murder of
Julius Brummer—no, I had to be punished for the fact
that in my whole life, the first solution that had come to
me, whenever I was faced with a difficulty that seemed in-
surmountable, had always been a violent one. A person
like myself belonged behind bars. I could see it now. I had

planned to take a human life, without pity and without remorse. What could be worse?

In the end everything seemed justified: that I wasn't allowed to see Nina any more, that nobody believed me, that I would be condemned, on circumstantial evidence and on the testimony of witnesses only, to life imprisonment. Undoubtedly. Even the fact that Nina and I would never be together seemed, in the last analysis, a just punishment. It was the worst punishment, but I deserved it. I would have liked to know if Nina, too, thought I had killed Brummer. And I would have liked to know who actually did murder him. On September fourteenth I was taken to Dr. Lofting for the last time.

6

He seemed more exhausted than ever that morning. With a tired gesture he indicated that I should sit down. Without looking at me, leafing through a file with his nicotine-stained fingers, he asked, half-aloud, "How are you getting along with your writing, Herr Holden?"

"Almost finished," I said.

"You don't have to write any more," he said, still fumbling around with the papers in front of him. "I am releasing you. You may leave the jail early tomorrow morning. If you feel so inclined, you can sue for false arrest, but I wouldn't advise it. Under the circumstances I don't think you stand much of a chance. The evidence against you was—"

"Just a minute," I interrupted him. "You—you are releasing me?"

"Yes."

"But that means—"

"That means that I no longer believe you murdered Herr Brummer. There's some water in a jug over there."

I got up and filled one of the glasses standing beside the jug with water, spilling half of it, and drank. I had to hold the glass with both hands. Then I sat down again. Lofting was toying with a paper knife. He said, "You know how consistently I have tried, in the past months, to find out where the poison came from that killed Brummer. I know now. It came from a former doctor who lost his license years ago for performing illegal abortions. He was an alcoholic. Recently, the people who knew him noticed that he suddenly seemed to have a lot of money. The police called on him. They found various deadly poisons in his apartment, among them prussic acid. He was given two weeks in jail for illegal possession of poisons. I heard about it quite by chance. I play skat once a week with some colleagues from the force. When I heard that poison had been found in the doctor's house, I had him brought in. I tried everything. I threatened him, I made promises . . . I got nowhere. He only laughed. He had never sold poison to anyone, said he. Three days ago he died of pneumonia."

"I don't understand a thing!"

"Two days before he died, he sent for me. He said he didn't want to die without telling the truth. Yes, he had sold poison to a man, in April, for a lot of money. He had filled some heart-medicine capsules with the poison. He explained how. He told me when and where he had met the man who had paid him to do this, and how he had packed the deadly capsules in a prescription box obtained from a friend's pharmacy, and sent them to Brummer in Baden-Baden."

"Who was the man who bought the poison?"

"He didn't know. He could only describe him. I proceeded to show him pictures of all the men who had had anything to do with the Brummer case, and pictures of you, the staff, Dr. Zorn—all Brummer's friends. All in all, approximately fifty photos. The doctor immediately pointed out one of them. Before he died he gave us a deathbed confession, under oath. He still had the post-office receipt for the registered package in which he sent Brummer the capsules."

"And who was the man?"

"Herbert Schwertfeger," Dr. Lofting said calmly.

"Herbert Schwertfeger . . ." I drew a deep breath. "Now I remember something. Brummer told Schwertfeger that his life was being threatened by a man who looked like me."

"When was that?"

"When Schwertfeger visited Brummer in Baden-Baden. A few days before his death."

Lofting nodded. "That's what I thought. That's when Schwertfeger got the idea. Brummer was blackmailing him, which forced him to accede to Brummer's demands. Of course he hated the man, and wanted to get rid of him. But with the documents that incriminated him in Brummer's possession, it was something he couldn't hope for. But if he killed Brummer, all suspicion would fall on you. So . . . he went ahead with it."

There was silence. It was raining. The drops fell on the windowsill, monotonously.

"I immediately authorized a warrant for Herr Schwertfeger's arrest, but he had been tipped off. The police came too late."

"Who warned him?"

Dr. Lofting's voice sounded resigned. "Herr Schwertfeger has many friends, friends from the days that idiots think lie behind us. One of these friends must have warned him."

"But . . . but then that friend must be someone close to you . . ."

"That's what I'm afraid of. The district attorney's office has already begun an investigation to find out who made it possible for Herr Schwertfeger to escape to Egypt."

"To Egypt?"

"He was seen yesterday in Cairo. We have asked for his extradition."

"And will they extradite him?"

He lifted his thin hands and let them fall again. "Let us hope so. One day Herr Schwertfeger's fate will catch up with him, as it catches up with all of us. However, I will probably not be here to interrogate Herr Schwertfeger."

"Why not?"

"I am a sick man. I have been advised to retire. In two months I shall leave office. It has become too much for me. Well, you'll read all about it in tomorrow's papers."

He rose, forced a smile and held out his hand. "I don't see any reason to apologize for having kept you under arrest for such a long time. You would have done the same thing in my place."

"Certainly," I said, and grasped his cool, dry hand. I pressed it firmly, but his remained slack. "And by the way, I have called Frau Brummer. She was very happy. I told her that quite a few people from the press would be at the gate when you were released. I believed it would be best therefore, for all concerned, if Frau Brummer did not come to fetch you."

"Of course."

"She understood too, and asks you to come to the Rhine when you are released. She will be waiting for you on a boat. She said you knew where. Why are you looking at me so strangely, Herr Holden?"

"I . . . I'm still utterly confused. You'll have to excuse me. And I keep thinking . . . you are retiring . . . what will happen to Schwertfeger, and all the others?"

"Yes. What will happen to all the others?"

"You said that in the end justice always triumphed."

Lofting turned away as if ashamed of something. "Ah yes," he said softly. "Justice . . . "

7

It rained on the following day too. A lot of reporters were waiting in front of the entrance of the jail. They photographed, asked questions, but I answered only a few. Then I got into a waiting taxi and drove to the Rhine. The leaves on the trees were changing color again, there was a smell of smoke and transience. The white floating restaurant was rocking gently. The taxi stopped. I paid the driver and saw the Cadillac parked along the curb.

I walked across the deserted deck to the glassed-in

347

cabin. Nina was the only guest. She was sitting at a table that was set for two breakfasts. There were flowers in a vase, and beside the vase lay a package, tied with string. As I entered the cabin, Nina rose. She was wearing her black and white checked suit and black alligator shoes. She had taken off her little black hat. Her hair was cut short, like a boy's. She was pale, and there were dark shadows under her eyes, and she looked as if she had been crying. She seemed relaxed, but exhausted, as after a long illness. We met in the middle of the room and embraced. I kissed her, and I could feel the boat rocking gently under my feet and hear the rain drumming on the roof.

We walked slowly back to the table and sat down side by side and held hands, and I too felt depleted. At the end of the room there was a narrow mirror. I could see both of us in it. We looked pale, worn out, enfeebled.

The white-haired old man with the white stubble on his chin stuck his head in and laughed. "Good morning, good morning! Here you are at last! So let's get going. The lady has ordered a *big* breakfast," and he disappeared.

Nina looked at me. "I thought you'd be hungry."

My legs felt leaden, my head ached, I could see spots before my eyes. My hand was lying on Nina's and I felt at peace, but I felt no joy. None.

"Are you hungry?"

"Yes, yes," I said, and thought of how long it had all taken, almost too long, hopefully not too long.

"Did you believe I had done it?"

"Never!" she said, and pushed the package across to me. "My letters," she said. "I wrote to you every day. You'll read them and know how much I love you."

"Do they say that you didn't believe I did it?"

"Yes, they do, Robert, yes," she said, her voice raised a little. I could sense that she was lying. "Why are you looking at me like that?"

"You did believe it, Nina."

She pressed her lips together, her nostrils quivered. Suddenly she nodded. Her voice had lost its timbre. "I believed it. Don't read the letters, Robert. Throw them away. I lied in them too. Yes, I believed you did it, and I was in despair. I could understand a man killing his wife out of jealousy, but a *planned* murder . . . that was something

348

else. Suddenly I was afraid of you, Robert. I could never have lived with you if you had done it."

"Are you still afraid of me?"

She shook her head, but her eyes couldn't lie.

I said, "I had resigned myself to the fact that they would convict me. I preferred it, to being free to live with you. I feel so guilty, so terribly guilty . . . my love wouldn't have sufficed either."

"But it has nothing to do with love," she said.

Suddenly my hands began to tremble, as if I had a chill. I pressed them together, I made fists of them, but I couldn't stop them from trembling.

"It will pass," said Nina. "We will forget it. You didn't do it. That's all that matters."

I looked at my hands and tried to stop their trembling, and thought: Will we forget it? Will it pass? Is the only thing that matters really the fact that I didn't do it? Will it ever be as it was? *Can it ever be the same again?*

Nina said, "We'll get married. We'll go away from here, to another city, another country. You must rest. You must give yourself time. And me. There's no hurry. Now we have all the time in the world."

But my hands were still trembling. "It's nerves," I said. "It'll stop in a minute."

"Of course it will," she said, and stroked my trembling hands and smiled. "It's stopping already. Just wait and see how much better you'll feel when you've had some coffee."

"Yes," I said. "After a cup of hot coffee I'll feel a lot better." And we moved closer to each other and looked at the heavy rain pouring down onto the river. The boat rocked gently, and below us we could hear the old man rumbling around in his little kitchen. Now there was a smell of coffee, and of eggs frying. I heard a few gulls screeching. They seemed to be circling over the boat. Nina moved closer to me. I laid my cheek on her hair. The rain was heavier.

"How do you feel, beloved?"

"Miserable," I said. "Absolutely miserable."

"It will pass," she said. "It will pass."

"Yes," I said. "I'm sure it will . . . "

Let these Get-Ahead books help you write better, read faster, speak more effectively!

DESK TOP REFERENCE LIBRARY

ONLY **$9.45**

A $30.30 HARD-COVER VALUE

Webster's New World Dictionary
664 pages packed with clear, complete, up-to-date definitions, pronunciations, usages, origins of words. Illustrated.

Webster's New World Thesaurus
An authoritative guide to writing and speaking accurately. Thousands of major entries with synonyms listed by frequency of use.

Speed Reading Made Easy
Proven-successful ways to increase your reading speed and help you understand and remember more.

A New Guide To Better Writing
Enables everyone to master the art of clear, concise-writing.

How To Build A Better Vocabulary
How to expand your vocabulary quickly. 30-day new-word-mastery technique.

The New York Times Guide To Reference Materials
Leads you through the maze of almanacs, encyclopedias, atlases, manuals, and all other reference materials.

Mail this coupon today and receive all six reference books in handy desk-top slip case.

All Time Bestsellers

Buy them at your local bookstores or use this handy coupon for ordering:

Reading Fit For A Queen

QUEEN-SIZE GOTHICS are a new idea. They offer the very best in novels of romantic suspense, by the top writers, greater in length and drama, richer in reading pleasure.

☐ THE FOUR MARYS—Rinalda Roberts	00366-9	1.25
☐ GRAVE'S COMPANY—S. Nichols	00252-2	1.25
☐ GRENENCOURT—I. Charles	00264-6	1.25
☐ THE HARLAN LEGACY— Jo Anne Creighton	03206-5	1.50
☐ THE HEMLOCK TREE—E. Lottman	00235-2	1.25
☐ INN OF EVIL—J.A. Creighton	00224-7	1.25
☐ ISLAND OF SILENCE— Carolyn Brimley Norris	00411-8	1.25
☐ ISLAND OF THE SEVEN HILLS—Z. Cass	00277-8	1.25
☐ KEYS OF HELL—L. Osborne	00284-0	1.25
☐ THE KEYS TO QUEENSCOURT— Jeanne Hines (Empress)	08508-8	1.75
☐ THE LAZARUS INHERITANCE (Large type)—Noel Vreeland Carter	00432-0	1.25
☐ THE LEGEND OF WITCHWYND (Large Type)—Jeanne Hines	00420-7	1.25
☐ LET THE CRAGS COMB OUT HER DAINTY HAIR—J. Marten	00302-2	1.25
☐ LUCIFER WAS TALL—Elizabeth Gresham	00346-4	1.25
☐ MIDNIGHT SAILING—S. Hufford	00263-8	1.25
☐ THE MIRACLE AT ST. BRUNO'S— Philippa Carr (Empress)	08533-9	1.75
☐ OF LOVE INCARNATE—Jane Crowcroft	00418-5	1.25

Buy them at your local bookstores or use this handy coupon for ordering:

Popular Library, P.O. Box 5755, Terre Haute, Indiana 47805   B-10

Please send me the books I have checked above. Orders for less than 5 books must include 60c for the first book and 25c for each additional book to cover mailing and handling. Orders of 5 or more books postage is Free. I enclose $_____ in check or money order.

Name_____

Address_____

City_____ State/Zip_____

Please allow 4 to 5 weeks for delivery. This offer expires 6/78.